San X
Sanders, Leonard.
In the valley of the
    shadow $ 20.79
1st ed.

IN THE VALLEY
OF THE SHADOW

IN THE VALLEY OF THE SHADOW

Leonard Sanders

Carroll & Graf Publishers, Inc.
New York

First edition 1996

Carroll & Graf Publishers, Inc.
260 Fifth Avenue
New York, NY 10001

ISBN 0-7867-0306-7

Library-of-Congress Cataloging-in-Publication Data is available.

Manufactured in the United States of America.

There is no bottom. There is no low. You never know what you're going to see next. There's no worst. It does amaze me what people do to other people . . . but there's no worst. You know what I'm saying?

Police Officer, quoted in *What Cops Know* by Connie Fletcher

IN THE VALLEY
OF THE SHADOW

1

Harold Appleby eased Sam's old blue pickup truck to the curb more than fifty feet from the intersection and turned off the ignition. To his left, traffic continued to roll by, drivers like zombies, eyes fixed, faces anxious, intent on where they had to go and how little time they had to get there. Watching them, Harold felt a rush of superiority as delicious as a mainline jolt of Mexican brown. All of his life he had been called dumb. Now he was making money and nobody told him where to go, what to do, or when to do it. He was his own man. He could take off for anywhere he wanted at the slightest whim and nobody could say shit or Shinola about it. So who was dumb?

He fished Sam's silver pocket watch from his shirt pocket and placed it on the dash. He turned in his seat and spread a road map, as if studying it. But his gaze was aimed over the map, across the fenced playground to the school. Patiently he sat and waited for the little bitch to appear.

He first had seen her two months earlier. Something about her long black hair, fearful big brown eyes, and matchstick legs had appealed to him. Twice during the past few weeks he had driven out of his way to stalk her. Now, unless something unexpected happened, he intended to take her.

At three-thirty by Sam's watch the younger kids started pouring out of the school, right on schedule. Still holding the map, Harold kept his eyes on the south door. Burdened with books and backpacks, the kids soon were strung out along the sidewalk all the way from the school to the intersection where Harold waited. An old man who carried a paddle-sized red sign that said Stop went to the center of the crosswalk and halted traffic. Cars stacked up bumper to bumper from the intersection back to where Harold sat, and beyond. Harold waited. Every few minutes the old man stopped the flow of kids and allowed more cars to go through the intersection. Harold remained motionless, watching.

The little bitch was almost to the crosswalk before he saw her. She was walking with a group of other children—with them but not of them. She kept her head down, sneaking occasional glances at those walking beside her, not taking part in the shouting, giggling, and horseplay of the other kids.

A loner—that was what first had caught Harold's attention two months ago. Maybe it took one to know one.

She walked on across the street and vanished among the stream of children. Harold kept his cool. He knew where she was going. He studied Sam's watch. Timing was everything. In seven minutes he would take her.

A small knot of stragglers crossed the street. That seemed to be the last of the children. The old man with the sign that said Stop walked to his car and drove away. Traffic dwindled to an occasional car or truck. Still, Harold waited, watching the long hand on Sam's old watch. When it reached the five-minute mark he returned the watch to his shirt pocket and started the pickup. He pulled back into traffic, signaling for the left lane. At the intersection he turned east, following in the wake of the children.

He next saw her far ahead, on the right-hand side of the street, alone. Today she had dawdled. He was a tad early. He slowed the truck and reached into the glove compartment for his .357 magnum Smith & Wesson. He clipped the gun and holster to his belt, carefully squared his Stetson, and pinned to his shirt the gold badge that said Deputy. Ahead, the little bitch turned down the shortcut toward her home. Harold allowed the truck to creep along to the corner. There he turned right onto the dirt road, following her.

The road dipped down across a dry wash and up a graveled hill. Open country lay beyond. Rank sunflowers and tall Johnson grass bordered the road on both sides, hiding the truck from view. When the little bitch heard the pickup she looked back anxiously, not yet showing fear. She eased to the far left side of the road, giving him plenty of room to pass.

Harold waited until he was almost upon her before braking to an abrupt halt. She stopped and stood rigid with fear, looking up at him with her big brown eyes. Harold stepped from the truck so she could see his gun, his cowboy hat, and the badge that said Deputy. "Hi," he said, hands on hips. "What's your name?"

Fear left her for the moment. "Catherine," she said. Her voice was high-pitched and whispery.

4

"Catherine how much?"

"Catherine Overby."

"Who's your homeroom teacher?"

"Mrs. Lansden."

Harold spat into the Johnson grass. The old bullshit came easily. "Mrs. Lansden says somebody's been stealing crayons from her desk. Know anything about that?"

She shook her head. "No, sir."

Harold took a step toward her. "Let's see that satchel."

She handed him her backpack. Harold unzipped it. Inside were two books, two sticks of chewing gum, half of a Hershey bar, two pencils, a small mirror, a comb, and some rubber bands. Harold put the bag under one arm. "I figured you'd be too smart to have them crayons on you. Mrs. Lansden is sure you're the one that's been taking them. You sure you don't know nothing about it?"

"No, sir."

"Well, let's go get your mama. We'll take her to Mrs. Lansden and get this cleared up right now." He gestured to the truck. "Hop in. Mrs. Lansden's waiting on us."

She hesitated only briefly. Harold felt fully in control. He had the gun, the badge. She climbed into the truck. The polite, cooperative ones were always the easiest.

Harold drove up out of the dry wash. At the next intersection he headed west, into open country. The little bitch turned to look out the rear window. "I live back that way," she said hesitantly, pointing.

Harold checked the rearview mirror. Nobody in sight behind, nobody ahead. He raised his right hand and brought it down like a club, knocking the little bitch off her seat. "Down!" he shouted. "Now!"

Again he raised his hand. But the second blow was not needed. She dropped to the floorboards and scrambled as far under the dash as she could go, whimpering and sobbing like a lost pup.

Harold felt a wave of disappointment. Another weeper. He wanted screamers.

He drove another eight or ten miles on the lonely road. He met no other car or truck. The constant whimpering and whining beneath the dash began to irritate him. He reached down and slapped her across the face. "Take off your clothes. Now!"

Still crying, she looked up at him and shook her head.

Again Harold raised his hand. "I'm warning you! Do it!"

She remained motionless, wailing, "No, no," over and over.

5

After making certain no other vehicles were on the road, Harold braked and pulled off into the bar ditch. "Okay. I'll do it for you."

He took his knife from its sheath at his belt, reached down, and slit her dress from the neck downward. She squealed but did not fight. He ripped off the rest of her clothes and threw every last scrap out the window. She lay on the floorboards, sobbing, trying to cover herself with her arms and hands. She was even skinnier than he had guessed. That was good. Sam liked them skinny.

"I want my mama," she cried. "You promised."

Harold hardly heard. Her crying and wailing had put him out of the mood for what he usually did at this point. He was thinking of the difficulties he might encounter on the long drive north to the barn.

He knew all the back roads. He would stay on them wherever possible. But some places he would have to travel a few miles on major highways. That would not be safe in daylight. Any guy driving an eighteen-wheeler could look down into the pickup.

Harold checked Sam's watch. Two hours until sundown. He could wait.

He drove into a creek bottom, to a place he remembered—a hidden cove where he had hunted and fished several times. There he parked and turned off the ignition. "Sit," he told the girl. "Don't move."

He changed clothes in the bed of the pickup, carefully packing his boots, pistol belt, hat, trousers, and shirt in plastic before stowing them in the toolbox behind the cab. He pulled on dungarees, a blue denim shirt, a gray gimme cap that said John Deere, and a pair of shit-kicker brogans. He kept the gun with him, tucked into his belt.

When he returned to the cab the girl was still crying. "My mama's going to wonder where I am," she said.

"We'll just let her wonder," Harold told her.

If all went well, her mama would be wondering for a long, long time.

The setting sun glinted off the windshield of the cop car at the intersection more than a mile away. Harold kept his cool, not slowing until he was over the hill and into the small valley beyond. He allowed the pickup to coast to a stop at the edge of the road.

He sat for a moment in panic, trying to decide what to do. He could not believe roadblocks had been set up so soon. Yet every instinct told him that the cops he had seen were hunting, and that he was the hunted. He tried to guess how much they knew. No one had seen him take her. He was certain of that. Odds were good they did not have a description of him or his truck.

Common sense told him he must get past that intersection, out of the net. He could not go back. No doubt other cop cars were back that way, closing off all roads. He knew he did not have time to fart around. The cop car at the highway intersection may have seen him. If he failed to reappear in the next minute or two, they probably would send someone to investigate.

"Shut up," he told the girl. "We're going to play a game."

She stopped sobbing and looked up at him. From the toolbox he fished out a roll of duct tape and a burlap bag. He taped her wrists, her ankles, and her knees together. He slapped her and shook her to get her attention. "Listen! If you make a single sound, I'll kill you. Understand?"

He taped her mouth without waiting for a reply. With one arm he lifted her and slipped her into the burlap sack. He tied the top securely and put the sack in the truck bed, nestled in the midst of the other sacks.

"You can breathe," he told her. "Don't do anything else, or I'll kill you."

He drove slowly over the next hill and down the slope toward the highway intersection. He placed his gun beside him, in the crevice behind the seat, within reach in case he needed it. He knew he would have to keep his cool. The cops would be alert. The odds were not in his favor if it came to a shootout.

As he approached the intersection, one cop stepped out of the patrol car and waved a flashlight The other cop remained behind the wheel. The sign on the side of the car said Oklahoma Highway Patrol. Harold eased the pickup to a stop. "Hi, officer," he called. "Something happen?"

The trooper ignored Harold's question. He took his time examining Harold and the truck. "Could I see your driver's license, sir?"

"Sure." Harold took Sam's old wallet out of his hip pocket and handed it out the open window.

"Just the driver's license, sir. Take it out of your billfold."

"Okay," Harold said. He knew the drill, but he wanted the cop to think it was all new to him.

"This your truck?"

"Yes, sir."

The trooper returned to the cop car and stood for a moment beside it, reading Harold's license number to his partner. Harold was certain the truck and license would clear a computer check. Sam had always made certain of that. Still he reached down to feel the comforting coolness of his gun.

But when the trooper came back he walked past Harold to peer into the bed of the pickup. "What you got in those sacks?" he asked.

"Snakes," Harold told him.

"Snakes?" He sounded dubious.

"Yes, sir. Rattlesnakes. That's what I do. Catch them. Want a look?" He stepped out of the truck, leaving the door open so the gun would be within reach. But he was convinced that the cops were not looking for the truck. Otherwise they would have made their move first thing.

The trooper reached for the nearest sack, hesitated, and withdrew his hand. Harold pulled a sack close and untied the top. He jiggled the burlap until a snake's head appeared, forked tongue testing the air. Harold knocked the head back into the sack with the flat of his hand. "Down, boy," he said. He rolled the sack, holding the top open so the trooper could see the writhing coils inside.

The trooper took a step backward. "Jeez!"

"I caught a good mess of them today," Harold volunteered. "In the mountains west of Lawton."

The trooper glanced back at the patrol car. Apparently he received a signal from his partner that Harold's license had been cleared by the computer. He handed the license back to Harold. "Have a good trip. Appreciate your stopping."

"No bother," Harold said.

He took his time driving off. Twilight had deepened, so he turned on his headlights. He drove north on pavement three miles before turning off onto a dirt road. A few minutes later he stopped the truck and lifted the girl out of the back. She was so quiet that for a moment he thought she had smothered. But when he put the sack on the floorboards and untied the top, she began to whine again. As he ripped the tape off she cried out in pain.

"Shut up," he said. "Or I'll hurt you a lot worse than that."

She quietened and crawled into the darker recesses beneath the dash. Harold drove on, worrying. For all he knew, there could be roadblocks on all the main highways. This was something new. Never before had they put up roadblocks.

He thought ahead, mapping in his mind the rural roads that went over or under the paved highways. Gradually he assembled an elaborate route that would get him home.

The extra distance would keep him driving most of the night. But Sam would be pleased. Sam was ready for another victim.

Then Harold would have to start looking for the next one.

2

Pain came first, welling up out of darkness, all-consuming. Light followed, blinding, blending into the pain. From a great distance came a male voice. "Mrs. Shelby? Mrs. Shelby? Can you hear me?"

Rachel tried to answer. She managed only a croak. Her mouth was dry, her throat numb, her nostrils assailed by sharp, unfamiliar odors.

The voice persisted. "Mrs. Shelby, do you know where you are?"

The question seemed ridiculous. Yet Rachel could not find the answer. "No," she said. The word emerged heavy with vowel and only a trace of consonant.

A form loomed over her, indistinct. Her eyes refused to focus. All was fuzzy-bright, spinning.

"You're in a hospital," the voice said. "In Oklahoma. You've been in an accident. This is important. Do you remember the accident?"

Rachel searched for such a memory and did not find it. "No," she said.

The word came out better this time.

"Well, don't worry. You're going to be okay. Do you understand?"

Rachel's yes emerged with a lisp. Again she attempted to focus her eyes. But the face remained a blur in a glaring field of white.

The voice was strong, reassuring. "We want you to rest now. Don't worry. You're in good hands. Your son was banged up a little. He's doing fine. He's right down the hall. Okay?"

Rachel tried to ask if Suzanne was hurt. She managed only unintelligible sounds. Her head was swimming. Waves of nausea swept over her. She could not form the words.

A hand closed reassuringly on her shoulder. "Everything's fine. Don't worry. Okay?"

He had mentioned David. Logic told Rachel that if Suzanne was hurt, he also would have mentioned her. "Okay," she said.

Two syllables, strung together. She felt an absurd sense of accomplishment.

The firm hand felt soothing on her shoulder. "Relax now. We'll talk when you feel better."

The hand, the intrusive voice, went away. Rachel retreated from the pain, the light.

She slept.

When she next awoke, her headache had dwindled to the level of a full-blown migraine. But agonizing signals now came from the rest of her body. She gasped as pain shot up her backbone.

"She's coming around," a female voice said.

Rachel opened her eyes. Squinting, she forced them into focus. Again the doctor loomed over her. His face was long, thin, and well-structured. He wore a close-cropped black beard. A young, handsome Abraham Lincoln. He even had the Lincolnesque look of sadness around his eyes. Hornrimmed half-glasses rode low on his nose. He took her hand. "Mrs. Shelby, I'm Dr. Peterson. How do you feel?"

Rachel wondered whether *nauseous* or *nauseated* would be most proper. She remembered that purists insist on a distinction, but at the moment she could not recall the specifics. Usually she remained above the fray and let the copy editor rule.

"Nauseated," she said. "Headache. Giddy. I hurt all over."

"I'm not surprised. You have cuts and bruises all over." He peered into her eyes with his little light, talking as he worked. "You're in intensive care, really an adjunct to the emergency room. We're a small hospital. Right now we need to check you over, find out what works and what doesn't. We'll start with your head. Do you remember the wreck now?"

Vividly she saw the big green car emerging from nowhere, gathering speed, heading toward her.

"Yes."

"Fine. Do you remember what happened before that? The last few minutes before the wreck?"

That picture also came to mind. They were driving along the access road, beside the interstate, looking for the Baskin-Robbins. Suzanne was in the front seat beside her, leaning forward, searching, still in high spirits from being recognized that morning and signing more than a hundred autographs. David, in the backseat, spotted the ice cream shop. He pointed to it. Rachel caught a glimpse of it just before the wreck.

"Yes. I remember."

"Good. That's a very, very good sign. Mrs. Shelby, you've received what we in the medical profession like to call a nasty whack on the noggin. Part of your scalp was torn loose. You cracked your skull. Literally. Not a big crack. Just a faint, hairline crack. But a crack nonetheless. Your left arm is broken, a simple fracture. That's the reason for the arm cast. You sustained a few other injuries we'll want to check into. But right now we're mostly concerned about your head. You see, the brain is like a big wet sponge in there. With a whack like you received, it tends to bunch up on one side, pull loose on the other, ripping nerves, blood vessels, and all kinds of important stuff. Extensive memory loss is common. And a bad headache. I can give you something for the pain if you need it. But I'd rather not. You see, if you got goofy on us, we wouldn't know if you were goofy from the medicine, or if your goofiness was a symptom we should know about."

With his solemn deadpan, Rachel was not certain how much of his spiel was humor. "You *are* a doctor, aren't you?" she asked. "Medical school and all?"

Behind him, a nurse snickered. Peterson smiled. His strong fingers worked Rachel's jaw, rotated her neck. "Tufts. Cornell Medical. Internship and residency at Bellevue, not far from your publishing house. I assure you, I'm competent enough to fix a simple whack on the noggin. You've had your appendix out. So you know that when we mess around in the tummy, the whole digestive factory shuts down for a while. When you jar the brain, it tends to do the same thing. We're lucky you're not into a lengthy coma. So don't be too concerned if your head doesn't seem to be hitting on all cylinders. The fact that you've regained short-term memory so soon is terrific news."

Rachel was acutely aware her head was not hitting on all cylinders. For a moment she could not imagine how he knew she was in publishing. Then she realized he no doubt had talked with David and Suzanne.

"How's David?" she asked.

"Awake and cracking jokes. I just left him a few minutes ago. He's going to be okay."

"How badly was he hurt?"

"This will sound worse than it is. Compound fracture of the left leg. Broken pelvis. Three fractures of the left arm. We called in some bone guys. They worked on him more than three hours, under general anesthetic. He should have been sick as a horse this morning. When he woke up he called for and ate a big breakfast. Claimed he missed dinner last night."

For a moment Rachel felt David's pain more than her own.

"And Suzanne?" she asked.

Peterson was moving her right arm, checking her shoulder. His fingers stopped working. He gaze went to the nurse, lingered, then returned to Rachel.

"Suzanne?"

Rachel felt her heart lurch. She struggled to sit up.

"My daughter! Isn't she here?"

Peterson held her firmly, forcing her back onto the bed. "Please, Mrs. Shelby. I'm sure there's an explanation. We were snowed last night in emergency. The authorities probably made accommodations for your daughter and neglected to mention it. How old is she?"

"Eleven. Almost twelve. But small for her age." Rachel attempted to elude his grip. "I've got to find her! What time is it? How long was I out?"

"Please, Mrs. Shelby," Peterson said again. "I don't want to have to give you a shot. There's nothing you can do that we can't do quicker. You're in no shape to be out of that bed. So just lie back and let us handle it."

A new wave of dizziness and nausea swept over her. She ceased struggling, consoling herself with the thought that Suzanne was adept in dealing with adults.

But where was she?

Peterson looked past Rachel to the nurse. "Have the desk call city and rattle their cage. Jeff worked the wreck. Tell them to get hold of him even if they have to call him at home. Get him over here pronto."

The nurse's shoes squeaked faintly as she hurried from the room. Peterson resumed his examination, exploring Rachel's upper arms and shoulders.

"In answer to your question, you were unconscious eighteen hours. It's now a few minutes after ten, Tuesday morning."

Rachel's common sense was screaming that something was badly wrong. She felt an overwhelming urge to assemble her family.

"Can I see David?"

Peterson frowned. "He's not mobile. Neither are you. Mrs. Shelby, I've joked around, but this is serious. I want you to lie flat. You show signs of intracranial bleeding. That could be dangerous. It bears close, careful watching."

The nurse returned. "They put out a code whatever. They said he'd be here in a few minutes."

Peterson acknowledged the message with a nod. He gently rolled Rachel onto her side, probed her ribs, and listened through his stethoscope while he thumped.

Rachel tried to make herself believe she might be overreacting. Both she and David had been unconscious for hours. The hospital would not have wanted an eleven-year-old underfoot. The normal procedure might have been for the authorities to make some provision for her.

Suzanne was a good kid. Obedient. Attentive. Unusually self-disciplined. But if someone had taken her somewhere for safekeeping, she would be driving them crazy by now to bring her to the hospital.

Officer Jeff had better have a good explanation.

"How did you know I've had my appendix out?" she asked Peterson.

He smiled. He was rotating her feet, testing the reflexes. "Oh, my dear lady, we examined you thoroughly, first thing. After all, this *is* a hospital. You'll find us nosy. They brought in your purse and we went through your papers. But we didn't learn much. Only that you're vice president and fiction editor of a New York publishing company."

"Was," Rachel said. "I'm now story consultant for a West Coast film studio."

"I told the nurses the minute they brought you in that we had us a live one. Usually all we get are farmers and ranchers and oil people. Boring. We're long overdue for someone interesting."

Rachel knew he was prattling to keep her mind occupied. In a way she was grateful.

He flexed her left leg. "That hurt?"

"Yes."

"That knee took a lick. We X-rayed it. Looks okay. I think it's only a bruise." He brought the leg up gently.

"My back hurts when you do that," Rachel told him.

He rolled her slightly and put his hand accurately on the exact spot. "There?"

"Yes."

"Spinal tap. That's how we know you're bleeding a little inside your head. The spinal fluid shows us. Otherwise we'd have to take a peek inside your head. We don't want to do that unless we have to. We're nosy, but we're not that nosy. Anyone you want us to notify?"

"Pardon?"

"All the whom-to-notify lines on your identification were blank. Is there anyone you wish us to inform that you're here?"

Rachel considered the complications such notification would bring. "No, thank you," she said. "I'll do that later."

Peterson flexed her other leg. "The people in accounting will be after you to fill out some forms now that you're awake. I'll hold them off as long as I can. They took your insurance card. They wanted me to ask if it's current."

Rachel had chosen the 120-day option for continued coverage under the publishing house plan, anticipating that would give her ample time to arrange new coverage in California.

"It's current," she said. "But accounting should be more concerned whether the other driver has liability."

"I'm sure that question has occurred to them."

Peterson rotated cranks at the foot of her bed, raising her head and shoulders. The room spun. Again Rachel had trouble focusing her eyes.

"How's that?" Peterson asked.

"The earth moved."

Peterson laughed to the nurse. "I told you we had a live one."

Minutes crept by, turned into hours, and still no one came. Twice Rachel sent someone to check, and both times word came back that the policeman was on his way. Rachel lay dizzy, hurting, desperately striving to contain the bubbling caldron of her panic. Again she tried to sit up, determined to go find a phone and get some answers. But the pain and vertigo were too much. She sank back onto the pillow and wept for a time in her helplessness, fear, and frustration. But gradually she found comfort in her recognition that thus far the medical personnel had been unusually caring and conscientious. She could see that for the moment she would have to trust them to help her.

She wiped her eyes on her skimpy hospital gown and rolled her head to examine her surroundings. She was the only patient in intensive care. The other two beds were vacant, posing the persistent but never-asked question concerning the last occupants.

The first nurse had left. A different one, a small, dark-haired woman, came in and insisted that Rachel try some tapioca rice pudding. Rachel ate half of a small serving.

A few minutes after one, the first nurse returned. Rachel almost failed to recognize her in street clothes. She was carrying a camera and smiling.

"I have a present for you," she said.

She handed Rachel an instant-camera snapshot. And there was David on a hospital bed, his left arm, left leg, and lower torso swathed in casts. He looked pale. But he was laughing.

Again quick tears came. Rachel knew she would never forgive herself for the wreck. Technically, it had not been her fault. But she had been careless, plunging into the intersection, blithely assuming no one would run the red light.

There were six pictures. In the last, David had raised his arm cast aloft. His thumb and fingers formed a duck's head.

Rachel had taught him how to make a duck shadow on the wall when he was two.

She could not stop crying. "Thank you," she said to the nurse. "Oh, thank you!"

"I have three of my own. I know how I'd feel. I don't live far. After a night like last night, it takes a while for me to unwind." She handed Rachel a box of tissues from the bedside table. "Now, dry your eyes and we'll take *your* picture. David's worried about you, too, you know."

Rachel was so grateful she felt awkward. "I missed your name."

"Donna. Donna Sewell. I'll just use this stepstool. Dr. Peterson would have my hide if I tried to sit you up."

As Donna stepped onto the stool, Rachel got her first good look at her. Probably in her late thirties, she was of above average height, lean, and willowy. Her dark eyes were quick, intelligent. Her thick straight black hair was feathered to just below the ears. She wore only a hint of makeup. Rachel judged she paid passing attention to her appearance but did not devote much time to it. Cleanliness and neatness prevailed. She wore a crisply starched denim skirt and white blouse. Tiny gold earrings, a little gold cross, and a wedding band were her only jewelry. There was an intensity, a directness about her Rachel liked.

Donna snapped pictures. Rachel wanted to send David a private signal. At first she could not think of one, but for the last picture she also raised her arm cast and with both hands made two ducks kissing.

Donna tossed the wet photos onto the bed to develop.

"I'm talking out of turn. But don't let Dr. Peterson's Jay Leno routine fool you. He's absolutely the best. I've seen them come and go. If I had something bad wrong with me, I'd run to him first thing. He's good good good."

She had an odd way of speaking, drawling out some words for emphasis, tripping through others so fast, the syllables overlapped. She said good good good as one word.

"He seems quite competent," Rachel said. "I don't think I've ever had such a thorough examination."

"He was off at seven, you know. He hung around until you came out of it. He's that way. Always on the floor, even after twelve-hour shifts in emergency. I don't know when he sleeps."

She gathered up the finished pictures, studied them one by one, and passed them to Rachel. "They came out pretty good. I overrode the automatic exposure. All that white seems to confuse it."

The photographs were a jolt. Rachel winced at the large dark bruises, her swollen face, black eyes, and the wrappings covering her head. "These may send him into shock," she said.

Donna laughed. She seemed to be wanting to say something else, but could not find the proper way. When she at last spoke, her manner was abrupt. "You haven't heard from Pryor yet?"

Rachel assumed that Pryor was Officer Jeff. "Not yet. I'm going crazy, waiting." She fought back tears. "I've never felt so helpless in my life."

For a moment Donna seemed at a loss for words. "Well, he should be along soon. I'm sure there was just a lack of communication somewhere. I'll get these pictures to David."

Rachel stopped her at the door. "Mrs. Sewell, I thank you with all my heart."

Donna gave a little shrug. "No trouble." She went on out.

Rachel picked up the photographs, knowing she would treasure them forever. Donna's return to the hospital to make them, after a busy night in the emergency room, was one of the kindest, most thoughtful gifts Rachel had ever received.

From the moment Rachel saw the policeman's face she braced for the worst. A man in civilian clothes was with him. They came into intensive care and stood beside her bed, hats in hand.

The policeman was short and skinny, with flaming red hair, big ears, and abundant freckles. He looked so much like an inept sidekick on a television sitcom that Rachel would not have been surprised to hear a laugh track. The man in civilian clothes was more imposing. He was solidly built, with blond hair trimmed short, a square jaw, good teeth, and blue eyes.

The uniformed officer made the introductions.

"Mrs. Shelby, I'm Officer Pryor. This here's Detective Lieutenant Hopkins. We'd like to ask you a few questions."

"First, I have one of my own," Rachel said. "Have you found my daughter?"

Pryor hesitated. "Not exactly."

Rachel could not contain herself. "What kind of answer is that? Either you have or you haven't!"

"We haven't," said Lieutenant Hopkins. His voice was low, self-assured. "That's why we're here."

Dr. Peterson eased into the room and leaned his lanky frame against the doorjamb. The officers looked at him questioningly.

"I think I should be here," he said.

Pryor turned back to Rachel. "Mrs. Shelby, you must understand. There was a lot of confusion after the wreck. We've now placed your daughter at the scene. But we haven't been able to trace her from there."

Again Rachel was consumed for a moment by heart-freezing terror. She attempted to push herself higher on the pillow and paid the price in pain. "Of course she was at the scene!" she shouted. "She was in the car with me! In the front seat!"

"Yes, ma'am," Pryor said. "We now have four witnesses who saw her after the wreck. Five, counting your son."

"Was she hurt?"

"We don't think so," Lieutenant Hopkins said. "Your son told us that after the wreck she was on her hands and knees in the front seat, trying to pull you out. Your air bag had deployed. But since the blow was from the side, it didn't do much good. You were jammed under it, between the steering wheel and the door. Your son said when she couldn't pull you out, your daughter crawled into the backseat, where he was. She didn't seem to be injured none. At least not bad."

Rachel's growing panic found an outlet in anger. "You questioned David? Without my permission?"

"Just general questions, ma'am. We didn't let on to him your daughter's missing. We told him we were trying to reconstruct the sequence of events."

"Your vehicle was on fire," Pryor said. "The driver of an eighteen-wheeler stopped, reached in, and pulled your daughter out so they could get to you and the boy. The truck driver said he set her down and went back for you. We don't know what happened to her after that."

"My car burned?"

No one had told her that.

"Yes, ma'am," Pryor said. "Your vehicle was totaled."

"The fire and your rescue held everybody's attention," Hopkins said. "Everybody knew the gas tank would explode any second."

Rachel listened in pure horror. "I had just filled it!"

Pryor nodded. "Yes, ma'am. It made quite a show when it went. That truck driver and two or three others did good work, getting you and your family out."

Rachel realized she owed her life, and David's life, to men she did not even know.

"No one remembers seeing your daughter after she was rescued," Hopkins said. "Like I say, all attention was on the car, on getting you and the boy out. Quite a crowd had gathered. Thirty or forty people, at least. The fire trucks and ambulances were coming. There was a lot of shouting and running around."

"Surely *someone* knows where she is," Rachel insisted.

"That's our thinking," Hopkins said. "We're going back, interviewing witnesses again, putting it all together. It's just taking us a little time. What we need to do now is eliminate some other possibilities. Could we ask you a few questions?"

"Of course."

Pryor and Hopkins pulled two folding chairs to the bedside.

"First off, where is the girl's father?" Hopkins asked. "Could we maybe talk to him?"

"He died five years ago of a massive coronary."

Never before had Rachel been able to put it so bluntly.

Pryor was making notes.

Hopkins nodded, "I see. What was his full name?"

"William Price Shelby. He was a stockbroker. On Wall Street."

"A witness at the scene rescued your purse from the car. Any reason why you were carrying two complete sets of ID?"

Rachel did not understand. "I beg your pardon?"

"Who is Rachel Mermin?"

Rachel could not see what that had to do with Suzanne's disappearance. But she answered the question. "That's my maiden name. My professional name."

"You kept credit cards, bank accounts under both names?"

"Yes. Mostly for business reasons."

"I see," Hopkins said.

But Rachel wondered if he truly did. "I was well established in publishing before I met my husband," she explained. "So I retained my professional identity."

"What about his folks?"

Rachel was growing more exasperated with each question. She

could not imagine how Bill's parents entered into it. She answered rather sharply. "They're retired, and quite elderly. They live in Florida. I can give you their phone number and address. But I hope it won't be necessary to alarm them at this point."

Hopkins shifted in his chair. "You see what we're getting at, ma'am. Lots of times, in fact, *most* of the time, when a child is reported missing, we eventually find it's a custody case gone sour. Is there anything like that here?"

"No! Absolutely not!"

"No family disagreements at all?"

Rachel was appalled. She wanted to get past this, to stop wasting time. "None! I talk with my husband's parents by phone every week or so. My mother-in-law is in bad health, almost bedridden. My husband, an only child, was born late in their lives. My own father is dead. My mother also is a stockbroker, with a firm on Wall Street. I assure you she's too busy to follow me all the way out here. I'll give you her phone number and address. But again, I don't want to alarm her unnecessarily."

"What about your male acquaintances? Any trouble there?"

That was too much. "Really! Is this necessary? From what you say, my daughter is apparently missing. Something terrible may have happened to her." Again Rachel could not stop herself from shouting. "We must find her! Can't we address that simple fact?"

Her anger left Hopkins unperturbed. "Ma'am, the quicker we get these questions out of the way, the sooner we can get totally into the search. We're bound by standard police procedure. We've got to ask these questions. We need your cooperation."

Rachel could not hide her fury. She wanted to get on with it. "I *am* cooperating."

"Then please answer the question. Is there a boyfriend?"

"No! Since my husband's death, I've dated from time to time. But there has never been anything really serious. Not a single instance! My children are my life."

"Would your daughter have taken this opportunity to run away?"

"At *eleven?*"

"We've had younger. Much younger. How was your relationship with her? Any trouble at all?"

"None."

"What was the purpose of your trip?"

Rachel sought some way to reduce the complexities to a few simple sentences. "I had just resigned my position in New York and accepted another on the West Coast. We shipped our furniture, personal belongings. There was no hurry to get there, so we decided to drive and to see the country.''

''Is there any reason you were carrying a considerable amount of cash in small bills?''

The police had been into the secret compartment of her purse! Again Rachel spoke with some heat. ''I wasn't aware I was carrying an excessive amount. I didn't know there was a law. We were going across the country. I wasn't sure automatic teller machines would be available when I needed them. I didn't want to run short. I suppose I should have used traveler's checks. But again, I wasn't sure what facilities I'd find between major towns.''

Hopkins took a notepad from his shirt pocket and thumbed through it. ''You left your motel room about daylight and didn't return until three. Right at checkout time. Where did you go during that interval?''

''We toured the Washita Battle Site, the Black Kettle Museum. My son is interested in Indians, the history of the Old West.''

''Did you see anyone there you knew?''

''No.''

''Anything unusual occur?''

''Only that my daughter was recognized and signed autographs for some schoolchildren touring on a chartered bus. But I wouldn't really term that unusual.''

''Recognized?''

''Suzanne starred in a movie that's currently in release. She has been recognized several times on our trip.''

Hopkins and Pryor glanced at each other.

''She's a movie star?'' Hopkins asked.

Rachel was not yet comfortable with that label. But she supposed it was accurate.

''Her first film has proved successful. She has been signed to do a sequel.''

''Mrs. Shelby, could she have been kidnapped for ransom?''

Rachel's brain truly was not hitting on all cylinders. That possibility had not occurred to her. She felt a fresh surge of panic. ''If that were the case, wouldn't we have heard something by now?''

''Not necessarily. Sometimes they wait. But if it's ransom, you were probably stalked. Do you remember seeing anyone that seemed to be following you, watching you?''

Rachel thought back over the hurried return to the motel before checkout time. ''No.''

''You didn't take any precautions? Her being a movie star and all?''

"No. Maybe I should have. But Suzanne's film career erupted so suddenly, I haven't had time to think about matters like that."

"What exactly happened up at the museum?"

Rachel reconstructed the scene, remembering details. "We were looking at the exhibits. This group of children came in. One of them became excited when she saw Suzanne, asked if she wasn't Suzanne Shelby. Suzanne said she was. The children crowded around. Suzanne spent the better part of an hour signing autographs. She has always been responsive to her fans."

"Mrs. Shelby, sometimes I get the feeling we're talking about an adult, not an eleven-year-old."

Rachel considered that observation carefully. She attempted to explain. "In a some ways, Suzanne *is* mature for her age. She has worked with adults in learning voice, dramatics, dance. She has dealt with directors, adult actors on a professional level. She's accustomed to being around adults. But because of these diversions, she may not be as mature as most children in some respects."

"Would that tend to make her run away? Like a five-year-old? Not aware of the danger?"

"No! She's dependent on me, on her brother, for *emotional* support. Her acting, all the other, is a make-believe world. Her brother and I are her reality. I don't know if I can explain that adequately."

"I think you have," Hopkins said. "Could you give me a description?"

"Auburn hair. A little more than shoulder length. Hazel eyes."

"Height? Weight?"

"Forty-nine and a half inches. About sixty-three pounds."

Hopkins hesitated. "Sixty-three pounds? At eleven?"

"I told you. She's small for her age. It's genetic. I'm small. My mother's small."

"What was she wearing?"

Again Rachel thought back, remembering. "Tan hiking shorts with shoulder straps. Pale yellow blouse with a muted pattern. Over-the-calf chocolate-brown socks. Ballet-style slippers. She was carrying a tooled-leather handbag."

"Jewelry?"

"A gold necklace chain with a heart-shaped pendant her father gave her. Tiffany watch. Gold."

"Earrings?"

Rachel could not remember. "I don't think so."

"You got a picture of her?"

"We had some in the car. In the trunk. Publicity stills. I don't know if they survived."

"No, ma'am," Pryor said. "Wasn't nothing in the vehicle that wasn't burnt up."

Rachel hesitated. The decisions were coming too fast. With her giddiness, she did not feel adequate to handle them. She had hoped to keep the studio in the dark about Suzanne's disappearance until more was known.

Now she could see that would be impossible.

"If you have a good fax machine, you can have a photo sent from the studio within the hour. Or you could get glossies by overnight delivery."

"I think, at this point, we should do both," Hopkins said. "Meanwhile, we'll continue interviewing witnesses. If we come up dry, we'll put the photos and description out."

Rachel gave him the name of the person to call at the studio, and the number.

Pryor and Hopkins stood, preparing to leave.

Rachel refused to let them go so easily. "What happens next?" she asked. "Will the FBI enter into it?"

Hopkins answered by rote. "All the facilities of the FBI are at our disposal. Officially, the FBI can't enter a case unless, one, we have proof that a crime has been committed, and, two, that the crime falls in their jurisdiction. At this point, Mrs. Shelby, we don't even know for certain a crime has been committed."

Rachel had reached the limit of her patience with the foot-dragging, the bad grammar, the country-hickness of Officer Pryor, the unyielding rigidity of Hopkins's attitude.

She did not bother to hide her anger.

"Let me make sure you understand, Lieutenant Hopkins. If my daughter is missing, her disappearance will receive national attention. A high-profile case. Isn't that the terminology? I don't think a small-town police department is equipped to deal with that."

The lieutenant's cheeks and ears turned a darker hue. "Mrs. Shelby, we've already pulled in six off-duty officers. We have nine men out interviewing right now. If we develop anything—anything at all—we'll call in the Oklahoma State Bureau of Investigation. They'll send in agents, specialists. In your bigger cities you'd probably have a half dozen cases competing for manpower. Here we've got one. You'd get no better work done anywhere in the country."

"I hope so, Lieutenant Hopkins. I just wanted you aware of what will happen if Suzanne's truly missing."

"Yes, ma'am. We'll cross that bridge when we come to it. We'd better get on. If we learn anything, we'll let you know first thing."

Hopkins and Pryor left. Rachel put her hands over her face and squeezed on the bridge of her sore nose, savoring for a moment the resulting pain. She could not hold back tears, but she fought to retain her composure. She knew she was dangerously close to unraveling completely.

Peterson had been standing by the door so quietly that she had forgotten he was in the room. He came to take her pulse. "How's the headache?"

"Better."

"The dizziness?"

"Not as bad. Doctor, you've got to get me out of this bed! You can see that, can't you?"

He did not answer immediately. He released her wrist and sank into one of the folding chairs. "If you tried to get up right now, you'd fall flat. You might finish cracking your skull."

"Put yourself in my place! How can I just lie here while Suzanne is out there God knows where?"

"What could you do?"

"I can use Suzanne's popularity to bring the FBI, every police agency possible into the search, and keep the pressure on until she's found."

Peterson shook his head. "We can't rush your recovery. There are too many risks."

"Like what?"

"To begin with, your scalp was torn over the skull fracture. Excellent avenue for bacteria. If you get an infection into the brain, it's Katie bar the door."

"I'll risk it."

"There's more. You've had—maybe still have—intracranial bleeding. Sometimes people get a whack on the noggin so slight, they hardly notice. They forget about it. Two weeks later they're dead from a cerebral hemorrhage. A goose egg like yours is nothing to play around with."

"I'll sign a waiver."

He seemed not to have heard. He went on, almost as if talking to himself. "I've treated head injuries no worse than yours where we had continued loss of memory, personality changes, difficulties with speech and gait, the whole smorgasbord."

"You said I've responded well. Maybe it isn't as bad as it looks."

"Maybe. Still, under ideal conditions I'd keep you under observation for a week or ten days, watching for any abnormality. Vision. Sense of touch. Muscular weakness. Indistinct speech. At the first hint of trouble, I'd have you on a plane to St. Anthony's in Oklahoma City. I don't often scare my patients. But I'm trying to scare you. Please understand *my* situation."

Rachel grasped his arm. "Dr. Peterson, I'm the only person who can do what needs to be done! I'm begging you to help me."

He was silent for a time. He frowned, as if struggling with a difficult decision. "I'll not promise anything. But perhaps I should take into consideration that you'll turn into a basket case just lying there, worrying. I'll meet you halfway. We'll see if we can cut a few corners. But I want you to do exactly what I say, and no more. Understood?"

"Yes."

"We'll see how well you do, and go from there. One other thing I should mention, even though it's not my place to do so. Your superior attitude was a smidgin too plain with those two cops. Lady, you need their help. So I'll give you some free, nonmedical advice. Don't look down your nose at the locals because of their rustic ways and bad grammar. I've made that mistake. You're in the land of the double negative. I know how it is in New York, with everyone trying to scramble up the pecking order. Around here the worst sin you can commit is to put on airs. Everyone guards against that. They toss in a double negative every once in a while to show they're just plain folks. The local brand of humor and fellowship. At least that's my theory. They know better. For your information, Lieutenant Hopkins holds a master's degree in criminology."

From what podunk college, Rachel wanted to ask. She refrained.

"Never get pushy, impatient. For instance, around here it's considered polite to ask anyone you reach by phone if he's got a minute. A New Yorker would take that as a gross insult, to suggest he had a minute to spare. It would ruin his whole day."

Rachel found herself receptive. She had sensed that she had performed badly with the policemen.

"But you do have a point," Peterson went on. "The local cops are limited in manpower. They'll be pulling double shifts, working sixteen-hour days. They can't maintain that pace long. Other local crimes won't come to a screeching halt. Like most of the country, we're up to our ears. The local police will give your daughter all they've got for a while. But if the early leads play out, they'll turn to the growing backlog."

Rachel could hardly bring herself to think that far ahead. But she assumed she should be prepared for any eventuality. "You have a suggestion?"

"I happen to know a fellow who retired three or four years ago from the Oklahoma State Bureau of Investigation. The OSBI. He's generally considered the dean of detectives in this state. He's on pension, social security. A widower. Kids grown. Bored. He wouldn't be costly. Probably not much beyond expenses."

"A private investigator? Wouldn't that antagonize the local police?"

"I doubt it. They've all worked with him. If the OSBI comes into it, he'll know everyone involved. He trained most of them."

"If they don't find her tonight, I'm starting a campaign to get the FBI into it."

"If I had a choice between Booker Reeves and the FBI, the FBI might lose."

"He's that good?"

"Yes."

"How do you know?"

Peterson's hesitation was brief. "I've seen him work."

Rachel opened her mouth to inquire further. Something in his face stopped her. "How would I get in contact with him?"

"He and I keep in touch. If you want, I'll call him. He can be here in two or three hours."

Rachel felt she should be doing something. Anything to preserve her sanity. "Doctor, I would be most grateful. Please tell him I'll pay half above his going rate."

Peterson had started toward the door. He stopped and looked back at her. "Mrs. Shelby, you must understand one thing. Booker won't come into it for the money. He says he has seen too much evil during his lifetime, and he doesn't want to see more. There's only one thing that'll bring him into it. Someone needing him. I'll only have to tell him an eleven-year-old girl is missing. If I know Booker, he'll be on the road in thirty minutes."

3

Sudden calls to duty in distant parts of the state had been an accepted way of life for Booker Reeves. Over years the procedure had become routine, now altered only by his changed circumstances. No longer was Betty available to do the necessary things, or to kiss good-bye. The responsibilities he once left to her he now farmed out to others. He telephoned his veterinarian daughter to come take custody of his coon hound, Hector. A neighbor promised to pick up the newspapers and mail. Booker packed essential clothing. Within twenty-five minutes of Peterson's call, he was westbound on the interstate.

The timing was fortunate—late enough to miss the afternoon rush hour, too early for the first stirrings of evening. Booker kept his radio tuned to a good country and western station. He deemed country music one of the few facets of life that had actually improved with the passage of time.

Traffic remained relatively light through the first hundred miles. Not until he entered the far western portions of the state did traffic thicken with a heavy surge of trucks and other dedicated overnight travelers.

Following remembered landmarks and the information Pete had provided, Booker slowed and exited the interstate to the access road that led to the intersection where the Shelby kid was last seen. During the final few years of his career he had worked five major cases in this part of the state, one an international oil field theft investigation that had lasted six months. He had been through the intersection dozens of times. He was familiar with it. But before he did anything else, he now wanted to study it in detail, to reconstruct in his mind what may have happened.

He found where Rachel Shelby's car had burned, almost directly under the overhead traffic signal, leaving oil stains and scorched

27

pavement. He left his car and walked out into the intersection to gain better perspective. At this time of night, local traffic was almost nonexistent. But a stone's throw to the south the interstate was a raging river, filling the air with diesel fumes and turbulent waves of sound.

At times Booker tended to think of the interstate's lanes as the essential veins and arteries of the national corpus, carrying nourishment to distant points, returning waste to be recycled. The interstate also carried a vast number of things he considered unhealthy—drugs and disease, trends and attitudes, change and ugliness. Circulation never ceased, not even while the body slept. Standing beside the interstate, day or night, and with only a little imagination, he sometimes thought he could hear the nation's heartbeat.

The prospect of again entering a major case had left Booker feeling pumped up. He was growing old in years but not, he sincerely believed, in essential ways. He felt no different now than he had at half his age. To the contrary, he was certain that in looking at the world from a high promontory of experience, he was far better equipped to deal with crime and criminals than ever before. After Betty's death, the OSBI had become his whole life. He had always liked putting the bad guys away. Never for a moment had he ever considered doing anything else.

His forced retirement had come unexpectedly, leaving him devastated and with a nagging sense that his career remained imperfect, unfinished. With more bad guys out there than ever, he had been put out to pasture.

The OSBI brass, secure in their relative youth, had been sympathetic but firm. They would not be able to understand Booker's viewpoint until they, too, were in the same fix, ten or fifteen years further down the road, when youth and new jargon began undermining their own hard-won knowledge.

A reprimand had been mixed up in it. In a drug bust Booker did not have time to notice that the shooter who came at him out of the dark was only fourteen years old, and the son of an influential family. Inferences were made in newspaper editorials and on the floor of the legislature that Booker could have found some solution other than shooting the boy dead. Legally, he was on firm ground. No charges were filed. But politically, Booker had embarrassed the Bureau.

It was so unfair. But a new, in-coming administration formulated new rules and declared them inflexible. The rules said Booker had to go.

The next four years had been hell on earth. All of Booker's closest friends were still working in the Bureau, immersed in heavy, ongoing caseloads. Booker's kids were grown, busy living their own lives. His grandchildren were preoccupied with their own full agendas, all their days organized to extremes never dreamed of in Booker's own childhood.

For the first time in his life, Booker became acquainted with loneliness and uselessness. Delayed grief for Betty hit him full-force. He now had leisure to remember all the small pleasures they had postponed because of Booker's work. He had abundant time to contemplate how Betty's life had been sacrificed for that work. The many plans they had made—for extended ocean cruises, a retirement cabin in the Ozarks, a motor home and scenic trips around the country—would never be realized. In his depression, Booker had believed that his life was over. Through long, dark nights he sat with pistol on his lap, going back over his grief-driven reappraisal of uncomplaining Betty, and the unthinking, selfish way he and the Bureau had treated her. In extensive retrospect, his career lost its luster. Unsolved, mishandled cases festered until he considered his career, on the balance, a failure. His depression became impenetrable. Several times he came close to suicide. He was saved only by his disgust with that solution; he had seen too many during his career.

After many months and much agonizing, he gradually came to terms with his situation. But the injustices—to himself and to Betty—still rankled.

He felt he had a lot to prove. So he relished this opportunity to demonstrate that the rules were wrong, that he was still as good a cop as anyone in the Bureau.

He stood on the street where Suzanne had disappeared and considered possibilities, cataloguing details.

On the northwest corner of the intersection, a string of shops formed a long strip mall—a convenience store, dry cleaners, Dunkin' Donuts, Baskin-Robbins, Eckerd Drug, and Cloth World. A Texaco station occupied the northeast corner. To the south a high embankment, broken only by the underpass, supported the elevated interstate. The access road provided travelers with more than a mile of motels, fast food restaurants, and service stations, and offered locals a way to get from here to there.

The crossroad served as a route to the downtown section on one end, and continued as a rural highway on the other.

Taking his time, Booker paced off distances. Forty-five feet from the car to the grass strip where Rachel Shelby and her son were taken after their rescue. The grass divider was twenty-five feet wide. Beyond, the parking lot in front of the strip mall was sixty-five feet deep. The first on-ramp to the interstate was a quarter of a mile to the west.

Rarely, travelers boosted clothing at the Kmart up the street, or drove away from restaurants or service stations without paying. But on the whole the interstate's contribution to local crime was nil.

During his long career, Booker had slept at most of the motels along this street. He had watched the travelers. He felt he knew them. Thousands hurtled past by day and by night, westbound, eastbound. Only a relative few made a pit stop for food, rest, gas. He had watched them in the motels and shops, as disoriented as cats suddenly tossed into the wrong social milieu. They spent a lot of time poring over maps. Their minds were fixed on distances and names like Amarillo, Albuquerque, Gallup, and Barstow, or, eastbound, Little Rock, Memphis, Joplin, St. Louis, and Nashville. They usually asked about good restaurants but invariably settled for the familiar. Big Mac. Whataburger. Fries. Big Gulp. Giant Slurp. Or maybe a Sizzler. They wrote postcards, packed and repacked their cars, fiddled with cameras, shopped for necessities, and drove on.

The interstate probably carried as large a percentage of wrong-doers as any cross-section of the population. Criminals fleeing justice. Mean bikers. Perverts. Con men. Armed juveniles. Runaways. Dopeheads. Drug traffickers.

But if the Shelby kid had been kidnapped, indications were that she had been a target of opportunity.

Logic and his gut feelings told Booker this crime was local. Long distance travelers, whatever their ilk, usually adhered to other agendas.

He returned to his car and continued to study the intersection, watching the traffic light change from green to amber to red, and back again. Far up the street a red neon sign proclaimed INDIAN CURIOS. Booker had gone into the shop once, just looking around. Most of the Indian curios were made in Taiwan. Booker's mingled Cheyenne and Arapaho blood had been profoundly offended. His great-grandfathers had fought George Armstrong Custer on several battlefields before smoking the peace pipe. They had been great warriors, incompetent bureaucrats, and piss-poor farmers. They had lost their reservation to Congress and its Dawes Commission. Their allocated lands went to back taxes. His family had subsisted below the poverty level long before the term was invented. He had pulled himself up by his moccasin straps, so to speak, through college and what he liked to think were his inherited tracking skills.

Otherwise, all he had derived from his Indian heritage were a propensity for diabetes and a gastric intolerance of cow's milk.

Yet his entire life had been circumscribed by the Indian thing. He regarded his origins with uncertain pride and a vague sense of loss. He envied his son who, only one-quarter Kiowa, enjoyed more identity with that close-knit tribe than with his three-quarters Cheyenne and Arapaho blood.

All of Booker's children had married Anglos. His son had gone into auto parts and was now phenomenally successful. Booker's elder daughter was the wife of a university professor who specialized in Greek poetry. His younger daughter had married a hospital administrator, and she herself had become a veterinarian. Booker's grandchildren were all Anglos. Sometimes he found himself searching his descendants for Native American traits among those of Scot, Irish, English, and other exotic European tribes.

He often wondered about a people who could go from the bow and arrow to auto parts in one short century.

He timed the traffic signal. He estimated the angle of sight from the service station, and from the various stores.

When he reached the point where he felt the intersection would tell him nothing more, he started his car and drove on downtown.

Booker pushed his way through the heavy glass doors into the small police station tucked into a corner of the faux art deco city hall. He recognized the bristle-blond, uniformed policewoman at the switchboard. Years earlier he had taken her to dinner two or three times. That had been during the time after Betty's death when he was still with the Bureau and thought he should make an effort to get on with his life. He had gone out with a number of women and still kept semiregular company with two or three. But he had found that new relationships paled in the light of forty years of marriage, the joys and trials of fatherhood, and thousands of shared memories. Booker liked to be around women, but none of the relationships had ever turned serious. The blond policewoman had been one of his early experiments. For a difficult moment he could not remember her name. Then it came to him. Terri. With an ''i.''

''Terri!'' he said. ''You're looking good. How's life treating you?''

She looked up at him with a half-flirtatious smile. ''Keeping me busy, is about all. We heard you retired.''

''I'm not quite dead yet. Is Hop around?''

Terri glanced over her shoulder to the empty reaches of the squad room. "Hop and Jeff came in a while ago. They're back there somewhere. Want me to ring?"

"If it's all right, I'll just wander on back."

A buzz at the switchboard rescued Booker and Terri from further conversation. As Terri answered the incoming call, she hit a button, freeing with a click the swinging gate to the squad room. Booker walked on through.

The police station had continued on downhill in the five years since he last had seen it. Upkeep never seemed to be a police strong point. The black and white tile floor needed a thorough mopping and waxing. The desks were scarred from long, hard use. Flesh-colored plastic foam showed through the seats of the chairs. An overhead fluorescent sang a note halfway between that of a mosquito and of an angry bee.

Hop Hopkins and Jeff Pryor were bent over a large crude drawing and a handwritten list of names. Booker recognized the drawing as an outline of the intersection.

Hopkins glanced up. "Booker! What the hell you doing here? I thought you was growing petunias, or whatever the shit retired cops do these days."

Booker perched his rear on an adjacent desk. "Word's out you have a hot one. Knowing the fuckups they call cops around here, I thought maybe I ought to drive down and see if I could help out."

"You back with the Bureau?"

"No. The kid's mother has asked me to take a hand in it."

Booker could see Hopkins assessing the complications of bringing an outsider into the investigation, and Chief Laird's possible reaction. Hopkins was ten times the cop Laird would ever be, and more or less ran his division and the whole police department the way he wanted. But when it came to the bottom line, Laird was chief. Hopkins had to listen to him.

"What you think of the mother?" Hopkins asked, apparently making a spot decision to deal Booker in.

"I haven't talked with her yet. I thought I'd try to get a feel for the case first."

"Far as I'm concerned, you might get off to a good start by checking out your client."

Booker was surprised. Pete had been full of praise for the woman. Booker wondered if Pete was wrong. He kept his poker face. "You got problems with her?"

Hopkins looked toward the door of Laird's darkened office as if judging how much he should reveal of an ongoing investigation.

"Jeff and I both came away feeling she's not leveling with us. First, she told us her husband died of a massive coronary five years ago. At the FBI Academy I bunked with a guy from the NYPD. I got him to make a quick check. The fellow in question OD'd on cocaine. Second, the lady was carrying two complete sets of ID and a little more than three thousand in small bills. Third, she doesn't act like a woman whose kid is missing. Never a tear in all the time we was talking with her."

"If one of my kids was snatched, you'd have to scrape my wife off the floor with a wheat scoop," Pryor said. "With this woman, we could've been talking about the weather."

"She told us the case is too big for us," Hopkins added. "Wants to call in the FBI."

"What's your thinking? Publicity stunt for the kid?"

"I'm hoping you can tell us. The studio did seem a little too quick on our request for a photo."

Hopkins handed Booker a fax sheet. The kid was good-looking, cute, and appealing. But Booker had found that true of most kids her age. "Pete seems to think the woman's telling a straight story," he said.

"She could have him conned. He's hovering over her like a mother hen."

Booker weighed Hop's argument. Maybe the case should be checked out from the beginning. "Could she have faked the wreck?"

"No. I keep coming back to that," Hopkins admitted. "The guy who hit her stated he was trying to squeeze through on amber. What he didn't know was, the Highway Department was out there last week and changed the timing. They'd been receiving complaints about slow lights. They cut the hang time on amber from about eight seconds to about three or four. So when this guy saw the light changing, he speeded up, thinking he'd have that extra few seconds to sail through, like he'd always done. He got red before the inter-section but couldn't stop. He plowed into your client's car right square in the middle of the intersection. I can't see any way she could have set that up, even assuming she'd risk getting killed. Her car torched on impact. Two or three other drivers got her out, unconscious, with only seconds to spare. No, whatever else, the wreck was legit. I'm not questioning that."

"You sure the kid was in the car?"

"We've got four witnesses who place a third person—a child—in the vehicle," Pryor said. "We're up to twenty-six witnesses at the scene. We're still finding more. Most arrived after the kid was pulled from the car.''

"We're slowly putting it together," Hopkins said. "Everybody's out interviewing. Understand, the case was almost twenty-four hours old before we got the squeal. We've had it less than six hours now. We're still playing catch-up.''

"Our best witness drove his rig on to California," Pryor said. "Straight through. He's probably loaded with caffeine pills or worse. But he gave us the best description of the first few seconds after the wreck. He said gas was already up underneath the car, burning. So he didn't even fuck with his fire extinguisher. He said he knew it wouldn't do no good. He concentrated on getting the passengers out.''

Hopkins consulted his notes. "The trucker said, 'I set the kid to one side and went back for the woman.' That was the way he phrased it. I asked him how far to one side, and he said about fifteen or twenty feet.''

"His eye for detail was good," Pryor added. "He told us that when he got back to the vehicle, the other two guys were trying to get the boy out. Bones were showing. They were afraid to move him. The truck driver said he shouted at them to hurry, then grabbed the woman under the armpits and pulled her out. He said he got a snoot full of smoke, and other people helped him carry her to the grass. Someone—we don't know who—reached in and got her purse.''

Booker looked at Hop's drawing, imagining the scene. "Exactly where was the last sighting of the kid?''

Hopkins pointed with a pencil. "So far, right here. Right where the truck driver put her. No one remembers her after that.''

Booker wished he were back in harness so he could go out, pull in some people, and interview them himself. He would have to play this cautiously. "I've been out of touch. Have you had anything like this around here in the last few months? Kids accosted? Attempts to lure them into a car?''

"Nothing. Oh, we have a couple of local wienie waggers. But we know them. They've never been aggressive.''

"Ransom? You done any thinking in that direction?''

"We've alerted the FBI, given them what we've got. We've put an extra recorder on incoming calls. About an hour ago we installed a recorder at the hospital for the switchboard operator to activate if she gets anything. The kid's mother is still in intensive care. No phone. Can you think of anything we missed so far?''

"No. Except maybe the film studio.''

"The FBI said they'd take care of that end."

"Doesn't smell like a ransom deal," Booker observed.

"Doesn't smell like anything that makes sense," Hopkins said. "If the woman's telling it straight, either the kid wandered off, or else we've got us a full-blown nut on our hands."

Booker studied the drawing. "What you working on now?"

"Correlating witness accounts. Trying to confirm we've got a genuine case."

"Starting so late, maybe we'd be wise to consider it genuine until we learn otherwise," Booker suggested. "Can I use your machine? I'd like to tap into VICAP."

Hopkins hesitated. "You on to something? Or is this one of your wild-ass theories?"

"Call it a hunch. I'm thinking she didn't leave that wreck scene by herself. She had help."

Hopkins chuckled. "I'd forgotten what it's like to work with you, Booker. Barking up every tree."

"Sometimes that's the only way to find the right one. It just occurs to me it may not be too early to see if we can find any connections with similar cases."

"What parameters?"

Booker considered. It was a good question. The FBI's Violent Criminal Apprehension Program housed material on most of the nation's major crimes. Unless the request for information was narrowed carefully, the computers would inundate him with bales of data he would have to winnow.

"Bold snatch," he said. "Females six to twelve. I doubt any older. I figure we're dealing with a short-eye. He's probably spooked by puberty. I'd bracket Oklahoma, Texas, Kansas, Missouri, Arkansas. Cases through the last five years."

Hopkins pondered the parameters. "I guess it's worth a try. Want to use my name?"

Booker was well aware he had edged into Hop's domain. Hop was the one who had received FBI training on the VICAP program.

"Some people up there owe me. You may have to deal with them later. I wouldn't want to interfere with that."

Hopkins did not insist. He seemed to have other worries. "Booker, already we're getting calls from the news media. And at this point I'm not even prepared to say the kid's missing, let alone abducted or kidnapped. Before we go to full cry, I'd like to have this thing better in hand. You can really help us by checking out your client. We need to resolve her inconsistencies."

"Soon as I finish with VICAP, I'll skim over your notes," Booker promised. "Then I'll go talk to her."

Rachel had long been intrigued with the way two men who admire and respect each other convey that fact in subtle, almost invisible ways. Nothing is revealed in the trite phrases "How you doing?" and "I'm okay. You?" She thought that perhaps the message is communicated through the deliberateness of the handshake, the sincerity given to the banal verbal exchange, the slow grins, the way they frankly study each other, searching for changes. She lay on her new bed in her new, private room and witnessed this male phenomenon transpiring between Dr. Peterson and Booker Reeves.

She had just concluded her first therapy session. Supported by Dr. Peterson and Donna, she had sat up on the edge of the bed, even taken a few steps. Her equilibrium was still awry, but the dizziness seemed to be fading. Physically, she felt stronger. Mentally, she was not faring so well. She sensed she was right on the edge, ready to fall apart any moment. It seemed intolerable that she was forced to go on with banal talk and situations while her child was missing, undoubtedly suffering untold horrors.

Peterson made introductions. "You two will want to talk," he said. "Donna and I will leave you alone for a while."

After Peterson and Donna closed the door behind them, Reeves circled the bed, pulled a chair close, and took out a small notepad. In deference to the late hour, the ceiling light was off. The only illumination came from the night-light over Rachel's bed.

Something about Booker Reeves reminded Rachel of the actor Spencer Tracy, especially in his later movies, such as *Judgment at Nuremberg*. Perhaps the impression came from his thick salt-and-pepper hair, cut short in the outdated style, from the abundant fine wrinkles around his eyes and mouth, from his compact, sturdy build, and from the way he seemed to feel the weight of the world on his shoulders. She sensed warmth, compassion in his chocolate-brown eyes. Although only of average size, he possessed what Suzanne's stage friends called strong presence. She felt from the first that he was an extraordinary person, that she could give him her total trust.

"I'm grateful you could come so quickly on such short notice," she said. "I'm relieved you're here."

His voice was deep yet soft. "I drove right on down. I knew I wouldn't sleep after Pete called. In a case like this, the first few hours can be crucial. We've already lost a lot of time. You feel up to talking?''

"Completely. I've been going crazy doing nothing. I want to get the police moving, get something done.''

Reeves nodded. "Lieutenant Hopkins kept good notes. He's made a good start. I dropped by to check signals with him.''

"Have they found anything? Anything at all?''

"They still have a number of interviews to conduct. What we're trying to do, right now, is pinpoint the exact time she disappeared. If we can reconstruct the sequence, maybe we'll know more.''

"I'm not familiar with the procedure in situations like this, Mr. Reeves. But shouldn't we talk about arrangements between us before we go into it?''

Again Reeves gave a brief nod. "Let me explain something. Under social security, in my age bracket half of my income beyond a small amount must be turned back to the government. Our national policy is to put retired people on the shelf, make certain they maintain a fixed level of poverty. That infuriates me every time I think about it. I've paid premiums on social security insurance more than half a century. I see no need to turn your good money over to the government. So what we'll do, I'll keep a running record of my expenses. When we wrap this up, I'll look at what the government limit will bear. It'll probably come out about minimum wage. Will that be satisfactory?''

"I wouldn't feel right about it. But yes, that's satisfactory, if truly necessary.''

"It is. And let's clear up something else right at the beginning. The initial investigation was slow to develop, first because you and your son were unconscious. That couldn't be helped. But second, you didn't respond in the way the investigators thought normal.''

Rachel was bewildered. "What do you mean?''

" 'Never a tear' was the way the interview was described to me.''

For a moment Rachel was almost beyond speech. How could they have misunderstood her so? "My God! If they wanted hysterics, I would've been happy to pitch them a walleyed fit! I may yet! I feel I'm about to explode! I just assumed that any self-indulgence on my part would be counterproductive.''

Reeves was studying her face intently. "Maybe they simply misread you. That happens.''

Rachel could hardly contain her fury. "Am I suspect in my daughter's disappearance? Is that what you're saying?''

"Ma'am, going into an investigation, everybody's suspect. That's just the way a good investigator thinks. What you do, you start eliminating. You don't get this impression from television or the newspapers, but a big percentage of the violence in this country is still family related. So you begin with the family, look for anything that might be considered not normal. Your lack of emotion caught their eye."

Rachel made an effort to keep her voice devoid of anger. "Mr. Reeves, for the last fifteen years I've been an executive in a highly competitive industry, with crises almost every day. A major author delivers his big fall book, one you've risked a lot of money on, and it's a pile of junk. The bindery calls and the signatures for a big, expensive coffee-table gift book have been printed out of sequence. There's no way to fold them, and the title has already been announced for the holiday season. Artwork commissioned for a dust jacket arrives, and it's terrible. The production schedule is thrown off, affecting selections by book clubs. An agent calls demanding the sky for your favorite author. You know you can't pay that much money, and the agent is threatening to take her to another house. I could go on and on. Mr. Reeves, if women in publishing cried every time they were upset, they'd have to put pumps in the basement. You have to maintain your public face. If you cry, you do it in private. I'm accustomed to self-discipline. I can't go around weeping. I've been dealing with a demanding profession, and with the responsibilities of a single parent, since my husband died five years ago."

"Let's go into that," Reeves said. "Why didn't you level with Hopkins and tell him your husband died of a drug overdose?"

Rachel closed her eyes, but only for a second. "Because the cocaine was only incidental. Bill wasn't a user. He was attending a bachelor party for one of his business associates. There was cocaine. You'd have to know my husband. He'd been in sports. Football. Track. Baseball. He felt driven to show he could outperform anyone. If it'd been arm wrestling, it would have been the same. No one at the party knew he was inexperienced with drugs. He didn't tell them. Neither he nor anyone else knew he had a congenital heart defect. The way his doctor explained it to me, his heart simply burst. So it *was* what I said, a massive coronary."

"The death certificate reads drug overdose. So does the NYPD blotter. Hopkins wasted a lot of time. Mrs. Shelby, don't try to put the best face on things, with me, Hopkins, or anyone in the investigation. Surely you see the problem. We must know you're who you say you are, that the things you say happened did indeed happen. When your answers don't quite match up, you give us reason to wonder."

Rachel did not respond. She had not known what was on the death certificate. Her lawyer had taken care of all that. But to explain now would sound evasive.

"After the family, an investigator turns to peripherals," Reeves went on. "Mistresses. Boyfriends. Close acquaintances. You've been single five years. And no boyfriends? A strikingly good-looking woman like you? Hopkins has plenty of reason to think you might have waltzed around the truth when he asked you if you'd had any serious male relationships. He thought you were overly defensive on the subject."

"I can tell you only what I told Lieutenant Hopkins. Since my husband's death, I've been totally absorbed in my work, in my children. Perhaps I've discouraged any gesture toward a close relationship. But I assure you, there has been none."

Again Reeves gave that abrupt nod, signaling that he accepted the answer. He paused and jotted a few notes before continuing.

"Mrs. Shelby, it'd help if you could tell me a little about yourself. I need to become acquainted with you, your situation, your children, everything. Just talk, and I'll listen. If you don't mind, let's start with your marriage. Tell me about your husband, how your marriage came about, your life."

Rachel hesitated, seeking a way to put years into a few words. She felt she could explain Bill best by describing the way she saw him, back in the beginning.

"Bill was from the South. Georgia. I first met him through my mother. At that time they were associates in the same brokerage house. We were introduced at a party. He was fascinated with New York, and I suppose I was about as New York as you could get. What first attracted me to him was his incredible energy. His enthusiasm. Suzanne is the same way. David takes after me, quieter, more introspective."

Again she hesitated, wondering how detailed an accounting he wanted. Remembering his earlier lecture, she decided not to hold back.

"My mother, my friends, were opposed to our marriage. We New Yorkers like to think of ourselves as worldly, sophisticated. But I suspect we may be more than a little clannish. I'm a Jew. Bill was reared Presbyterian. My mother, my friends, thought that two people of such different backgrounds could never make a successful marriage. Bill and I proved them wrong. We had a very good life. We shared an interest in music, art, theater, books. Bill was brilliant. Time after time I saw so-called intellectuals try to put him down because of his southern accent. He would start slipping arcane words and concepts into the conversation, without ostentation, and cut them off at the knees before they knew what was happening. He was a fascinating man. Eventually my mother, all my friends, came to love him.''

Reeves made notes. Rachel wondered what she had said that was of significance.

"Lieutenant Hopkins didn't quite understand why you felt it necessary to carry two sets of ID—credit cards, bankbooks.''

"I tried to explain that. I had the feeling I wasn't communicating. You see, I was well known in publishing before I met Bill. I had my own imprint. Rachel Mermin Books. I operated under the umbrella of a publishing house, but my name was known. So I kept that identity, professionally and on credit cards and bank accounts. Why should I have to explain at book conventions, and elsewhere, that I was really Mrs. William P. Shelby, and forego the name recognition? I saw no need. Can you give me any reason why I should?''

Reeves gave her the hint of a smile. "No, ma'am, I don't. But I can see how it caught Lieutenant Hopkins's eye. If Hop's wife started running around using her maiden name on everything, he'd probably straighten her out in a hurry.'' He returned to his notepad. "Do you normally carry so much cash?''

"No. As I attempted to explain to Lieutenant Hopkins, I was uncertain what facilities would be available in the smaller towns we would be driving through. I knew it was risky, and not wise. But I didn't want to run short.''

"Tell me about Suzanne, how she came to be a movie star.''

Rachel tried to keep the explanation simple, when in reality so much was involved.

"Bill and I had agreed, early, that we didn't want to stint on our children's education. We selected a school for them that offers a curriculum heavy on the arts. Two years ago, a Broadway musical auditioned children from the school for some walk-on parts. There was one speaking role. Suzanne won it. She was mentioned in the reviews. Then came the film. The script was clever—half comedy, half serious—with Suzanne playing a pint-sized detective. Song and dance numbers were worked into the plot. I combined my vacation with a short leave of absence, and we went out to the Coast to make the film. While we were there I received several job offers. I think most were only polite gestures. But one studio persisted even after we returned to New York. The film was released and the reviews were overwhelming. The box office has been good. So the offer came for a sequel. I had to make a decision.'' She hesitated. ''Mr. Reeves, I don't know how much of this you want to hear . . .''

''All of it. You're doing fine.''

''Several years ago my publishing house was acquired by an international conglomerate. Young people, well-educated but with very little experience, were placed in supervisory positions. Frankly, most of them didn't seem to know what they were doing. Many of my longtime associates—friends—were let go. I love that work, can't really imagine myself doing anything else. But conditions were becoming more and more difficult. I looked around and found that matters were not much better elsewhere.''

She paused, collecting her thoughts. Booker Reeves's dark brown eyes were locked on her.

''And I had to think of Suzanne,'' she went on. ''I realize that almost all parents think of their children as special. But with Suzanne, this is not just my opinion. She has tested extremely high on every IQ test she's been given. The film critics are calling her another Shirley Temple. And she is ambitious far beyond her years. She sees herself as another Jodie Foster, progressing from juvenile into mature roles. And who am I to say she can't? I worry about it. I want her to have a normal life, whatever that is. Yet I don't want to deny her what she has her heart set on doing. She has read books on film techniques, and understands them to a surprising degree. She has picked up adult perspectives. Already she says that someday she wants to direct. She owns tapes of most of the Jodie Foster films and studies them, scene by scene. Same with Barbra Streisand. Take a movie like *Yentl*. Suzanne can dissect it from beginning to end by memory, what each scene was designed to accomplish, the camera angles used, the lighting, the dialogue. I suppose she's a film prodigy, if such a thing exists. Even the professionals consider her a phenomenon. During delays on the set she spends every spare minute talking with the cameramen, the writers, the lighting technicians, the set designers. I'm not saying she can talk on their level. But they respond to her earnestness, her enthusiasm, her perceptive questions. Because of her precocity, she often is not accepted by children her own age. But she truly made a friend of almost everyone connected with the film. So when her career blossomed into the sequel, I felt I shouldn't stand in her way. And it seemed a good time for me to leave publishing, at least for a while. So I accepted the studio offer and signed Suzanne to do the sequel.''

Reeves made an entry on his notepad. ''Why did you decide to drive across country? Tell me about that.''

"In a way, it was a whim. I've flown East Coast to West Coast and back at least twenty or thirty times. But I've never really seen what lies in between. Oh, I've attended book conventions in Chicago, Atlanta, Dallas, Las Vegas, other places. And sales conferences here and there. But you know how that goes. You see only airports, taxis, hotels, and exhibit halls. Suzanne and David had seen even less of the country. For the last two years Suzanne has been totally immersed in her career. I had been more and more engrossed in my work. David also is perhaps a bit mature for his age. He's involved in western history and computers. But after all, he *is* a child. I know I haven't given him the attention he deserves. We had six weeks. I thought that in driving across country, we would have the opportunity to get to know one another again. One of my fondest childhood memories is of a trip down the East Coast to Florida with my parents when I was eight. I wanted to re-create that for Suzanne and for David. And it seemed to be working, until this happened."

Rachel almost lost it then. Her eyes watered. She stopped to regain her composure.

"So there are no peripherals, Mr. Reeves. No boyfriends. No shady associates. Suzanne would not have wandered off or run away. Someone has kidnapped her. I have no doubt. I can't see why anyone else has any doubt. No other possibilities exist! My insides are in total panic. I read the newspapers. I know what may have happened to her—what may be happening to her."

Reeves did not respond.

"So what do we do now, Mr. Reeves? Where do we go from here? I want to know everything. Every clue, every theory."

Reeves grimaced. "Mrs. Shelby, on a case like this, a disappearance, there's so much garbage. Suzanne's picture will be in the newspapers, on the television news. We'll receive tips from people absolutely certain they've seen her at a shopping mall. We'll go out and canvass the salesclerks, review security cameras. Another person will claim to have seen her getting into a car somewhere, and maybe we'll put out a description of the vehicle, do some hunting. Most tips will come from people genuinely wanting to help. We'll hear from the psychics, and we'll have to listen to them, because sometimes they're right. But we'll also hear from the crazies. We'll probably get a bogus ransom demand or two. There'll be tips from the sadistic, claiming God knows what, and we'll have to check out all of them. We'll study similar regional crimes, and that won't be pretty. We'll take a close look at every sexual deviate we've processed in the last five years. Mrs. Shelby, there's probably more moral degradation out there today than at any time since the Middle Ages. A case like this just eats you alive, even when you're not personally connected. I don't think you should be subjected to that. Not needlessly."

"Mr. Reeves, she's my daughter. Some of those outré tips might make sense to me when they wouldn't to anyone else. I might be able to say yes, that's exactly what Suzanne would do in those circumstances."

Reeves raised his eyebrows, acknowledging her point. He remained silent for a time, as if reconsidering.

"Understand, a lot of what we get will be confidential. But I'll make you a deal. If there's anything I think you might help us on, however remote the chance, I'll bring it to you."

Rachel knew she had won a concession. She sensed she should not push for more at the moment.

"Tell me about the wreck," Reeves said. "Describe it from your perspective, from the time you first got into your car."

Again Rachel thought back to the last hurried moments at the motel. "Checkout time was three. With Suzanne signing the autographs, we barely made it. Suzanne and David packed and loaded the car while I went to the front desk. That's a trick we use to fudge when we're running late."

"You see anyone hanging around? Anyone showing any interest in you? Anyone at all?"

"Not that I remember. Of course, I wasn't paying attention to anything like that. After paying the bill, I returned to the room. David and Suzanne were searching, making certain we'd left nothing behind. That's our routine. They do that while I make sure everything's stowed properly in the car."

"Anyone else checking out nearby?"

"No. I think I'd have noticed. That whole wing of the motel seemed deserted. We got into the car and drove to the service station right below the motel. The bays there were empty. We were the only car. I'm sure of that. I drove into the full service lane. A nice-looking young man filled the gas tank, checked the oil and the tires. He did joke with David about the New York license plates, but I don't think he was especially interested in us."

"He's been interviewed. Hopkins says he's all right."

"By then it was getting toward four. Too early for dinner. We studied the map. The next big town, Amarillo, looked to be more than two hours away. We debated what to do. Then David challenged us. He said, 'I can tough it out to Amarillo on ice cream if you guys can.' "

Reeves laughed. With his deep voice, it was a good sound.

"So we agreed on that. David said he'd seen a Baskin-Robbins in a strip mall just down the street. He couldn't remember exactly where. We set out to look for it. I drove to that intersection. The light was red. I stopped. There was a van, about the size of a Federal Express delivery truck, in the left-turn lane. I pulled up beside it in the center lane. A car or two crossed the intersection on green, but no one else was stopped at the light. We were looking across the intersection to the mall, hunting the Baskin-Robbins. David saw it just as the light turned green. I drove on into the intersection. I remember being vaguely aware that the van beside me didn't move, even though he had the left-turn arrow. I should have been alerted by that. But I wasn't. The van blocked my view until I was past it and into the intersection. Of course by then it was too late. This big green car ran the light and hit us. That's the last I knew until I woke up here. Anything you can tell me about what happened, I'd appreciate. Especially anything about Suzanne."

Reeves thumbed back through his notepad. "Let's take it chronologically. Two witnesses actually saw the collision. The driver of the van you mentioned, and a security guard parking his car at the strip mall. Both ran toward the wreck. Both saw Suzanne still in the car. Two other witnesses also saw her in the car. The driver of an eighteen-wheeler, the one who pulled her out. And an office supply salesman who also stopped and helped in the rescue."

"And David."

"And David. So we've definitely got her in the car after the wreck. She wasn't thrown out. Fire was evident from the first moment. The way the pavement slopes, the gasoline leaking from the ruptured tank was running up underneath your car. Suzanne was trying to pull you out. The driver of the eighteen-wheeler reached in and got her, walked her six or eight steps away, set her down, then went back for you. The security guard and the salesman were pulling David out, hurrying, but being careful, because it was plain he had compound fractures."

Rachel winced.

"Now, here's what I think is a telling point. See if you agree. They carried you and David to a grassy strip beside the road, right next to the mall parking lot. Two or three people knelt beside you to see if they could help. Not one remembers seeing Suzanne. I'm thinking she was diverted, taken, between the time the truck driver set her down and the time you and David were carried to the grass. Somewhere within those two or three minutes. Otherwise, I believe she would have made her way to you and David."

"Definitely."

"But she didn't. Any ideas why?"

Rachel thought for a time before answering. "I see only two possibilities. Either she *was* injured and wandered off in a daze, or else someone took her by force or talked her away with a ruse."

"We have an anomaly here," Reeves said, looking at his notes. "The truck driver guessed her age as about seven or eight."

"She's very small for her age. I told Lieutenant Hopkins that. It's hereditary."

Reeves studied his notepad. "You told Hopkins that Suzanne can function as an adult on some levels, but that perhaps she's below her age level in other ways. What exactly did you mean?"

Rachel hesitated. "That's difficult to explain. For the last few years she has been in a special class of unusually talented children. Music. Dance. Drama. That's her world. Those children don't even play in the normal way. It's all sublimated into artistic expression. Her intense interest in this field and the time she devotes to it have robbed her of the practical experiences most children acquire. She has been overly protected. Everywhere she goes, she's accompanied by an adult—me, her instructors, her grandmother, an au pair. She travels by taxi, limousine. Never by bus or subway. In hindsight, I can see that maybe I've been wrong, protecting her so totally. But that was what I meant. She tends to live in films, drama, make-believe. She has seen little of the real world."

Again Rachel paused, uncertain how far to go. She remembered that Reeves had warned her about putting the best face on matters. "You see, Suzanne hasn't yet recovered from the loss of her father. In some respects, she's still a deeply troubled child. Onstage, or in front of the camera, she has confidence in abundance. But offstage, she lacks this assurance. She can deal with adults in her profession, but she has never learned the proper skills for interpersonal relations with children her own age. I hope I'm making myself clear."

"You are," Reeves said. "Later, we may want to go into that in more detail, when we have the time." He studied his notes for a moment. "Why did you go up to the national grasslands? Any specific reason?"

"That was mostly David's trip. He's intrigued with Indian lore. I think *Dances With Wolves* started it, or maybe just intensified it. And of course *The Last of the Mohicans*. I've bought him books. He knew all about the Washita Battle Site, showed us how Custer's troops attacked Black Kettle's village from different directions. He was excited about it. He identifies with the Indians."

"Maybe David and I will get along. I'm part Arapaho, part Cheyenne."

Now that he had mentioned it, Rachel could see Indian features in his high cheekbones, thick hair, Roman nose, and chocolate eyes.

"While you were up at the grasslands, did you notice anyone paying a great deal of attention to you?"

"Just the children from the buses at the museum. They were all of grade-school level, I would say. Their interest in Suzanne seemed quite normal."

Reeves gave his abrupt nod. "The adults on the bus tour have been interviewed. Doesn't seem to be anything there. Anyone else that you remember?"

"No."

"What about David's relationship with Suzanne? They get along all right?"

Rachel looked at him for a moment. "Surely David's not a suspect."

Reeves seemed a trifle embarrassed. "Mrs. Shelby, I'm trying to become acquainted with you and your family as fast as possible. Forgive me if I was too blunt. It occurred to me that with a famous sister, and David less than three full years younger, there might be resentment. Friction. If so, I should know about it."

"There's been none so far, that I can see. Irritation, maybe, when our plans are interrupted. Some amusement when Suzanne's fans carry on over her. But not resentment. Please understand, Mr. Reeves, Suzanne's career has soared so fast. David's still adjusting. *I'm* still adjusting."

"Sounds like he's handling it well. But I'm also thinking that if there *is* a problem, however well hidden, this may make it tougher for him, with Suzanne receiving even more attention. You might want to think about that."

"I have. I've thought of a lot of things in the last few hours. But understand, Mr. Reeves. Part of my concern with David is that he's too caring at times for his own good. And he certainly doesn't take a backseat to his sister. Suzanne's interests are focused. David's are varied. Computers, history, popular music, astronomy. I feel—sincerely believe—that he is headed toward becoming an interesting, well-rounded person."

"Has he been told yet?"

"No. But Dr. Peterson says he's curious, asking about her. I can't put it off much longer."

"With your permission, I'd like to talk with him after he's told."

46

"You have my permission. What I want to know is, what happens now? Can we force them to bring the FBI into it?"

Again Reeves grimaced. "Mrs. Shelby, the FBI isn't the monolithic problem-solver most of the public assumes. The FBI will be represented, at least in an advisory capacity, until we learn what we have here. The new crime act of 1985 gives them more latitude to enter these cases. If we establish that Suzanne has been abducted, they can come into the case twenty-four hours later on the assumption she may have been taken across state lines. But they're relatively limited in manpower on something like this. What we need are the *facilities* of the FBI—access to their files, their labs, their experts, their communications. We already have all that. The big plus as far as we're concerned is that the locals are calling in the Oklahoma State Bureau of Investigation—the OSBI. The Bureau is stretched thin. It's the Bureau's job to take on major crimes in the state that are beyond the capabilities of local law enforcement. They've had plenty of practice, and they're good at it. They're accustomed to working with the FBI and local departments. You'll probably have as much investigative manpower at work here tomorrow as you'd get in a similar case in New York."

Rachel remembered that Lieutenant Hopkins had said essentially the same thing. "With so many organizations working on it, won't there be confusion?"

"Twenty years ago, on a case like this, there might have been infighting, competition for turf, undercutting. But not anymore. If the soaring crime rate has done anything positive, it has succeeded in bringing police organizations into a closer working arrangement. It'll dovetail rather smoothly."

A soft knock came at the door. Dr. Peterson opened it and stuck his head in. "Maybe you both should know. The hospital switchboard has been solid red for the last hour. Chief Laird called from the police station. It's the same there. Camera crews are on their way from all over."

Rachel felt beleaguered. She had not yet had time to call her mother, Bill's parents, or Suzanne's film studio.

"How will we handle this?" she asked Reeves.

He shook his head in exasperation. "I wish we had more time." He was quiet for a moment. "I'd say let's use them. Someone, somewhere, may have seen something. It might be good if you made a personal plea for help, offered a number to call."

"Chief Laird suggested a press conference early tomorrow morning," Peterson said. "He wanted to know if you could attend. I told him you're in no shape to go over to the police station. I suggested we might conduct it here at the hospital. I wouldn't want you out of a wheelchair, but maybe you could read a short prepared statement. Chief Laird could do the rest. I don't think you should try to take questions or do interviews. Booker, what do you think?''

''Sounds like the best way to handle it, if Mrs. Shelby feels able.''

''I do,'' Rachel said. ''I'm feeling much stronger. I want to do something. Anything.''

''I'll have to get an okay from the hospital administrator,'' Peterson said. ''We can block off the north part of the waiting room, set up a table, keep it short.''

''Dr. Peterson, I really should tell David about Suzanne before I do this.''

''I agree. When you're ready, I'll have someone take you down to his room.''

Rachel thought ahead to the ordeal of facing the cameras. ''Donna said the dress I wore in here was beyond salvage. I have no other.''

Peterson grinned. ''Donna can find you a fresh hospital gown. A little top-of-the-line number.''

''What will I tell the media?'' she asked Reeves.

''The truth. Don't shy away from it. Your daughter's missing. They'll ask if you think she's been kidnapped for ransom. You can say you understand that the police are considering that as a possibility.''

''Is that what you think, Mr. Reeves? She was taken for ransom?''

Reeves hedged. ''I believe we should use that as a ploy. I'm sure Laird and Hopkins will go along with it. She was probably taken for other reasons. But if we suggest ransom, maybe the kidnapper will go for it.''

Rachel did not ask about the other possible reasons.

She was not yet prepared to think about them.

The overhead light was off. Only David's bed lamp was on. Rachel first thought he was asleep. From her angle in the wheelchair, his eyes appeared to be closed. She had raised her hand to signal the nurse to stop when she caught a glint from David's eye and saw that he was playing with a video game.

''Ten minutes!'' she said. ''I want you out of that bed and dressed in ten minutes!''

That was the way she got him moving almost every school morning. He laughed and turned in bed so vigorously, she feared he would dislodge the mechanical apparatus that held his leg aloft. She left the wheelchair and joined him in bed, hugging him to her.

He began crying. She held him, thinking of all the times through the years she had comforted him for lesser hurts.

But she had not been there this time, when he really needed her.

"Baby, are you in pain?" she asked. "If you are, Dr. Peterson can give you something to help you sleep."

He wiped a palm across his eyes. "No. I'm just tired of lying here."

"That makes two of us. This is my first trip out of my room. But Dr. Peterson is letting me get around a little. He said he'll start you in therapy tomorrow. You'll be up hobbling around in no time."

He laughed. Rachel saw his question coming and raised the subject first. "David, I have something terrible to tell you. I want you to be brave."

"About Suzanne?"

Rachel was thrown off stride. "You know?"

"I only know no one will talk about her, or answer my questions. Is she dead?"

Rachel was jolted to the edge of panic. She grabbed David's hand. "Oh, no, baby! We just can't find her. She has simply disappeared."

David's eyes widened. "Disappeared?"

"Right after the wreck."

David spoke excitedly. "I saw a man take her out of the car! I told the police!"

"That man was rescuing her. The same man came back and rescued me. David, did you see Suzanne at all after she was taken from the car?"

"No. They were pulling me out. It hurt. I didn't think to look for her."

"Of course you didn't. I just thought there might have been an incident or something you noticed."

"I should have looked!"

"No! No! You mustn't think that. There was no reason for us to think she was in danger."

Again David started crying. Big tears rolled down his cheeks. "Why can't we find her?"

"David, the police say they're preparing the largest search ever conducted in Oklahoma. Maybe in the whole Southwest. In the morning I'm going on television to ask the public for help in finding her. I'll arrange for you to watch on your television set. We're going to find her. We have to believe that."

David had paled. The full impact was just beginning to hit him. "What could have happened to her?"

Rachel had been dreading that question. Both Suzanne and David had received child abuse training at school. Both had been warned about sexual deviates. Some of the parents had protested that the information they had been given was too detailed, too scary. Rachel had attended a meeting where the content was explained to parents.

She answered his question obliquely.

"David, we have no way of knowing what happened to her."

"Could she have been kidnapped by a crazy person?"

"We can only pray she wasn't."

"If she was, I'll bet she's picking up some great bits."

Rachel was unable to speak for a moment. Suzanne was always adding to what she called her "bits." Two nights ago, on the southwestern edge of Missouri, they had stopped at a roadside café for late dinner. The place was almost deserted. Closing time was only thirty minutes away. The waitress, deep into her behind-the-counter clean-up, had not wanted to be bothered with late dinners. Rachel had been irritated by the woman's attitude, but paid little attention.

Quietly Suzanne had monitored the woman's every move. Afterward, back at the motel, she pinned up her hair, slipped on a long robe, and gave Rachel and David a hilariously accurate replay. Standing hipshot with pad poised, talking out of the side of her mouth, she performed the whole routine, only slightly exaggerating the woman's foot-shuffling, pencil-wiggling impatience.

David spoke in a thin voice. "Mommy, I'm scared."

"So am I," Rachel said.

She slipped her good arm under his head and held him. With a gesture, she dismissed the nurse.

Cuddled awkwardly in the hospital bed, Rachel and David comforted each other through the remainder of the night.

4

Booker carried the stack of folders to the tiny room Hopkins had set aside for him at the rear of the police basement. The files were fresh off the fax and smelled of developer. He was dreading the next hour or so, for he knew the nature of the material he must absorb. The FBI's impartial electronic VICAP had disgorged eighteen cases adjudged possibly similar to Suzanne Shelby's disappearance, all occurring during the last five years within a five-state region—Oklahoma, Kansas, Arkansas, Missouri, and Texas.

His interview with Rachel Shelby left him deeply disturbed. Suzanne already had assumed shape and personality in his mind, and he knew the odds against recovering her alive. He felt close rapport with the woman and her suffering. Clearly this was going to be a horrendously tough case.

He placed the folders on the bare, unused desk and arranged his hat on the metal top of a file cabinet. He lowered himself into the creaking swivel chair, arranged notepad and ballpoint, and began reading.

For the next two hours he studied in minute detail information that literally made him sick. He could not understand a society that allowed such crimes to happen to children. He often wondered how he would react if one of his children—or now one of his grandchildren—became such a victim. As he read, he felt the full agony of every one of those eighteen kids, and of their families.

Of the eighteen, seven demanded closer study. In the reading, he had stacked those seven to one side. He picked them up and again reviewed them, this time more slowly.

Kathy Simpson. Six. Thickest of the files because more information was available. Disappeared from her school bus stop in the small community of Fairmont in north central Oklahoma. Early morning. Full daylight. No witnesses or indication of struggle. Last seen leaving home for school. She was not at the bus stop when the school bus came and went. Unclothed body found by fishermen twelve days later in shallow water on the edge of Kaw Lake, up on the Kansas border. Estimated time of death: forty-eight hours before discovery.

The son of a bitch who took her had kept her alive approximately ten days.

Why?

Booker could only imagine.

Cause of death, suffocation. Telltale petechial hemorrhage in the eyes. But an anomaly here—the something different you always hunted. She was not strangled. No trauma to throat, nose, mouth. No damage to the soft membranes. No toxicity in blood or soft tissues. To all physical appearances, she simply had stopped breathing.

What the hell would cause that?

Had she been scared to death?

Booker shuddered.

Ligature abrasions on the right ankle. The medical examiner observed that the marks appeared to be from a chain or hasplike object, not the usual burns from rope, tape, or plastic tie. The only other marks on the body were double rows of shallow punctures on the left shoulder. Faint hooklike indentures. The medical examiner had made a drawing. The broken double-row pattern reminded Booker of a dog's tongue, only bigger.

What the hell could have made those punctures?

Had the son of a bitch whipped her with a cactus spine?

If so, some of the spines should have broken off, been recovered.

No, it was something else.

But what?

Kathy's vagina had been intact, undamaged. But deposited sperm and rips in her anus revealed that her body had been sexually assaulted at some time after death.

"Thank God for small favors," Booker said aloud.

He made notes. He was acquainted with Kathy's case agent. He would call and ask about those puncture wounds. Something weird there. The state medical examiner probably would not remember the autopsy. He performed hundreds each year. But his files might contain more detailed notes. Booker would check.

He put Kathy's folder to one side and picked up the next.

Cindy Gardner. Seven. Disappeared while camping with family in Mark Twain National Forest in the southwest corner of Missouri.

Beautiful country. Booker once took two of his grandsons fishing there.

Skeletal remains found five months later in an abandoned coal shaft near Joplin. Animals had been at the body, scattered the bones. Not much physical evidence on little Cindy.

Booker vaguely remembered news accounts, confirmed by the sketchy information in the file. Cindy had left her two brothers to return to camp alone. She never arrived. Early afternoon. Full daylight. A massive search had been conducted.

Booker wondered whether Cindy's case could be connected to the others.

His gut feeling said it was. But he had nothing solid. He put Cindy's file on top of Kathy's and went on to the next.

Brenda Wallace. Seven. Vanished from a trailer park outside Plainview in the Texas Panhandle. Body found partially buried six weeks later on Beaver Creek in Kansas. Two boys hunting jackrabbits saw Brenda's feet sticking out of the ground. Body in poor condition. Cause of death undetermined. Decomposition too extensive to identify trauma.

But again, something different: the upper portion of the body was covered with a substance that did not appear to be mold. The notation read "possibly organic."

What the hell did that mean?

Brenda had been visiting a playmate. She left to return home, less than a quarter mile away. She never arrived. Full daylight. Road in sight of houses all the way.

The case had the same feel. Booker added it to the short stack.

Renate Estraca. Eight. Vanished from shopping mall parking lot in Tulsa. The family had gone into a store. Renate had forgotten her purse and money. She went back to the car to get it and never returned. Saturday afternoon. Full daylight. Body found twenty-six days later in a ravine near Russell, Oklahoma, by a rancher hunting a strayed steer. The body had been dismembered and scattered by animals. Time of death unknown. Cause of death unknown. Trauma unknown.

But the son of a bitch who took her had hauled her from one corner of the state to the other.

Why?

Renate sure as hell deserved more than she had received from state law enforcement.

Booker retained the file in the short stack.

Patsy Gray. Eight. A more recent case. Disappeared while riding bicycle near rural home southeast of Shamrock in the Texas Panhandle. Bicycle left on road. Body never found.

Booker added the brief file to his stack. Patsy was out there, somewhere. Someone might find her bones any day.

Gaye Monroe. Nine. Even more recent. Vanished from street in Midwest City, Oklahoma. Her mother had sent her to a nearby convenience store for milk. Gaye never arrived. No witnesses. And, as yet, no body.

Catherine Overby. Eight. The latest case. Disappeared a month ago on way home from school. Traced by witnesses to within a block of her home on the edge of Frederick. Taken on dirt road she habitually used as shortcut. Granddaughter of county sheriff, so police went to full cry within an hour of disappearance. Roadblocks set up on all main roads. Nothing. Body not yet found.

Booker went back over his notes. All females. All white except Renate, labeled brown. Daylight each instance. Bold snatch, at sites possibly observed.

Booker checked the dates. No overlap. If all seven were done by one guy, as Booker was beginning to believe. the son of a bitch wanted only one plaything at a time.

But the disposal pattern bothered him. Shallow water. Dry ravine. Creekbed. Mine shaft. Two unknown. Not the consistent MO expected of a single perpetrator.

The details were too vague. He could not get a feel for the perpetrator on any of the cases. He was sure of only one thing: distances between abduction and disposal varied up to more than two hundred miles.

If the seven crimes were all committed by one perp, the son of a bitch moved around. He had wheels.

Of the other eleven cases gleaned from VICAP, one aspect or another suggested they did not fit. On some, investigators had found family friction that indicated possible custodial kidnapping or domestic violence. On others, some evidence pointed to a known suspect, but not strongly enough to make a case. On the remainder, all from rural areas, the child had merely disappeared, with no solid indication of foul play. Searches had been conducted, but no bodies found.

Booker went back over the eleven. Three might possibly fit with the seven he had selected. Not enough information was available on them, but Booker put them with his original seven.

He glanced at his watch. Time for the morning network news shows. A portable TV faced him from atop a file cabinet in the corner. Duty cops probably popped down here to catch ball games on quiet days. Booker walked over, flipped on the set, adjusted the volume, and returned to his seat.

Suzanne Shelby was the lead-off item. The newsreader called her "the stunning new child star" and spoke of her disappearance in grave tones. A still picture of Suzanne came onscreen. Booker left the set tuned to the one network. He figured the others would be offering much the same.

Hopkins and Pryor came to the door, saw Suzanne on the screen, and took chairs. None of them spoke, not wanting to miss a word.

The newscast abruptly cut live to the lobby of the hospital. Rachel Shelby was in a wheelchair, flanked by Peterson and Police Chief Laird.

Pryor snickered. "I figured he'd work his way into it."

The camera moved in close on Rachel Shelby, and in that moment Booker felt her pain in his gut. He found himself wanting to be there to protect her, give her comfort. She was the most womanly female he had met in years and he found himself responding. Battered and without makeup, she remained poised, projecting strong character and a unique allure. The white head wrappings and hospital gown made the bruises on her face even more pronounced. She seemed nervous but determined. For a moment the press conference was lost in confusion and noise. Apparently someone off camera gave Chief Laird a cue. He leaned into the microphones and introduced himself, Rachel, and Pete.

"First, Mrs. Shelby will read a statement," he said. "Then Dr. Peterson and I will take a few questions."

Laird was more than competent in his martinet uniform and carefully squared cop-hat. He was a handsome guy, and spoke well. Few among America's television audience would suspect that he was more politician than cop.

Rachel read her brief statement in a firm voice. She said Suzanne was missing, presumably abducted, possibly for ransom. She urged anyone with information to contact the authorities. The police station number came onscreen.

"Shit," Pryor said. "We're in for it now."

Pete took it from there. He said Mrs. Shelby had sustained a severe concussion, a slight fracture of the skull, and had remained in a coma for eighteen hours. He described David's injuries. He said both were recovering satisfactorily.

Booker thought Pete handled himself superbly. He looked like a competent, take-charge guy. No one would have recognized him for the shattered, broken man Booker first met six years ago. Booker felt good knowing that he had helped Pete find his life again.

Chief Laird said he had asked the FBI and the Oklahoma State Bureau of Investigation for assistance, and that both agencies had responded. He took a few shouted questions. Yes, they had some leads. No, he could not talk about them. He said most of his department was pulling double shifts. He was proud of the way his men had responded.

"Wait till the overtime hits," Pryor said.

Still answering questions, Laird said his department was exploring the theory that Suzanne had been taken for ransom. No, they had not heard from a possible perpetrator. They were busy developing several lines of inquiry.

"Meaning we got zip," Pryor said.

The screen went back to the network in New York for a recap of the wreck and the disappearance. Three-second clips of the intersection, the burned-out car, came onscreen. Then came longer clips from Suzanne's movie.

Booker's earlier nausea returned. Suzanne was the best kind of cute—totally unaffected.

From the folders in front of him, he knew what she might now be enduring.

If his blossoming theory was correct, the son of a bitch liked to keep them alive about ten days. Unless he could put it all together soon, come up with something solid, her file would join the others.

The network newsreader in New York ended the segment, saying that Rachel Shelby was posting a ten-thousand-dollar reward for information leading to Suzanne's recovery.

The police number returned to the screen.

"Shit," Pryor said again.

When the screen went into a commercial, Hopkins walked over and turned the set off. "You really think this Shelby woman's playing it straight?" he asked.

"Yeah," Booker told him. "After talking to you, I went over there about fifty-fifty. I came away ninety-nine point nine. Pete says she's a tough lady. I agree. I think she's just holding it in. Better than I could."

"You don't get any feel for something ragged around the edges? A weird boyfriend? A drug deal?"

"No."

"What about the extra ID?"

"Hop, if you're not careful, they're going to stuff you and put you in a museum. You're living in the stone age. That's not unusual. Maiden names. Hyphenated names. In her world, that probably was common even before women's lib."

"So you think she's exactly what she says she is?"

"Yes."

"Shouldn't we run her through the polygraph, just to be sure?"

"Hop, she's in no shape for that. We have the basic facts: the kid was there, then she wasn't. We need to work on that. Later, if you still have doubts, we can put her on the machine."

In his present situation, with no official capacity, Booker did not feel completely comfortable offering advice. But Hopkins had been deferring to him from the moment he arrived, just like in the old days.

Years ago, back when Hopkins was with the county sheriff's office, they had worked three major cases together—the robbery murder of an elderly farm couple, a drug bust involving brown heroin flown in from Mexico, and a multimillion-dollar oil equipment theft that eventually stretched from Oklahoma to Iran.

Booker was reluctant to speak out. But he did not want the investigation to go off in the wrong direction. "Look at it this way. You agree she couldn't have faked the wreck. The background check from your buddy in the NYPD looks good, except for the drug overdose. And she has explained that. With a famous kid, she's in the spotlight. There are big bucks riding on this film sequel coming up. I don't think she'd be messing with drug deals or any hanky-panky. That's my feeling."

Hopkins glanced at the folders. "You come up with anything?"

"Seven possibles, three maybes. I'm ready to take these first seven and run with them. If anything pans out, we might factor in the other three." He gave Hopkins a thumbnail sketch of the seven cases. "That might be enough for the FBI profilers," he concluded. "What do you think?"

Hopkins had been trained in profiling at the FBI Academy at Quantico. He thumbed through the folders. "Hell, Booker. Missouri to West Texas. Up into Kansas. That's a lot of country. And not much correlation that I can see. Dumps all different. Every one."

Booker nodded. Hopkins might be right.

Still, he felt his gut feelings should be explored.

"Let's try this for size," he said, voicing the possibilities as much for himself as for Hopkins. "Suppose we do have a serial child-killer at work here, and this son of a bitch is out cruising, looking for a target of opportunity. He heard the wreck, maybe saw it. He went—maybe drove—to the scene. He got there just in time to see Suzanne pulled out of the car and set to one side. No one was watching. All eyes were on the burning car, the rescue of Mrs.

Shelby and David. Our perp simply put an arm around Suzanne and took her."

"In the middle of a crowd? And no outcry?"

"Maybe he fed her a line of bullshit and walked her away from the scene. If anyone saw it, maybe they thought it was part of the rescue. Chances are, nobody saw it. They were watching the drama at the burning car. If Suzanne made outcry, nobody heard. The fire wagons and ambulances were coming, full sirens, honking and yelping their way through intersections. People at the scene were shouting. And all of this right next to the interstate, with all the diesel trucks and shit. Plenty of noise and movement. People were distracted. Maybe we shouldn't be surprised no one saw the snatch."

Hopkins was still looking at the folders. "If this guy exists, and these cases are connected, it'd be the first time he snatched from a crowd."

"We know he's a bold son of a bitch. He took Renate in a shopping mall parking lot. A Saturday afternoon. Brenda within sight of her own home. Gaye from a street. Catherine a half block from her home. Maybe this guy takes them where he finds them. Maybe he just doesn't give a shit."

"Disorganized?"

Booker was aware of the new theories flowing from the FBI's Behavioral Science Unit during the last decade. He did not entirely agree that killers can be so neatly labeled. He felt that many fall through the cracks.

"Hop, they need another category. Organized. Disorganized. And plain mean sons-a-bitches. I think this one is a plain mean son of a bitch. Born mean."

Hopkins laughed.

"Whatever happened to the concept of evil?" Booker insisted. "Some assholes don't need a reason, like a missing father and a cold-hearted mother."

"The devil is alive and well and in possession of men's souls," Hopkins said. "If I remember right, we got pretty drunk on that argument one night."

Booker remembered. That had been after the murder of the elderly farm couple. A rough case. Body parts scattered throughout a six-room house. Booker had argued—and still insisted—that anyone who believed in God also had to acknowledge the existence of the devil, and evil.

Hopkins turned back through the folders. "Booker, I really can't see the correlation. None of the cases have much in common."

"They're all bold snatches."

"Even that's not consistent. Some urban, some rural."

"Well, I'll play around with it," Booker said. "Unless you've come up with something else for me to work on."

"Pryor's right. We've got zip. We've about played out our string with the witnesses."

"You thought about hypnosis?"

"I guess that's next. Think we could get Patricia?"

Patricia McMahon was a forensic psychiatrist retained by the OSBI. Both Booker and Hopkins had worked with her.

"Hell yes. You heard Laird say he's requesting OSBI assistance. With all the media attention, you only have to ask. One thing we might do to get ready for her would be to chart where each witness was standing in relation to the burning car, and to where the truck driver put Suzanne down."

"I'm working on that. We're going back and reinterviewing witnesses now." Already Hopkins's mind seemed to be on something else. "You don't really believe the kid was snatched for ransom, do you?"

"No."

"I don't either. The chief's been big on it from the first. Movie star. Ransom. But I don't think so."

"Hop, I'm beginning to think we're hunting a son of a bitch that likes little girls. And his life is so screwed up, he can't even get it on with them until after he kills them. And maybe not then."

"Socially inadequate," Hopkins parroted from the textbooks.

Booker was equal to that game. "Minimal interest in the news media. Probably doesn't know yet that he snatched a movie star."

Hopkins gestured to the folders. "You really want to go ahead with this?"

"Yeah," Booker said. "Maybe you're right. Maybe the cases aren't linked. But on the other hand, maybe they are."

5

Exhausted from the long, restless night and the tension of the press conference, Rachel went to bed and for a time napped fitfully. She awoke wondering how in God's name she could have wasted three hours in sleep.

She punched the button for the duty nurse. A few minutes later an LVN acknowledged the call. She was full of announcements.

"Dr. Peterson left orders. Mrs. Shelby, you're to eat a good lunch, get some strength into you. Then we're to give you telephone privileges. Therapy is scheduled at two. Dr. Peterson will be by to see you when he comes in at four."

Rachel discovered she was truly hungry. While she ate, the nurse returned carrying a stack of callback slips. Rachel searched through them over coffee.

Most were from television networks, tabloid shows, talk shows, and print journalists. Rachel put them into three separate piles—those she would call first, those she would call later, and those she might not call at all.

Many of the slips bore names and numbers of friends, acquaintances, and former professional associates. She put those into another pile.

She was left with three sets of duplicate slips bearing notations of repeated calls from her mother, from Suzanne's producer, and from Bill's parents in Florida.

The nurse brought a phone, plugged it in, and left Rachel alone.

In her work, Rachel always made a practice of tackling the most difficult task first. In keeping with that habit, she dialed her mother's direct line at the Wall Street office.

Judith Mermin came on frantic. "Rachel, why didn't you call? I didn't even know until someone here said they had seen on you *Good Morning America*. Is that the way to treat your mother?''

Rachel spoke sharper than she intended. "Mother, I *couldn't* call. I was *unconscious*. I'm only now beginning to regain my senses."

"You were on CNN a few minutes ago."

The implication was that if Rachel was able to conduct a press conference, she could have called her mother. Rachel did not respond.

"You looked awful!"

That meant she had allowed herself to be seen in public without makeup and in institutional clothing. Again Rachel remained silent.

"How badly are you hurt?"

"Concussion, cracked skull, broken left arm, and bruises."

"You seem to be recovering. You spoke strongly. Where *is* Suzanne? Why haven't they found her?"

"The police are doing all they can. I've hired a private detective."

"They said David was hurt."

Rachel described David's injuries. As she expected, Judith immediately took charge.

"Rachel, the market's in free fall today. I must make some calls. But I can be on a plane by six. Do they have an airport out there?"

Rachel braced herself. The last thing she needed was a running battle with her mother. "Please don't come right now," she said. "It isn't necessary."

"Well, excuse me for insisting. But, Rachel, I *should* be there."

"There's absolutely nothing you could do. David's heavily sedated. He must lie quiet and heal. I'm busy with therapy, dealing with the police, the media."

"I could help hunt for Suzanne."

With a jolt, Rachel realized that Judith had not yet grasped the true situation. She obviously thought that Suzanne was merely lost, wandering around like a missing cat.

"Mother, we don't know where to *start* to look. Don't you understand? Suzanne's not lost. She apparently was abducted. Kidnapped. Taken somewhere by someone."

"But why?"

Living in New York, in the midst of it, Judith had always handled crime by blithely ignoring it. Not six weeks ago Rachel had upbraided her for walking through Penn Station late at night alone.

Judith, at her steamroller best, had insisted serenely that she had been in absolutely no danger.

Rachel was determined not to soften the reality. "Suzanne *may* have been taken for ransom. Some of the police think so. But we must face the fact that she *may* have been taken for whatever some men like to do to young girls.''

Judith's gasp came clearly over two thousand miles of wire and microwave relay. ''Oh, my God! Rachel, I'm going to be sick!''

''That's why I looked awful. I may look a lot worse before this is over.''

''Should I send money?''

The old standby. Still, Rachel appreciated the gesture. ''No,'' she said. Then she reconsidered. ''At least not yet. I haven't had time to think of what all this will cost.''

''Rachel, I want to help. But I don't know what I can do if you don't want me there.''

At this point Rachel was expected to fold, to say come on out, God yes, I need you.

Mother-as-victim was a whip that had always worked.

But not this time.

''Mother, right now I'm working very hard in therapy to get my feet under me. I'll be talking with the police, the press. There's nothing more to be done. Maybe it'll change later, and I'll need you here. When I do, I'll call you.''

On that note the conversation ended.

It was one of the few times in Rachel's life that she had success-fully fended off her mother.

But she felt no sense of satisfaction.

The conversation with Bill's parents went easier. They had been living in South Florida ten years. Rachel and the children had gone to Florida to visit only three times since Bill's death. Bill's parents had not visited her in New York. So in a way the exchange was more like a social call. The Shelbys expressed their shock and dismay, and asked how they could help.

But they did not suggest boarding a plane for Oklahoma.

Rachel promised to keep them informed.

She dreaded the call to the producer. But it had to be made.

In the past she had found Al Gold well insulated behind layers of secretaries and underlings. This time he came on almost immedi-ately.

''Rachel, we've been sitting here listening to the terrible news. Are there any new developments?''

''No. I'm just taking it moment by moment.''

''We want you to know the entire studio shares your concern and anxiety.''

Rachel was sure that was an understatement. No doubt the sequel moneymen had been on the phones from the moment they heard the news.

Rachel thanked him for calling and explained that she had been unable to get back to him earlier.

He asked about her injuries. She tried to minimize them.

For Suzanne's sake, she wanted to sound positive.

"I've hired a private investigator," she said. "He's a veteran detective. Very experienced. He knows and has worked with the FBI, the state police, everyone. I'm hopeful he'll be able to help."

"Do they have any indication of what has happened to her?"

Rachel refused to lie. "Nothing so far."

"I see. Well, we're trying to decide what to do. Of course our primary concern is for Suzanne. But we're thinking that after this experience, she might not feel like going ahead with the production."

Rachel fought down an immediate flare of anger. She put all the conviction she could muster into her voice. "Mr. Gold, if Suzanne emerges from this breathing, she'll want to go ahead. For her, nothing could be a greater tragedy than not making this picture."

"Yes, I understand. But, Rachel, we must be realistic. As you probably know, we're heavily into preproduction. That's terribly expensive. Locations. Sets. Equipment. Costumes. Contracts. Under the circumstances, we're wondering whether to go forward."

Rachel wanted to tell the man what a bastard he was. She paused for control. "Mr. Gold, at this point I really can't relate to your problem. All I can think of is getting my daughter back."

"Of course. Of course. Has there been any hint of ransom?"

"No. I wish it were that simple."

"Perhaps it could be. Frankly, considering the money the studio thus far has invested, we're thinking in terms of making an offer of a reward of sufficient size that we might elicit a response from the kidnapper."

Rachel felt a surge of hope. "That's very generous. Of course I'm sure we should clear whatever we do with the police."

"Yes. Naturally, we would expect to work with the police. I've called in some advisers. They suggest it might be best if the offer came from you, personally. The studio may not have pockets as deep as the kidnapper might assume."

Rachel found herself in a role she had played many times. "How much money are we talking?"

"We can go a million or so. But the thinking here is that maybe we shouldn't lay it all out up front. We're thinking a half mil for starters. That'd leave room to negotiate, if it comes to dealing with the kidnapper.''

Rachel did not want him to think she was impressed, or that she would be operating out of her league. Only two months before she had closed with an author's agent for 12.2 on a two-book contract.

''Mr. Gold, that's small potatoes compared with the money Suzanne brought in with the first movie. The sequel should do even better.''

The line was silent a moment. ''If necessary, we could go a mil or two higher. But frankly, we figure we're probably dealing with some creep who never saw that much money in his life. My advisers think too much might scare him off.''

Rachel recognized that as a valid point. She felt the psychological aspects should be considered carefully. And she assumed legal barriers would have to be overcome.

She was not even sure such an offer was possible.

''Let me talk with my own advisers and call you back.''

''I'll be awaiting your call. And for the moment the thinking here is that perhaps we should put the production on hold and await developments.''

Rachel assumed that the alternative was to scrap the project entirely. ''Thank you,'' she said. ''Suzanne will be most grateful.''

Rachel's growing relationship with the local police had not deterred her from placing all of her trust in Booker Reeves. From the first she had liked his quiet demeanor, his implicit empathy, and his ever-present aura of confidence. After her talk with Al Gold she immediately placed a call to Booker at the police station and told him of the conversation. ''Would that work?'' she asked. ''Could we offer a ransom?''

''Not a ransom,'' Booker said. ''Not directly. But there might be a way . . .'' The line remained silent for a moment. When Booker again spoke, his words came slowly and softly, almost as if he were talking to himself. ''This guy might go for it. We'd have to play him very, very carefully. Like a big fish on a light line.''

Again he was silent a moment.

Again Rachel waited.

''Do you think the studio would be willing to pump some money into a sort of sting operation?''

Rachel reviewed what she knew of Gold. Any film producer was basically a gambler. She felt she knew the type.

"I believe so. Suzanne safe would mean millions to the studio."

"Understand, there's no way we could make a flat offer to pay a ransom. That's illegal, for one thing. But we might find a way to work around it. No law enforcement agency could be involved. We'd have to do it on our own, play it subtle, based on what we can learn about this guy. Let me talk to some people, see what we can do. I'll get back to you on this."

Rachel felt she was ready to ask. "You don't think Chief Laird is right, do you? You don't think Suzanne was taken for ransom."

Booker's hesitation was brief. "No, I don't. But we might put the idea into his head. The trick will be to reach him. He probably doesn't watch television or read the newspapers."

"You sound as though you know who it is."

"I don't know him. But I think I'm just beginning to get a feel for him."

Rachel threw herself into the therapy session with all her energy, performing the exercises even faster and more vigorously than the therapist requested. The giddiness was gone. She felt her strength returning minute by minute.

Dr. Peterson arrived in time to witness the last of the session. As the therapist gathered her equipment for departure, Peterson motioned Rachel onto her bed for a physical exam.

"Dr. Peterson, I'm ready for release," she said. "Can't you see? I can find my nose with my eyes closed. I can walk a straight line. I can touch my toes with my good hand without losing my equilibrium. Dr. Peterson, I've *got* to get out of here!"

Peterson checked her pulse and blood pressure. He looked into her eyes with his little light. He then dropped into a chair and toyed with his stethoscope. "It's hardly been twenty-four hours since you couldn't stand by yourself."

"Haven't I improved much faster than you expected?"

"Yes. But we don't know what's going on inside your skull."

"I can tell you." She gestured to the callback slips. "I'm busy prioritizing my time among the networks to get the most exposure possible. I'm planning how I'll print and distribute fliers all over this state, all over this part of the country. Booker says someone somewhere is bound to know something that will help. I've got to reach that person."

Peterson frowned. "You're not anywhere near ready for that."

Rachel felt hot tears. "Dr. Peterson, I can't coddle myself. Not with Suzanne out there enduring God knows what."

Peterson looked away. For a moment he studied the floor. Rachel waited, torn by indecision on what to do if he refused.

She could sign herself out. She was not a prisoner.

But she had confidence in this man. She felt badly in need of his support. And she could not ignore the fact that his dire warnings of the dangers were probably valid.

When he spoke, his voice contained a new intensity. "Okay, I'll release you. Tomorrow morning. But on firm conditions. First, I want you to consider yourself an outpatient. I want you back here every morning for a complete checkup. Two, I want you to pace yourself. Don't try to do too much. When you tire—and you will— walk away from the pressure, if only for a few minutes. Realize that we can't have your blood pressure soaring. And three, I want you to promise that at the slightest symptom—any of the signs we've talked about—you'll come straight to me. The switchboard will be alerted to your situation. They'll know what to do. Promise?"

"I promise."

"Have you given any thought to where you'll do all this work?"

Rachel nodded. "I'll rent office space, furniture, and hire temporary help."

"I know a man who has vacancies in a strip mall. I could call him if you'd like."

"I would be eternally grateful."

"He also could help with the furniture. And you'll need special service to get phones installed. Usually there's a considerable wait. I know the regional supervisor. I can call him, explain the circumstances."

Rachel smiled at him. "You've been thinking ahead too. I thank you. I'll never forget this."

Peterson folded his stethoscope, stuck it into his lab coat pocket as if to signal that the examination was completed, and that their conversation was now on a different level.

"Mrs. Shelby, there's a good reason medical doctors are trained to keep professional distance. Emotional involvement can affect judgment. But from the first, I've been empathetic to your situation, *angry* over what has happened to Suzanne. What I'm trying to say, if I can help in *any* way, just let me know."

"I will, Dr. Peterson. You, everyone here, have been so good to me. Every stitch of clothing I own is sitting packed away in a California warehouse. Right now Donna is out shopping for me, on her day off. I learned this afternoon that some of the administrative staff have been staying late, helping to field telephone calls. There's no way I can repay such generosity.''

''Nor should you. I think you'll find that the community feels partly responsible for what has happened to Suzanne.''

Rachel was puzzled. ''In what way?''

''They're aware of how much our society has deteriorated. They feel guilty that we've allowed this to happen. They want to fight back.''

Rachel felt like confiding in him. ''If anyone had told me, months ago, that I'd be in this situation, I would have thought I'd be paralyzed, helpless. But now I can't wait to get started. I didn't know I was capable of such rage. That's what's driving me. Anger. I've never felt more capable.''

Peterson nodded his understanding. His face bore that deep sadness Rachel had seen in him at odd moments.

''You're probably at a peak,'' he said. ''There's a theory that God never sends you anything you can't handle. I'm not so sure about that. But I do know that once you're faced with it, you can endure almost anything.''

''I hope so,'' Rachel said. ''For Suzanne's sake.''

Donna arrived shortly after dark, loaded with packages. ''I probably went overboard with your money,'' she said. ''I settled on a dress *and* a blouse and skirt. I just fell in love with the blouse.''

Rachel had been hoping only for something adequate to wear out of the hospital. She was genuinely surprised by Donna's selections. The dress was simple, neat, stylish. The blouse was of a subdued floral design that would look good on television. Obviously Donna had chosen with care.

''This is perfect,'' Rachel said. ''But I can see you spent too much time hunting.''

''I enjoyed it. I was just afraid I'd get arrested in petite.''

Rachel broke the news that Peterson was releasing her. She told of his help in finding facilities for her.

Again she expressed her thanks for all Donna had done, and for how kind everyone in the hospital had been.

''I thought you might like to know,'' Donna said. ''Last night, the pastor of our church said a prayer for Suzanne. Not mixed in with the prayer for the ill and the infirm and all that. A special prayer. Just for her.''

Rachel was momentarily disturbed. An image came to mind of

those ridiculous Protestant ministers on television, waving their arms, shouting, threatening God's wrath if they were not sent money.

She shoved the thought aside.

Donna was more intelligent than that.

"Afterward, some of the church women came to me and asked what they could do to help," Donna went on. "They know, of course, that I work here. What I was thinking, you mentioned hiring temps. Most of the women I'm talking about have worked in offices. They would love to help you."

Rachel was reluctant to commit herself to a situation she might not be able to control. She hedged. "That's a thought."

Donna had a way of frowning, cocking her head, and looking intently into a listener's face. "Would you like to talk to my pastor? I know if I were in your place, I'd sure want to talk to someone."

Rachel did not know what to say. Donna had been so helpful. She did not want to hurt her feelings. She evaded the question by asking another. "What denomination is your pastor?"

"United Methodist."

"I'm a Jew," Rachel said.

"Oh."

Donna did not seem to know where to go from there.

Disturbed by Donna's unease, Rachel sought to soften the moment. "I really should say I was reared Jewish. I haven't practiced my religion as I should."

That had been another facet of her life she had postponed. She had planned, at some point, to introduce Suzanne and David to their rich heritage. But with work, and the daily responsibilities of a single parent, she had let those good intentions slide.

"I didn't mean to intrude," Donna said. "It's just that the church is such a big part of my life. I couldn't do my work without it. Every time someone dies right in my arms, I go home a basket case. These old people, dying all around you of horrible diseases. The children brought in burned, hurt. It really gets to you sometimes."

"I'm sure it does."

Donna still seemed bothered by what she apparently considered a gaffe, and was trying to fix it without making it worse. "I just wasn't thinking. I've never been around Jews. I didn't recognize the name Shelby as Jewish."

"My husband was Christian," Rachel said. "We had a mixed marriage."

She was not accustomed to such personal talk. In her milieu, it was just not done, most especially with casual acquaintances.

But maybe Donna was right. She felt the need to talk to someone.

"Donna, I'm experiencing difficulties I suppose are regional. Dr. Peterson warned me that I would. We New Yorkers are notorious for stepping over dead bodies in the street, for ignoring anyone in trouble, for never becoming involved. I feel uncomfortable with the generosity I've received here. I know it's mostly for Suzanne. Still, I don't quite know how to handle it."

Donna gave her that frowning stare. "Mrs. Shelby, helping others is the most *human* thing anyone can do. People *want* to help, feel human. You shouldn't deny them that!"

"What should I do? Just say thank you?"

"Yes yes yes! You've done that very well."

"I hope you'll bear with me," Rachel said. "I've been so panic-stricken over Suzanne, I haven't had time to assimilate all this. I know something extraordinary is happening to me, the way people have responded. But I'm frankly puzzled. In my experience, strangers don't act this way. Take Dr. Peterson, for instance. Few people in my life have been so kind, so generous. He devotes so much time to me, I feel I'm his only patient."

Donna smiled. "There are at least six patients in this hospital who would say the same thing. The young man who hit you has a crushed chest, jammed knees. He may never walk again normally. The girl with him wasn't wearing a seat belt. Her face was smashed. She'll be undergoing plastic surgery for years. There's a sweet old lady dying of cancer up on Two West. Dr. Peterson hovers over all of them. That's just the way he is."

"He's such a nice man," Rachel said. "I like his humor. But he seems so sad. I'd like to understand him better because I owe him so much."

Donna's frown deepened. "I thought you knew. But I guess there's no way you could." She glanced at the closed door and lowered her voice. "His wife was murdered about five or six years ago. She was pregnant with their first child."

Rachel was shocked speechless. That revelation explained much about him. "How absolutely awful!" she managed to say.

Donna's voice dropped almost to a whisper. "That's not all. Dr. Peterson was charged with her murder. It was a big news story for weeks and weeks and weeks. It was on those true crime television shows where they act things out. You see, he was a cardiac surgeon in Oklahoma City, very well known. We sent him patients. The doctors around here said he was as good as anyone in Houston,

Johns Hopkins, or the Mayo. But he was in jail, bond denied, about to go to trial, when Booker Reeves found the real murderers. I don't know all the details. Dr. Peterson was released. But, of course, his life was ruined.''

For the moment, placing herself in Dr. Peterson's place, Rachel almost forgot her own troubles.

''I think he felt his friends, the hospital, didn't stand behind him the way they should. He quit practice, resigned from the hospital.''

''No wonder he looks so sad,'' Rachel said.

''I saw a news story—this was back before I dreamed I would ever know him. He was quoted as saying he'd never practice medicine again. And I felt, oh, such a loss! Because I knew how many people he'd helped. Then, about eighteen months ago, he showed up here.''

Donna hesitated, as if uncertain how much to tell. Rachel waited.

''Dr. Woods, who founded this hospital, died suddenly. Massive stroke. One day he was here, making his rounds, and the next he was gone. There are other doctors who have privileges, attending physicians who have patients here and perform surgery. But Dr. Woods *was* the hospital. There was no one to take his place. Then they brought in Dr. Peterson.''

She paused, as if remembering events, selecting what she needed.

''For the first year or so Dr. Peterson was quiet, just did his work. Remote. He worked night and day. He bought a place—a ranch—a few miles out of town. He still spends all his spare time there. He never attends parties, social gatherings. None of us ever felt we got to know him. Only in the last few months has he begun to open up. He has talked, joked more with you than he has with anyone since he came here.''

Rachel thought of the pain in those dark eyes. Now she felt even more drawn to him.

''Don't let on I told you,'' Donna said. ''Ordinarily I'm not a gossip. But I thought you ought to know.''

''I'm grateful you told me,'' she said.

''Well, I should let you get some rest. Dr. Peterson would have my hide if he knew I was keeping you up. What time do you want to start in the morning?''

Donna's implication was that she would be ready anytime Rachel designated.

''Donna, you've done so much. I can't ask you to do more. I'll rent a car, first thing. Then I'll be able to take better care of myself.''

Donna held up a hand, palm outward. ''I'll be up anyway. I can run you out to the car place, show you where everything is. Eight o'clock? I don't imagine you'll be able to get anything done before then.''

Rachel opened her mouth to protest the kindness. Then she remembered Donna's lecture on accepting help.

''Eight it is, then,'' she said.

6

"Booker!" Nate Noonan squeezed his bulk past the clotted desks and chairs in the squad room. "I thought we'd finally got rid of you."

"Not hardly." Booker reached up to shake Nate's hand. "This case must be setting off alarms in high places to get you out from behind a desk."

Noonan dumped a sheaf of material onto a desk and lowered his weight into a chair beside Booker. "You'd better believe it. Governor was on the phone to the director before the first newscast was over."

Around them, officers from several agencies were crowding into a room designed to accommodate a sixteen-man police force. Many disparate groups were represented—the FBI, OSBI, Highway Patrol, U.S. marshal's office, sheriff's office, and volunteer officers from several surrounding counties.

Booker had been only half joking. He was surprised to see Noonan, who had climbed so high up the OSBI administrative ladder that normally he no longer went into the field.

Booker and Noonan had worked closely together for eighteen years. They felt no affection for each other, but no strong antipathies either. Booker thought Noonan sometimes tended to fluff off on details, and to talk when he should listen. Noonan thought Booker came up with too many wild theories and piddled around too much with the insignificant. Yet they had worked through the years without serious friction. Booker had not seen Noonan since retirement. Noonan had gained another fifteen or twenty pounds, pushing him close to two seventy-five.

Booker kept the needle working. "You just get in?"

He knew that Noonan had worked all night.

"Been on my feet since ten o'clock yesterday. If I'd known they were going to be late with this meeting, I would've stopped for breakfast."

"How many people here from the Bureau?"

"As of this morning, ten." He named them. Booker knew all but one, who had joined the Bureau after his retirement.

"I thought maybe Patricia would be here."

"If we're lucky, she'll be down this afternoon. We've got four witnesses lined up for her to work on. But she's subpoenaed on a murder case in Ada. Lawyers for both sides promised they'd be through with her by noon. But you know how that goes."

Booker made an effort not to show his disappointment. He needed Patricia's advice, and he could see that she faced a rough day. After testifying several hours in a murder trial, she would drive halfway across the state to question four witnesses under hypnosis. She would be too tired tonight to listen to his esoteric theories.

"Who's case agent on this?" Booker asked.

"For better or worse, you're looking at him."

"I guess that's a tad better than worse," Booker said.

He reassessed his own situation. As OSBI case agent, Noonan would be directing the entire investigation. Booker's relationship with Hopkins, and even with Chief Laird, had been good. He did not know how Noonan would regard an unauthorized investigator sticking his nose into a hot case—especially one who had left the Bureau under a bit of a cloud.

Noonan glanced at the folders in front of Booker. "You got an angle?"

Booker nodded. "It occurred to me that this subject probably has some priors. I pulled files for five years to see if I could find any connections."

"All the kid disappearances?"

"Yeah."

"Good God, Booker. We've been up the hill and down again on that a dozen times. We've never come up with anything."

Booker felt he should persist. "Who worked it last time?"

Noonan frowned. "Seems to me Fletcher tried again for a connection when that Tillman County kid was snatched. I forget the name."

"Catherine. Catherine Overby."

"Right. Fletch came up with zip. You might talk with him."

Booker did not know if Noonan was saying to talk with Fletcher and go ahead with it, or to profit by Fletcher's experiences and drop it. He did not ask.

"Where is Fletcher?"

"He's working that sniper incident on Eye-Forty-Four down by Randlett. You could try and reach him through Lawton."

Booker had his answer. Noonan apparently thought the theory important enough to interrupt an agent involved in an ongoing investigation.

"I'll do that." Booker decided to push his luck. "I also need to talk to Patricia."

"What about?"

Booker explained the film studio's willingness to pay up to a million for ransom if some sort of deal could be arranged.

Noonan's reaction was immediate. "Shit fire, Booker. You know we can't participate in anything like that."

"No. But I'm thinking we might find some way to plant the idea. Get him to thinking money."

"I don't know," Noonan said. "If the kid's really been snatched, we may be dealing with a real sicko. That could be the wrong thing to do."

"That's why I need to talk to Patricia."

Noonan was rescued from making a reply. Chief Laird borrowed a policeman's baton, rapped on a desk, and brought the meeting to order. He raised his voice. "It's been a long night. I know you're all tired. But we felt we ought to get together, map out where we're going with this investigation."

The room quieted. Laird thanked everyone for their work. He introduced the two FBI agents, Tom Simmons and J. H. Todd, and explained that their role would be more or less advisory and liaison at the moment, until the nature of the case was determined.

Booker was pleased to see that Simmons was the SAC—special agent in charge. Booker had never worked with Todd, but Simmons and Booker had spent many long hours together on the oil field equipment theft that had turned federal when it led to Iran.

Laird said Hopkins and Pryor would be coordinating personnel and assignments.

"We've made formal request for the OSBI to take the lead in the investigation," he said. "Those of you just coming aboard should know that Senior Inspector Nate Noonan is case agent. Nate, you want to bring us up to speed on where we are?"

Perhaps not wishing to burden his tired feet further, Nate remained seated. "At this point I think we've worked the wreck scene fairly well," he said. "What we need to do now is follow through on the tips that are coming in. We've had three men on the phones all night. We've screened them fairly close. But we figure we've got forty, maybe fifty that need looking into. That's one thing I hope to get done today.''

He opened a folder and poked at the reports. ''I don't know what to tell you on how far to go with these. You can use your own judgment. If one opens up, and you need help, just ask. We'll go back over everything later, make sure we haven't missed anything.''

''How will we make assignments?'' Hopkins asked.

''Grab bag, I guess. Some of our OSBI people are out now on two or three that look the most promising. Frankly, most of this looks like pure unadulterated crap, the kind of thing you usually get on cases like this. But we've got to follow through. This afternoon Dr. McMahon will be interviewing four witnesses under hypnosis. If she comes up with even a hint of a description, we'll go back and reinterview the wreck-site witnesses. We're now up to forty-two witnesses at the scene in the proper time frame. There may be more we haven't found. So we'll need all the legwork we can get.''

''We should have the FBI preliminary profile by tomorrow,'' Hopkins said. ''That may give us some work.''

''Right. The second thing I hope we can get done today is the physical search. We've made a half-assed stab at it around the intersection. Today we'll walk the whole town. Organized door-to-door search. Every street. Every alley. We'll go through all the trash in the town's one hundred and sixty-two Dumpsters. I want you to look for anything that doesn't belong. Look especially close behind the Dumpsters, and in all outbuildings and toolsheds. As you work, ask around. Anyone seen this kid? Anyone seen anybody odd hanging around? Hop and Jeff will coordinate the ground search. If you find anything, for God's sake follow proper investigative procedures. We don't want any heavy hands on the evidence. Anything at all suspicious, report it, back off, and we'll check it out. Any questions?''

No one responded in the brief interval of silence that followed.

Then, to Booker's amazement, Nate put a hand on Booker's shoulder and squeezed, just like they were old asshole buddies. ''Most of you know Booker Reeves here. Retired agent. He's into this, working with the victim's mother. If any of you need to ask her something, you might ought to go through Booker. Understand, I'm not denying access. It's just that the lady was hurt pretty bad in the wreck, and she's got all this on top of her. Booker maybe can answer your questions, or pave the way if he can't. He's old and decrepit, but we might as well use him.''

The room erupted in laughter. Booker grinned to show he could take a joke. Nate waited for quiet.

"Booker, how'll they reach you?"

"I'll be here most of the time."

"And if you're not. You got a beeper or something?"

"No."

"We can lend him a radio," Chief Laird said.

"Good. You can reach him through the PD switchboard. Booker, you got anything else to add?"

Booker felt one point needed to be stressed. "Only that I think we can anticipate some of what we're going to get in the FBI profile. We can guess that the subject will be a white male, eighteen to twenty-six . . ."

Again the room erupted in laughter.

Booker had not intended to be humorous. The ages varied slightly. But it was true that the FBI profiles usually started out with that phrase.

Simmons and Todd did not appear to appreciate Booker's parody, even if unintentional. They did not smile.

Booker ignored the interruption. "If the kid was snatched—and apparently she was—this subject probably will be ordinary-looking. He'll be driving an ordinary-looking car or pickup. Otherwise, someone would have noticed him. He may be scroungy, or he may be handsome, but not so much so one way or the other that you'd give him a second glance. Otherwise, someone would have noticed him. He blends in. I mention this because I suspect our witnesses may think we're looking for someone with two heads and horns. I think we should tell the witnesses that this guy may be a monster, but he probably doesn't look like one. They may even know him."

"I'll buy that," Nate said. "Nobody noticed him because he didn't look like much of anything. You might mention that." He glanced at Booker. "Anything else?"

Booker hesitated. He now was leaving logic behind and edging into theory, gut feeling. But he was beginning to feel strongly about it. "I think this guy travels a lot. He has a job that keeps him on the road. He may not cruise all the time. But when he sees a target of opportunity, nothing stands in the way of his taking advantage of it. So he's not into a structured job, appointments, reporting in, all that. He's probably self-employed at whatever he does. To a kid, he probably looks like an authority figure—schoolteacher, cop, maybe a minister. That might put him on the older end of the profile. Mid to late twenties."

Clearly Nate did not buy these embellishments. "You have anything solid behind that?"

"Only that it was a bold snatch. That tells me he's had practice. He's been doing this a long time. Could be he has a minor record—wienie wagging, peeping, groping. But now he's older and he has gotten better at it. I doubt he's ever taken a serious fall. He's probably not in VICAP."

"Well, that's certainly something to think about," Nate said. "But we probably should keep all our options open. Let's look for anything that might fit." He glanced around the room. "If nobody has anything else, those of you who will be working this morning can check with Lieutenant Hopkins on what needs to be done. We'll come back here and check signals again about six o'clock this evening."

As the meeting broke up, Noonan rose and moved away. Booker was aware that he had been put down rather solidly for voicing pure speculation to the troops. But he was not especially bothered. He felt what he had said needed to be said.

He went to Chief Laird and was provided with a desk and phone. He was in luck. Fletcher returned his call within twenty minutes. Booker cupped the telephone mouthpiece in his palm, a habit acquired long before to prevent broadcasting his end of the conversation to an entire office.

"Fletch, how you doin'?"

Although Fletcher was in the field, his voice came through strong and clear. "Today, not worth a shit. Nothing to go on. I can't find the handle. And they're chewing my ass."

Fletcher also was working a high-profile case. Booker had read about it on the front page in the morning *Daily Oklahoman*. Someone northbound on Interstate 44 had sprayed oncoming traffic just north of Red River with 9mm rounds from an automatic weapon. Three trucks and four cars had been hit. No one had been killed, but five persons were wounded and one was in critical condition. There were no leads.

As case agent, Fletcher was drawing the heat.

"Let me tell you something, Booker. When *I* retire, they'll never get me back into it."

Booker was not surprised that Fletcher knew he was working on the Shelby case. In the course of business, OSBI agents scattered around the state talked to each other. And when they talked, they also took care of Bureau gossip. Booker felt extreme satisfaction to be back in the loop. For four years he had been out of it. He warmly welcomed the camaraderie of dealing again with a live case.

"I got into this before I knew what a circus it'd be," he said. "We're mounted up and riding off in all directions."

"Nate's good at that."

"I noticed you worked the Catherine Overby and Gaye Monroe disappearances. Nate said you did quite a bit of work on them. You ever make any connections?"

"Nothing to hang your hat on. Nate got pissed I spent so much time on that angle. When I read about this Suzanne Shelby case, I thought about getting on the horn and suggesting there might be a pattern. But then I heard Nate was case agent, and I doubted he'd be receptive. He could be right. I didn't find much there."

"He's not exactly ecstatic I'm looking into it. But I pulled the files, on the parameters as I knew them. File says this little Overby girl was taken right off the street."

"Within a half block or so of home. On the edge of town. Very quiet. No traffic. No sidewalks. I figure the subject probably pulled right up beside her. No outcry. Nothing. We interviewed every person for blocks around. All her schoolmates. No one remembered anything."

"What do you figure?"

"Very effective MO. Maybe he's playing cop. Shows a badge, gun, or something. 'Get in the car, little girl.' "

"Yeah. That's what I'm thinking."

"I went up to Fairmont, out to Plainview, Shamrock, and Childress. The Estraca family had moved from Tulsa. I never tracked them down. The Gardner case up in Missouri was also transient. I think the family was from Illinois, best I remember. I didn't go back and interview on those two, but I did on the others."

"Childress?"

Booker knew of no disappearance from Childress.

"Becky Foster. Eight. Disappeared from a church picnic at Medicine Park. Body dumped in a ravine out in the Texas Panhandle. She wasn't found for a while. We didn't get much out of the autopsy. ID'd through dental records."

"The computer didn't pick her up."

"She may not be in VICAP. That case may predate. You're getting back toward the eighties there. If you remember, those VICAP forms were so complicated back then that a lot of investigators said fuck it. Some cases weren't entered."

Booker made notes. "She snatched from a group?"

"Last seen one morning in choir practice. Had solo part, so ID certain. Choir practice ended about fifteen minutes before noon. No one saw her at lunch."

"Traffic?"

"Well, you know that campground. People coming and going. The church group was situated back a ways. But no one paid much attention to who was wandering around."

"Brenda Wallace. Plainview. Had some unknown substance on upper body. You look into that?"

"I would've liked to have done more. I talked to the medical examiner, is all. He said the body was in bad shape. He first thought this stuff was slime mold. But he was puzzled because it had dried, and that kind of mold usually doesn't. He said he determined it was dried enzymes, but he lacked the time and facilities to pinpoint what it was from."

"Enzymes?"

"Like in spit. That's what he thought it was. You know digestion really starts in your mouth when you chew. Your saliva has enzymes that help turn this into that. When the food goes on down, the pancreas, liver, and other organs pump out about a zillion more kinds of enzymes to help digestion. But the medical examiner thought this was the kind found in saliva. He was still working on it. I can't remember his name."

"I've got it." Booker told him. "I'll give him a call, see if he found anything,"

"It was so unusual that he'll probably still remember the case. You got a drawing of the bite marks on the one found up in Kaw Lake?"

"Yeah. Kathy Simpson. From Fairmont. What did you make of that bite?"

"Beats the shit out of me. Too big for coyote, anything like that. Not from regular teeth, anyway. Double row. More like a spiny bite from a fish. But it'd have to be a hell of a big one. And how would a fish that big get into the shallow water where she was found? She wasn't a floater. She was dumped right there."

"Did the medical examiner venture any guess on the bite? Anything he didn't feel comfortable putting down in black and white?"

"No. Claimed he had no idea."

Fletcher paused. His voice took on a more strident tone. "Booker, when I was into that, I had myself about half convinced that we had us a runaway serial killer at work. I still lean in that direction. But I couldn't come up with enough of a pattern to sell the idea. I had nothing but a gut feeling."

"That's about where I am now," Booker said.

"If you lay it out chronologically, maybe there *is* a progression. The early victims were buried. Then they were just dumped. Then there's the enzyme thing. And the bite marks. After that, the last year or more, there've been snatches, but no bodies found.''

Booker had not yet reached that point in his thinking. ''You're saying he's getting better at it.''

''Right. I don't buy that shit that the MO never changes. I think they try this and they try that until they find what works, what feels good.''

''And now he's found what works, what feels good.''

''Right. No more bodies. And something else. Have you noticed how all the victims are small, even for their age? Thin. You'd think that from the law of averages, he'd pick up a tubby kid occasionally. But they're all small. Every one.''

''Yeah. I've noticed that. You have any theories on it?''

''Makes disposal easier. Or maybe small kids fit his fantasy. I don't know. Could be any number of reasons.''

''Yeah,'' Booker agreed. He had not been able to pin a definite theory to it.

He thanked Fletcher for his help and ended the call. He then phoned the medical examiner in Texas, who quickly confirmed Fletcher's memory.

''Last I heard, medical science still hadn't broken down all the digestive enzymes,'' the medical examiner said. ''I sure as hell don't have the facilities to do the qualitative analysis myself. But I played around with it some. It wasn't like anything I'd encountered before, or since.''

''And it looked like saliva?''

''That's an educated guess. Understand, we're talking about something awfully complex. Could have been almost any kind of digestive juice. Like I said, I have no way to break it down. I'm just going by what clues I could pick up.''

''Any way I could maybe send a sample off somewhere, get a major lab to break it down for us?''

''There wasn't much of it to begin with, and I used what I had, running tests. I don't have a specimen.''

''If we exhumed, would we be apt to find some?''

''I doubt it. Deterioration was well along, even back then. And like I said, there wasn't much.''

Booker asked him a few questions about possible injuries to the body. The pathologist's memory was not as good on that. Booker thanked him and terminated the call.

Behind him, Hopkins and Pryor had completed assignments. They were discussing the relative merits of the tips that had not yet been assigned.

"Is Slewfoot still working?" Booker asked Hopkins.

Pryor laughed. Slewfoot had been whoring along Interstate 40 for years. Others came and went, but Slewfoot stayed. She was not bad-looking, but tough. Every cop knew her.

Hopkins took Booker's question seriously. "Far as I know, she's still working the truck stops west of town. We told her not to do business within city limits. I haven't seen her in a while."

"Old flame, Booker?" Pryor asked. When he became animated, Pryor's freckles seemed to stand out.

Booker ignored him. "One of these kids had dried spit all over her upper torso. Lots of it. Ever hear of anything like that?"

"No."

"I have," Pryor said. "They call it a tongue bath."

"I'd imagine you'd be an expert on that," Hopkins said.

"No. But there's a little secretary in the dean's office at Southwestern I'd like to learn on."

"Hop, if you don't need me, I think I'll go out and talk to Slewfoot," Booker said. "I'm assuming that if there's anyone around with that perversion—aside from Pryor here—she'd probably know about it."

"Probably," Hopkins agreed.

"Dr. McMahon on line three," Terri called to Hopkins.

"Hop, I'd like to talk to Patricia a minute after you're through," Booker said as Hopkins picked up the call.

From Hopkins's end of the conversation Booker gathered that she and Hopkins were estimating her drive time, and how to arrange her four hypnosis sessions. At last they agreed on a working schedule, with witnesses brought in at ninety-minute intervals.

Hopkins passed her on to Booker.

"How'd it go?" Booker asked, meaning her morning on the witness stand.

"About as bad as it gets," she said. "I try so hard to remain neutral. Just the facts, my conclusions. Then the defense implies with every question that I'm a hired gun for the state, trying to railroad his poor, impoverished client. The lead defense lawyer is a real bastard. I'm just furious."

"It's all a game with them," Booker sympathized. "Knowing you, I'd bet they lost more ground than they gained. Juries usually see through that."

"Well, I've got to put it out of my head, think about this next one. I saw Pete on television. He really looked good."

"He's apparently doing well," Booker reported. "Folks around here say he's a workaholic. Seems to be trying to lose himself in his work."

"That's not necessarily good. He's bound to be repressing a lot of unvented anger."

Booker knew the comment was made by Patricia the concerned friend, not Patricia the psychiatrist. "He seems to be handling it," Booker said. "Look, I know this is turning into a rough day for you. But I need to talk to you in the worst way. Do you suppose we could get together? After you've finished with the witnesses? It's important."

The line remained silent for a moment. Booker assumed she was considering time frames.

"I won't be in there until three. An hour to familiarize myself with the case, then four ninety-minute hypnosis sessions. Booker, we're looking at ten or ten-thirty at least, after a hellish day. I won't be at my best."

"Your worst is good enough for me. What I had in mind was more like a ménage à trois. You, me, and Jack Daniel."

"Why didn't you say so? Okay. But, Booker, I don't know where I'll be. Hop said the town's full of news people, that the motels are full as far east as El Reno. Check with him. He's trying to find accommodations for me."

"I'll do that. And I'll see you then."

"Could you give me some idea of what it's about? So far I've received absolutely no background on this Shelby case. All I know is what I've read in the newspapers and seen on television."

"At this point there's not much else," Booker told her. "I've developed a working theory. So far, not many people around here are buying it. I need to get your input."

"What do you see? A pattern?"

"Yeah. If I'm right, we're dealing with a four-barreled monster, and the Shelby kid's probably the same as dead. But there's a slim chance I may be on to a way to save her."

7

Once again Suzanne forced her mind back to the movie, away from reality and the paralyzing terror. She stepped backward onto the metal-framed cot for perspective. The big snake's cage would have to be moved to make room for the camera. A low dolly shot, almost from the floor, would bring into frame the chain and padlock on her ankle. She could think of no other way to work them in. She experimented, sitting on the bare mattress, bringing her right heel up against her tush. Low was not her best profile, especially with the wide lens required to work so closely. But she could lean into the shot, head down, looking up, and that would get her eyes, ankle, chain, and padlock in frame. With her head lowered, her hair would bunch on her shoulders, and that was good. She would put a soft red filter on the key light, slightly above the camera, to bring out the amber in her hair and to darken the icky green of the wall behind her. And she would need some rags to cover the essentials. She did not object to nudity if it fitted a story purpose, like swimming or taking a shower. Anything in character she would do. But her favorite screenwriter, Mort Miller, once told her that too much bare skin tends to distract from the emotional context of a scene. And coming right down to it, her tush was not all that great. She envisioned herself in tattered tan hiking shorts and a frilly slingshot top. But she was not sure that costume would be in character.

She would have to get some advice on that.

In the shot, she saw herself carrying on an exchange in dramatic confrontation with the snake man. She had not yet worked out the dialogue. But she would be resisting, showing her courage. He would slap her hard, and she would give him the Jodie Foster laugh from the breakfast scene in *Taxi Driver*. That would play. But as yet she could not find a way to stay within bounds of taste when he started acting ugly.

That would have to be suggested some way. Suggested without going porno. She was not sure how to do that.

Maybe somebody older could give her advice. She would be too embarrassed to ask Mort. He was a super guy. She could not imagine talking with him about anything like that. Maybe she could find someone else to ask.

She had already worked out the opening. The atmosphere and mood of this place could be conveyed from the first fade-in. She envisioned a long establishing shot, introducing the setting just as she first saw it from the snake man's truck—a wild, brush-covered canyon, with the camera traveling in on an old red rock-and-metal barn behind a fallen-down, vacant, unpainted house. The shot also would frame the old car parked to the left of the door. Bright lighting and sharp shadows would create the sense of the sun baking the old metal building. Mort had shown her film clips to demonstrate how that was done, conveying a feeling of heat, using nothing but light.

In this opening shot, the snake man would drive up in his rattly old blue pickup truck, take a bag of snakes out of the back end, go through the noisy business with the chain at the door, and carry the sack inside. A reverse angle shot would show him coming into the barn, sweating, wet patches on his back and under his arms, unfastening the sack, and dumping the snakes into a pit in the corner.

For a while she had been stymied on where to go from there, how to immerse the viewer totally in the setting. Then she remembered Mort talking about that terrific device of the music room scene in *Five Easy Pieces*. That was her absolute favorite of old movies. She always got excited, just thinking of that music room scene, and Mort talking about the way it turned your mind around. Up to that point in the movie, Jack Nicholson had been an oil field worker with crummy friends. He was with Karen Black, and she was trying so hard to be uncrummy, she made your teeth hurt. Then Nicholson drove home to Oregon or Washington State or somewhere real woodsy, to this classy old house full of arty people. As Mort said, no viewer would have bought that plot twist—this almost-crummy oil field worker as a former concert pianist. But they made it work with this fabulous camera device. Nicholson is lounging on a classy leather couch when Susan Anspach comes in with a terrific arrangement of flowers. As she crosses to place them on a piano, the camera gives an overview of the marvelous old room with its hardwood floors and high, old-timey fireplace. She turns and asks Nicholson if he would do her a favor, if he would play something for her. Nicholson gives a faint nod and goes to one of two facing pianos, and the slow way he looks at the keyboard lets you know that a zillion memories are going through his head. At last he starts to play a haunting piece, and the camera starts an agonizingly slow pan to the left, past polished violins, past an enrapt Anspach, past gold-thread draperies that must have cost a fortune, to pictures along the wall—Nicholson as a boy, chamber groups, Nicholson's sister, young and carefree-looking, Nicholson when he is older, portraits of composers, Nicholson's sister at the keyboard, a formal portrait of Nicholson's father. Nicholson is still playing, a devastatingly perfect piece, as the camera completes its 360-degree pan back to Anspach. By the time the camera finishes this unhurried pan, you know that yes, this guy once belonged here. You can guess at all the crap he took, growing up here, and you even understand, a little bit, why he left. Your mind goes the full circle with the camera, from unbelieving to believing.

Suzanne had thought it all out. She would flat steal that device to introduce the snake man, to take the audience from the known to the incredible. Like Jack Nicholson's room, the interior of the barn would not be meaningful in bits and pieces. She would give them the whole 360-degree smear.

She would start with the big snake, Sam, framing in on the dark at the top of his cage, so at first you would think you were seeing a log, maybe, or a roll of carpet. Then the snake would move, and that big head would come around—the handlers could probably make him do that—and you would have a real oh-my-God shot to set the mood. Then the camera would start panning to the right so slowly, you would want it to hurry, and the cages with the almost-as-big snakes would come into view. From the stillness you would get a sense of the hot, airless closeness of the old barn. Maybe the camera would go up, and you would see the underside of the roof, where the light bulbs glowed day and night in their metal reflectors. Of course there would be no way to convey the god-awful smell. You would see and hear the chickens pecking and clucking at the bottom of the cages and wonder about them, but you would not know about them until later. The camera would creep on past the worktable with the test tubes and glass beakers, on past the long hooks and wires and stuff, and you would know that all that gear had something to do with the snakes, but maybe not what. Then the camera would pan slowly on to the rattlesnake pits, and you would see the big lumps that looked like knee-high mounds of spaghetti. You would wonder for an instant what those lumps were, then you would know in another oh-my-God shot almost as good as the first. The pits would keep crawling by, and you would wonder if there were really that many rattlesnakes in all the world. The pits would end, and you would have paint-flaky old wall until the rattlesnake skins, row on row, and you came to the snake man himself in his old broken-down recliner held together with ropes, his sleeve up, doing dope.

From there Suzanne was not sure what the pan would show, for she had not seen that corner of the barn. But the camera would look, then come on past the door, past the stalls filled with hay and junk, to frame in on this little waif, soaked in sweat, chained to the wall next to the big snake.

Envisioning the scene, Suzanne could see that the fluffy slingshot top would not do. Much too playschoolish. A raggedy pullover, maybe, in a color contrasting with the icky wall. And maybe she would wear a cap, something like Barbra Streisand's in *Yentl*.

But that might be too much. Too cutesy.

She would have to think about it.

The snake man had been away all day. Left alone, giving away to the terror of her situation, Suzanne had tried for more than an hour to pull her foot out of the chain. Now her ankle was pinched and bloody. Her leg ached. Sharp pains came each time she moved. And she was hungry. Last night the snake man had tossed her a cold Big Mac. But this morning he had left without feeding her.

The snake man said her mother was dead. She did not really believe him. He was like a blustery five-year-old, always telling lies. She had seen her mother and David carried to the grass. People had knelt beside her mother, fussing over her. Suzanne doubted they would have done that if she was dead.

Still, she could not be sure. Maybe her mother had died later, and the snake man was telling the truth.

She had no way of knowing, and not knowing made things even worse.

The snake man was much like a kid who had appeared briefly in her class three years before. The kid had been bigger than the other students, and started shoving them around. Suzanne had understood from the first that the big bully got pleasure from scaring people, and that he picked on those who were scared the most. He was so mean he even frightened the teachers. When they tried to discipline him he threw temper tantrums, turned red of face, and smashed things.

The entire class had been terrified of him. But in two or three weeks he was gone. Some of the boys said he was sent off to reform school. But Suzanne did not believe everything she heard.

The snake man was much like that mean kid, for he, too, seemed to get pleasure from frightening people, and he threw temper tantrums and smashed things.

At school Suzanne had given the mean boy her cocky-kid routine, the character Jodie Foster often played in her early movies, and it seemed to throw him. He had avoided her. But when she tried that same routine on the snake man, he had slapped her flat. Several times she had sensed that in his tantrums he was dangerously close to punching her with his fists. She knew that if he ever did he would scramble her brains, for he was well muscled, and adult-sized.

Yet he was also childlike, and dumb.

She knew that if she worked at it, she could outsmart him.

And if her mother were truly dead, outsmarting him might be the only way she could get out of this mess.

Suzanne put an ear to the metal side of the old barn. From somewhere near she heard the meadowlarks singing, out in the grass and open fields. Suzanne, David, and her mother had seen hundreds of them on the trip to the national grasslands before the wreck. Her mother stopped the car and the birds were singing all around.

Suzanne's mother had not known the name of the bird. But a teacher with the touring children had identified them for Suzanne.

"Those are meadowlarks," she told Suzanne. "*Western* meadowlarks. They look almost exactly the same as your eastern meadowlarks. The only way you can tell the difference, the western meadowlarks have a greater repertoire of songs. You see, here in the West, they have more to sing about."

Everyone had seen the New York license tags on their car. The students around them laughed. Suzanne recognized it as gentle teasing, so she laughed too.

Then the woman knelt beside her. If she knew Suzanne was a movie star, she kept it to herself. "If you listen, you can hear their favorite song. They say, '*Oh, yes, I am a pretty little bird.*' Do you hear it?"

Suzanne listened, and she did.

That was exactly what the flutelike notes seemed to be saying.

Meadowlarks were plentiful here too, especially in the late afternoons. Suzanne spent hours each day listening to them singing outside the old red barn.

She found comfort in knowing that the larks were free to fly anywhere they wanted.

The rustlings within the old barn stilled. The chickens ceased pecking corn in the bottom of the cages and stood alert, listening. Even the refrigerator cut off. Then, with her ear to the metal, Suzanne also heard the faint whine of the snake man's truck. Instantly the paralyzing terror returned.

Most of the time she could think about her movies and the meadowlarks and block out what was really happening to her. But not all the time, because deep down she knew what the snake man planned to do. He had made no bones about it. Each time reality forced its way into her mind her legs and arms went limp, her stomach drew into a knot, chills shot up her spine, she peed helplessly, and could not stop crying. She kept those moments at bay the best she could with her movies.

But now she could not ignore the fact that the snake man was back. After his long trips he always acted ugly. She could do nothing to avoid him. Again she was made aware of her nakedness, her helplessness. There was no place to hide.

Except for the slaps, he had not yet hurt her. But she never knew what might come next.

The truck groaned and squealed to a stop outside. A door scraped open and banged shut. A moment later came the click of the padlock and the ear-shattering racket of the chain pulled through the metal doors. The snake man entered, carrying a sack of rattlesnakes. He set the sack on the floor, untied the top, and dumped the snakes into a pit. He wiped the sweat from his face with his sleeve and returned to the truck for another sack of snakes. He dumped them on top of the others.

He was wearing jeans, blue work shirt, and a cap. In that costume he did not remotely resemble the man who had kidnapped her. But he was the same man. She now had seen him change clothes several times.

She remained quiet, hardly breathing, hoping he would forget about her. But he was in a playful mood. He came toward her, shucking off his clothes. In less than a minute he was naked too.

He was so fat around the middle that she wondered how he managed to look so tall and slim in his other outfit. Even his face looked different. Before, he had been square-jawed. But now his face was almost round. His mouth was odd, just a long slit, giving him the squashed-in look of a Cabbage Patch Kid. As usual, his mouth was full of tobacco. A brown streak dribbled from the left side down to his chin. He never seemed to comb his long brown hair. It was matted down over his ears.

"Hey!" he yelled, banging on the cages, trying to get at least one of the snakes to wake up and eat. The chickens squawked in panic and ran around the bottoms of the cages.

As if following orders, one of the middle-sized snakes swung his head down from the bare branches at the top of the cage. With his movement, the clamor of the chickens grew louder. The snake dropped on lower. Chicken screams filled the old barn. All the snakes stirred.

Suzanne felt the now-familiar tingling along her spine and the terrible knotting in her stomach.

The ugliness had started.

The snake man hurried to his worktable. He lit a burner and cooked the dope. Suzanne had never seen it done before coming here except on television. But some of the kids at her school had talked about it. She watched the snake man fix the needle and go to his old recliner. He circled his upper arm with a big rubber band and shot the dope into his elbow. He then put his head back and closed his eyes.

In the cage the bedlam continued as one of the big snakes stalked the chickens. Suzanne wanted to cover her ears, but she forced herself to watch, listen, and not miss a thing. She had been taught that all good actors collect key moments, internalize them, and store them away to be used later. All the rest of her life, when a script called for fear, she would have the pain of the chain cutting into her ankle, the chicken screams, and the snake man. She would never have to fake fear. This was real. She could tap into it any-time.

So she made herself concentrate on the action and sound as the snake pursued the chickens. She tried to imagine what the chickens were feeling as they frantically fled from one corner of the cage to another, screaming, tumbling over each other as they tried to avoid the snake.

The snake man left his chair and sat down on the bare cement floor in front of the cage and watched the stalking like a kid in front of a television set. He chortled as the snake crowded all the chick-ens into a corner.

Breaking into flight, bumping into each other, they again eluded the snake.

The uproar seemed to last forever.

But at last the deadly game ended. The snake struck and seized one. He quickly enveloped the bird in his coils until only splayed tail feathers showed. The coils moved, tightening. The other chickens quieted, secure in the knowledge that this time they had been spared.

Slowly the snake worked the chicken into his mouth and began the messy process of swallowing it.

The snake man sat fascinated. Not until the entire chicken disappeared into the snake did he stand.

Suzanne steeled herself.

Her own ordeal was beginning.

He came to her with four short lengths of rope and bound her spread-eagle on the cot. This time she did not resist. He was bigger and stronger. Her earlier struggles had only gotten her slapped around. Instead, she concentrated on working herself into character—the cocky kid Jodie Foster played in *Alice Doesn't Live Here Anymore.*

This time she would just leave off the dialogue.

By the time the snake man loomed over her she was solidly into character. She looked up at him, refusing to show her fear.

He wanted her scared, crying, begging. She was sure of it. That was what the mean kid in school had wanted. She was certain the snake man was the same.

He wanted her to scream like the chickens.

She concentrated on staying in character, closed her eyes, and remained silent while he did his stuff.

The ugliness seemed to go on forever. Numb, Suzanne held her breath, fearing that at any moment the snake man might do something new, something far worse.

Then the ordeal ended. The snake man went away, staggering to his chair. There he would sleep for several hours, leaving her tied spread-eagle.

She remained motionless, not trying to twist and turn to wipe the sticky stuff from her stomach. She had learned that if she allowed it to dry, it was easier to scrape off.

In the cage beside her, the big snake Sam stirred, aroused by the feeding, by all the noise. Sam never seemed to sleep. His eyes were always open, looking at her. Sam had not been fed in all the time she had been chained next to him. There were no chickens in his cage. She did not know how long Sam had gone without eating.

The snake man had said he wanted Sam real hungry, because he was saving Sam a terrific treat. He said Sam had swallowed six little girls, and was about ready for another.

The snake man's claim filled her with fear so great that there were times she could not contain it, for she was certain he was not joking. He did not seem to be the stand-up type.

8

Years ago, when Rachel was fresh out of college with honors in English literature, she first broke into publishing as a publicity assistant. In those days the bottom-rung assistant position was viewed by many as an entry-level job that provided the brightest candidates with a good introduction to the broad field of publishing. They were expected to go on into future careers in editorial, marketing, advertising, or management, if not in publicity administration. But Rachel found work in the publicity trenches so exciting that even after three years and a prized opening in editorial she had almost declined to leave. Daily she dealt with well-known authors and with the often even-more-interesting lesser-knowns. She achieved first-name acquaintance with key people at newspapers and television stations all over the country.

That was far in the past. But as she put her own office into operation, she was amazed how quickly the skills and terminology returned. Soon she was deeply immersed in her campaign to make Suzanne's disappearance known to the nation, and to the world.

She had not managed much sleep, but the day started off well. While Donna and her minister organized the office, Rachel shared a packed press conference with Chief Laird in the town's council chamber. At least four hundred journalists and camera people had arrived. More were on the way. Laird read a general statement and took most of the questions. Rachel limited her role to making the announcement that her office for media relations would open at noon. She told the media that they should depend on Chief Laird for hard news concerning the progress of the investigation, but that she would be available to help them with background information on Suzanne. She gave the assembled journalists the address and phone number. She failed to see signs of incipient trouble.

By the time she arrived at her new office, all seemed to be coming together marvelously. The four-room suite had formerly housed an insurance agency. Desks, word processors, faxes, and duplicating machines were in place. Technicians were installing the phones. Many of the volunteer workers had brought fresh-cut flowers. The office had already assumed a disarming look of permanence.

Donna's pastor was a rotund, pleasant man with a winning intensity about him. He said he was familiar with desktop publishing. He promptly set to work designing and producing a flyer with Suzanne's picture and description. Donna made assignments and otherwise organized the office. Rachel was pleased to see that Peterson's friend had anticipated her needs. An attractive sofa graced one corner of her private office. Artfully arranged with cut flowers, the room provided a more than adequate setting for her television interviews.

With the noon opening deadline rapidly approaching, Rachel cloistered herself and wrote material for a press kit, aimed especially at the area's smaller newspapers and radio stations lacking facilities to do their own research. She devoted most of her attention to a biography of Suzanne, listing her Broadway roles, her other accomplishments. She also included remembered quotes from Suzanne's reaction to her series of successes. Rachel wanted everyone to see Suzanne for what she was: an extremely talented, clever, personable, likable little girl. She wrote a brief sketch of Suzanne's family, and a sidebar description of Suzanne's last few hours before the wreck—touring the Washita Battle Site and Black Kettle Museum, signing autographs for the group of Oklahoma schoolchildren. The words came almost effortlessly. In just over two hours, Rachel completed the background handout.

She delivered the material to Donna's helpers. Soon they were running off copies to be assembled with photographs in a press kit.

For the first time since Suzanne's disappearance, Rachel felt a sense of accomplishment.

Then it was noon, and the circus began. Television trucks and equipment filled the parking lot. Cables ran through the office doors, front and back.

Rachel had allocated her time carefully, giving top priority to satellite interviews with television network anchors. Next came the print newsmagazines on their weekly deadlines. She also gave high priority to regional television stations, on the assumption that they would reach local viewers who might have critical information the police needed.

But within minutes she knew she was in trouble. She discovered that in the years since she last dealt with the media, one essential ingredient—courtesy—had been lost. She had envisioned an orderly procession through the office as the press kits were disseminated. But the journalists and technicians crowded into the outer offices, jostling and bumping each other mercilessly. Camera lights came on, and they began shouting questions at her, questions she could only refer to Chief Baird.

The clamor became so great, there was no way Rachel could conduct her scheduled interviews. Her staff could not continue their work. Upset, Rachel banned the media from the front offices to await their turn in the heat of the parking lot. But some defied her, shouting that she was showing favoritism.

Rachel went to the phone and called Chief Laird. He sent a policeman to maintain order.

The result was not the atmosphere Rachel had envisioned. The journalists and cameramen stood outside in the hot sun and grumbled. But Rachel was able to continue, albeit on a delayed schedule.

The interviews moved by in rapid succession. By late afternoon Rachel was almost back on schedule.

She knew she was approaching exhaustion. But only a few on-camera interviews were left.

The young woman from the television entertainment newsmagazine had been gracious and patient despite the delay. Rachel especially wanted to do well on the taped sequence for the show, for it was one of Suzanne's favorites.

The woman was new but adept. She was honey-blond with an appealing pixie face. She sat quartered to Rachel on the couch and asked her questions in an almost leisurely, unhurried manner.

She began by asking Rachel about Suzanne's career. They covered all the familiar ground, going from Suzanne's early roles to Broadway and, finally, the movies.

Rachel felt she should emphasize one point. "So you see, Suzanne's career didn't happen overnight. She has been working very hard, really since she was five or six years old, with this goal in mind. She saw other children onscreen, and believed she could do it too. She has thought of little else."

"Are you a typical stage mother? Have you encouraged her? Urged her to accept bigger and bigger roles?"

Rachel recognized the negative undercurrent in the question. But she knew that hesitation on camera can be deadly.

"Definitely not," she said. "Not in the usual sense. From the very first I've had great trepidations about her career. If anything, it's been the other way around. Suzanne has led me into it."

"And now she's missing. Tell me, how do you cope?"

"I'm just taking it moment by moment."

"Have the police given you any reason at all to believe she's still alive?"

The callous insensitivity of the question was too much. Rachel's anger was instantaneous. She felt herself falling apart on camera. Tears came, and there was nothing she could do to stop them. "Of course she's alive!" she said, her voice rising.

The woman backed off with a soothing comment. But she did not bother to hide her faint smile of satisfaction. She had succeeded where the others had failed, bringing forth tears, making Rachel weep into living rooms all over America.

The interview went downhill from there. Rachel was led into relating anecdotes from Suzanne's early childhood. But with the continuing tears, what should have been endearing instead came out maudlin. Rachel could not regain the self-confidence that had driven her throughout the day. She felt she was in Sylvia Plath's bell jar, cut off from the world around her. Words had ceased to have meaning.

She cooperated on the reverse-two shots, with the cameraman filming from behind her to catch the back of her head, focusing on the interviewer re-asking the questions.

But after the woman and her crew left, Rachel put her head down on her borrowed desk and wept.

Donna came to see why Rachel was not picking up. She felt Rachel's pulse and reached for the phone.

"I'm calling Dr. Peterson."

"No!" Rachel said. "I'll be fine in a few minutes. Please don't call him."

"He'd have my head on a platter if I didn't. You're showing some kind of reaction, and God knows I'm not qualified to judge. Just stay quiet until he comes."

Donna went away. Rachel's phone stopped ringing. Donna returned and sat with her until Peterson arrived.

He came into her office carrying his bag. "I knew you'd overdo it," he said. "That was a calculated risk."

While Donna stood by, again a dutiful nurse, Peterson monitored Rachel's pulse and blood pressure. He looked into her eyes with his light and felt along her throat and temples.

"Any symptoms? Headache? Anything at all?"

"No," Rachel told him. "I'm just tired."

"Exhausted is a better word. Okay, you've made this sleepy little burg hum like the Big Apple for a day. But that's it. You're up against the wire. No more. You can hang up your cleats for the night.''

Rachel protested. ''I must make arrangements with the crime shows. They're sending in crews tonight.''

''Tomorrow will be soon enough. You have half the town working for you out there. Let them handle it. They've been scheduling Little League teams for years. This is duck soup for them. Did you remember to eat lunch?''

''No.''

''Nothing since breakfast. Okay, you're having dinner at my place. I'll call my housekeeper and tell her to set another plate. That way I'll know you remembered to eat. Then it's to bed for you. Where are you staying?''

''Booker managed to get me a motel room.''

''Get your things. You won't be coming back here.''

Suddenly Rachel felt weak and helpless. She did not protest further.

Peterson sent Donna out to announce that Rachel would be leaving for the day.

As Peterson escorted her out into the front offices, she was met with a curious reaction.

Her volunteer workers stopped what they were doing, rose, and applauded.

The moment seemed spontaneous. Rachel was bewildered. She felt she should be applauding them instead of the other way around. But she was too tired to sort through her emotions.

Again tears came too easily. ''I love every one of you for what you have done,'' she told them. ''I can't thank you enough.''

The policeman escorted them through the crowd in the parking lot. Then she was in Peterson's car, driving away from her office toward the main part of town.

Peterson drove easily, effortlessly. Rachel was still trying to regain her composure. She did not understand what happened back at the office. She felt confused.

''Why were they applauding *me?*'' she asked.

Peterson gave her his sad smile. ''Today they saw a woman who should be flat on her back in the hospital put in a day that would kill a television professional. How many one-on-one interviews did you do today? Ten? Twelve? And you wonder why they applauded.''

''They did most of the work. They designed and printed the flyer. They distributed them. They handled the phones. I'll never be able to repay those people from that church.''

''They weren't all from Donna's church. I saw Baptists, Church of Christ, Lutherans, maybe an Episcopalian or two. You have a good cross-section of the town out there.''

Thinking back over the day, Rachel felt she had not done well, that she should have done much more. ''I underestimated what the pressures would be,'' she admitted. ''I let those television people run over me.''

''The way I heard it, you moved mountains.''

''I should have given more time to hard news. *Time*, for instance, said they're considering the cover, tying Suzanne's disappearance with crimes against children nationwide. On short notice I couldn't supply all they wanted. It was much the same with *Newsweek* and the larger newspapers. I should have hired a professional PR firm.''

''I warned you not to try to do everything in one day. There'll be ample time tomorrow.''

''And the bottom line is that now I don't know if I'm helping Suzanne or not. Booker said it'll help apply pressure, bring in more investigators, more tips. But I picked up indications that some of the police think it will only generate false information.''

''I'd listen to Booker.''

The route Peterson was driving confirmed her earlier impression. Actually, there were two towns. The newest had grown up along the interstate to service travelers and was filled with motels, service stations, fast food outlets, and a few discount houses. Now they were entering the older part of town, which Peterson said served the local ranchers, wheat farmers, oil field workers, and permanent residents.

Rachel caught glimpses of men in the alleys. They were gathered around the Dumpsters, pawing through trash. With a breathtaking jolt she realized they were searching for Suzanne's body.

The unexpected sight was devastating. For an interminable moment, in the depths of shock, Rachel felt herself losing control. It was as if she were standing to one side, watching herself fall apart. She was helpless to avert the disintegration. She turned her head to the car door and was racked by agonizing sobs.

She was only vaguely aware that Peterson braked the car and pulled to a stop at the edge of the road. She felt his hand on her wrist, letting her know by his touch that he was there to help. But he did not try to stop her sobbing. Minutes passed before he spoke. His voice was soft, intimate.

''Rachel, one of the most difficult lessons you learn from tragedy is that the world goes on, that you must accept the changes in your life. To preserve your sanity, you must understand that.''

"I just feel so inadequate," Rachel managed to say.

"That's ridiculous. You're doing all any human could expect to do."

"No. I could do more. I should be out there helping those men hunt for Suzanne."

"What could you do that isn't being done? And by professionals? If you remember, when I released you, I warned you to pace yourself. You can do only so much. The body can tolerate stress, even anxiety. But in panic situations, the body releases endocrines—adrenaline, all kinds of compounds, some we probably don't even know about. They keep you going for a while. But then you reach the limits. You have gone much further than most."

She wiped her eyes. "I'm all right now. I just lost it there for a minute or two."

But he was not through. "Rachel, think of it this way. If you drive yourself back into the hospital, you haven't helped anyone, especially Suzanne. The days ahead may be just as rough. You must take care of yourself, for your sake, and for Suzanne's sake. You need to spend time away from it. Now, let's go have a good dinner and get you ready to tackle it again tomorrow."

Rachel felt he was speaking not only as a doctor, but also from depths of personal experience. "Okay," she said.

"Lean back if you want. The seat reclines."

Rachel pushed the lever and arranged herself more comfortably. He put the car back into gear and returned to the road. They soon left the outskirts of town and were into the country, moving along a narrow blacktop road. Green hills stretched away into the distance. The lush vegetation of the fields spilled into the ditches beside the road. There were no fences. The land seemed open, free.

"I had no idea this part of the country was so lovely," Rachel said.

"Eye of the beholder." He remained silent a moment. "I grew up here. Product of a broken home. I was reared by my paternal grandparents, about fifteen miles over in that direction." He pointed. "All of this was a lot different then, before the interstate. The highway was Route Sixty-six, the one Steinbeck made famous. His Joads came right by your motel on their way from Sallisaw to Salinas. This country was so isolated then. Oklahoma City was an impossible distance. New York was as far off as the moon. I couldn't wait to get away. A couple of Rotary scholarships were my ticket."

He drove for several minutes without speaking. Rachel knew she was hearing rare revelations. She did not push.

"Now I wonder why I ever left," he said after a time, almost as if to himself.

They passed a grove of trees. On the far side Peterson made another right-angle turn. They entered through an arched gate and drove up a lane bordered by white railings.

The modern brick house was low and rambling. Down a hill to the right, at what Rachel assumed to be corrals, stood large metal tanks and a row of heavy machinery. Peterson parked in the drive at the front of the house and came around to open her door. "We'll have a glass of wine on the patio and give my housekeeper a little more time with dinner," he said.

"I shouldn't have come," Rachel said. "This is too much of an imposition on her."

"To the contrary. Miata will be beside herself over the chance to serve you a good dinner. She knows about Suzanne."

The living room was spacious, with a big stone fireplace and cathedral beams. Indian art hung over the mantel and along the walls. Pastel blues and brilliant reds seemed predominant. Intriguing figurines contributed to the updated-*Bonanza* decor. Peterson gave Rachel little chance to absorb details. He ushered her on through to the dining room, where french doors and paneled windows looked out on a sweeping expanse of green pasture.

Peterson called into the kitchen. His housekeeper, a tall, thin woman in her early thirties, came out for introduction. She seemed extremely shy. She blushed as she promised that dinner would be ready in a few minutes.

"Make it fifteen, at least," Peterson said. "Give us time for a leisurely drink."

He poured Chablis and led Rachel through the french doors onto the patio. There she stopped, overwhelmed by the sheer beauty of the landscape.

The house sat on the edge of a bluff. A small creek ran below the patio. Walking to the railing and peering down, Rachel saw fish swimming in the clear water. The creek flowed gently toward a pond. The rampant greenery swept away to distant hills. Beyond the pond, cattle and horses grazed.

Peterson followed through on the introduction. "Miata takes care of the house and does most of my cooking. Her husband, Ramon, looks after the place. He does most of the work. They have two teenage boys and a daughter, who help out."

"This is all yours?" Rachel asked, gesturing to the view.

This was a side of him she never would have suspected.

"Most of what you see."

"It's so gorgeous! It looks like a well-kept park."

"Counting a half section I lease, it's slightly larger than your Central Park. And it has one definite advantage—eight million fewer people."

"What are those cattle?"

"Brangus. A blend of Brahma and Angus, combining the best qualities of each. The horses are Arabian."

"The bull looks different. That is a bull, isn't it?"

Peterson laughed. "Purebred Brahma. You start with pure breeds to get the proper strain. It gives me a chance to use what biology I've learned."

"He looks huge. Is he dangerous?"

"Only because he's affectionate. He weighs close to a ton and thinks he's a lapdog."

Miata announced dinner. They went inside. For a time conversation centered on the food. Peterson explained that the dishes were authentic Mexican, as differentiated from the fiery Tex-Mex.

Rachel thought the dinner superb, and said so.

Peterson suggested they have postprandial coffee and brandy on the patio. As they walked out, the sun was setting on distant green hills. Colors had deepened, becoming even more vibrant. Rachel could not stop marveling over the sheer beauty of the rolling landscape.

"Dawn is best for color, especially after a heavy dew," Peterson said. "But sunsets are livelier."

Scores of birds were coming in to the nearby pond to drink. Peterson handed her a well-worn pair of binoculars. "I'm not a birder. But I understand we're in a flyway from Canada to South Texas. We have a lot of visitors."

Rachel focused the binoculars. She recognized several species— killdeer, sparrows, kingbirds, mourning doves, and long-legged cranes. There were others she did not recognize. But most common were the meadowlarks, with their mottled brown wings, yellow breasts, and black bibs. Robin-sized, they were fearless and lively, and offered a repertoire of loud, cheerful songs.

"When we went up to the national grasslands just before the wreck, we saw meadowlarks everywhere," she told Peterson. "Suzanne was quite taken with them. They must be abundant around here."

"And coddled," Peterson said. "They're rather careless birds. They build their nests on the ground. In the spring you see farmers climbing off their tractors to move the nests, to keep from plowing over them."

"Do they continue to use their nests after they're moved?"

"I don't know. The farmers seem to think so."

The beaks of the meadowlarks were open as they blended their flutelike songs with those of the other birds. For a time Rachel listened to the concert, totally enthralled. She thought of how Suzanne would respond to the scene.

And with that thought the agony again overwhelmed her. She handed the binoculars back to Peterson. "This is absolutely surreal. I shouldn't be here, enjoying dinner, this sunset, the birds. I must be going crazy!"

"Easy, easy," Peterson said. "Pace yourself. Charge your batteries, get ready for tomorrow."

They sat together in silence for a time while the red of sunset deepened.

Again Peterson spoke softly. "This place is therapeutic. Moving out here was one of the smartest things I've ever done. Here you can get away from the bad in the world, and renew yourself with the good that most people have forgotten exists."

The statement did not seem to require an answer. Rachel remained quiet, basking in the beauty of the birds and the sunset.

Booker selected a corner booth that gave him a complete view of the restaurant. By the time the waitress arrived, the mingled aromas from the kitchen reminded him that he had not eaten since his early breakfast. He ordered the chicken fried steak blue plate special. He was on his third cup of coffee when Slewfoot came into the restaurant and looked around uncertainly.

Booker raised a hand. She approached, lowering her head, studying him. "Booker?"

He stood and gestured her into the booth. "Pauline," he said. "You're looking good. You didn't recognize me. Have I changed that much?"

She slid into the booth. "Man, it's been ten years at least. You were back here in the dark. All the gray hair fooled me."

"Fools me, too, every time I look in the mirror. Can I order you something?"

Slewfoot glanced over her shoulder, toward the front of the restaurant. "Ahmed doesn't like for me to be in here."

"You let me worry about Ahmed. What would you like?"

"A Coke is all. I've already eaten."

She insisted she wanted nothing else. Booker signaled the wait-ress, who managed to take the order without looking at Slewfoot.

"Booker, you ought to use a rinse on that hair," Slewfoot said, still studying him. "Use some vitamin E on those crow's-feet. It'd take twenty years off of you."

"Wouldn't make me feel twenty years younger."

"It might surprise you. The way people treat you has a lot to do with it."

Booker was piling up insights too fast to absorb. He estimated that Pauline—better known as Slewfoot—must be into her mid-forties. Her hair had been the same golden shade, cut in a shoulder-length Dutch-boy bob, through all the years he had known her. No crow's-feet were evident around her button black eyes. Her skin was freckled, but smooth and without blemish. She was tall and lean, and nimble and athletic, probably from climbing in and out of trucks. She had always looked like your best friend's tomboy kid sister, the one you liked but was always off limits.

Maybe that was what made her so popular.

The waitress brought the Coke and placed it on the table, again without making eye contact.

"I shouldn't be in here," Slewfoot said. "What do you want with me."

"Pauline, we're looking for a guy who may be a little bent. We have a corpse—a little girl—that has what looks like saliva all over the upper torso. You ever hear of anything like that?"

To Booker's surprise, she giggled. She looked at the ceiling and blew air up her nose. "Booker! You know me! I'm straight arrow. Try anything kinky with me, I'm gone."

"I just thought you might have heard something. We think this guy may be a short-eye."

"The little actress?" Slewfoot guessed. "Is that what you're working on?"

"Yeah," Booker admitted. "There's a chance this earlier case—the one with the saliva—may be related."

Slewfoot looked at him in silence for a moment. "Booker, I'm sitting here wondering why I should help you. Maybe you've forgot. I sure as hell haven't. I did six months in the Choctaw county jail because of you."

Booker was surprised. He had not known she did time in that bust.

"Hey, that wasn't just me," he said. "That was a big operation. We had to shut Templeton down. You just got caught up in it. That wasn't anything personal."

"Six months in jail is personal. The DA threatened me with conspiracy if I didn't turn state's evidence and testify against Templeton. That really put me in a bind."

For a moment Booker shared some of her anger. That was indeed a cheap trick on the part of the DA.

"Believe me, I didn't know," Booker said. "There was no reason for him to do that. Templeton was our target. We got him cold."

Pauline made a sound that could be considered a snort. "You got Templeton. But you didn't get the biggie."

Booker inclined his head, acknowledging the point. Templeton had been running a large truck stop just north of Red River, dealing in drugs, prostitution, gambling, and stolen goods. But they failed to collar the guy behind him. In hindsight, Booker could see that he should have developed Pauline as a source. Prostitutes usually know more of what is going on than most anyone.

"That prick of a DA had me in a bad squeeze," Slewfoot said. "If I had talked, I would've fed the fish in Lake Texoma."

That was probably true.

"Pauline, I'm truly sorry you got caught up in that. We should have followed through, protected you. I just assumed it would be a simple bust for you, nothing but a fine."

"Well, what the hell, that's downriver. But you're wasting your time anyway, Booker. I don't know anything about anyone hung up on spit."

"What about a short-eye? You know or hear of anything in that department?"

"No."

But something clicked in her eyes. A memory had come to her. Booker did not know how he knew, but he knew.

"Pauline, it's important," he said.

She looked away. Booker remained quiet, giving her time to think about it.

She looked at him, searching his face. "Booker, I've always trusted you. If I told you something, could you leave me out of it?"

He nodded. "Confidential source. No one need know."

"I can't have it get out I've told this kind of stuff."

"Hey, this is me. I just told you, confidential."

Still, she hesitated. She glanced behind her to make sure they were truly alone. She lowered her voice. "This was about two months ago. There's this long-hauler that comes through every two or three weeks. Plumbing supplies out of Philly, headed for Fresno or some damn place out there. He usually overnights here, or in Tulsa, to log some sleep."

Booker nodded. Cross-country truckers were required to rest occasionally. Federal regulations.

"I've only seen this guy two, maybe three times. Anyway, he stopped here, got a room, and called me. While we were fooling around, he reached into a zipper bag and brought out some pictures. I didn't think anything about it. Lots of guys use pictures to prime the pump."

Again Booker nodded, waiting. He knew Slewfoot would not be disturbed by simple pornography.

"Most of the pictures were the usual stuff. But mixed in with them, toward the bottom, were some kiddie porn. There were these two little girls. One looked to be about four, the other maybe a year or two older. They seemed to be asleep. But their little jammies were pulled down, and this hand was doing things to them."

Booker shook his head to show that he was appalled. And he was.

"I don't think this guy intended for me to see those pictures. He was kind of embarrassed. I didn't like it worth a damn, and I let him know it. So he comes out with this story. He said the pictures really weren't his. He even tried to make a joke out of it."

She paused. Booker waited.

"He said that this friend, after his wife leaves for work, baby-sits the kids. He wakes them up and gives them downers. Then, while they're out, he does anything he wants with them, and nobody ever knows."

Booker considered the information. This guy was probably a bona fide short-eye. If he did that to his own kids, what would he do with other people's kids, given the chance?

"Booker, I recognized the ring on the hand in the pictures. It isn't this guy's friend. It's him!"

Booker had already assumed that.

"Later, when he went to sleep, I looked in the bag. He has a bunch of pictures of other kids. A lot of kids."

"This is around Philly?"

"He trucks out of there. Probably lives in some dump within commute of there. He's through here regular. I hear he's always loaded with uppers and downers and sometimes other stuff. He keeps his stash in the little blue zipper bag with the pictures. He carries it rolled in a tan army blanket in the sleeper."

"You got a name?"

"Name, company, truck number, whatever you want."

Booker took out a pad and extended a ballpoint pen.

Slewfoot shook her head. "No. You write it."

Booker wrote as she rattled off the name and numbers.

"He'll probably be through, westbound, toward the end of this week, or maybe the start of next," she said. "Get the bastard, Booker."

Booker closed his pad and put it in his shirt pocket. "We will, Pauline. Someday there'll be stars in your crown."

Again she snorted. "A crown? For a snitch?" She made a face. "I've never done this before in my life. But those pictures made me so fucking mad. They really took me back, Booker. I grew up in foster homes. I've been there."

Before he could think of a suitable reply, she was out of the booth and gone.

Booker drove back into town and to the police station. The squad room was filled with tired and disgusted cops. The day-long ground search had been futile. None of the tips had produced a promising new lead.

Booker borrowed a typewriter and wrote a report of his interview with Slewfoot, unidentified except as a confidential source. He took it to Nate, who first scanned it briefly, then went back over it more slowly.

Nate looked up at him with red-rimmed and bloodshot eyes. "You don't really think this is our guy, do you?"

"Probably not," Booker admitted. Slewfoot's John did not fit the profile of Booker's theory. A long-hauler had to account for every minute of his time on the road. He would never have been able to stalk and pick up victims unnoticed and at random, especially on country roads.

Nate scowled. "Booker, you haven't changed a fucking bit. Here we are up to our asses and you go out and bring in more shit."

"What are we supposed to do?" Booker asked. "Walk away from it?"

For a moment Nate appeared to be thinking of doing just that. But he relented. "Okay. We'll bounce it to DPS. They'll love us for it."

"Nate, I'm thinking there could be a connection. If this guy's so heavy into kiddie porn, he might have pictures of one of the priors. It could be a breakthrough."

Nate frowned, thinking. Booker kept quiet, allowing Nate to follow the logic. All over the country, kiddie porn creeps swapped pictures like baseball cards. There was a vast network. Trusted friends introduced trusted friends. Contacts were made in the slammer. There were computer bulletin boards that specialized in kiddie porn. And they recognized each other. Booker knew a cop who claimed that if two short-eyes were put into the crowd at the Super Bowl, they would find each other and be swapping pictures before halftime.

"Maybe our guy is into the swaps," Booker suggested. "Maybe that's why he keeps them alive for a while. Maybe he's a shutterbug. It could be that he has traded pictures with this trucker."

Nate rubbed his eyes. "Booker, I just wish I had half as much manpower as you got theories. That's such a fucking long shot, and you know it."

"I'll put my own time into it," Booker promised. "I've been through all of the files. I might recognize one of the priors, where maybe someone else wouldn't."

"You'd go to the bust? Even if it's up by Tulsa?"

Booker considered the complications. Tulsa was a four-hour drive, eight both ways. The chances were slim, and the trip would cost him most of a day.

But someone familiar with photographs of the prior victims should be there to go through the trucker's little blue bag, just in case.

"Even if it's up by Tulsa," he said.

"Okay. We'll tell the troopers to alert us to the bust," Nate said. "And if it doesn't pan out, at least we'll get rid of you for a day."

9

Rachel awoke to the ringing phone. Middle of the night. Hardly anyone knew where she was staying. She rolled to the edge of the bed and answered.

Booker's bass voice rumbled in her ear. "Sorry to wake you. I tried to call you at your office and just missed you. Are you okay?"

Booker's voice contained a warm sincerity that conveyed he was not asking an idle question. Rachel was beginning to value him not only as a protector, but also as a friend. She answered with suitable honesty. "I'm much better now. I just lost it for a while this afternoon."

"Understandable. We've been worried about you. If you need help, don't hesitate to call me, anytime."

Rachel felt a rush of affection for Booker. His courtly manner was reminiscent of her husband, and the gentle qualities that first attracted her to him. "Booker, I appreciate that more than you know," she said.

He hesitated. "Reason I called, we really need to talk. And there's someone I want you to meet. We're in room one fourteen, right down from you. If you can come, I'll walk over and be waiting at your door."

Rachel glanced at her watch. Almost one in the morning. She had been asleep five hours.

"Give me twenty minutes," she said.

But she was ready in ten. Makeup could not cover the extensive bruises on her swollen eyes and cheek, so she made no attempt. With her hair shaved or cropped and stuffed beneath turbanlike bandages, she did not even need a comb.

When Booker arrived, she was shocked and dismayed by the changes in his appearance since she had last seen him. He seemed older. The lines in his face had deepened. His eyes were bloodshot from lack of sleep. She remembered his saying at their first meeting that "this type of case just eats you alive." Clearly the effects were taking a toll.

Booker offered his arm and they walked in close companionship to one fourteen. He pushed open the door. A tall, willowy woman with long, dark hair stood in the middle of the room. "This is Dr. Patricia McMahon," Booker said. "Forensic psychiatrist."

McMahon took Rachel's hand. She had quick dark eyes and an easy smile. Her navy blue woolen skirt proclaimed itself part of an expensive business suit, and her white blouse probably bore an impressive label. She had kicked off her shoes and was in stocking feet.

"We have Jack Daniel's, Coke, and coffee," Booker said, moving on past Rachel. "What would be your pleasure?"

Rachel felt the need of something stronger than coffee. "I'd love bourbon and water. But I had some wine earlier. I'm not sure if that much alcohol would agree with the antibiotic I'm taking."

"What is it?" McMahon asked.

Rachel handed her the bottle of pills.

"Alcohol is contraindicated," McMahon said. "But I assume Pete served the wine hours ago. If I know Pete, he'd say another drink now wouldn't hurt."

Rachel was not certain she approved of the no-secrets familiarity. She wondered about the obvious closeness of Dr. Peterson, Booker, and McMahon, and how it came about.

"Bourbon it is, then," she said to Booker.

The room was arranged the same as her own, with two full-sized beds, two armchairs, and a straight-backed chair by the mirrored dresser. All was modern motel-functional. McMahon gestured Rachel into one of the armchairs and pulled the straight chair over by the bed, facing her. Booker mixed the drinks at the small bar that divided the room from the lavatory and dressing area. Rachel judged from their relaxed manner that they were into their second or third drinks.

"Patricia's in the dumps tonight," Booker said. "She testified all morning in a murder trial. Tonight the jury turned the guy loose."

"It was frustrating," McMahon said. "There was so much the state couldn't introduce. So much I couldn't say. The man has a long record, a terrible history. But we couldn't let the jury know that."

"Can't use one crime to prove another," Booker said. "Basic credo of our legal system."

"I'm convinced he's a very dangerous person," McMahon said.

Booker served the drinks. "He'll kill again. That's for sure. And there's nothing anyone can do about it."

Rachel felt they were giving her a glimpse into their lives—preparing her—for a purpose. She was affected by the dimensions she sensed in them: Booker and his decades of pursuing, catching, and convicting criminals. Patricia McMahon, this cool, intelligent woman, trained to look unblinkingly into the criminal mind. Rachel was intrigued, yet frightened by the depravity she knew they faced routinely. She strongly suspected that if she became familiar with their world, she would never be the same.

Booker eased into the other armchair. On his gesture, they leaned forward and touched glasses. "To Suzanne," he said. "May God keep her safe."

The drink was strong. Rachel soon felt the warmth spreading.

"Patricia interviewed four witnesses under hypnosis this evening," Booker said. "We didn't get much. But we may have a partial description."

"One witness was a good subject," McMahon said. "I have a lot of confidence in what she told us."

"Can you tell me?" Rachel asked.

"She said the man she saw was tall, with a khakilike outfit she thought might be a uniform," Booker said. "Western-style hat. Security guard, maybe. She had the impression of a big wide belt with something attached. She wasn't sure what. Knife, maybe. And snakeskin boots. She was sure of that. Not many snakeskin boots around anymore."

"The witness is a real estate agent," McMahon said. "She was on her way to show a house, when she came upon the wreck. She stopped in the shopping mall parking lot and walked over to the edge of the crowd. You had just been carried to the grass. She was on her way over to see if she could help. Her impression was that this little girl, who may have been your daughter, was a few feet ahead of her, and starting toward you when this tall man took her arm, leaned over, and said something to her. He moved the child to one side. The real estate lady walked on past them. She didn't get a look at the man's face."

"We have quite a few security guards around here, for all the oil field equipment," Booker said. "This gives us something to work on. Now that we know the direction of the suspect's movements, we'll go back and do repeat interviews with everyone who was at the scene, ask them if they saw him."

Rachel fought down her excitement. This was the first indication anyone had seen Suzanne after her rescue.

"You're certain it was Suzanne?"

"Virtually certain," Booker said. "She was standing in about the same location where the truck driver set Suzanne down."

"We have charts showing the movements of every witness," McMahon said. "I'll question several more under hypnosis today."

"Maybe somebody will remember something that will lead us to something else," Booker said. "That's the way you build these cases. Bit by bit. It's slow, and it drives you crazy."

"The lady today was such a good subject," McMahon said again. "It's a shame she didn't get a view of his face."

"The reason we called you, Patricia and I have been talking over some possible actions we might take to bring this guy out into the open," Booker said. "I wanted to get Patricia's thinking before I mentioned it to you. There's risk involved. So we feel you should be in on the decision."

Rachel now understood the reason for the earlier shop talk. They wanted her to see the situation from their perspective.

"Understand, this is just theory," Booker went on. "But the fact is, eight other young girls have disappeared within three hundred miles of here under similar circumstances within the last thirty-five months. Let me stress that the cases may not be related. But I'm about three-quarters convinced that they are. Patricia's about half convinced. Opinions within the OSBI are mixed. The FBI profilers say there's not enough evidence to make a judgment."

Rachel felt she must ask. "Were any of those eight found alive?"

Booker met her gaze and studied her a moment before answering. "No. But remember, none had anywhere near the search we're mounting for Suzanne."

Rachel wanted to be sure she understood. "You tend to think that the same man who took all those other girls also took Suzanne?"

Booker nodded. "Yeah. I do. Again, I could be wrong. There's not much to go on. The MO seems the same in some ways, vastly different in others."

"The FBI admits the cases make an interesting statistical cluster," Patricia said. "But they may be just that, and nothing more."

Patricia left the straight chair and made herself comfortable on the bed. She placed pillows behind her, leaned against the headboard, and stretched out her long legs.

"Anyway, if this is the same guy—and I'll admit that's a fairly big if—we may know a few things about him," Booker said. "That's Patricia's department."

"I'll give you some background," Patricia said. "We in forensic psychiatry are still working our way into a new area. A little more than ten years ago a maverick FBI agent, Robert Ressler, began interviewing convicted killers. Ressler had spent a career in military intelligence. He had the right background. He was teaching hostage negotiation and related subjects at the FBI Academy. He also was helping the then-fledgling art of criminal profiling, taking facts about the victim and the crime scene and projecting a description of the criminal. Ressler quickly saw that they didn't know much about repeat murderers. So on his own, he started interviewing killers. Others came into it. Initially, they interviewed thirty-six serial killers."

"*The Silence of the Lambs*," Rachel said.

"Right," Booker said. The liquor seemed to be making him more talkative. "The killers in *The Silence of the Lambs* were composites. Ressler was interviewed by the guy who wrote the book. I forget his name."

"Thomas Harris," Rachel said.

Patricia ignored the interruption. "Ressler and his colleagues found some interesting correlations among the first thirty-six. Later, more serial killers were interviewed. Last I heard, they were up to about one hundred seventy subjects. And the initial findings held up. It was a major breakthrough. For the first time we were into the minds of killers. We psychiatrists came in. It's a fast-growing field."

"They still haven't answered all the questions," Booker said. "A lot of people have identical backgrounds and don't turn into killers. I think there's something in killers at the beginning. They're just born mean. Natural killers."

"That may be," Patricia said. "But the FBI interviewers found that almost invariably, serial killers have certain backgrounds in common. A cold-natured mother. Or at least emotional distance. A missing or nonfunctional father. Aside from the Ted Bundys—the organized, rare ones—they're loners. They live disorganized, crappy lives. No friends. Quiet. Nonentities. People you could be around every day and not remember. But most important, the interviewers found that every one of the serial killers had a fantasy, nurtured from childhood right into adulthood, refined all the way. Usually a fantasy of getting even. If the killer dreams of cutting up women, eventually he does. He starts trying to make life as exciting as his fantasy."

"That's why pornography's so dangerous," Booker said. "Your

average guy can look at it and no harm done. But a killer gets off on it. Works it into his fantasy.''

"The FBI studies were almost all of killers of adults," Patricia went on. "We still don't know much about child killers. We suspect they're much the same. But we lack the empirical evidence on them that we now have on killers of adults.''

"They're the same," Booker said. "Just locked into an early stage of sexual growth. Like the child molesters.''

"That's one theory," Patricia said. "But the statistics on children are misleading. Three hundred and fifty thousand children disappear in this country each year. I know that's hard to believe. But those are FBI figures. Of those, they estimate that almost three hundred and forty-five thousand are custody kidnappings and runaways. Even if we accept those figures, that leaves five thousand unaccounted for. A few wind up with the pimps, sex rings, the child porn scene. The large numbers obscure the fact that there are some who disappear and we never know what happened to them. We have no accurate statistics. We're operating in the dark.''

"Even their own parents do away with them sometimes, and there's no outcry," Booker said. "I've seen that.''

Rachel remembered Peterson quoting Booker as saying he had seen too much evil in his career and did not want to see more. She felt she was beginning to understand this driven, grim man.

"So when we have missing children like these eight, we can't say for sure," Patricia went on. "When a child disappears, Booker and his colleagues look at the family and make a judgment. If the disappearance doesn't seem to be family related, it's put down as possible abduction. But we're seldom sure. Some eventually turn up in the larger cities. Others may be murder victims—more than we realize. The bodies may never be found. We may never know.''

"We found five bodies out of these eight," Booker said. "I'd guess that's about average.''

Every revelation sent Rachel's horror soaring. Yet she knew they were preparing her for what was to come, something even worse.

She forced herself to sit quietly and listen.

"So if this is one man—if he exists—we can postulate certain facts about him," Patricia said. "Again we're playing with the statistical odds, the preponderance of serial killers who present the same characteristics. Do you see what I'm saying? All of this is extremely nebulous.''

"Yes. I understand," Rachel said.

"Most likely, he will live alone. He has minimal social interaction. No friends, few acquaintances. He can function, but he has almost no personality. People tend not to remember him, even those who were in school with him, who have worked with him. He is thoroughly isolated. He doesn't watch television or see newspapers.''

"He probably doesn't know Suzanne is a film star, that the whole country is aware of her disappearance," Booker said.

"He may be ignorant, but he won't be stupid," Patricia went on. "He has been abused, dumped on all his life. As a loner, rejected and starved for attention, he is natural prey for pedophiles and molesters throughout childhood. Chances are very good that he has been used in this fashion, and again abandoned. Probably several times. It's a pattern. And it makes him a survivor. He has found ways to cope. He'll be extremely crafty. He'll have an almost animal cunning.''

"You hear a lot about street smarts," Booker said. "There's also such a thing as country smarts.''

"Still, he's isolated," Patricia said. "Our main problem would be how to reach him. Booker may have come up with a possible way." She looked at Booker. "Your department.''

"If we're right, this guy travels a lot," Booker said. "He covers long distances, so he probably uses the main highways, the interstates. He may ignore television, newspapers, radio. But there'd be no way for him to miss billboards. Would the studio bankroll some billboards?''

Rachel thought about the question. If he wanted, Gold could write off the expense as institutional advertising. "I believe they might.''

"From what we can hypothesize from the pattern, we think this guy keeps captives alive ten or twelve days," Booker said.

Rachel's mind raced with that revelation. Suzanne was seized Monday afternoon. They were now entering Friday morning.

If Booker was right, Suzanne might have only six more days to live.

"I haven't had time to look into how long it takes to put up a billboard," Booker said.

"Normally, about fifteen days to three weeks," Rachel told him. "But if we'd pay for overtime, we might get it done in forty-eight hours.''

Booker and McMahon looked at her questioningly.

"I used to do book publicity and promotion," Rachel explained. "Sometimes, on certain books, we did outdoor advertising. If there was a time element—a movie tie-in or some kind of breaking news recognition—we would rush the exposure. We paid for special handling and got them up in two days.''

"Would enough billboards be available?" Booker asked.

"I think so. Outdoor advertisers stay slightly overbuilt. They give the extra space to charity—United Way, whatever. With the current economy, I'm sure space would be available."

"Now we come to the risk," Patricia said. "I can't minimize the danger. When this man sees Suzanne's picture up on a billboard, his already fragile grasp of reality will be severely jolted. There's no way to be sure how he'll react."

"He might panic," Booker said. "Kill her just to get rid of her."

Rachel felt her heart seize. A wave of nausea swept over her. She had to wait a moment before she could speak. "Then why risk it?"

Booker ran a hand across his face before answering. "To establish contact. Start a dialogue. That's basic in any hostage or kidnap situation. It buys you time. And maybe it gives you the avenue to find him."

"Would that be worth placing Suzanne at such risk?"

Booker's dark eyes met her gaze and did not waver. "Mrs. Shelby, if this man is the type we think, he is already locked on to a track that will end with him killing her. We've got to jolt him off that track and find him. Maybe we can do that by putting dollar signs in his head."

"We would want to *imply* we'll pay ransom," Patricia explained. "A large ransom might fuse into his fantasies. Our theory is that with his abductions and killings, he's seeking what he has never had in life. Power. Power over human life. And money translates into power. I believe there's a good chance he'd take the bait. But I want to talk with other psychiatrists today and see if they concur."

"The wording would have to be subtle," Booker said. "We can't make a flat offer to pay ransom."

"That would make us a participant in the crime," Patricia explained. "Prosecutors claim they'd have big problems with it."

"I only want Suzanne back," Rachel said. "I don't care about making a case."

"Deep down, I think we all go along with that," Booker said. "But the official argument will be that if we start paying ransom, we'll instigate other kidnappings, and there'd be no end to it."

"Why can't we predict how he might react?"

Patricia glanced at Booker before answering. "Because we're into this gray area. We know about serial killers. We know about sex rings and child pornography. Some good work has been done in those areas. We know about pedophiles. Molesters. Abusers. But we don't know much of what's in the mind of the serial child-killer. In a way, he may be closer to the serial rapist in that he's seeking power over the victim, not necessarily sex.''

"But he's a killer," Booker insisted. "Basically, he's a killer."

Rachel felt this was an old argument between them.

"A *different type* killer," Patricia said. "I may be wrong. But I think that deep down, in one part of him, he's still a child. He's the school-yard bully gone berserk."

"In the body of an adult," Booker said.

"He's not a classic pedophile or child molester. He's of a completely different nature."

"I'm so ignorant about all of this," Rachel admitted. "Parents are told to be watchful of male adults taking exceptional interest in their children, boys and girls. I've always assumed that boys must be protected from irresponsible homosexuality, and girls from over-sexed males who can't control themselves."

"No!" Patricia said. "True homosexuality has absolutely nothing to do with pedophilia. It's more complicated than that. Pedophiles have their own code of conduct, just as heterosexuals and homosexuals do. Pedophiles are a separate entity. Some excellent investigative work has been done on that by Dr. Ann Wolbert Burgess and her associates at the University of Pennsylvania."

"Short-eyes have a peculiar outlook," Booker said. "When they have sex with children, they honestly don't think they're doing them any harm. You should hear them when we bust them. They say, 'You're arresting me for that?' They've been doing it so long, they've convinced themselves that sex with children is normal. Pathetic people."

"Our man probably has all the requisites of a serial killer," Patricia went on. "Emotional estrangement from mother. Missing or nonfunctional father. Deficient personality. He's a failure sexually. Most of the public assumes that with a serial sex killer, we're dealing with a virile, insatiable maniac. Our man isn't like that at all. Often, masturbation is about as far as he can go with a live victim. He has never—not in his entire life—had a normal relationship with a woman. He's all fantasy. There's still debate on the origins of his fantasy. I believe it probably starts with the basic home situation in his childhood. He tries to assert himself, resolve his anger and frustration, on what he *can* control, just as the rapist does. Often there's a pattern. He may start with inanimate objects. He sets fires. He destroys property. He steals and ruins prized possessions of others. Then he may turn to animals. He poisons, disembowels dogs. Sets cats on fire, ties cherry bombs to their legs.

He establishes *control* over animals. Then at some point he turns to children.''

"Oh, God," Rachel said.

"He wants a plaything," Booker said. "But there's a bright side. This guy we're hunting seems to want to keep them alive for a while. He seems to have the facilities to keep them longer than most."

"Ordinarily, we'd certainly spare you all this," Patricia said. "We'd wait, and if it turned out badly, you'd never need to know the details. If we recovered Suzanne, we'd then deal with her psychic trauma. But we have this decision to make, and you by necessity must be a participant. We felt you should know all that's involved."

"We talked to Pete after he brought you back to town," Booker said. "He said he believed you could handle it."

Rachel remembered that Peterson had said that if necessary, one could endure the unendurable.

But this?

"We don't know what this guy's fantasies are," Patricia said. "I've given you a worst-case scenario. He may not be a sadist. Suzanne may not be subjected to extensive abuse."

"But you don't believe that."

"No," Patricia said softly.

"You see our quandary," Booker said. "We think this would move the guy in the right direction. But we're not sure."

"No doubt he has succeeded in depersonalizing her," Patricia said. "At the moment, she's just an object to him. He probably doesn't even know her name. If we succeed in making her into a valuable person, in his mind, by placing a dollar value on her, that might help prevent him from killing her."

"So that's where we are," Booker said. "I feel we should do this. The investigation is moving along. But I'm not greatly encouraged by developments thus far. I think we need to shake this guy's tree."

"I want to do more research," Patricia said. "But at this point I think it's a good plan."

Booker and Patricia remained silent, waiting for Rachel to respond.

Patricia also appeared totally exhausted. Rachel thought of what she knew of Patricia's long day. She glanced at her watch. Two-fifteen in the morning.

She now fully understood that this horrible event in her life was routine for Booker and Patricia. They were brought face-to-face with the unspeakable most every day.

"Let me make sure I understand," she said. "You both think

that if we don't do this, and if the police don't find him in time, he will tire of Suzanne and kill her. Is that right?''

"Yes," Patricia said.

"As far as we know, that has been his pattern," Booker said.

"Then I don't see we have an alternative. I'll call the studio the first thing this morning. I'll also contact the outdoor advertising people, find out what's available. I'll order the blow-up of Suzanne's picture. Then, if the studio cooperates, all we'll need is the exact wording for the sign."

"Booker and I will work on that," Patricia said. "We should have it for you by noon."

"Try for billboards along the interstates," Booker said. "From western Missouri to the Texas Panhandle. From north Kansas to central Texas. If we know anything at all about this guy, we know this: He gets around."

Booker walked Rachel back to her room. On the way, he monitored the cars in the parking area. He went into her room ahead of her, searched it, and checked the locks on her door.

"Keep that cross-bolt in place," he said. "Don't open the door to anyone unless you're certain of the identity. Today I'll see about getting you more protection."

Rachel had never for a moment considered that she herself might be in danger. "Do you think that's necessary?"

"When we put up the billboards, we don't know what this guy will do. Let's establish good habits now."

10

Through a one-way mirror, Booker watched Patricia work. The sound came from a speaker at his elbow.

"Let's start at the beginning," Patricia said. "You are in your store and you hear a loud crash. You look out the front window. What do you see?"

The woman's head was leaning forward, her chin almost on her chest. Her hair was gray and she looked to be in her mid-sixties. She was the sixth in a string of witnesses subjected to hypnosis during the day. Patricia had put her under quickly. Booker had hope that unlike the first five, she would be a good subject.

"Fire," the woman said.

"Where."

"The car. Burning."

"You saw that a car was burning. What did you do next?"

"Dialed nine-one-one. Told them."

"Could you still see the burning car? From where you were using the phone?"

"No."

"Your view was blocked?"

"Yes. Behind the counter."

"You couldn't see, because you had to go behind the counter. Is that right?"

"Yes."

"Mrs. Parton, what did you do next? After notifying the police?"

"Went out front."

"You walked out the door to the front of your store. Is that right?"

"Yes."

"Can you now see the burning car?"

"No. More cars. People."

118

"Cars have stopped, people have gathered, blocking your view. Is that correct, Mrs. Parton?"

"Yes."

"So what do you do next?"

"Lock the store. Walk over to where I can see."

"You lock the store and walk across the parking lot. Is that correct?"

"Yes."

"Do you now have a good view of the wreck?"

"Yes."

"Is the car still burning?"

"Yes."

"Do you see the accident victims?"

"Yes. On the grass."

"They have been rescued and placed on the grass. Is that correct?"

"Yes."

"What is happening to them?"

"People are taking care of them."

"Mrs. Parton, I want you to take your time and describe the scene. Do you see a child anywhere? A little girl?"

The woman frowned. Almost a full minute passed. "No," she said.

Booker found that he had been holding his breath.

He had thought for a moment that Patricia was about to score with this one.

"You don't see a little girl anywhere? What about a man that looks like he might be a security guard? Maybe a sheriff's deputy?"

Again the long wait while the woman searched the scene in her mind's eye. "No," she said.

Patricia led the woman through a description of the crowd and the arrival of the ambulances. The answers were repetitious, almost exactly what Patricia had obtained from other witnesses.

Booker was preparing to return to the squad room when the interview took a different turn.

The woman suddenly flopped in her chair, her face contorted in fright.

"Mrs. Parton, what happened?" Patricia asked.

"He almost hit me!"

"Who almost hit you?"

"An old pickup."

Booker returned to his seat. Patricia was taking her time, carefully planning her next question.

"Mrs. Parton, where is this truck headed?"

"Out."

"Out of the parking lot?"

"Yes."

"The ambulances are coming. Other cars are stopping. But this one pickup is leaving?"

"Yes."

"Mrs. Parton, do you know the reason why he almost hit you?"

"Wasp," Mrs. Parton said clearly. "Or dog."

Patricia stood for a moment, grappling with that. Booker wished the glass were two-way so he could signal her. He had already made the association. A moment later, Patricia did.

"He's distracted by something in the truck? Is that what you're saying?"

"Yes."

"What makes you think it is a wasp? Or a dog?"

"Slapping at it."

"He is slapping at something inside the cab. Is that correct?"

"Yes."

"What part of the truck almost struck you?"

Booker recognized that as an extremely skillful question. The answer would define the lady's position relative to the truck.

"Left front bumper," Mrs. Parton said.

"So he is passing close to you. Mrs. Parton, do you see his face?"

"No."

"Shit," Booker said.

"Why not?" Patricia asked.

"He's turned. Slapping."

"His back is to you and he's slapping at something inside the truck. Is that correct?"

"Yes."

"How is he dressed? Tell me what you see."

"Cowboy hat. Pearl-toned. Brown shirt. Light brown. Epaulets."

Booker took out his notebook and wrote down that answer. The description fit.

She had seen the son of a bitch.

"Where does the truck go?"

"Out. To the freeway."

"The truck leaves the parking lot, headed west, onto the interstate. Is that correct?"

"Yes."

Booker recognized that Patricia had made an error, jumping ahead, destroying the sequence. She quickly realized this.

"Mrs. Parton, I want you to think back to the moment the man almost struck you. Do you see the truck now?"

"Yes."

"What does the truck look like? Do you see anything different about it?"

"Big pipe. On the front."

Again Booker wished for a two-way glass. Some farmers and ranchers welded five-inch oil field pipe to the front of their trucks to serve as heavy-duty bumpers. But Patricia was an observant woman. After a moment she also made the connection.

"There is a large pipe where the truck's bumper should be?"

"Yes."

"Do you see anything else different about the truck?"

"No."

"Now he has missed you. And he's driving past. Do you see the driver now?"

"Yes," Mrs. Parton said after a moment.

"From his position in the truck, how would you describe him? Short? Tall?"

"Tall."

"Now the truck is driving on past you. What color is it?"

"No color."

Patricia hesitated, struggling with that answer. "Faded? Is that what you're saying?"

"Yes."

"What color do you think it might have been when it was new?"

"Blue."

"The truck is passing you. Do you see anything in the back end? In the pickup bed?"

"Gunnysacks."

"Does there seem to be something in them?"

Mrs. Parton paused. "Yes."

"Why do you think so?"

"They're tied. At the top."

"How many sacks are there?"

"Three. No, four."

"Anything else that you see in the pickup bed?"

"Toolbox. White."

"A white toolbox. Is it a small toolbox? Or a pickup box?"

"Pickup. All the way across."

"Up next to the cab?"

"Yes."

"All right. The pickup has passed you. It's moving away. Please take your time and concentrate, Mrs. Parton. Can you see the license plate?"

Again the frown, the long pause. "Yes."

"Is it an Oklahoma plate?"

"Yes."

"Mrs. Parton, can you read what is on that plate?"

Again Booker stopped breathing. At that moment he would have killed for the image in that woman's head.

Her frown deepened and her closed eyes squinted. "H . . . B . . . J."

She stopped and shook her head slightly.

"And the numbers? Mrs. Parton, can you read me the numbers?"

Anguish was plain on Mrs. Parton's face. She battled with the image for a full minute. "I can't see them. Trailer hitch."

"Shit," Booker said again.

But that was a bit more information. Faded old blue truck with a white cross-bed toolbox and a trailer hitch. License beginning HBJ. That narrowed the search.

Patricia moved on to other, easy questions. She returned to the license plate several times, trying again for the numbers. But the trailer hitch still blocked Mrs. Parton's view.

Patricia went into the routine of bringing Mrs. Parton out of it, giving the posthypnotic suggestions to remove any lingering effects. Booker rose and went into the squad room. Nate was on the phone. Booker gave him the cutoff sign. Nate said something to the party on the other end, held the receiver against his chest and looked up at Booker with his this-better-be-good scowl.

"Patricia got a partial," Booker told him. "HBJ. No numbers. Old faded pickup, probably blue. White fitted toolbox. Three or four burlap sacks in back, tied at the top. Trailer hitch partially obscuring license. The witness didn't see his face, but her description matches."

"The kid?"

"She didn't see Suzanne. But the subject was slapping at something in the cab. Mrs. Parton thought it might be a wasp. Or a dog. But he was probably beating the shit out of the kid."

For the first time since Booker had known him, Nate's expression came close to revealing compassion. He had moved the phone away from his chest, making the person on the other end of the line privy to the conversation. From Nate's demeanor, Booker thought he knew that person's identity.

"Does this description sound solid?"

"You'll want Patricia's evaluation. But for my money it's good." Booker raised his voice a notch for the benefit of the person on the line. The expense of retaining Patricia had been the subject of considerable OSBI budget controversy. "You should have seen Patricia at work. She played that witness like a Stradivarius."

"Could it be suggestive?"

That was a valid question. Sometimes, wanting to help, witnesses were *too* cooperative. Feeding on hints from the interviewer, they made up information. In Texas a born loser named Henry Lee Lucas once successfully confessed to several hundred murders before doubters began to notice that many of the crimes occurred in the same time frame in vastly different sections of the country. Lucas simply had been exceptionally adept at feeding the questions of the interviewers back to them as positive answers. Such feedback was always a hazard.

"Definitely not," Booker said. "All information came from the witness. The tapes will show that."

Nate frowned. "This is still so fucking iffy. Bottom line, we have a witness who saw what may have been a security guard near what may have been the victim. Now we have a witness who saw an old truck, with the driver slapping at what may have been the kid. We still don't have solid evidence of an abduction." His frown deepened while he considered the problem. "I guess it's all we have," he said. "Okay, go ahead and give it to Hop. Tell him to get it out. I'm on the phone with the director. Soon as I'm off, we'll talk, see where we stand."

"Right," Booker said in a tone that conveyed a heel click to the director.

He took the information to Hopkins, then wandered over by the dispatcher and made sure that what went out was complete and accurate.

He felt the heady high that always comes with a possible breakthrough in a tough case. Law officers all over the state would now be looking for the truck and driver. Word would go out to surrounding states. If any justice was left in the world, someone would see the son of a bitch, make an apprehension.

That progression of events could not be left to chance. A platoon of agents would go to work on the partial. Somewhere in the vast files of vehicle registration a number combination would match up with the description of the truck and agents would go out to investigate ownership.

But nothing was for certain. The truck might be stolen. Maybe the subject would resist arrest and go down hard. If so, Suzanne might never be found, and they would never know all they needed to know in order to close the other cases. Or maybe the subject would lie low, all leads would play out, and Suzanne would die.

And there was danger that the investigation might be turned in the wrong direction by the new information and hamper efforts on other fronts.

But Booker felt they should not let up anywhere.

Time was not on Suzanne's side.

11

Before contacting the studio, Rachel talked with the outdoor advertising companies to gain some idea of availability and cost. She was still gathering this information when Al Gold reached her.

From the first moment she sensed that his attitude had changed. His voice was brusque as he asked about the progress of the investigation.

Rachel told him there was nothing new. Before she could introduce Booker's idea for the billboards, he took the conversation in a different direction.

"What are you doing, Mrs. Shelby?" he demanded. "I've seen you on all the networks. You're quoted in all the papers. People here are upset."

Rachel was taken aback by his tone of animosity. "I don't understand what you're asking."

"With the circumstances, we don't object to your responding to questions from the media. But clearly you've hired a public relations firm. Mrs. Shelby, we have people here who handle media relations."

Rachel thought she understood. It seemed to be a matter of turf. "Mr. Gold, I have *not* hired a public relations firm. I've done all that has been done with the help of local volunteers. I'm working with the police. They *want* the publicity in the hope it will generate information they can use."

"I don't think you understand, Mrs. Shelby. Timing is very important in a project like this. Too much beforehand, and you take away from exposure on the film's release. We must think of image. I'm told the networks are running spots promoting crime show segments scheduled tonight. Mrs. Shelby, we don't want the picture associated with that type of programming."

Rachel now understood. It all came down to money.

She made an effort to keep her voice level when she wanted to shout at him. "I don't think *you* understand, Mr. Gold. Those shows have the reputation of catching criminals. We're trying to catch a criminal. The criminal who has kidnapped my daughter. That's my sole interest. Getting my daughter back."

Gold hesitated. "Mrs. Shelby, we're not objecting to the publicity. But it must be controlled, balanced. We can help you. I'll have a team in there this afternoon to handle the public relations."

Rachel did not have to think about her reply. She answered automatically, putting all the force she could muster into one word. "No!"

The line was silent a long while.

"Mrs. Shelby, I must remind you. It's in the contract. The studio handles, or approves, *all* publicity."

Rachel's impulse was to tell him to go ahead and sue. But she felt he was viewing the situation from too narrow a perspective. "Mr. Gold, the studio grossed several hundred million on the first film. You know, and I know, that the second should do even better. But without Suzanne there will be no second movie. You would never find an adequate substitute. Suzanne is unique to the role. The studio has invested considerable money in her. I believe it would be in the studio's interest to do all possible to get her back. We have a large number of dedicated policemen here working around the clock to find her. They tell me publicity helps them in their work, that it may reach a person who has knowledge they can use. So I will continue to do all I can to get that publicity."

"Then you won't cooperate with the studio public relations team?"

"I'm receptive to advice. But I've already made commitments. I have a schedule to keep. I won't step aside."

Again the line was silent. Rachel sensed that she had won the argument.

"Then I'll offer you some advice," Gold said. "Back off. You've reached a peak level of exposure. Feed them but don't force-feed them. Too much is too much. You'll start getting diminishing returns. Go more for quality. Ration your availability."

"I've been thinking along those lines," Rachel admitted. "And, Mr. Gold, I've talked with some people here about posting the reward. They see a way it might really help. You are still planning on that, aren't you?"

"We're assembling the money. We've encountered some difficulty obtaining that much in unsequenced bills. But it should be ready this morning."

Rachel described Booker's idea for the billboards and Patricia's evaluation of the possible effect.

"How much will the billboards cost?" Gold asked.

Rachel gave him the figures.

"I'm sure we can come to agreement on that," Gold said. "But on the ransom itself, I must make our situation clear. We have certain fiduciary requirements. You've declined our help on public relations. But we must keep control of the money. I trust you won't object if I send an assistant along to handle the money."

Rachel felt a moment of apprehension. But she understood that the studio could not release the money with no strings attached. "I won't object," she said. "In fact, I'm most grateful that you are putting up the money."

"We would not expect to do less. Our man should be there sometime this afternoon. Is there a vault anywhere near you?"

"There's a small bank just down the street. I'll see what's available."

"Good. He'll be contacting you."

Rachel spoke quickly to keep him from signing off. "Mr. Gold, time is a prime consideration on the billboards. We really should be making arrangements."

"I understand. You can go ahead and do that."

"Thank you, Mr. Gold. I will."

She ended the call without telling him that she already had done so.

Booker went to Nate and suggested that he and Patricia drive to Oklahoma City during the afternoon to review records of parolees from sexual crimes. Booker explained that he and Patricia would make the perfect team for the job, with his memory for names and faces, and Patricia's trained eye for deceptively insignificant detail. After a brief pro forma argument, Nate grudgingly agreed to release Patricia for the afternoon.

She insisted on taking her own car. Ordinarily Booker disliked riding with other drivers, especially women drivers. Patricia was an exception. Her skill behind the wheel was commensurate with the other competencies in her life.

She waited until they were several miles eastbound on the interstate before raising the topic he knew he would have to face with her. "Booker, we haven't had a chance to talk, to get caught up with each other," she said. "How you been doing?"

For a moment Booker considered whether it was Patricia the friend or Patricia the psychiatrist asking the question. He decided it was the friend. "Not worth a damn. I'm just not gaited for idleness."

She gave him an analytical sidelong glance. "I knew it would be rough on you. Betty's death and your retirement came too close together. I was hoping you'd get into something else, find other interests, make new friends."

"I guess I should have found something else," Booker admitted. "But I had too many loose ends from the Bureau rattling in my head. That was my only interest. I don't make friends easily."

"Sure you do," Patricia said.

"Think about it. How long have you known me?"

Patricia was silent a moment. "Ten years. I met you right after my first case with the Bureau."

"And when did we get to know each other?"

"The Peterson case."

"Right. We worked together because we were the only two people in the Bureau who thought Pete was innocent. I'm too plain-spoken. I have a lot of acquaintances but few friends."

"I had every intention to look you up after you left the Bureau," Patricia said. "But routine kept interfering."

"Believe me, I know how that is," Booker assured her. "I gave my life to the Bureau, mostly at Betty's expense."

"I should have called you. I'm sorry I didn't."

"I think I'm over the worst of it," Booker said. "Climbing back into the saddle on this case has helped. How about yourself? Any serious boyfriends?"

Patricia winced. "Booker, I don't know where I'll be tomorrow, the next day, or next week. I rarely have a moment to myself. How can I establish a meaningful relationship under those circumstances?"

"Don't hand your life to the Bureau, Patricia. Life's too short. When you're growing old and look back, it seems like your life was shot out of a cannon."

"I'm thirty-eight," Patricia admitted. "I've been awfully aware lately of the biological clock. I want children of my own. I've considered quitting this work and opening a pediatric practice in psychiatry. But I really feel I'm making an important contribution with the Bureau, the courts, prison system."

"Patricia, I'll give you the benefit of experience. There's no loyalty left anywhere anymore. You'll get nothing back from all your sacrifices. Read the newspapers. People are being booted out of their jobs in their fifties, after thirty years of service to their companies. In these times you have to look out for yourself. If I were you, I'd think hard about that pediatric practice."

"Maybe I will," Patricia said. "And thank you, Booker. Thank you for caring."

They were approaching El Reno, where feeder roads soon would begin to increase traffic on the interstate. Booker wanted to clear up a few questions in his mind before Patricia became totally involved with driving. "You gave Rachel a good rundown on our probable subject. But I felt you held back a few angles. Is there anything else I should know before we plunge into those records?"

Patricia considered the question for a moment before answering. "I described to her the type of personality I think we're dealing with. There are other types. I could be wrong."

"He could be older?" Booker guessed.

"By a few years. Or he possibly might be the regressive type. Some pedophiles function fairly well through adolescence, even get married, have children of their own. Then they regress, seek younger sexual outlets. I don't think our subject is of that type."

"What's your reasoning?"

"The continuity in age of the victims. They're all within a year or two of the same age. No progression."

"Suzanne is older."

"But small enough that people mistake her age. And there's a randomness about the abductions that makes me think our subject is younger, willing to run more risk. I think an older subject would be more cautious."

That had been Booker's thinking. "What other types are there?"

Patricia sighed. "The totally sadistic. They take children for torture, physically or mentally. They're more interested in pain and mental anguish than power or sexual pleasure."

Booker thought of the ten to twelve days the subject usually kept his victims. That might fit the plan of a sadist.

"Some are mixed," Patricia went on. "I think that if you mixed sadism with a power trip, that would be the worst combination imaginable."

"I hate to say it, but that sounds like our man."

"The pattern fits," Patricia agreed. "I've been thinking more and more in that direction. I just hope to God I'm wrong."

They drove on to the Department of Corrections in mutual silence.

Do you feel like talking?'' Patricia asked. ''If you could come over, I have fresh coffee and a pint of frozen yogurt. If you don't come, I'll have to eat it all by myself and suffer.''

Rachel was grateful for the invitation. Her worst moments came at night, when she was alone and had time to think random thoughts. ''Give me ten minutes,'' she said.

''Make it five. The yogurt is melting.''

Patricia answered Rachel's knock wearing a long robe, her long, dark hair wrapped in a towel. Rachel assumed she had just stepped out of the shower. She gestured Rachel into a chair and hurried back to the dressing alcove. The aroma of fresh coffee was comforting with its vague associations of other times, other places.

''The worst drawback to my work is constant travel,'' Patricia said. ''I hate motels. I hate living in other people's filth. You know how the maids clean these rooms? They pour detergent into the commode and use it as a basin for a long-handled brush to go over the tub and lavatories. I've caught them at that. No wonder hepatitis and other diseases are again flourishing.''

''I intensely dislike motels,'' Rachel agreed. ''But I suppose they're necessary.''

''I've learned to cope,'' Patricia said. ''Of course you can't clean the whole room. But I've discovered that if I spread clean newspapers, I can make one corner my own. I carry a portable coffeemaker and a small microwave. The motels seldom protest. I ask for clean towels every day, and unless I'm stuck long in one place, I put the Do Not Disturb sign on the door and try to keep the so-called cleaning people out.''

Rachel recognized that Patricia was offering survival tips in a noncondescending way. She was grateful. She had been disturbed over the way her few possessions had been tossed around.

''Forgive the plastic cups and spoons,'' Patricia said in serving. ''My motel phobia doesn't quite extend to carrying my own china and silver.''

She sat facing Rachel, and for a time they spooned the strawberry yogurt in silence. Rachel was aware that Patricia was covertly studying her.

''How are you doing?'' Patricia asked. ''Are you bearing up under all of this?''

Normally Rachel would have considered the question intrusive. But she now was becoming accustomed to expressions of genuine concern. She answered honestly. "Most of the time now I'm just numb, emotionally. I make it through the day fine, while I'm working. But at night, when the pressure's off, I tend to fall apart."

"Are you getting any sleep?"

"Only when exhausted. Even then I sleep only an hour or two. Then I wake up and can't go back to sleep. So I don't feel I've really slept. That doesn't concern me. I don't have time for sleep."

"You must get your rest. Do you have any medication for sleep?"

"Dr. Peterson gave me some sleeping pills. I haven't used them. Whatever else, I want to keep a clear head."

"How did today go?"

"Fairly well, I suppose. I finished with the crime shows and was interviewed by the film trade publications. I followed through with the newsmagazines. All of that's mostly into Chief Laird's department now. The studio's representative arrived. The money is in the bank, waiting. We have the billboard material working."

"Booker and I have just returned from the city," Patricia said. "We went through about two hundred and fifty case histories of known sexual deviates, searching for anything that might help us."

Rachel felt she could ask. "You find anything?"

"Twelve recently paroled convicts who have proclivities in that direction. The OSBI will check on them, along with another fifteen or twenty who also could be candidates." She paused. "Do you feel up to talking for a while about Suzanne?"

"Yes," Rachel said.

And she was surprised to find that she did. Reviving memories of better times seemed to be good therapy.

"You mentioned that Suzanne is a troubled child. Tell me about that. When did you first notice anything unusual?"

Rachel considered the question a moment before answering. "I suppose my first inkling came not long after we enrolled her in school. The administrators routinely give the children something they call the Stanford-Binet to see how well they may perform with schoolwork."

Patricia nodded. "The Binet is standard. It's older, perhaps more reliable. The Stanford is the updated American version of the original, based on Binet's perception of child development."

"They said Suzanne tested completely off the scale. So they gave her what they called the Wechsler to see if the first results were a fluke."

Again Patricia nodded. "That was probably the Wechsler Intelligence Scale for Children. I'm surprised they would give her that. It's specifically designed for adolescents and older children. I use an abbreviated form of the Wechsler adult version in my work to evaluate convicted criminals and prison inmates in order to advise judges in presentence reports and appeals. It's about as reliable as any we have."

"She scored high on that, even though it was above her age level. The psychology firm that does the evaluation was quite excited. They made a special project of Suzanne. They gave her the Goodenough, the Vigotsky, others I never identified."

Patricia shook her head, conveying her dismay without putting her criticism into words.

"Understand, I wasn't told about this," Rachel explained. "The first I knew was when Suzanne came home crying one afternoon. The test results were being discussed by the teachers. The students had overheard, and were treating Suzanne like a freak, calling her disparaging names. She was terribly upset."

"How did you feel about that?"

"Angry. First, because the school had put Suzanne in that position and, secondly, that they had not informed me or asked my permission to administer the additional tests. I talked with the school director. He promised there would be no more tests, and that Suzanne would be treated normally, no different from the other children."

"How does Suzanne feel about it now?"

Rachel searched for the right word. "Sensitive. She's proud of her high IQ. But she resents being treated like a freak. So she usually tries to downplay her intelligence."

"Has the situation created any problems between her and David?"

"None I'm aware of. Really, David doesn't kowtow to Suzanne in that department, even though he tested only a few points above average. He's more practical. He corrects her occasionally and doesn't hesitate to call her stupid."

Patricia laughed. "They get along okay?"

Rachel remembered that Booker had asked that question. She expanded her answer. "They fuss at each other every once in a while, like most siblings. But yes, I'd say they get along exceptionally well."

"How do you feel about her film career?"

"Terribly uncertain. I'm not at all sure I'm doing the right thing." Rachel hesitated. She had never talked in depth about this. She had to feel her way into the subject. "Suzanne is a sensitive, delicate child. She has severe developmental problems. I know that. I fear her sudden success may be doing her more harm than good."

"In what way?"

Again Rachel searched for words. Patricia waited patiently, her expression receptive.

"I'm told that the death of Suzanne's father came at a critical time in her life, and that she hasn't yet recovered. She was very much a Daddy's girl. She doted on Bill, and he on her. Then suddenly he was gone. Afterward, I would hear her crying in her sleep. I thought this was a phase, that eventually it would stop. But it didn't. So I consulted a pediatric psychiatrist. Suzanne went to her once a week for more than a year."

"Can I have her name? I would like to talk with her."

"Of course," Rachel said.

"What were her conclusions?"

"She said that basically Suzanne has a strong, well-integrated personality, but that the loss of her father and her treatment as a freak by her peers came too close together. She felt there had been some psychic damage. She found that Suzanne tends to sublimate reality. When Suzanne's faced with a problem, she just puts it out of her head and turns to creative fantasy. The psychiatrist said this is an artistic trait—turning reality into art—and that she wasn't sure it should be tampered with. Suzanne spends a lot of time making up movies. The final diagnosis was that we shouldn't worry unless her fantasies interfered with her schoolwork or daily life."

Patricia did not respond. Rachel wondered if she disagreed.

"Booker said Suzanne sees herself as another Jodie Foster."

Rachel nodded. "At the moment her career means everything to her. You asked how I feel about it. I'm afraid her sudden success may turn out to be only a bubble, and that she may be in for traumatic disappointment. That's my biggest worry. Or was, until this."

"I haven't seen her movie. From what I've read and seen on television, she apparently has talent to spare."

"But my worry is, can she go beyond childhood roles?" Rachel explained. "I think the critics are wrong in comparing her to Shirley Temple. In those old Shirley Temple movies, the adult roles and the situations were written down to a childish level. I don't know why the critics pick Shirley Temple. I believe comparison would be more apt with the early work of Elizabeth Taylor, Margaret O'Brien, Natalie Wood, Tatum O'Neal, Drew Barrymore, other childhood stars. I think audiences see Suzanne as a child—a troubled child. Her hurt seems to come across onscreen. Audiences recognize it as authentic, and respond. Will she keep that appeal, that vulnerability, on into adulthood? I don't know."

"You told Booker she studies Jodie Foster movies. *All* of them? I ask, because as I remember, some aren't exactly children's fare. I don't know about the ratings, but *Taxi Driver*, for instance, and *The Silence of the Lambs*. And that one where she's the victim of gang rape."

"The Accused."

"And that one where she lived in a house alone, involved with dead bodies and murder."

"The Little Girl Who Lives Down the Lane. That's one of Suzanne's favorites. Yes, I banned some of them for a while. But Suzanne can be very persuasive. Eventually I allowed her to study them. She runs them over and over. But, you see, Suzanne is involved with the devices of characterization, the acting, the camera angles, lighting, dialogue, the structure of scenes, the way the story is told. She has a good VCR and studies them frame by frame. She focuses on techniques and effects, not the sex and gore. She knows that Hannibal the Cannibal is only Anthony Hopkins chewing up the scenery."

Patricia gave Rachel a mock wince over her unintentional play on words.

"Perhaps I indulge Suzanne and David too freely," Rachel admitted. "I was denied self-expression when I was a child. Maybe I overcompensate. But children are exposed to adult-level fare today no matter what you do. I now feel that introduction in a controlled setting may be the best way to go."

"You could be right," Patricia said. "I would appreciate it if you would call Suzanne's psychiatrist the first thing tomorrow morning and pave the way, giving verbal permission for her to release Suzanne's records to me."

"I'll do that," Rachel promised. She wrote out the name of Suzanne's psychiatrist and the phone number.

"I don't know yet what use we may make of this," Patricia said. "But it will help us to know Suzanne, to understand what she might do in different situations. It'll be more ammunition. We need all we can get."

With the billboard project well under way, Booker had not yet obtained clearance from everyone concerned. Well-versed in bureaucracy, and assuming that the case soon would go federal, he put in motion a squeeze play. First he called the U.S. Attorney in Oklahoma City to gain approval for the wording. The DA initially objected to the plan. But eventually Booker convinced him that in the interest of saving Suzanne's life, legal concessions were in order. Finally the DA agreed.

Booker then called the state's regional district attorney and made the same pitch. The state DA also objected. Booker explained that the case undoubtedly would go federal, that the U.S. Attorney concerned had already cleared the plan, and that time was growing short if they hoped to save Suzanne's life. Ultimately, the DA gave his approval.

Armed with his fait accompli, Booker took the wording to Nate, who spent several minutes considering it.

"I'm uneasy about it," Nate said. "But if you've got clearance from the DAs, and if Simmons goes along, I'll recommend it to the director."

To Booker's surprise, FBI Special Agent in Charge Simmons was more receptive. "Maybe it'll stir the pot, give us a break," he said. "If the case goes federal, I'll probably take some heat about it. But I can stand it if it'll do any good."

While Nate called the OSBI director, Booker talked with Police Chief Laird about protection for Rachel. Laird said he was stretched too thin, but he would see what he could do. A few minutes later he returned Booker's call, saying a compromise had been reached: The police department would continue to guard her office throughout the day. Sheriff Bates had offered two shifts of deputies to give her protection each night at the motel.

Booker then made arrangements with the telephone company for an emergency dedicated hookup. He was promised immediate action.

Nate reported back to Booker that his attempt for clearance with the director had been only partially successful.

"We'll not stop you," Nate said. "But the director told me to make it plain: This is *your* idea. The responsibility rests with you, the studio, and Mrs. Shelby. The OSBI has absolutely nothing to do with it."

Booker drove over to Rachel's office. The Methodist minister working with Rachel had already completed the layout for the billboard. Booker gave them the legally cleared wording and the new telephone number.

Booker and Rachel stood behind the minister while he set the type and moved it onto the layout on the computer screen. The result was put through the color printer.

To Booker's eye, the printout was exactly what he had envisioned when the idea first came to him.

After they checked and double-checked for errors, Rachel faxed the completed layout to the outdoor advertising company.

Afterward, Booker felt drained. The dispatch of the layout left him in a sort of postpartum depression.

Rachel seemed to share his mood. The color print of the billboard lay on her desk. Tears welled in her eyes. She could not take her gaze off it.

Booker felt moved to do what he could. Patricia was away on a presentence hearing. She would not be back until midnight. Pete was on duty at the hospital.

"We could both use a good dinner," Booker suggested. "I know a place that serves good barbecue."

Rachel did not look away from the picture. "Booker, I feel I should stay by the phone. Maybe we could have something delivered."

"Chief Laird gave me a police radio and beeper. If anything happens, they'll let me know."

Rachel acquiesced. Booker led her out to his car, ignoring the cameras, the shouted questions.

The restaurant was forty minutes away on the interstate. Booker and Rachel rode most of the way in silence, locked into a mutual somber mood. For Booker, every billboard they passed was a reminder of those that would be going up all along the interstate. He assumed that Rachel's thoughts were in the same vein.

Booker was troubled by old, familiar stirrings. None of the women he had gone out with in the years since Betty's death had come anywhere close to taking her place. But with Rachel, he was beginning to feel a telltale tenderness.

Logic told him the thought was ridiculous. He was more than old enough to be her father. Yet, he could not deny his feelings.

At the restaurant he guided her to a corner banquette, where her bandages and now well-known face would not attract so much attention. He waited until they were into coffee and brandy before broaching the subject that had been heavily on his mind all evening.

"Don't get your hopes up too high on a breakthrough from the billboards," he warned her. "Keep remembering that this is only one string in our bow."

She looked at him with an enigmatic expression. "Are you telling me you're afraid it isn't going to work?"

"I'm only telling you there's no way to know where a break may come in a case like this. We can't put all of our hopes or efforts into one basket."

"What are those other strings in our bow?"

"The description of the old blue truck. You can bet that all over Oklahoma and surrounding states cops are looking for that truck. Most of them have kids. This case will be very much on their minds. Any one of them, at any moment, may collar our man and lead us to Suzanne."

Rachel closed her eyes but remained silent.

"That's the most likely scenario," Booker went on. "But there are other ways we may find him. We have platoons of people working on the partial license plate. Every slight hint of a matchup is investigated. It's slow, hard work. People move, trade cars. We're making progress."

"But we have so little time left," Rachel said. "Two days! Two days!" She began to cry.

"That's just theory," he reminded her. "Time frames are difficult. We may have more leeway than we figured."

"Or less," Rachel said, sobbing. "That's what you're saying."

Booker reached for her hand. "I'm just telling you there's a broad reason for hope. The billboards are only a part of it. We're looking at every sexual deviate in the state. I'm going back over all those cases that may be related, hunting anything we might have missed. Local police, sheriff's offices, parole officers, state troopers, other agencies, are helping. I'm calling in a lot of old markers on this. What I'm saying is that with all we're doing, a break will come eventually somewhere."

"But will it come in time?" Rachel said. She turned her face to the wall and sobbed helplessly. "Oh, God! Will it come in time?"

Unable to offer further encouragement at the moment, Booker held her while she wept.

12

Rachel had just awakened and was preparing to leave for the office when the phone rang. Booker's voice sounded cool, unemotional. "We have something we'd like you to examine. We could come out now, unless you'd prefer to come down here."

Rachel felt her heart lurch. Booker had helped her through a difficult evening, calmed her enough for sleep. Now his voice sounded so somber. An interval passed before she could speak. "Booker, what is it?"

"I'd rather you told us. We can be there in five minutes, if that's all right. Or I can come get you, bring you down here."

Rachel considered. She had washed out some things and the room was a mess. But she did not feel up to facing the cameras and reporters hanging around the police station.

"Come on out," she said.

"I'll be bringing Patricia, Nate, and Simmons. We'll see you in a few minutes."

Simmons of the FBI? Rachel again felt uncontrollable panic. She had to know. "Booker, is it something bad?"

The line was silent a moment. "I'm not sure. It might be to the good. Let's keep that thought in mind."

Abruptly he hung up. She hurried around the room, picking up, putting things in order, blocking her mind from useless speculation. But she knew it was something serious. That was implicit in Booker's tone, and in the fact that he was bringing those in charge of the investigation.

When the group arrived, she followed the procedure Booker had decreed, not turning the bolt until she saw him in the peephole.

From their faces as they entered, Rachel gathered that regardless of what Booker had said, it was bad. Patricia took Rachel's hand, touched her arm. Inspector Noonan was carrying an ordinary grocery sack and a rolled-up section of newspaper. He went to the back bed and spread the newspaper across the coverlet. Booker turned on all lights. The four of them gathered around the bed.

Booker's voice was abrupt, businesslike. "Mrs. Shelby, we would like you to tell us if you recognize this."

Noonan reached into the sack and pulled out a clear plastic bag. He unfolded it on the newspaper.

In it were Suzanne's tan walking shorts, blouse, and one stocking.

Rachel felt her knees folding. Then Patricia had her by the shoulders. Booker brought a chair and they eased her into it.

"Ma'am, are those articles of clothing what your daughter was wearing?" Noonan asked.

Rachel was beyond speech. Her mind froze, not yet ready to accept the horrible possibilities.

She nodded.

Booker put a hand on her shoulder. "This may not be as bad as it looks," he said.

"A young high school couple found these articles about daylight this morning on a back road," Noonan said. "Near a creek. About eighteen miles from here. They remembered the description we put out. They sacked them and brought them in."

Rachel reached out and spread a palm over the plastic bag, feeling the texture of the cloth, seeking comfort from it. She looked up at Booker. "How could this possibly be to the good?"

"It gives us the direction he took. We can narrow the search. And this is more or less solid proof that she was abducted. Now it's a federal case."

"This gives me authority to bring in special agents from all over," Simmons said. "We'll have more manpower at work."

"Basically, nothing will change," Booker said. "We've all been working together from the beginning—local, state, the feds. We'll continue to do so. This just means that the FBI will take the lead, give us more expertise, help in our coordination with other states."

Rachel could not put aside the reality. "But doesn't this mean he may have . . ."

She could not form the words.

"Not at all," Booker said quickly. "I think he threw the clothing out when he drove by that spot. He and Suzanne are probably long gone from there. But we'll make sure. You remember Patricia's speculative profile of the guy? This fits the pattern."

"More of us are buying into Booker's theory, connecting the earlier cases," Simmons said. "If Booker's right, and I'm personally coming to believe he may be, we still have some time on our side.''

Noonan gestured to the clothing. ''Mrs. Shelby, you haven't examined them closely. We'd like you to make certain.''

The plastic cleaning bag was sealed with transparent tape. Rachel raised one end and hooked a finger under the corner. ''May I?'' she asked.

''I'd rather you didn't,'' Simmons said. ''We'll rush this to the FBI labs. They may find hair, fiber, other trace evidence that could help us later on.''

Patricia held the plastic bag so Rachel could use both hands to manipulate the clothing inside. For the first time, Rachel noticed that the shoulder straps were still buttoned. She looked closer. ''These straps were torn loose,'' she said.

Booker spoke hesitantly. ''They appear to have been cut. Probably with a knife. The FBI labs can tell us for sure. The blouse is also either cut or torn, or possibly both. But again, you shouldn't jump to conclusions as to what that means.''

''Remember, this guy isn't a rapist,'' Patricia said. ''He's probably incapable of normal sex.''

Rachel examined the torn blouse. The fabric there appeared to have been ripped, not cut. Pinching the thin plastic, she pulled cloth aside and exposed the labels.

''These are Suzanne's,'' she said.

''I have to ask you,'' Noonan said. ''How can you be absolutely sure?''

''That's the label of an exclusive shop on Fifth Avenue,'' Rachel explained. ''I assume the mathematical odds would be infinitesimal against finding that label, and that particular design, on a rural road in Oklahoma.''

Noonan nodded his acceptance of that and carefully returned the plastic bag to the grocery sack.

Rachel wanted to keep the clothing. She felt the need to have something, anything, of Suzanne's, to hold on to. She remembered the day they purchased the outfit, and Suzanne's enthusiasm, her concern over achieving the proper look, the perfect fit.

''Mrs. Shelby, are you all right?'' Patricia asked.

Rachel nodded. ''What happens now?''

No one answered her for a moment.

''Today, as soon as we get organized, we'll go out and make a search of that creek bottom,'' Booker said. ''We'll cover the ground for at least two miles in every direction, searching for further evidence.''

Rachel was not misled.

Again they would be searching for Suzanne's body.

Suzanne was toying with the first glimmer of a complete plot. In the late morning, with the snake man gone and the sun baking the metal sides of the old red barn, she lay sweltering on the filthy mattress in a half stupor and thought about her movie.

She now felt the story should center on the young daughter of a famous person. For a while she considered the idea of the father being the president, or maybe a senator. But eventually she settled on a high-ranking diplomat.

Two years ago her class had made a field trip to the United Nations. The UN contained some great interiors. That would be where the father worked. He would be the United States ambassador to the UN. He would be a big man, robust, full of laughter, a fun guy, just like her own father had been.

To accommodate this new story line, she had revised her original opening. The movie instead would begin on a day when something really important was happening, something involving all nations and world peace. The father would be wearing a terrific suit, speaking at the podium in this awesome auditorium, and there would be reverse shots of all these impressive-looking men listening to him. The daughter also would be there, of course, in the audience, sitting beside her beautiful mother, seeing her father at work on this really important day.

Her screenwriter friend Mort Miller once told her that one of the biggest mistakes commonly made in movies was to fail to tell the story behind the story. Mort said all too often characters seemed to exist only for the purpose of the story, and you were never given a feeling for their lives before or afterward. Suzanne was determined never to make that mistake in her movies. Mort had said that the story behind the story should be implied, woven into the dialogue and action, so you never needed flashbacks.

She felt her new opening contained these essentials.

From the father's eloquence, the viewer would know he was well-educated, a high-class guy. From his size and the way he moved, the viewer would know, without really thinking about it, that he had been a star in sports—football, baseball, and track. His smooth, confident demeanor would show he was accustomed to doing really important things. From the mother's beauty and impeccable styling, the viewer would sense her background and breeding, that in growing up she had been surrounded by all kinds of handsome suitors, and that she had chosen the father because he was far and beyond the best of the best. And from the way the daughter listened, the viewer would know that she was intelligent, understood all the really important stuff, and worshipped her father.

Then the speech would be over and the important men would be congratulating the father on his terrific ideas. But the father would be hurrying things along. You sensed he wanted to get away, and to be alone with his family.

From that establishing sequence, an exterior shot would open up the story. Mort had said that every good movie contains certain scenes you remember, scenes that support the thread of the story. This would be one of those memorable scenes, with the ambassador's family walking hand in hand out of the UN. The limousines and flags would be in frame, so you would know where you were. From that long perspective, Suzanne would cut to a medium shot, with the ambassador, daughter, and mother walking into the camera. The daughter would be between her parents, holding her father's hand, wearing a heartstoppingly elegant, simple, grown-up–looking dress, and maybe a small, brimmed hat.

It would be such a perfect picture that you knew something awful was about to happen.

Then you would hear the gunshots.

The terrorists would fire from several angles. The father would have no chance. He would fall, horribly wounded, with blood all over. The mother would be hurt, too, and people would hurry and carry her to safety. There would be a close-up of the daughter, uninjured, clinging to her father, begging him not to die.

Then a man in uniform would lean over the daughter and talk into her ear, telling her they must move out of the street to make way for the ambulance. Sirens would be wailing all over, and people would be shouting, and she would believe the man. But after he walked her to one side, he would scoop her up and put her in his truck, and she would see that his uniform was cheap and fake and that he was the snake man. He would tie her wrists and ankles with plastic and slap her to the floor of the truck.

Then he would drive away with the ambassador's daughter.

She felt that for story purposes the camera should stay with the ambassador. The viewer would see him being rushed to the hospital and the medical people all looking concerned. There would be shots of famous surgeons working over him and he would almost die. The beautiful mother would be there, wounded but recovering, holding his hand, praying for him, and he, too, would recover.

After thinking over the possibilities, Suzanne felt that the cameras should continue with the ambassador. A series of dramatic scenes would show how his life had been shattered because his daughter was missing. And from those scenes the viewer would know that his daughter was the most important thing in the world to him.

His recovery would be slow. But as soon as he regained his strength, he would search for his daughter. He would get out thousands of photographs, making his daughter famous, asking everywhere if anyone had seen her. He would put her picture on milk cartons, in the newspapers, and on television.

Mort said when you had two parallel stories running, you stayed with one until you reached a logical place to leave it, then switched to the other, just like beginning a new movie. So at this point Suzanne would go to the opening she had devised earlier—the establishing shot of the canyon and red barn, the snake man coming in the door, the slow pan of the interior, coming to frame on the ambassador's daughter chained to the wall by the cot in the corner, next to the big snake.

Suzanne had thought and thought, and as yet she did not know where to go from there. She had taken care of all the ingredients Mort said must be contained in the first quarter of a movie—a definition of the dramatic situation and introduction of all principal characters. She had put the heroine in danger. She had introduced the viewer to the family, the snakes, and the snake man.

She was still working on the rest of the story, and how it would end.

She knew she needed to show the story behind the story of the snake man. But she could not imagine what had made him so angry. Once she had tried to ask him some questions about himself. But he said only, "Shut up," and slapped her.

She had not tried again.

For the most part, he ignored her, treating her as if she were a piece of furniture. The only times he seemed to notice her were when he acted ugly.

In school they had taught her that your body is your own. They had brought in a special teacher to tell them what to do if someone did something to you that was wrong. The special teacher said that the person who would do this might be someone you knew well, maybe a friend or even a member of your family. But she said that sometimes sick people took advantage of children. She said to always watch out for Mr. Stranger Danger.

Suzanne decided that the snake man was her Mr. Stranger Danger.

Stymied as to where to go with the daughter's story, she took the cameras back to the ambassador. She would have shots of him hounding the police, and on a horse leading men on searches of rough, western-looking country. There would be long shots of him in boots and outdoorsy clothes, walking vast stretches of landscape, searching, always searching. He would tell his story to Barbara Walters and the whole country would grieve with him.

Imagining it, Suzanne wept for this man whose life had once been so full of fun, now searching for his missing daughter.

She felt weak. She had not eaten for two days. She had managed to hide the heart-shaped pendant her father had given her. She fished it out from under the mattress. Forgetting for the moment about dialogue and camera angles, she held the pendant against her lips and wept in paralyzing fear while the snakes slithered restlessly in the heat of the old red barn.

Booker stood with his back to the wind, the sun warm on his face, waiting beside Nate for the last of the officers to arrive. He felt uncomfortable. His jeans, flannel shirt, and boots had been stored in the trunk of his car for years against outdoor emergencies such as this. The jeans felt tighter than he remembered. The boots were stiff and the shirt was musty.

"Booker, you shouldn't have been so optimistic with the lady," Nate said. "You know damned well what we're liable to find out here."

"I was being honest with her. I don't think the kid's been dumped yet."

Cars and pickups were parked almost bumper to bumper on both sides of the road, on both sides of the creek. County, city, and volunteer officers lounged on the bridge, waiting. Simmons and his specialists were down at the creek with the high school senior who had found the clothing. The boy was talking with Simmons, pointing, showing where he and his girlfriend had walked, and exactly where they had found the clothing.

"I'll give it fifty-fifty odds we'll find the body today," Nate said. "The guy didn't stop at this bridge for tea and cupcakes."

Booker did not answer. He had already stated his belief.

Nate took his silence as argument. "Booker, according to your own theory, he buried one and dumped several others on open ground close to a road. That may be what we'll find here."

Booker was rescued from response by Sheriff Bates, approaching with two deputies in tow. The sheriff wore a big hat that made his head seem small. His pants were tucked into lace-up boots, and his neon-blue nylon jacket was buttoned to the collar against the wind. He spat into the dirt and looked up at Nate. "I count thirty-eight here now," he said. "I believe this is all that's coming. Where you want us?"

"Let's wait till Simmons and his men get through," Nate said. "Then we'll start our sweeps." He looked at Booker. "Thirty-eight men will give us about a hundred-yard swath. That ought to do it, don't you think? Any more than that, they'd be stumbling over each other. Be hard to control."

Booker nodded agreement. He did not add that he would have preferred only a few hand-picked men. To his way of thinking, thirty-eight were too many.

Simmons and the boy came out of the creek bottom, climbing back to the road. The FBI specialists were still at work. Simmons came toward Nate and Booker, the boy following. He was a good-looking teenager, clean-cut, soft-spoken, and polite, the type that gave Booker yet some hope for the country's future.

"We're about through," Simmons said. "You can start any time now."

"Find anything?" Nate asked, watching the specialists.

"Not really. Ground's hard down there. No footprints. We're just gathering comparison samples of soil, pollen, plants, in case they're needed."

Nate spoke to the sheriff. "Okay. Let's get the men over here, and we'll get organized."

The sheriff motioned and the officers came to the end of the bridge and gathered around.

Nate raised his voice. "Most of you have done this kind of thing before, so you know what to expect. For those of you who haven't, here's the way we'll work it. First we'll go up this side of the creek. We'll form a line, with intervals just close enough you can join hands with the man on either side of you. Look for footprints, any clothing or trash, anything that doesn't belong. Keep a sharp eye out for soft dirt, any place where it looks like anyone may have done any digging. We'll take it slow and easy. This isn't a race. We don't want to miss anything. Check out every inch. If you see anything, stop right where you are and sing out. We'll give the FBI forensic people a first look at it. I guess that's it."

"What kind of pattern will we follow?" Sheriff Bates asked.

"We've already searched along the road here," Nate said. "We'll now go downstream to the next section line, cross over the bridge there, and come back the other side of the creek. We'll do the same going upstream. Then we'll spread out from there."

Silently the officers walked down the slope from the bridge, climbed over the barbed-wire fence, and began to form the line. The three deputies in waders who were to walk the creek stood together in the water, helping each other make last-minute strap adjustments.

"Shit," Nate said.

Booker followed his gaze. Television trucks were coming over a hill in the distance.

"Anybody got yellow tape?" Nate asked.

"I have a roll or two in my car," Sheriff Bates said.

"It'll take more'n that," Nate said. "Let's string it from each end of the bridge and along the fences, both sides of the creek, as far as we got tape. Let's declare this whole pasture a crime scene. Corral them here on the bridge."

Sheriff Bates called to deputies and walked toward his car. Booker did not want to hang around to be a part of the hassle with the media, especially not in clothing with five-year-old smells and wrinkles. He walked down the slope and joined the search.

He chose the end of the line nearest the creek. Walking there would be more difficult, but he believed that if any evidence was found, it would be along the creek, and he felt himself far more qualified to find it than the younger officers.

The line was formed, the intervals tested by joining hands. Then they began moving slowly.

The ground was broken by abundant dry washes. Booker stopped and knelt often, studying the ground carefully before going on.

Farther downstream, tangled brush and vines made progress difficult. The pace was slowed by the men wading the creek, who stumbled along over rocks, sunken tree limbs, beer bottles, and other trash on the uneven bottom.

By the time the line reached the next bridge, they had acquired a harvest that consisted mostly of cans, plastic bottles, condoms, and abandoned fishing gear.

They found nothing that appeared to have any bearing on the case.

The sweep back on the opposite side of the creek took even more time. The news contingent was waiting with cameras trained from the bridge. Booker arrived back at the cars tired, joints aching, his feet blistered from the stiff boots. But he made himself stay with the search through the sweep upstream, and back down again.

Toward noon, dogs were brought in—long-eared, sad-eyed bloodhounds. They sniffed the hillsides and ridges. They found two dead 'possums, but no trace of Suzanne's body.

13

Harold slowed in front of the post office, braked, and turned the wheel to park at the curb, carefully adhering to the white stripes on the pavement. TEN MINUTE PARKING, the sign said. He checked Sam's watch but continued to sit in the truck another full minute, assembling his courage. Even after three years, every time he went to look in the post office box he half expected to be stopped and questioned. He was ready with a story, just in case. But that did not make it easier.

He took a deep breath, left the truck, walked up the wide steps, and entered through the big, high doors. People were coming and going and there was a long line in front of the windows where you bought stamps. No one was anywhere near Sam's box in the corner of the lobby. Harold walked to it, peeked in, and saw nothing. He opened it and felt inside, just to be sure.

He returned to the truck disappointed but relieved. When the box contained letters, he liked the feeling of communication, and he badly needed new orders. Sam's money was about gone. At the moment he had only the order from the man in Phoenix who wanted a hundred big rattlesnake heads to put in Lucite cubes for the tourist shops. Only seventy heads were left in the freezer. Most were just average. He must now go out and find at least forty or fifty giant rattlers. He could not risk sending the smaller heads. Sam always said competition was so keen, you should always deliver top-class merchandise.

Harold had learned the hard way that Sam knew what he was talking about. Two months ago the big laboratory had refused to pay for a bad batch of venom. They had not sent an order since. And the man who bought skins had complained that many in the last batch were not properly preserved. Harold knew he must be more careful and deliver exactly what they ordered. If this man in

148

Phoenix wanted big snake heads, that was exactly what he would get. Harold knew of two good places to find them—in the Wichita Mountains, and in the Texas Panhandle at a place just below the Caprock.

Trouble was, the days were now too hot. Sam had told him that snakes could not tolerate extremes in temperature. When they got hot, they hunted shade. In the Wichitas they went down beneath the big boulders, too far to be driven out. But Sam had showed him canyons out in the Texas Panhandle where snakes did not have good places to hide. They squeezed into crevices and crawled under rocks and roots. Sam had showed him where to look. A squirt of gasoline mist always brought them out.

So now he was on his way to the Texas Panhandle. There he would snare maybe fifty or more of the really big fuckers. Big enough that the man in Phoenix could not complain, and would have to pay. The trip would take a couple of days. By the time he returned, Sam would be half starved, hungry enough to eat and digest the tough little bitch.

Harold grinned in anticipation, imagining how it would be when he shoved her into the cage with Sam.

He drove to the interstate entrance ramp, flicked his left blinkers, and mounted the access road into the westbound lanes. Big trucks roared past him, doing seventy and eighty miles an hour. He accelerated to find a comfortable niche among them.

The miles sped by so fast that he arrived at the turnoff for home before he had sufficient time to consider whether he wanted to go that way. He was tempted to drive down by the old place. Not to visit. He had not been home to talk to anyone in three years. But two or three times a month he drove down there and sneaked up to the house in the evenings, just to see what the hell was going on.

He had spied on his family hour after hour, and they never dreamed he was within a hundred miles.

His sisters were growing up. But his mother was the same.

She had not changed in all the time he had known her.

He eased into the right lane and almost made the turn onto the exit ramp. But at the last moment the thought came to him that he had no time to fart around on this trip.

He had to get those snake heads off to the man in Phoenix.

He drove past the exit and continued on west.

Still, he liked to think about home, the way it had been in his early years. Some good memories were mixed in with the bad.

When he thought hard, he could still remember his father. Thick, dark hair, heavy black eyebrows, and that slow, go-to-hell grin. In his oldest, best-preserved memories, Harold could see him, dangling a hand-rolled cigarette from the corner of his mouth, one eye slightly closed against the smoke, while he worked with his hands, making leather wallets, belts, watch fobs, and such shit.

He had taught Harold how to hand-roll cigarettes. He always let Harold lick the paper to seal the roll. Sometimes he let Harold have a puff or two.

Life had been good then. His father had kept Mom in her place. When arguments flared, his father always won.

But there were bad times, too, like when his mother whipped him almost every morning for wetting the bed. Harold still remembered how it had been, peeling off his wet pajamas, knowing what was coming. His mother kept a willow switch as big as his thumb. Every morning she would flay his naked backside, leaving him wailing in pain. Often she threatened to tie his penis shut with a cord. He would run and hide, knowing she might. But she never did. Every night he would stay awake as long as he could, trying to keep from wetting the bed. But every time he would drift off and awake in a puddle and again feel the willow switch lashing his butt.

That happened hundreds of times.

Eventually his mother put newspapers down on the cement floor of the back porch and told him he must sleep there until he became housebroken. She fed him there, too, on the back porch, like a dog.

Then Harold's sisters came along like a string of firecrackers. They were all skinny like his mother. Carbon copies. Beverly, Marla, Linda, and Jonell. His mother cooed and carried on over each baby until it began to grow up and the next one came along.

Suddenly the house was full of women. His two grandmothers lived nearby. They were in the house every day, all day. His aunt Helen left her husband, moved back home, and she was usually there too.

His father was gone more and more, and each time he returned, there was a big cuss fight. One night after a big argument that lasted until morning, his father stomped out.

"You're a hopeless bitch," he told Harold's mother. "I can't live with you anymore."

And that was the last time Harold ever saw him.

Harold's grandfathers had died long before he was born. He had no brothers or uncles. He was left alone with eight women in the small house. And all eight were on his ass every waking moment. *Tuck in your shirttail! Comb your hair! Tie your shoelaces! Stop running through the house! Close your mouth, you look like a moron! Quit standing like that, it'll give you round shoulders!*

Don't you have a handkerchief? How long have you worn that shirt? We're busy. Can't you go outside and play?

They were a solid clique. They always had something going on and he was left out of it. He did not seem to know how to make friends. The rejection he received at home followed him around like a cloud. Growing up, he spent more and more time alone.

So when Buster Claybough showed him some pictures and invited him over to his house by the school, Harold did not have to think twice.

The pictures were of a girl about seven, and she was naked. In most of them she had her legs spread, and she was laughing into the camera, having fun.

Harold looked at the pictures spellbound. Buster said he had more that Harold might like to see, of girls doing everything imaginable.

From the first, Buster had established firm rules: Harold could come over to his house anytime between the end of the schoolday and nine in the evening. He could help himself to the Cokes and beer in the refrigerator, and to the candy, crackers, and potato chips in the pantry. He could look at the pictures anytime he wanted, as long as he put them back in the bedroom drawer.

Harold had known Buster for years but had hardly noticed him before. Buster drove the school bus and did janitor work. Now Harold could see that Buster was a smart guy, maybe smarter than any of the teachers.

Buster wore khakis like a uniform. His shirt and trousers were always clean and sharply creased. He was a neat guy, and good-looking, with a square jaw, lean build, and deep blue eyes.

One hot afternoon Harold lay on the bed, looking at the pictures. Buster reached over and stroked him. "Let's take the edge off that," he said.

Almost as if in a dream, Harold concentrated on the pictures and allowed Buster to do whatever he wanted.

He liked what Buster did. But at the same time he was repelled. He did not know what to think.

Buster always offered Harold a treat. At first there were pills that made him feel good. Sometimes they smoked grass. Buster said he had a straight pipeline to the border and could get anything he wanted. After a time, they did heroin. Buster showed him how to cook and mainline the stuff.

Floating on a cloud of heroin, Harold became more at ease with the different things Buster did. He just put his mind into neutral and left it blank.

Buster asked him to bring other boys over. Harold showed some pictures to three boys in his class and they also began to visit Buster's house.

Harold watched the other boys go through the same experiences—pills, marijuana, the weird sessions on the bed.

Almost every afternoon for a year they partied, drinking beer, eating potato chips, watching television, doing pot or heroin. When Buster messed with the other boys, Harold felt both relieved and jealous. Watching Buster at work, he began to see the effectiveness of Buster's line of bullshit. Buster could make kids do whatever he wanted. Sometimes, when they were all high on dope, Buster would take pictures of them fooling around. He said he had friends in other parts of the country who refused to believe they had so much fun.

Word got around. Other kids came.

Harold began to feel that he was beyond some of what was happening. He started imitating Buster, manipulating the younger boys. Buster got a big kick out of that. He praised Harold for "learning real quick."

Then, after more than a year, someone squealed. Harold never knew exactly who. The cops came, gathered up all the pictures, and put Buster in jail.

Buster had told Harold that this might happen someday. He said not to worry, that the cops would try to scare them, but that the cops could do nothing. Harold halfway believed Buster. So when the police took Harold down to the station and questioned him, he said they had just looked at the pictures and fooled around. He denied he ever saw any of the things the cops claimed.

But the cops talked to everyone, including Harold's mother. She pitched a temper tantrum and whipped him, this time with one of his father's old belts. She was madder over the embarrassment than about what he had done. She said the whole town knew and that she, his sisters, and his grandmothers would be the ones to suffer.

In the end, Buster won, just like he said he would. The cops could do nothing. The parents of the other boys refused to allow them to testify. Harold's mother also refused. So the cops were forced to turn Buster loose. The only charge they brought against him was for possession of the pictures.

After Buster hired a lawyer, they dropped that charge too.

During the time Buster was in jail, the school board fired him. After he was released, he threatened to sue, and the school paid him a bunch of money.

"They could've done more to me for spitting on the sidewalk," he told Harold, laughing. "With the money they paid me, I could take that kind of trouble every day."

But Buster said the cops were watching and it might be best if Harold did not come around for a while.

A few weeks later Buster disappeared, just like Harold's father.

After that, life was different. Everyone in town knew what had happened at Buster's house and who was involved. Two of the boys were taken to another part of the state by their parents. The others told around that it was Harold who got them in trouble. People shied away from him. No one at school would speak to him or acknowledge his presence. The teachers never called on him. He might as well have been an empty chair for all the attention he got in class.

One night at a baseball game, a bunch of girls gathered around a praying mantis clinging to a light pole. They were giggling and squealing over the human-looking face, and the way the mantis followed them with its eyes. On impulse, Harold reached past them, grabbed the mantis, popped it into his mouth, chewed it, and swallowed it.

The girls went into hysterics. Some threw up. The commotion stopped the ball game. The school principal came and lectured Harold, telling him that what he had done was disgusting, uncivilized.

But the next day at school Harold found everyone talking about it. There were doubters. So Harold ate more bugs to prove the story true. Afterward, he would eat a bug for a quarter and, for fifty cents, a live cockroach.

He made money for a while, doing that. There was a trick to it. He learned to bite them in two early so they would stop kicking. And if you chewed them good before touching them with your tongue, the taste was not bad.

Eating bugs brought him a lot of attention, but no friends.

At home his situation grew worse. His sisters started calling him Harold the Horrid. They must have told it around, because soon that was what everybody called him.

But he found a way to get even. While his mother was at work he masturbated in front of his sisters, chasing them all over the house while they ran and screamed and cried.

Each time he did it his mother whipped him. He savored the pain, knowing that like Buster, he was winning.

And each time, she threatened to call the police.

But of course she never did.

One afternoon while he was chasing his sisters a bunch of stuff shot out, scaring him until he remembered that Buster had told him it would happen someday.

His hatred grew with every beating.

At night he would take his hunting knife, slip into his mother's room, and stand over her while she slept. Hour after hour he held the knife over her, thinking how easy it would be to stop the beatings.

He knew that some night he would do it. Only one thing stopped him: He relished the sense of holding her life in his hands. If he killed her, that would end.

He invented other diversions. At night he crept into his sisters' rooms and masturbated into their hair. The screams and wailing the next morning as they washed their hair was more than worth the beating his mother gave him. His sisters would be late for school and his mother late for work. She would threaten to call the police, but again she never did.

At fourteen he quit school. Nobody seemed to notice. He felt great relief. No longer was he required to face that wall of silence every day.

His only real problem was money. He did odd jobs on surrounding farms, cleaning barns, clearing brush, loading hay. He racked balls and swept out at the pool hall. He fixed flats and greased cars at service stations. No job lasted long. He was forever broke.

In his fifteenth summer, during the annual Rattlesnake Derby, he learned that he could make money catching rattlesnakes.

Every year during the derby a carnival came to town and set up their rides, game booths, and sideshows. There was a downtown parade, and at night on the square they had an old fiddlers' contest, hog calling, pig kissing, and whatever else stupid the merchants could think up.

Harold had been hanging around the derby almost since he was in diapers. But not until that summer did he learn what it was all about.

Dealers came and bought rattlesnakes by the pound. Harold knew shit about snakes, but he figured that if other people could catch them, he could. He went out into the mesquite brakes west of town, snared a few, and sold them.

At night he hung around the carnival rides and snake pits, listening to the girls squeal.

It was at the snake pits that he met Sam, who was there paying top price for the best rattlers.

A small man, rotund and red of face, Sam was first and foremost a talker. He opened his acquaintance with Harold by asking a barrage of questions. Of course most of Harold's answers were lies. He said his father had been killed in Vietnam, and that he was just farting around, waiting until he was old enough to join the marines.

Sam said he had a bad heart and could not do heavy lifting. He hired Harold to load the snakes he had bought. Talking all the time, he showed Harold how to handle them without getting bit. Sam said he was on his way to another rattlesnake festival.

He offered Harold a job.

Harold learned more in his first few weeks with Sam than he had from eight years of formal education. Sam talked almost incessantly. During the three years Harold was with him, Sam probably described every significant incident in his life, along with the lessons he had learned.

He was a man of firm opinions.

"Never have anything to do with banks," he warned over and over. "The government will be down on your ass in a minute. Always take cash, money orders. Never give anybody your social security number or your address. That way the sons of bitches can never find you."

Sam taught Harold how to hunt and snare snakes. In a few hours they would bag more snakes than Harold had been able to find in all his hunting before he met Sam.

Traveling around, Sam taught him the snake business. Sam sold the rattles and heads to the curio trade, the skins to the leather industry, the venom to the scientific laboratories, and the meat to the specialty food companies.

"They sell most of the meat to Europe, Japan," Sam said. "Those Japs will eat fish heads, anything."

He taught Harold how to pack, ship, and bill for each shipment. He allowed Harold to sleep in the red barn with the snakes.

Sam lived in a small rented house in town.

"Never own property," Sam said. "You have to sign away your fucking life. In the long run, rent's cheaper. And nobody gives a shit who you are."

Sam carried a little tin box in his shirt pocket and kept popping pills from it. Harold thought they were speed, until one night Sam told him what they were. "Nitroglycerin for my heart. If I ever pass out on you, just put one of these under my tongue. It'll bring me around."

Over the months Sam grew sicker. Harold performed more and more of the work. He milked the snakes of venom, skinned them, and trimmed and packed the meat. The people at the dry ice place and in the freight offices came to know him as Sam's assistant.

In season Sam and Harold drove into the Wichita Mountains, the rough country below the Caprock in the Texas Panhandle, the canyons along the Cimarron and Canadian rivers, anywhere there was rough, sparsely inhabited country.

"That's where you'll find snakes," Sam said. "They don't like to be around people. Shows their good sense. If I ever come back in another life, I want it to be as a snake."

Sam would take Harold to a mountain or canyon and give him a hand-drawn map showing the best snake dens. Harold received the full benefit of Sam's thirty-five years of snake hunting.

Sam liked to visit whores. He said it was the only way to have sex without being saddled with a woman. He tried to get Harold to go with him. Twice Harold did. Both efforts were failures. Harold could not get rid of his fear that if he stuck his penis in there, he might not get it back.

If Sam knew of Harold's failures—if the whores talked—Sam never mentioned it.

Then came the night that Sam passed out. Harold put one of the little pills under his tongue. Sure enough, Sam came around. But he looked terrible. His face was pale and his lips blue.

"This one's bad," Sam whispered. "Maybe you better drive me to the hospital."

They were in Sam's car, not the truck. Sam remained conscious long enough to give directions. But when Harold drove into the ambulance port at the hospital, Sam was out cold. Harold ran inside and got help. They wheeled Sam into the hospital on a stretcher. Harold told the hospital people Sam's name and nothing else. They searched for Sam's billfold. Harold knew Sam kept his billfold stuffed under the seat in his car. But he did not tell the hospital people. The billfold was full of information Sam always kept to himself.

To avoid more questions, Harold left the hospital.

Late that night when he phoned, a woman at the hospital said Sam had died. Harold did not return to the hospital. He did not ask what they did with Sam's body. As far as he knew, they could have chopped him up, packed him in dry ice, and sold him to the Japanese.

Harold drove Sam's car back to the red barn. Not knowing what to do, he did nothing.

After two weeks he drove the pickup into town and past the place where Sam had lived. The house looked different. Two men were painting it. Someone had hauled off the junk Sam kept at the back.

But no one came to the red barn. So Harold stayed.

After a month he got up enough nerve to go look in the post office box. He knew its location, because Sam usually avoided climbing the post office steps and sent him in to get the mail.

The box was full of orders. At last Harold knew what to do.

He went to work, filling them.

So he had kept the snake business going, just as if Sam were still alive. He shipped the goods. The money orders came back. They were in Sam's name, but Harold had Sam's identification. If anyone asked, he planned to say he was working for Sam.

And in a way, he was.

Not long after Sam's death a notice came saying the rent on the red barn was due. The realty firm wanted a lot of money. Harold dug out Sam's cash box, buried in the corner of the barn, and sent them money orders. Every few months he found a slip in the post office box saying the rent on it was due. Each time, heart pounding, Harold went to the counter and paid in cash.

Thus far, no one had asked any questions.

But after the first few months, the old familiar loneliness returned. Around Sam's constant talk, Harold had never been required to have a thought of his own. Now he again was surrounded by silence. His head was empty. He had nothing but his fantasies for entertainment.

It was like after Buster left, when his sisters and everyone started calling him Harold the Horrid, and he had felt so terribly alone.

One night he went back by home, parked the truck down the street, and slipped up to the house in the dark. They were all there—his sisters, his grandmothers, his aunt, his mother. He stood in the dark for a long time and listened to their shit.

Later that night he sneaked in and stood over his mother for a long time, holding the knife, listening to her breathe, feeling the power. His sisters were sleeping soundly. He lingered in their bedrooms much of the night, masturbating into their hair.

He had no idea what happened the next morning. He did not wait around to see. But when he went back two weeks later, deadbolt locks had been put on all the doors. Burglar bars guarded the windows, and he could not get in.

During the first spring after Sam's death Harold made all the rattlesnake derbies and festivals. The activity helped take his mind off his loneliness. At each festival he set up Sam's canvas pits and bought snakes, following Sam's practice of paying top price for top quality. He attracted crowds by working in the rattlesnake pits barefoot, pants legs rolled up, showing off. When coveys of girls squealed and squirmed at the sight, he picked up rattlesnakes with his bare hands and pretended he intended to toss them into the group. He did it just to hear them scream. Festival officials came around and told him to quit doing that. Once a girl's boyfriend threatened to whip him.

In the midst of the crowds, Harold felt ever more alone.

Pressures he did not understand built in him.

One afternoon in late summer he stopped at a Sno-Kone stand. He had been in the Wichita Mountains all afternoon and he was hot and thirsty. A group of kids was lined up at the window. A girl of about six stood off to one side, crying. Remembering Buster's line of bullshit, Harold asked her what was wrong. She said she had lost the money her mother had given her for a Sno-Kone.

Harold bought her a Sno-Kone and told her to get into the truck. She did. No one was paying any attention. So he simply drove off with her, just as he had daydreamed of doing maybe a thousand times.

When she began crying and tried to jump out of the truck, he told her to shut up and knocked her to the floorboards.

He kept her in the truck two days. Again he felt that incredible sense of power he had known standing over his mother, over his sisters. This was even better. He had this one completely under his control, crying and whimpering.

But he knew he had done a dumb thing. He had not planned ahead. He could not take her back and turn her loose. She could describe him and the truck. He thought of taking her to the red barn, but Sam was not long dead. Someone might come nosing around. In desperation he finally hit her in the head with a rock and dropped her body in a storm drain on the outskirts of Lubbock, in a new development where streets and curbs had been built, but not the houses.

He doubted the body would ever be found.

In the days that followed he kept thinking about it, reliving it. Sometimes he would drive hundreds of miles without being aware of his surroundings, fondly remembering how it had been, standing in his mother's bedroom, and how it had been in the pickup with the weepy one on the floorboard.

He was determined that next time he would not be so dumb. He would plan ahead.

Gradually he was becoming more confident in running Sam's operation. Twice at festivals some old farts asked about Sam. Harold told them that Sam was not feeling good, and had sent him to buy the rattlesnakes. The explanation seemed sufficient. And no one had come around the barn asking questions.

Slowly he worked the red barn into his fantasies.

Then he set out to turn his fantasies into reality.

He installed a ring bolt in the corner by the spare cot where Sam sometimes slept when he was too drunk to drive home. At hardware stores hundreds of miles apart, Harold purchased lengths of chain and padlocks. Using Sam's tools out of the box in the pickup, he knocked holes in the pipe-framed front door and snaked a chain through.

Now he kept the red barn chained shut while he was away, just in case anyone came nosing around.

The barn was well isolated. The nearest neighbor was almost eight miles away.

By the end of that first summer, Harold felt he was ready.

He took the next one from a traveling carnival at Pawhuska. She was Indian-looking and a fighter. But when he got her back to the red barn and chained to the wall, she was subdued. She refused to eat, cried all the time, and became sickly. He beat her to death with his fists because she would not do what he told her.

But again he had not planned ahead. He hauled the body around in his truck two days before he found a good place to dump it.

That winter he picked up and killed two more, one up in Kansas and the other in Arkansas. But the experience was never as good as he thought it would be. They died too easily. He wanted them screaming and begging.

Then one night at a carnival near Antlers he saw a twenty-foot python. He overheard the owner bragging that the snake could kill and swallow a good-sized hog. The man said that in India and in South America pythons killed and swallowed full-grown oxen.

The man said pythons would not eat anything they had not killed themselves. He explained that they did not kill by crushing, like most people thought, but by suffocation, squeezing steadily to prevent the victim from breathing. He said that every time the victim exhaled, the snake tightened his grip, preventing any intake of breath.

Excited, Harold saw that as the perfect solution. A big python would scare the shit out of them, make them scream, do the killing, *and* dispose of the body.

He searched the classifieds in Sam's snake magazines and found that pythons were not rare. Carnivals, tent shows, and zoos swapped them all the time.

The only difficulty was that most were too small.

Harold kept hunting. Eventually he found a twenty-two-footer.

He tried that one with mixed results on a girl of about seven he picked up in Kansas. The snake stalked her around the cage for two days, but never attempted a kill.

Harold, for once jaded with all the screaming, finally had to do the job himself.

The owner had told him that the snake had been raised on chickens, and that anything else he fed it should smell like chickens. Harold tried using chicken blood, chicken manure, and chicken feathers, but the snake refused to be fooled. Harold concluded it had never attempted to kill and eat anything bigger than a chicken, and did not know how.

He went in search of a larger snake. He found several and bought them.

All proved equally disappointing.

One, a twenty-two-footer, did manage to kill a seven-year-old he had picked up at a trailer park near Plainview. The snake tried to swallow her. But when she was halfway down, the snake threw up and would not try again, leaving Harold with a slimy, saliva-covered mess he buried more than a hundred miles away.

That same snake tried again with a six-year-old he picked up on a country road early one morning near Fairmont. The snake stalked her for hours, and eventually killed her. But he would not try to swallow her. Harold dumped the body in a lake, hoping the fish would eat her.

Then he heard about a huge snake for sale in Alabama. He drove there to look at it. The owners—dispersing a bankrupt sideshow—claimed the python was thirty-two feet long. Harold was sure they were lying. He doubted the snake was more than twenty-eight or thirty. But on first glance he knew he had found a giant among snakes.

The owners said the snake had killed and eaten grown hogs for years.

From the first, Harold had felt a strange rapport with the big python. But not until he brought it back to the red barn and installed it in its own cage did he understand why.

The snake's eyes eerily duplicated the way Sam had looked at him hundreds of times. The resemblance was so strong that Harold half expected the snake to start talking. And the more he was around the snake, the more he became convinced that Sam Chambers truly had returned to life in the form of a snake, as he had wished to do.

That had been more than a year ago. Since then, Sam had killed, swallowed, and digested six little bitches.

Now Sam was hungry again, ready for the next.

Ａs Harold drove on west toward the state line, a half-formed worry nagged at the corners of his mind. For miles he sought the source but could not grasp it. Then it came to him: He had not changed the license plates.

At the next exit he left the interstate. He remembered stopping there once before. A crossroad ran under the highway. Big pilings, connected by concrete braces, supported the overpass. Behind the tall foundation for the pilings ran a road where, Harold supposed, teenagers came to do dope and make out.

He drove up behind the pilings and circled around until the truck was hidden from the crossroad.

Interstate traffic continued to thunder overhead, unseen.

He climbed into the bed of the truck and dug in the bottom of the toolbox. There he kept six sets of license plates, filched from used car lots, parked trucks, and salvage yards. He made it a practice to put on bogus tags for a few days when he thought there was any possibility that the cops might be looking for him. That was what had been bothering him. He had not remembered to change the tags since grabbing the little tough one near the burning car.

Flipping through the metal plates, he selected a set he had not used for quite a while. Taken from a used car lot, the tags probably had been forgotten by the cops.

After changing the tags, he peeled out of his khaki uniform, folded it neatly, slipped it into its protective plastic wrappers, and placed it in the toolbox. He put his hat into its bag and returned it to the toolbox along with his snakeskin boots. He pulled on dungarees, a blue work shirt, and the gimme cap that said JOHN DEERE. He fished his shit-kicker brogans from the toolbox, slipped his feet into them, and laced them up.

He had hard, sweaty work to do in the Texas canyons. He did not want to muss his good clothes.

The idea for the uniform had come to him not long after Sam's death. Driving along the interstate one day, his attention had been seized by a cigarette billboard. In it a big cowboy-looking guy that reminded him of Buster was gazing into the distance, holding a cigarette. Harold had pulled onto the shoulder of the road, stopped, and studied the picture. Up close, the guy looked even more like Buster. But what intrigued Harold most was the guy's clothes. The shirt was especially neat, and seemed to convey authority. It was much like Buster's uniform, but better. Harold liked those button-down things on the shoulders and the creased, starched look. The hat, too, was different, with higher crown and wider brim than most of those in cowboy movies.

During the next few weeks Harold searched through the stores, but found nothing resembling what he wanted. Then, a month later, in a sporting goods store near Amarillo, he found a salesman who knew instantly what he was talking about.

"I have just the shirt," the man said. "The Swiss Army shirt. Epaulets. Four-button cuffs. Patch pockets. I can fix you up."

He led Harold to the back of the store and there it was, the exact same shirt he had seen on the cigarette man.

Harold bought a half dozen, along with matching trousers. The guy even told him a good place to have the outfit laundered and ironed to get the sharp creases.

"Those shirts are popular with law officers," the guy said. "I sell quite a few of them."

Harold later found the hat in a western outfitters. And in a pawn shop, he bought the badge that said DEPUTY.

Dressed in his new clothes, Harold felt like a different person. He had more self-confidence. People seemed to treat him with more respect. And when he told the little bitches to get into the truck, they did.

He now wore the outfit most of the time while traveling. But sometimes he grew tired of the watchfulness it imposed. At times the outfit came close to attracting too much attention.

To relax, and for work, he liked to go back to the way he was before Sam died. In dungarees, work shirt, gimme cap, and brogans, he blended in. Nobody noticed him. He always wore his old clothes when he went prowling around in the small towns. And prowling had become a big part of his life.

He had learned to hide Sam's truck or car by parking at all-night cafés, or around used car lots and garages. He then went on foot, snooping through a town in the dark, never allowing himself to be seen.

In his snake hunting, he had noticed that jackrabbits, snakes, and lizards can hide by remaining perfectly still, becoming a part of their surroundings.

Imitating them, he often stood at the back of houses, sometimes for hours, listening and watching what went on inside, figuring out relationships, what was what, who slept where. He always carried some snake meat laced with strychnine to take care of any dogs that bothered him.

Over the years he had come to know several towns well. He knew houses where widows lived alone. Sometimes he slipped in, stood over them with his knife, and listened to them sleep. He liked to do that. He was sure nothing on earth could top the heady power of permitting the old bitches to live another day, another week. Sometimes he stole a clock or a vase, or maybe moved some shit around just to show them he had been there.

He also knew where little bitches lived, and where they slept, in a dozen towns.

He had not yet taken a little bitch from her home. But he thought a lot about it.

Eventually, he probably would.

Not long after Sam died, Harold bought a .357 magnum Smith & Wesson Model 66. The guy who sold it to him claimed the gun had been made especially for the FBI. Harold kept it with him in the truck. Sometimes he daydreamed of going back home some night and wiping out his whole family, blowing their heads off one by one.

At other times he daydreamed of using his knife on them, going from room to room, slitting throats. That was probably what he would do some night.

But on this trip he needed to concentrate on making money. He had squandered almost all of Sam's cash buying the pythons. Sam's old pickup was wearing out. The car was not in much better shape. Soon the rent would come due again on the red barn. That would take another big chunk of money. His carelessness in sending the bad venom and the half-tanned skins had cut his income almost to zero.

But if he could find some quality snakes on this trip, he might squeeze by.

He estimated that this trip would take two days.

When he returned, Sam would be plenty ready to eat.

Thus far, the little tough one had been a disappointment. She seldom made a sound. He had yet to get a single scream out of her.

He drove on west, daydreaming of what was to come. He would see if the little tough one could keep from screaming after he shoved her into the cage with Sam.

14

Healing nicely," Peterson said. "No sign of infection."

Rachel lay reclined on the examining table, her head on a level with Peterson's chest. He had removed her bandages, donned fresh surgical gloves, and was now cleaning the scalp wound. A nurse was at his elbow, passing the swabs.

"I'm afraid to ask for a mirror," Rachel said. "It must look bizarre up there."

"Actually, it's rather appealing," Peterson said. "You could start a new style on MTV, get an electric guitar, jump around, and make a lot of money."

"I may do that," Rachel said. "I hate wigs. I never thought I'd ever wear one."

"I'll bet you'd look super in a gamin cut," the nurse said. "You should grow out to that in no time."

Peterson finished with the cleaning and applied new dressings and bandage wrap. He finished by tapping her on the shoulder. "That should do it. When you're ready, come on into the office."

He walked out, closing the door behind him.

With her broken arm, Rachel encountered difficulty leaving the examination table. The nurse helped her.

Rachel was tired and emotionally drained. She had been on the phone most of the night, returning calls long overdue to her mother, to Bill's parents, and to friends and acquaintances in New York. Her longtime protégé at the publishing house wanted to take a leave of absence and come to Oklahoma to help. Rachel eventually convinced her that the trip would be futile. But it had been a long, emotionally draining conversation. Other friends had wept and commiserated with her at length.

She had emerged depressed. In all, she had managed less than three hours of sleep.

She found Peterson seated at his desk, scribbling on records she assumed to be her own. He gestured to a chair without looking up. He also looked tired. Rachel knew he had just completed a twelve-hour shift, then stayed overtime for her examination, missing dawn from his patio. His long, angular face was intent. He looked up at her, his expression still serious. "You're coming along much better than we could have expected," he said. "Your scalp is closing nicely. That's a relief. Your arm and shoulder look good on the X rays. I feel easier about the concussion. No news in that department is good news."

"What about this swelling and discoloration on my face? Dark bruises were bad enough. This sickly green is worse."

Peterson smiled. "Count your blessings. If the cheekbone had collapsed, you could have lost that eye. Under the circumstances, green looks good to me."

"I guess I can live with it," Rachel said. "Lord knows I have no time for vanity."

Peterson leaned forward and studied the records. "You're still losing weight. That worries me. You're down almost ten pounds from the time they brought you in. You don't have that much to spare."

"As I've told you, all of my mother's family are thin."

"Thin is thin, and gaunt is gaunt. You're burning more calories a day than you're taking in. How many meals are you skipping a day? What do you have for breakfast?"

"Toast and coffee."

Peterson grimaced. "Lunch?"

"Someone brings me a sandwich."

"Dinner?"

Rachel hesitated. Her night out with Booker had been an exception. Mostly she had been going to bed without eating.

Peterson did not wait for an answer. "Take time for your health. You owe it to yourself, to Suzanne."

Rachel nodded, signaling she would. "How's David doing?"

"Physically, ahead of schedule. We made an X-ray series yesterday. His bones are knitting. But I'm now worried about his mental condition. His therapy is painful, wearing. He's bored. He has nothing to occupy his mind except to lie there and worry about his sister. He doesn't have the outlets you do."

Rachel had not yet had time to think through all that. "What can I do?"

"Do you have family?"

"Only my mother, along with aunts and cousins. My mother wants to fly down. I've discouraged her. Should I tell her to come?"

Peterson dodged the question. "Why did you discourage her?"

Normally Rachel would never have discussed her relationship with her mother. Even in psychotherapy that had been a difficult subject. But she felt the need of advice. "Mother's a very strong person. Pushy. She tends to take charge. I didn't want to have to contend with her, along with everything else. I have all I can do as it is."

"How is she with David?"

Rachel was not sure how far she wanted to go in taking Peterson into her confidence. But after brief reflection she decided he might tell her if she was doing the right thing. "Mother doesn't seem to know much about children. I don't know why. She never treated me as a child even when I was one. It's complicated."

He waited, making no comment, allowing her to say as much as she wanted. She made a snap decision to go all the way.

"My father committed suicide when I was barely nine. He lost his money almost overnight in commodities and couldn't face it. My mother was forced to go to work. She put me through college. My debt to her can never be repaid. But she has always treated me as an adult—more like a younger sister than a daughter. I had no childhood. I don't mean just more responsibilities at an early age because of the circumstances. It goes beyond that. In therapy, years later, I came to realize that my mother didn't know *how* to treat a child. She refuses to tolerate weakness in herself or in others. She views childhood as a period of weakness and stupidity. She treats David and Suzanne as adults and ridicules their childish ways. She's puzzled when they respond as children."

"Then you're probably right in keeping her at bay. David badly needs parental attention right now. He's a scared little boy. He needs to be treated as one."

"So what can I do? I know I should be spending hours with him every day. But I can't. Surely you can see that."

"I have a suggestion. It wouldn't take much of your time. Why don't you just call him two or three times a day. Tell him what you're doing. Maybe ask him questions about Suzanne, what she'd do under certain circumstances. He probably knows her as well as anyone. Give him a role in all of this."

Rachel lowered her head into her free hand. "I didn't realize I was neglecting him so. I feel suitably chastised."

Peterson raised a palm. "No! I didn't mean it that way. It's just that I'm in a position to see things you're not. The other night one of the nurses found David crying for his sister. For a time he was inconsolable. That moved me. It moved all of us here at the hospital. He's a bright, intelligent, lovable boy. He has a good idea of what's happening, and he can guess the rest. He's frightened. He needs reassurance.''

"And I have so little to offer. I should be sleeping in his room instead of in that motel.''

"No. You need your rest. I know the hours you're working. David understands the demands on you. It's just that two or three phone calls a day would mean much to him.''

"I'll do that,'' Rachel promised. "Starting today.''

"When he gets more mobile, I'd like to take him out to the ranch for visits if it's all right with you.''

"That would be very kind. I would appreciate that.''

"Consider it part of the therapy. His, and mine.''

Never before had Dr. Peterson referred even obliquely to his own tragedy. Rachel left his office wondering if by word or gesture she had inadvertently violated Donna's trust, and given Peterson some hint that she was aware of his own pain.

Rachel reached David's room just as he was finishing breakfast. The nurse's aide was gathering up the debris. She picked up the tray, acknowledged Rachel with a smile, and left the room. Rachel leaned over David's bed and hugged him. She felt his hot tears on her cheek. "Are we going to find Suzanne?" he asked.

Rachel squeezed him tighter, prolonging the moment, trying to think of an honest yet encouraging answer. She cupped his face in her one good hand. "David, we must believe we will. We have so many wonderful people working so hard to find her. We have to be brave. You and I know that wherever Suzanne is, she's being very brave.''

"She can *act* brave," David said. "She can give them her Clint Eastwood bit. But underneath, she'll be scared too.''

Rachel could find no answer to that. She did not try.

"I never thought I'd want to hear more of her stupid movies," David added.

Rachel felt the need to take as positive a stand as she could manage. "David, when we *do* get her back, she'll need us more than ever. Let's remember the love we're feeling for her right now, hold it, and give it to her when we find her. You're just as important to her as she is to you. She'll be depending on her brother for help.

We'll have to be strong for her, give her a lot of attention. Do you understand?''

David nodded. ''You're saying I should listen to all the stupid movies she wants to tell me.''

Rachel laughed. ''That. And maybe let her have the pulleybone without argument, the last drop of lemonade. A thousand ways to show her you love her.'' Rachel shifted to a more comfortable position on the bed and bumped into a video display on David's bed table. At first she thought it was a television set. Then she saw that it was attached to a joystick.

''What's that?'' she asked.

''A new Nintendo Dr. Peterson gave me. It's really neat.''

The computer game looked moderately expensive. ''He gave it to you?''

''He said maybe it'd keep me quiet enough for my bones to heal. He comes around to see me four or five times a day. He's a lot of fun.''

''You two seem to have hit it off. He was very complimentary about you too.''

''Did he say when I could get out of here?''

''Not yet.''

''I could help hunt for her, you know. I'm not banged up as bad as you.''

''Not as badly. And that's not true. I just look worse. Aside from this arm, and what Dr. Peterson calls a nasty whack on the noggin, I was hardly hurt.''

''On television you look like a fighter who's been whipped real bad—badly—and you're fighting the world with one hand. Suzanne would like that. She'd build a movie around it.''

Rachel found herself momentarily amused. If they got Suzanne back, a lot of movies would come out of this experience. She glanced at her watch. ''I have to go.'' She remembered Peterson's advice. ''We have a big day coming up. We're going to announce a half-million-dollar reward.''

David's eyes widened. ''A half million? From Grandmother?''

Rachel laughed. Her mother often talked in Wall Street numbers. ''From the studio. They said they'll go a million, maybe more. We're trying to make it sound like a ransom. Return Suzanne, and no questions asked.''

''But they'll get the guy, won't they?''

''I hope so. At the moment that doesn't seem important. I want Suzanne back. They can get the guy later.''

''A half million!'' David said again.

Rachel fished for a way to involve David as Peterson had suggested. Then she saw how he truly could help. "David, I want you to do something for me. Think of some secret that only you and Suzanne would know. If this guy calls, we'll want to make sure Suzanne's all right before we give him the money. So we'll tell him to ask Suzanne a question. And only we will know the answer. Do you understand?"

David studied her request for a moment. "Like a joke between the two of us?"

"Exactly. Something where she'll know the question came from you. And you'll know the answer came from her."

David chewed on his lower lip. "I can think of several right off. But maybe I can remember a really good one."

"I'll call you later today and we can talk about it. We'll work on it till we have something foolproof."

She kissed him and hurried out. The special phone was being installed this morning. She wanted to be there.

Senior Inspector Nate Noonan leaned his bulk forward in the folding chair and put his forearms on his knees. "Mrs. Shelby, we all agree that the chances of this guy calling are remote. You understand, don't you, that nuisance calls may be all we'll get?"

"Yes," Rachel said. "I understand."

"But we feel the effort is worth making. What I'm wondering, are you sure you want to take the calls? If this man is holding your daughter, and if he does call, we'll probably only have one shot at him. That's quite a responsibility for anyone to assume. I know how you feel. But you shouldn't allow your emotions to guide you in this. I personally think you should allow the FBI specialists to take the calls."

Rachel and Patricia McMahon were seated on the couch. Noonan, Hopkins, Simmons, and Booker sat on folding chairs pulled into a semicircle facing them, Noonan on the left, then Hopkins and Simmons, and Booker on the right. The door was closed, blocking sounds from the front offices. The new telephone apparatus was centered on Rachel's desk a few feet away, dominating the room with its silent potential.

For a moment, surrounded by professional law officers, Rachel almost yielded to doubt.

Was she really capable of dealing with this maniac?

The question had kept her awake most of the night. But she knew if she showed the slightest hesitation, the experts would be chosen to take the call. She made her voice firm. "Inspector, I'm *not* being guided by my emotions. Mr. Gold's advisers insisted that the family—not the police—should deal directly with the kidnapper to keep from frightening him off. I don't know who his advisers are. But I do know he put up the money on that basis. I'm obligated to him. I would be going against our arrangement if I allowed the police to handle it."

Simmons also leaned forward. "Mrs. Shelby, I assure you this is a most unusual arrangement. These plans had been implemented before the case fell within our jurisdiction. We're willing to allow them to stand. But frankly, we'd feel better if a trained negotiator handled the phone."

Rachel felt the vague stirrings of memory. "The books about the Patricia Hearst case said that Mr. Hearst dealt with the kidnappers."

"Under direct FBI supervision. We've had new laws and new techniques since then. But in general, the method is determined on a case-by-case basis."

"Then why don't you and the police keep your distance and allow me to negotiate to get my daughter back?"

"A crime has been committed, Mrs. Shelby," Noonan said. "It's our job to bring this man to justice."

"You also have a responsibility to protect the victim," Rachel shot back. "I can't stress this too strongly. Gentlemen, if the police and the FBI interfere, and it costs Suzanne's life, I'll hold you responsible."

Noonan reddened. After a long silence, Booker spoke. "I think we can do this without coming to loggerheads over it. Nate, we've already discussed this at length. Tom, you've gone along with it. Patricia thinks Mrs. Shelby can handle it. So do I. There's no question but that the subject will feel far more comfortable dealing with her than with an FBI agent or the police. And I hate to mention it. But neither the FBI nor the OSBI could pay ransom, legally."

Patricia looked at her watch. "I've got to get on the road."

Booker had explained earlier that Patricia was to be leadoff witness today in a rape case in Muskogee. Jury selection was in progress. The judge had given Patricia dispensation on reporting until two P.M., allowing her time to brief Rachel. Muskogee was a hard four-hour drive.

"Where are we on the billboards?" Noonan asked.

"The first are to go up this morning," Rachel told him. "They promised they would have all up by tomorrow noon."

"Booker said you'll be announcing the reward at a press conference. When?"

"At ten," Rachel said. "That's plenty of time to make the noon news, the P.M. papers."

"Then if this subject happens to see one of the first signs, we could be receiving a call any moment."

Rachel felt her heart quicken. "Yes."

Noonan glanced at Patricia. "Maybe you'd better go ahead and brief Mrs. Shelby. We don't want you cited for contempt."

Patricia turned on the couch to face Rachel. "We have a lot to cover. I've written some of it down. Areas to avoid. Tricks to keep him interested. But there are important points I should discuss with you."

Rachel gestured to the apparatus on her desk. "First, how exactly will this equipment work?"

Booker gave the explanation. "This phone and the one at the police station will both ring. Hopkins and the FBI specialist will take turns manning the one at the police station. If you don't pick up here by the third or fourth ring, one of them will take the call. Otherwise the man there will just monitor. Both phones have tape recorders. If one fails, we still have the other. We can expect calls from flakes. Hopkins and the specialist will assess whether you're talking to the right guy."

"There's a red light on your phone," Hopkins said. "If I'm fairly sure it's a bogus call, I'll activate it. You can take that as a signal to make your demand to know if Suzanne's all right. If the caller backs off, starts waffling, we can be almost certain it's bogus."

"We believe the bona fide kidnapper will consider your double-check only as an inconvenience." Booker said. "He'll be irritated. But he'll go along with it."

Again Patricia looked at her watch. "Please!" she said.

Noonan grinned. "Go ahead."

Patricia handed Rachel several typewritten pages held together by a clip. "First, never forget for a moment that this man has never had a normal relationship with a woman. So don't expect the usual man-woman framework. Pick up what cues you can on how he regards you. Respond to them."

"How?"

"That depends. If he seems to consider you an authority figure, be cautious about falling into the role. This man is driven by anger,

171

irrationality, frustration. He has been rebelling against authority most of his life. We don't want him rebelling against you.''

"If he insists on making you an authority figure, be the most reasonable one he's ever met," Hopkins intervened. "Listen to him. Respond to him. Chances are no other authority figure has ever treated him as a normal person. In hostage negotiation, we're taught to build rapport on that.''

Patricia nodded agreement. "For the same reason, don't lie to him. He would pick up on it immediately. He has been lying all his life. He's an expert on lies. You want to build trust.''

"What if he shows his anger?" Rachel asked. "How should I handle it?''

"Firmly but not threateningly. Stress the rational. Make it plain that you and he are two people making a trade, and that it doesn't go beyond that. Keep him on that track. Don't allow any distractions.''

"How should I introduce myself? First name?''

"No. Maintain distance. You're Mrs. Shelby. You might go to Rachel if good rapport develops. But as a rule, distance is best. He's second person singular to you, unless he chooses to identify himself some way. Hop, do you agree?''

"Definitely. If you were a male, you might try for the buddy-buddy, us against them. But with a woman, that wouldn't work. He'd never get buddy-buddy with a woman.''

"In that vein, let me give you some general ground rules," Patricia said. "Personify Suzanne. Always. Use her name at every opportunity. At this moment she's as inanimate to him as a plastic doll. You must make him see her as a person—a valuable person.''

"Should I mention that she's a film star? Booker said he probably doesn't know.''

"Yes. He may not believe you. So offer proof. Tell him to look at newspapers, television.''

"I figure him as a doper," Booker said. "He may be hard to reach, spaced out.''

"And never forget he's acting out a fantasy," Patricia went on. "We don't know what it is. If Booker's right—and I think he is—this man's fantasy involves keeping his victims alive for a while. Most of his kind don't. They want to turn a live, unmanageable body into a limp doll they can play with, do things to. So they kill rather quickly. This guy has a different fantasy, a different thrill. I wish we knew what.''

"Should I probe for his fantasy?''

"No! That's the deepest part of him. Chances are he'll never confide that to anyone. Not without extensive therapy or hours and hours of sympathetic treatment. But be alert for the unusual in his attitude. Any aberration may give a hint. Nate and Hop will phone the tapes to me. I'll go over and over them for any clues to his thinking.''

"How will we set up the swap?"

"Talk to Nate and Booker about that. But I suggest you allow the subject to set it up. That'll make him feel he's in control. And we should have an alternate plan or two, in case he doesn't come up with one.'' She started gathering her material. "I must go. If you have any questions, or want to talk further, call me tonight. Hop will have my Muskogee number.''

"Thank you," Rachel said. "I will.''

Patricia hurried out. Through her office door Rachel saw that camera crews had gathered outside the front offices for the press conference.

"Hop, you have anything to add?" Noonan asked.

Hopkins was looking over the material Patricia had left for Rachel. "Only a few items. Mostly about the mechanics. Patricia seems to have covered everything.''

"It's almost time for my press conference," Rachel reminded the men. "Inspector, would you like to help make the announcement?''

Noonan rose. "No, thank you. This is your show. I just hope you know what you're doing. You said if we scare him off, you'll blame me. Mrs. Shelby, I'd like to leave you with a thought. If you blow it, you'll blame yourself for the rest of your life. You might want to think about that.''

Nate, you shouldn't have been so blunt with her," Booker said. "Can't you see she's barely holding it all together?''

"She threatened us first. I just don't want there to be any room for doubt in her mind as to how serious this is.''

"Good God, Nate! She's the one with a kid on the line. She damned well knows it's serious.''

"I'd still feel better with Hop or one of the FBI boys on the phone. I'm afraid she may crack right at the wrong moment.''

Booker did not respond. He felt he had made his point. "How many people we got working on the prior cases?" he asked.

"As of this morning, nobody," Nate said. "We're just spread too fucking thin, reinterviewing the witnesses, following up on tips that are still coming in, cleaning up on the clothes dump, running checks on the partial, you name it. We just don't have enough people.''

Booker absorbed that information. Shifts were changing and the squad room was crowded. Hopper and Pryor were at the center of the confusion, inundated with incoming reports.

''Nate, if this guy doesn't call, I still feel our best shot lies with the earlier snatches. We may have missed something.''

''Shit, we don't even know if it's the same guy,'' Nate argued. ''Even if it is, I think we've milked about all we're going to out of those cases.''

Booker always believed the younger agents failed to ask enough questions. He remembered dozens of cases that seemed about played out, when someone just happened to ask the right question. ''If you don't mind, I'd like to stay on them,'' he said.

''Do as you please,'' Nate said. ''I don't see anybody giving you orders one way or another.''

Nate moved off to talk with some of the returning OSBI agents. Booker went to the desk assigned to him by Chief Laird.

He decided to start with the last known abduction before Suzanne was kidnapped. Within minutes he had Sheriff Overby on the line.

''Booker, I heard you'd retired,'' the sheriff said.

''Not completely,'' Booker told him. ''I'm working with the family on this Suzanne Shelby case. I've been struck by the similarities of your granddaughter's disappearance and the Shelby case. Is there anything new on your granddaughter?''

The line was silent a moment. ''Not a thing,'' the sheriff said. ''Nothing from the first day. It's just like she dropped off the planet earth.''

''I was sure sorry to hear about it. Of course, I was out of the Bureau by then.''

''Fletcher was the case officer on it originally. He seemed to think it might tie in with several other abductions. But Scott called me a few days ago in connection with this Shelby case. He didn't seem to think there was much linkage.''

''Opinion's divided on it,'' Booker told him. ''I tend to agree with Fletch. We're up to ten possibles on it, all speculative. Cases are widely spaced, MOs different. But they're all sudden disappearances, like your granddaughter.''

''I'm still spending most of my time on it,'' the sheriff said. ''Can't sleep. I keep thinking something will turn up somewhere.''

''I have Fletcher's notes. But I don't have all the details. What exactly happened?''

Again the line was silent a moment. "My son and his wife almost lost Catherine three years ago to double pneumonia. Maybe they've been a little overprotective of her. She's all they have. My daughter-in-law always insisted she come straight home from school. Catherine is a good kid. You could set your watch by her every day by when she got home. When she was ten or fifteen minutes overdue that day, my daughter-in-law knew something was wrong. She called around to the other kids who walked most of the way with Catherine. They all said Catherine left them as usual at the shortcut she always took, a dirt street that runs down across a dry wash. My daughter-in-law went out and looked down that street. When she didn't see her, she panicked and called me."

"What time was that?"

"I logged it at four-eighteen. Probably less than thirty minutes after she was kidnapped. Right off I remembered some of those other cases—the little girl taken up at Medicine Park, the Midwest City child, and the one at Fairmont. And I knew Catherine. I knew she wouldn't just wander off somewhere. So I got roadblocks set up within an hour."

"How many?"

"Counting my men, city police, and the highway patrol, fourteen. We had this town boxed off. Later I went over everybody's notes. No one went through those roadblocks who looked unusual or couldn't give a good reason for being there."

"They take down license numbers?"

"Some did, some didn't. I ran a check on all we had. About two hundred. Nothing cropped up."

"Could you fax me a copy of those license numbers and the notes you have? I'd like to see if they match anything we've developed in the Shelby case."

"Sure. I'll get them off this afternoon."

"Did you turn up any physical evidence at all?" Booker asked, thinking of Suzanne's clothing.

"Only one thing. I found a place in soft dirt where little Catherine stepped off the road, kind of into the weeds, like she was making room for somebody to go by her. There were tracks where she stood for a time, moving around like she was talking to somebody. Then she walked back up onto the road. The ground is firmer there. I couldn't make out any other prints."

"Tire treads?"

"The ground was just too solid, with gravel in a few places. And the tracks were mixed up. Fletcher tried for a cast, but never came up with anything."

"Any strangers reported in town that day?"

"I canvassed all along Main Street, around the school, the teachers, Catherine's schoolmates. Nobody remembered a stranger or anything strange. All seemed normal right up to the time she disappeared."

"No clothing? Schoolbooks?"

"Nothing. I find myself wishing we'll find her body. Almost two months now. Common sense tells me she's dead. Her body would help put a closure on it. Both my son and his wife are in bad shape, not knowing."

Booker assumed the sheriff was also in the same mental shape. He felt he should give the sheriff the benefit of his theories. "The last six cases or so, we haven't recovered a body," he said. "In the early cases, if this is the same man, we had dumps. Shallow burials, an old mine shaft, ravines, and a lake. But no trace at all on these last few cases."

"That's plumb spooky."

"It is," Booker agreed. He thanked the sheriff ahead of time for faxing the material. He promised to keep in touch. "We have a lot of men working on this case up here. If the two cases are connected in any way, we may find some answers for you."

"I hope to God you do," the sheriff said.

Booker ended the conversation needing a drink. He had fully felt the sheriff's pain and that of the son and daughter-in-law.

That was the way it had always been. Booker had poured his emotional life into his work, with little left over for Betty and the children. Thinking back over the years, and scores of emotion-draining cases, Booker almost lost his composure right there in the squad room, surrounded by cops and cop activity. He forced himself to go on with the telephone work.

He had finished reviewing the Kathy Simpson and Cindy Gardner cases before the faxed material came in from Sheriff Overby. He immediately began work on the license numbers assembled from the roadblocks. After thirty minutes he could not escape the obvious conclusion: Not one bore the slightest resemblance to the partial obtained from the witness under hypnosis. Booker's disappointment was almost more than he could handle.

Once again he was back to square one.

15

Harold nearly missed seeing the sign. He barely caught a glimpse. By the time he turned his head to look, the sign went past too fast to see, like the flash cards Mrs. Beasley taught the alphabet with in kindergarten.

It seemed incredible, but Harold was almost certain he had seen a picture of the little tough bitch up there where the cigarette man used to be.

He braked and tried to pull onto the shoulder so he could back up. But three big trucks were running nose to tail in the right lane. They swept him on past, too far for any chance to pull off and back up.

He drove on five and a half miles to the next exit, crossed under the highway, and went back. He kept looking for the sign, driving less than forty. Traffic piled up behind him, the drivers blowing their horns as they changed lanes and breezed on past.

When he again saw the sign, it was pointed the wrong way and too distant, across four lanes of traffic. Again he caught only a glimpse.

He drove on west four miles, crossed the highway by an overpass, and returned eastward.

This time he stayed on the shoulder, traveling no more than thirty while traffic whizzed and roared past. When he came to the sign he pulled even farther off the road, into the grass, and stopped.

It was the little tough bitch. There was no doubt. Her photograph took up half the sign. She was laughing and her hair looked different. But it was her. To the right of her picture, on a red background, big black letters said REWARD. Underneath that it said $500,000. Beneath that was a phone number.

Under the picture it said SUZANNE SHELBY.

Harold turned off the ignition and sat for a time looking at the

177

sign, trying to fathom its meaning. He had been out of school so long, he had lost the art of reading big numbers. But he could not see a period anywhere. He remembered that all to the left of the dot was folding money and all to the right was shit. Counting carefully, he figured where fifty dollars would be, then five hundred, five thousand, and fifty thousand. He concluded that the reward was for five hundred thousand dollars.

He felt disoriented. Who would spend so much money on that little lump of bones and hair?

Had he grabbed a little rich bitch?

He tried to remember the make and model of the burning car. He had not paid much attention to it. But he was sure it was no limousine. And the clothing he had cut off her had seemed ordinary.

Yet here was this sign.

He knew he would not be able to remember all the numbers. He could not find a pen or pencil. He fished a .357 cartridge from the box in the glove compartment, sharpened the lead with his knife, and wrote onto an old envelope all it said on the sign.

He sat for a time trying to imagine how the sign came to be there, and what it meant. On the highway, a passing truck driver blew at someone and jarred Harold back to where he was.

Caution set him in motion. Cops did not like people to stop on the interstate. If they saw you, they nosed around and asked what you were doing. He did not have a story ready to explain why he was parked beside the reward-money sign.

Hurriedly he folded the envelope into his shirt pocket and drove on.

A thousand thoughts seemed to be going through his head at the same time. Nothing made sense. The little tough bitch was the sorriest he had grabbed. She refused to do anything right. If Sam had been hungry enough, Harold would have fed her to him days ago.

Who would have believed she was worth five hundred thousand dollars?

He thought of all he could do with that much money. He could replace Sam's old wornout truck. He could just walk into the showroom and plunk down the cash. He daydreamed for a while about that, and it made him feel good.

No longer would he have to worry about enough money to pay the rent on the red barn. And if someone wrote complaining about the quality of the skins or venom, he could just write back fuck you.

But he wanted nothing to do with the cops. He was sure the phone number would be connected with them in some way.

Driving on toward home, he hunted for a way to outsmart the

cops and get the money. Surely they would not be able to identify him if he used a pay phone somewhere to call, talked only a minute or two, left no fingerprints, and got the hell away as soon as he hung up.

Yet, in the back of his mind, there remained a nagging worry that they already might know something about him and be watching. He thought back over the last few grabs, searching for any hint they might have gathered about him.

He had switched the license plates faithfully each time. He had worn the cigarette man's outfit on each grab. If anyone saw him, that was what they would describe to the cops. Now, as always, he felt he was a totally different person in his gimme cap, dungarees, and clodhoppers. If the cops knew anything at all, they were probably hunting the cigarette man.

He stopped for a Whataburger, his mind still on the sign. When he finished, he ordered a burger to go and, on impulse, added a shake and fries.

The extra was for Sam. He deserved some flesh along with the bones.

As Harold drove on home over dirt roads, he kept close watch in the rearview mirror. When he reached the dirt track leading up to the red barn, he stopped, got out, and studied the ground, reassuring himself that the road had not been used since he last drove over it two days ago.

At the red barn he unchained the front doors and carried in the bags of snakes. His hunt in the Texas Panhandle had been successful beyond expectations. Forty-five of the rattlers he had captured bore exceptionally large heads. The other twenty-two were above average.

Sam always said the trick to finding snakes was knowing where to look.

Sam had been full of smart sayings like that.

The thought about Sam reminded Harold. He went back out to the truck and brought in the Whataburger sack. The little tough bitch was sitting on the cot, legs drawn up, calmly watching him. He tossed her the sack. She peeked inside as if suspecting a trick. Slowly, she took out the food and began eating.

Harold walked over to Sam's cage and slapped his hand against the metal. "Hey! Sam!" he shouted.

The python's bucket-sized head came up and turned to look at him with the same beady, expressionless stare Sam always used whenever Harold did something stupid or crazy. Harold laughed.

He was more sure than ever that it was Sam in there, inside the snake.

The little tough bitch was eating the burger and fries in her dainty way. Her prissiness irritated him. He knew she was bound to be hungry, for she had not eaten since he left two days ago. The milk shake had melted. She sipped it anyway.

He thought of the sign, the money. "Hey, you! What's your name?" he asked.

She looked up warily. For a moment he thought she did not intend to answer. He was ready to knock her into the middle of next week. She waited until her mouth was clear of food. "Suzanne."

"Suzanne what?"

"Suzanne Shelby."

That was the name on the sign.

Even though he had been certain, the proof was a jolt. "Your folks rich or something?"

She continued to look up at him, studying him. Harold could see wheels turning inside her head. He had seen that before, back in school, when all the little bitches made a special effort to show him up dumb.

"My family has money," she said. "I don't know how much. I have money too. I'm a movie star. I'm paid oodles of money for that."

Harold hooted. He had told some windies in his time. This was a prize winner. "Horseshit," he said.

"It's true! Go buy a newspaper. Look in the entertainment section. You'll see! I have a movie currently in release. I'm sure it's being screened somewhere around here."

He felt odd talking to her. He had never talked with one beyond the usual bullshit to get them in the pickup. Her use of big words angered him. He knew she was doing it to confuse him. "Shut up," he said. "I don't have to stand here and listen to no lies."

He went back to the rattlesnakes. Distracted, he had forgotten to dump them into the pits. Sometimes they smothered when left too long in the sacks. He did not want that to happen with this good batch. Hurriedly he set to work.

Needing room, he moved the smaller rattlers—those he had been milking—from the corner pit into the one beside it. He erected a plywood barrier to separate them from a batch ready to skin. With the corner pit cleared, he dumped the sacks one by one. He used a rake to separate the snakes until they covered the bottom of the pit. For a time he stood admiring them, laughing over the way they struck at the rake, their rattles sounding a steady chorus. A half dozen were among the biggest he had ever caught. He wanted to take them to the other end of the barn and show them to Sam. But he was reluctant to play the fool for the little tough bitch.

He had planned to work all night processing the snakes, getting the heads ready to ship to the man in Phoenix. But his mind kept returning to the sign and the money.

He was unable to concentrate. Upset, he decided to put the work off until morning. He had scored a fresh batch of brown in Amarillo. After preparing a needle, he sat in his old recliner and mainlined a good fix.

When the initial nod wore off, he was better able to think.

Going back over the situation from every direction, he could not see any risk in making a quick phone call just to see what the fuck was going on. He needed that money.

Yet he could not escape his certainty that the cops were involved. He knew they had all kinds of electronic gadgets now. The damned phone might even take his picture, for all he knew.

He remembered Sam saying many times, "Never give the sons of bitches any excuse to look you over."

Yet there was the money just for returning the little tough one.

He saw the flaw in that. She could describe him to the cops. And she knew about the snakes.

It would take a dumb cop not to track him down once they learned he was in the snake business.

He wondered if there was any way to feed the little tough bitch to Sam and still get the money.

The more he thought, the more confused he became.

He did not know what in hell to do.

The next morning, after the snake man drove away, Suzanne set to work. She was confident that if she dug long enough and hard enough, she could free the ringbolt from the concrete.

The only tool she had found was a small nail she managed to pull from the wall. For a while she scraped furiously. Before long her hands were bloody and she had made only a slight dent in the concrete. Discouraged, she climbed back onto her cot and tried to determine what was different about the snake man.

Never before had he shown the slightest interest in her as a person.

Why, after all this time, had he suddenly asked her name?

After thinking for a while, she decided he must have seen or heard something during his long absence that made him curious about her.

Going back over her scene with him last night, she could see that she had handled the dialogue badly. She should not have told him she was a film star. Maybe if she had strung him along instead of trying to wow him, she could have come to know him, learned to handle him without being slapped flat.

She still believed that if she planned carefully and thought things through, she might yet be able to noodle her way out of this. Playing back the scene over and over, she felt that he had known her name before he asked and was only seeking confirmation.

At first she thought maybe he had seen her name in a newspaper or on television. She felt sure that at least some stories had appeared in newspapers concerning her disappearance.

But she soon recognized the fallacy in that theory.

If that was where he saw or heard her name, he also would have learned she was a film star.

So he must have learned her name somewhere else.

But where?

Maybe he had seen her picture on milk cartons. Suzanne had no idea how much time was required, after one disappeared, before the information showed up on milk cartons. But that seemed to be a possibility.

The theory raised her hopes. If her name and picture were on milk cartons already, her mother would have been the one to get it done. David would not know how.

That thought made her feel much better, because it meant her mother was not dead or injured badly in the wreck and fire.

Thinking of her mother, she began to get the first glimmer of the next segment of her movie.

She liked her earlier opening at the UN. She would keep that, along with the establishing shots of the red barn and the slow, 360-degree pan of the interior, with the ambassador's daughter in the corner next to the big snake.

After that the ambassador's daughter would be knocked around some, and you would see a hint of the weird stuff the snake man did—whatever she could get away with onscreen. There would be close-ups of Sam the snake, his eyes always open, always staring at the ambassador's daughter.

Then you would learn with an oh-my-God rush that the ambassador's daughter was going to be fed to Sam the snake whenever the snake man got around to it.

Mort always said that once you establish a situation, and posed the threat, you leave it there and pick up the other thread of your story.

So Suzanne would leave the ambassador's daughter in peril and return to the father and his desperate search.

Scenes would show that he had not recovered from his injuries. A succession of dramatic situations would make the audience see that the worry and long hours were doing him in. Doctors would warn him. But he would ignore them and continue his search for his daughter.

He would fall gravely ill. Reaction shots would show doctors gathered around, shaking their heads, saying his heart was broken because of his missing daughter and there was nothing they could do.

This would set up a great death-bed scene. Suzanne intended it to be one of those you remember, and maybe cry over, long after seeing the movie.

She would get Mort to help with the dialogue. It would have to be perfect. She would shoot the scene under soft lighting, almost like candlelight. And in his last moments the father would talk about his love for his daughter, and he would make the mother promise to carry on with the search.

The audience would recognize that the father had sacrificed his life for his daughter. Everyone would remember what an important man he had been in the beginning, a real fun guy, and know how he had given up everything in his love for his daughter.

Envisioning the deathbed scene and the way it would be done, Suzanne wept for a time before she could go on with her movie.

Mort always said that each tragedy not only moves the story along, but also redefines the focus of the movie.

Suzanne could see that the camera now would follow the beautiful mother as she fulfilled the death-bed promise and took up the search.

The audience would see the change in her. Instead of the high-fashion outfit she wore in the United Nations scenes, she now would appear in neat business suits. She would buy one of those snub-nosed pistols and there would be scenes of her learning to shoot.

Instead of searching canyons and fields, she would go around asking people questions, trying to pick up clues.

Disturbed, Suzanne saw that she was edging into the territory of Jodie Foster and *The Silence of the Lambs*. Mort always said you could steal story devices and camera tricks but never dialogue or scenes.

Jodie Foster had gone around asking questions until she found the guy, and then she shot him. So that had already been done. The mother would have to do something different.

Suzanne was not sure exactly what.

And she would have to show some way that her own situation was a lot different from that of the senator's daughter the crazy guy kept in the well—the crazy guy Jodie Foster was hunting. The senator's daughter had to worry only about being killed and skinned, not being chased down by a snake, crushed, and swallowed like a screaming chicken. Overwhelmed by fear, unable to make her mind go back to the movie, Suzanne drew herself into a small knot and cried uncontrollably.

Booker went back through the photographs one more time. He had driven up to Tulsa in the early morning, facing into the sun most of the way. His eyes were bothering him. Even with the magnifying glass he was forced to squint. Altogether, he counted seventeen little girls in the pictures, and two little boys. The quality of the photographs varied. Some were amateurish. Others were professionally done. Not one of the kids resembled any of the possible priors. But there might be more photographs somewhere. "You think maybe this guy would talk to me?" he asked.

The vice captain laughed. "He'd talk to a fence post, tell it how innocent he is. He doesn't seem to realize the fix he's in with the drug charges, not to mention this stuff. His biggest concern is getting his kiddie pictures back."

"I'd like to talk to him."

"You really think he's connected with that little actress?"

"No. But he may know someone who knows something."

"I'll have him brought up. They also took a briefcase full of letters off him. Did they tell you that?"

Booker was still vague about the way the arrest was handled. The DPS, OSBI, Tulsa police, and the sheriff's office seemed to be involved. But for his purposes, the details were unimportant. "No. I just got in a few minutes ago," he said. "I haven't been able to get ahold of the trooper who made the stop."

"We've got the letters in property. I'll get them for you if you want."

"I'd appreciate it," Booker said.

"His wife is on the way down here. She's a deputy sheriff up there somewhere in Pennsylvania. Ain't that a hoot? I'll bet she'll burn his ass."

The captain went on out. Booker returned to the pictures, trying to imagine the mind-set that would make a man risk his marriage, his job, his freedom, and self-respect in such behavior. In some of the photographs the girls were arranged in poses common among swimsuit and Hollywood pinups. Most were blatantly pornographic.

The captain returned apologetic. "The cells are in lockdown right now over a fistfight. It'll be a few minutes before they send your man up. Here are the letters. We haven't disseminated them yet. We may bring the postal inspectors, the FBI, others into it. Several other perps are involved. There could be five or six good busts out of this one."

The captain left Booker alone with the letters. Booker estimated there were at least fifty or sixty. A few were typed, but most were handwritten. None was subtle. Booker began reading at random:

> I received the photo of Diane. She is *beautiful*. I fell in love with her in the first minute. In return, I'm sending you a snap of Jill, taken a year ago when she was six. If she grabs your fancy, I have others I will send. I'm working on my collection, and if you will send me the names and addresses of men who share our interests, I will reward you with some of my best. Please have Diane write me a letter. I would treasure it forever. And if you have any photos of her a little younger, maybe about six, I would love to see them. In the meantime, kiss her in an appropriate place for me.

"Jeez," Booker said to himself.

He thumbed through some of the other letters. All were of the same ilk. Words and phrases were interchangable.

For the next several minutes Booker devoted himself to copying down names and addresses. Most of the names were probably fictitious. He would not follow up on them immediately, because he did not want to interfere with the ongoing investigation. But a remote chance still existed that one of the names might crop up in the Shelby case. Nate had been right. Booker now was convinced that this was a dry run. He regretted wasting a full day. He should have stuck with the Shelby case instead of going off on this thousand-to-one shot.

The captain returned. "I put your subject in Interrogation Room Two-A. Ring me when you're through with him. Are you finished with this stuff?"

"Yeah," Booker said. "If I find a connection, I may ask for a copy of some of those letters. But right now I don't see one."

He walked down the hall to the interrogation rooms.

Bart P. Hill sat at a small table. He was wearing jailhouse coveralls and sported a shiner that had closed one eye.

Apparently word had gotten around among the jail population that he was a short-eye, arrested for groping his own daughters. Jailbirds need someone to look down upon. In jails and prisons, short-eyes provide an outlet for a lot of anger.

Booker introduced himself.

"I've already talked to a dozen cops," Hill said.

"I'm working on a different case," Booker told him. "I'd like to ask you a few questions."

"You offering me immunity?"

"I can't do that. But I can tell the DA that you cooperated in the investigation of another case. That might help."

"Go to hell. All I've done is love my children. Is there a law against that? This is a different world. Children have to grow up fast these days. You've got to teach them things."

Booker remained silent.

"They want it," Hill insisted. "They enjoy it. Don't children have any rights? You won't find any children anywhere that get more loving than my daughters."

Booker sidestepped argument. "In your correspondence with males of like interests, did you ever encounter the name Brenda Wallace?"

Hill blinked with his good eye. He thought for a moment. "No," he said.

"Gaye Monroe?"

"No."

"Renate Estraca?"

"Hey, what is this?"

"Just answer the question."

"I'm not answering any more questions until I know what the fuck this is all about."

"These are children who have been murdered. There's a chance you've corresponded with the killer unknowingly. You could help us by telling us if these names were ever mentioned in the photographs and letters you've received. Renate Estraca. That name mean anything to you?"

Hill shook his head. "No."

"Patsy Gray?"

"No."

Booker went through the rest of the names. Hill denied recognizing a single one.

Booker remembered the medical examiner's findings of ligature marks on the ankles in some cases. "You ever correspond with anyone who was into bondage?"

Hill shook his head more emphatically. "Good Lord, no."

"Did you ever correspond with anyone who expressed an interest in snuff films?"

Hill struck the table in front of him. "Hell no! What kind of man do you think I am?"

Booker did not bother to answer.

Suzanne awoke to a terrible crash as the snake man ripped the chain from the metal doors and stormed back into the building. She sat up. He crossed the barn to his worktable and slammed down a newspaper.

Suzanne almost cried out her joy. He had bought a newspaper! Now he knew she was truly a film star, and that she had not lied.

For a while he paced up and down the far side of the barn, slapping the snake cages, cursing. The snakes stirred. The chickens squawked.

Suzanne was more certain than ever that something had changed. Why was he so angry?

She pulled herself into a small ball and lay back on the cot, hoping he would forget about her. But after a time he threw his cap onto the worktable and came straight to her. "What're you doing here?" he asked.

The question sounded crazy. Suzanne answered guardedly. "You're the one who brought me here!"

"I mean here. Oklahoma."

Suzanne understood. He must have seen a news story that said she was from New York. Or maybe California.

"We were on our way from New York to California when we had the wreck," she explained.

"Who's we?"

"My mother, my brother, and me."

He walked away, slamming the flat of his hand against Sam's cage. Suzanne waited. After stomping back and forth a few times, he returned. "You don't look like no movie star."

Suzanne let that pass. Mort always said that when you receive criticism, just consider the source.

"How'd you get to be a movie star?"

That now seemed so long ago. Suzanne had to stop and think back. "I was on Broadway. Only a walk-on. Then it got better."

She saw by his puzzled expression that he did not know what she was talking about. She tried again. "I was in a stage play. Some movie people saw me. That led to the offer of a role in a movie."

"They pay you a lot of money, huh?"

He had mentioned money when he first started talking to her. He seemed to have money on his mind. Suzanne decided to work on that without trying to wow him. "Quite a bit."

"How much?"

"I don't know," she answered honestly. "My mother takes care of all that. There are percentages, points, gross, net, a lot of things I don't understand."

He appeared to accept that. He stood looking at her with his face screwed up, thinking.

At that moment, in a burst of clarity, Suzanne guessed a reason for his preoccupation with money. Maybe her mother had offered a ransom. He wanted the money but was afraid to try for it. That was why he was angry!

Maybe she should encourage him. "They'll pay good money to get me back," she said. "You can count on it."

She was not sure that was true. But she felt it was a good point to make.

He pounded a fist against his hip. "If I did, you'd spill your guts!"

Suzanne opened her mouth to promise not to say a word. But she hesitated. That would be a lie, and it would sound like a lie.

Again he walked away. "I've got to think about this." He stopped and looked back at her. "What does your daddy do?"

"He's dead. He died when I was six."

"Your mama work?"

Suzanne nodded affirmatively. "She's in publishing. Books. Or was. She accepted a position as a story consultant for a film studio."

"What about your other folks?"

Did he intend to rob them?

She did not see how he could. She felt she should answer, try to get to know him. "My grandmother is a stockbroker in New York. She sells stocks and bonds. My other grandparents are in Florida. They're retired."

'No brothers or sisters?"

"Just David. He's eight. Almost nine."

Suzanne did not know what was in his mind, but obviously he was working hard on it. He was frowning, his head lowered, biting his lower lip. "Your mee-maw in New York. She make a lot of money?"

"I don't know," Suzanne said honestly. "I think she does. We always seem to have enough."

"What's her name?"

Again Suzanne was hesitant, but she figured any communication between the snake man and her family could only be a plus. "Judith. Judith Mermin."

"You know her phone number?"

"Yes."

The snake man went to the worktable and returned with the stub of a pencil. He pulled a folded envelope from his pocket. "Give it to me."

"Home? Or office?"

"Both."

Suzanne gave him the numbers, adding the area code.

"Spell her name."

Suzanne did. As he wrote, she could see scribbling on the bottom side of the folded-over envelope. She saw her name and a long number with several zeros. She could not make out the number.

The snake man put the envelope back in his shirt pocket. "I got to think about this," he said again.

He returned to the worktable. There he cooked heroin and prepared a needle. He went to his old recliner and gave himself a shot. Suzanne watched, wondering how the dope felt when it hit you. She supposed she would have to do that eventually, so she would know how to act if she ever signed to play a doper.

The snake man leaned back in the chair and closed his eyes. Suzanne curled into a ball and thought back over the dialogue.

The only reason she could see for the snake man to telephone her grandmother would be to start negotiations for the ransom.

For a while she felt good, imagining the phone call, all that would follow.

But the more she thought about it, the better she understood why the snake man was so worried.

If he collected the reward and freed her, and if the police showed her mug books like those she had seen on television and in movies, she would be able to identify him.

The devastating fear returned. She began to cry.

She could see that even though the snake man wanted the money, he would never let her go alive.

16

The special phone remained silent through the first day. The tension Rachel first felt over its presence gradually faded. By evening she was beginning to suspect that Inspector Noonan and the other officers were right, and that Booker's ploy would prove a failure.

But on the second day seven calls came in. They were of a pattern. Each caller began hesitant and uncertain. When Rachel asked questions, the caller kept repeating that he had "some information." Then the red light would glow and a moment later Hopkins or the FBI specialist would come on the line.

Booker said that of the seven callers, two provided information that might prove useful. The other five were only seeking the reward.

On the following day Rachel was able to answer the special phone without a rush of adrenaline. The first two calls again were of the tip variety.

But from the moment she picked up on the next, she knew it was different. After her hello, there came only a lengthy silence. Then a male voice asked, "Who is this?"

Rachel heard overtones of aggression, perhaps belligerence.

"I'm Rachel Shelby," she said. "I'm Suzanne's mother."

Again the silence. Rachel waited. Patricia had said to make the subject do the talking, if he would.

"You got the money?" the voice asked.

From that instant Rachel knew she was talking with Suzanne's kidnapper. Yet she managed to speak calmly, matter-of-factly. "Yes. I have the money. Do you have Suzanne?"

Both Patricia and Hopkins had warned her not to push him into a corner. She had jumped ahead to the showdown on sheer instinct.

For one reason or another, this seemed to be a man of few words.

Once again came the long silence, followed by the most chilling words Rachel had ever heard in her life. "Yeah, I got the little bitch."

And there was something else. A snicker? The shift of something in his mouth?

Rachel fought down the horror of the moment. She forced her voice to be strong, unemotional. "Then we can do business, you and I. A half million dollars for Suzanne, safe and sound. Even swap."

Again she was defying instructions. Inspector Noonan had said that for prosecution purposes, she must make the kidnapper demand the money. But at the moment she cared nothing about prosecution. She read this as a simple man. She felt she should put all cards on the table.

"I don't want no cops," he said.

"Nor do I. This is strictly between you and me."

"Where's the money?"

"As I told you, I have it."

"In money orders?"

That threw her for a moment. The last she had heard, postal money orders were limited to a maximum of seven hundred dollars.

He seemed to be mesmerized by the money. On impulse Rachel devised an enticing description. "In bills," she told him. "Three thousand one-hundred-dollar bills. Two thousand fifty-dollar bills. And five thousand twenty-dollar bills. Five hundred thousand dollars. A half million. In two big, heavy suitcases."

Again there was a long pause. When he spoke, the tone of belligerence was back. "Okay. Listen up. Leave the money. Under the river bridge. On the way up to Leedey. South side. Then I'll turn her loose."

Rachel hesitated. She was fearful of setting conditions, but she knew she must. "It won't be that easy," she said. "I have to know for sure you have her, and that she's all right. You see, you could be anybody, as far as I know. So I have a test question for you to ask Suzanne. You can call me back with the answer, and then I'll know, and we can go from there. Okay?"

He thought that over for a moment. "Okay," he said.

"Fine. Ask Suzanne what was her secret name for Mr. Peabody, the headmaster of her school. Mr. Peabody. You got that?"

A rustling came over the line. "Spell it."

"P-e-a-b-o-d-y."

"Okay, I got it."

"Ask Suzanne her secret name for Mr. Peabody. Call me back with the answer. Then we'll decide how to do this. Okay?"

"Okay. But no cops."

"No police," Rachel said. "I promise."

The line clicked and a moment later the dial tone came on. Rachel hung up and started trembling uncontrollably. She could not stop. She lowered her head into the crook of her good arm.

Her office phone rang. She answered.

"Very good," Hopkins said. "You handled that extremely well."

Booker was on an extension. "No one could have done it better. This is a real breakthrough. And I truly believe she's still alive. Otherwise he would have weaseled out on the test question."

"We'll shoot copies of the tape to Patricia and to Washington," Hopkins said. "Specialists will vet it for accent, background noise, word use. It'll tell us a lot about him."

"We already know a hell of a lot more," Booker said. "He's local. The way he said 'the road to Leedey.' An outlander would have used the highway number. He said 'the river.' He knows there's only one, the Washita. And he's got either an accent or a speech impediment."

"The specialists will know," Hopkins said. "I've got to get this moving." Rachel heard him hang up his phone.

"Mrs. Shelby, let's not forget that this is a federal case now," Booker said. "Tom Simmons will be wanting to talk with you as soon as he studies the tape."

"Mr. Reeves, I don't want them interfering in the negotiations. I promised this man no police. I meant it."

Booker did not answer for a moment. "We'll give this subject some room," he said. "But, Mrs. Shelby, you should understand that the police investigation is still our best chance of getting Suzanne back unharmed. The reward has served its purpose. It has flushed him out, started a dialogue. But I must tell you. I genuinely doubt a ransom deal will work."

Rachel struggled to make sense of that.

Booker Reeves had been the one who devised the plan, pushed it through.

"Why won't it work?"

"Suzanne knows too much about him. He didn't have ransom on his mind when he took her. So he probably hasn't protected his identity around her. Now he can't afford to let her go."

Rachel felt faint. "Then why in God's name are we doing this? Why did we go to so much trouble? And why is he going along with it if he doesn't intend to go through with it?"

"He thinks he can outsmart us and get the money without delivering. We've got to keep him thinking that right up to the moment we find him."

"Mr. Reeves, it's been more than a week! You haven't found him yet!"

"In the last two days the investigation has opened up considerably. You remember that early on I told you I was discouraged on the slow progress? Well, now I'm encouraged. And this today gives us a great deal to work with."

Rachel's dismay was turning into anger. "Mr. Reeves, I feel betrayed. I was led to believe we could buy her back. Mr. Gold put up the money on that supposition."

"It's possible we can. But at the same time we must be realistic."

"You've known all along, haven't you? Even when you came up with the plan for the billboards!"

"Yes. But look at what we've accomplished. We've learned for fairly sure that she's alive. An hour ago I would have placed the odds at much less than fifty-fifty. Now, as long as we keep him going for the money, he won't do away with her. He knows we may demand further proof at any time."

Rachel felt sick. "You thought she was dead? You never told me that!"

Reeves sighed audibly over the phone. "Mrs. Shelby, I've investigated more than three hundred murders. Many of the victims were children. I've seen what some people are capable of doing. I always hope for the best, but I tend to expect the worst. I try not to let it interfere with my work, so I don't go around talking about it."

Rachel had no answer for that. She supposed she should be grateful that he had agreed to help, when apparently he fully expected that Suzanne would be yet another victim of the evil he had seen.

Still, she believed he was wrong on the chances the ransom would work. "Can't we try for an exchange seriously? He's hungry for the money. I sense that. And he's simple-minded."

"If you remember, Patricia predicted he might be dumb but extremely crafty. I think that's what we've got here. Sure, we'll play along with him. Maybe even try for an exchange. But let's not underestimate him. I doubt he'll go through with it."

Rachel did not agree. She fully intended to do all in her power to bring about the exchange.

"And on the subject of not underestimating him, I want a twenty-four-hour guard on you, beginning now. Let us know where you are at all times. Never travel alone. Call, and either I or somebody will

drive you wherever you need to go. We'll have policemen or deputies at your office and at your motel room guarding you around the
clock.''

Rachel thought that excessive. ''Why?''

''Maybe it's more of my pessimism. But you've told this subject
you've got the money. He's shown himself to be extremely interested in the money. And if I read him right, he's a cold-blooded
killer.''

I don't know whether this asshole is smart or lucky,'' Nate said.
''I don't guess it matters which. Either way, he's sure making mon-
keys out of us.''

Booker and Nate stood near the front cash register at Love's and
watched the FBI work. The giant-sized convenience store just off
the interstate west of town supplied truckers, travelers, and locals
with an impressive array of goods and services. As usual, the place
was crowded. A full-time fry cook was busy preparing everything
from bacon and eggs to ornate sandwiches for waiting diners. Other
customers prowled the grocery section for detergents, canned
goods, and assorted essentials. Farther back were souvenirs and
auto accessories. The other side of the building contained a huge
curio shop. At the front, to the left of the register, a bank of public
telephones looked out on the large parking lot so truck drivers
could keep an eye on their rigs while they reported their location to
their companies, and to their wives and girlfriends.

The kidnapper had used the telephone on the far end of the row.
Simmons and his specialists were trying to lift prints. Two other FBI
agents were interviewing customers and store employees.

''I just hope the asshole's not hanging around watching this,''
Nate said. ''He'd probably split his sides.''

The phone in the middle of the row rang. An agent answered and
handed the receiver to Simmons. Each phone was equipped with a
swing-out seat, but Simmons remained standing throughout a long
conversation. The person on the other end seemed to be doing most
of the talking. Simmons's replies were brief. At last he hung up the
receiver, spoke briefly to one of the agents, motioned to his partner
Todd, then came to Booker and Nate. ''I think we're about
wrapped up here,'' he said. ''It's a wash. Not one of the employees
saw anything unusual. No one remembers seeing anyone answering
our description. J.H., you got anything?''

J. H. Todd was a few years older than Simmons and bordered on portly. Booker had always thought they made an odd pair—Simmons tall, athletic, and brash, and Todd round-bottomed, slow, and reticent.

"Two latents and a partial palm print. But I expect they'll turn out to be from one or two callers who tried to use the phone after the subject was through with it."

"We should've put people in all of these Love's places," Nate said.

"Probably wouldn't have done any good," Booker said. "Is there any chance we'll get anything from the security camera at the cash register?"

"Quality will be shitty," Simmons said. "But we might find something."

"Maybe we could take all the photos from the proper time frame and show them to the wreck-scene witnesses," Nate suggested.

"If we get anything decent, we might," Simmons agreed.

"I'm almost to the point of thinking there may be two people involved in this," Nate said. "If he's still wandering around in his cowboy suit, it seems someone would have noticed him."

"I've been thinking along those lines," Booker admitted. "Maybe he looks more nondescript without his deputy sheriff outfit."

Nate laughed. "Like Chief Laird without his uniform. You ever see him in civvies? I damned near didn't recognize him."

Simmons did not even smile. He appeared tired, impatient. "I just received a preliminary on the telephone tape," he said. "The analysts think he either has a speech impediment, or else there was something in his mouth. Snuff or tobacco. He didn't talk long enough for a good fix on education, but they peg him at about eighth-grade level. His accent pins him to within two hundred miles of here. The profilers picked up a lot of anger, aggression. They told me to put out a warning for everyone to be careful. They believe this subject will take a hard fall."

"I hope to God I'm there to see it," Nate said.

"We may get more from the tape, but I doubt it," Simmons went on. "So I guess we'd better decide where we go from here. Anyone have any ideas?"

"He'll call back," Nate predicted. "Probably tomorrow. You can almost hear him panting for the money. I think we should blanket every public phone for a hundred miles in every direction."

Booker had been fearful that was Nate's intention. "Nate, that's too big a risk. We'd just scare him off. I'd rather see us string him along. He won't turn loose of the kid. That's for sure. But we might flush him out.''

''That'd be a tough sell in Washington,'' Simmons said.

''We should keep in communication with him if we can,'' Booker said. ''A stall is the only way I see to do it.''

''I guess you're right,'' Simmons said. ''Okay, I'll try to sell it. I'll take a little more heat if I have to.''

''What about the bite on the kid up in Kaw Lake,'' Booker asked. ''Your people got anything on that?''

''Nothing yet,'' Simmons said. ''But they're making the rounds with it.''

''Booker's had a hard-on about that bite from the first,'' Nate said. ''Now it's beginning to bother *me.*''

''It could be significant,'' Simmons said. ''I talked quite a while with one of the profilers. He suggested there's a possibility that this subject may be so disorganized, so screwed up, he hasn't fallen into the usual mold. He said the way the subject jumped for the money shows he's not entirely locked into his psychosis.''

''So what do we do now?'' Nate asked.

Simmons considered the question only briefly. ''We'd better go talk with Mrs. Shelby. If we run the stall, she'll need a lot more coaching.''

Harold guided Sam's old car to the curb, stopped, got out, and raised the hood. Across the street, people were milling around in front of the place where the newspaper said Rachel Shelby was running her campaign to get her daughter back. A uniformed policeman stood at the door. Small panel trucks with radarlike things on top were parked up against the building. Lettering on the side of the one Harold could see said WKY-TV.

He thought about walking over and mingling with the group. But he decided against it. If Sam was along, he would cuss a bunch and tell him it would be a dumb thing to do.

After watching the people for a time, Harold turned his attention to the engine of Sam's old car. He was not entirely play-acting. The carburetor was tuned too rich, and the idler was set too low. He had been intending to make adjustments for weeks.

He restarted the car and gunned the engine a few times to bring gas up into the carburetor. Then he allowed the engine to settle down. With a screwdriver, he tightened the idle. After the engine was running steadily at the new speed, he adjusted the setscrew on the gas mixture, fine-tuning it until the engine sounded right.

Only occasionally did he glance across the street to see what was going on.

He had finished, and was thinking of leaving to keep from becoming conspicuous, when a car drove in and parked near the building. A stocky man got out and walked toward the door. He was an old guy with gray hair. But everything about him said cop. And sure enough, the policeman waved to him. The two talked briefly before the old guy went on inside.

Harold figured he should hang around a while longer. Something seemed to be happening.

He killed the engine, dropped to the pavement, and crawled underneath Sam's car. He had been intending for weeks to seek the source of a slow drip. It seemed too far back to be from the oil pan, and too far forward to be from the transmission. After his eyes adjusted, he ran a hand up between the engine and the transmission and found the answer.

Main bearing. That was bad news. It could only get worse.

Like the pickup, Sam's old car was about shot.

From beneath the car the view across the street was not as good, but he could see all he needed and no one would be paying any attention to him. He lay quietly and watched.

After a few minutes the old cop came out with a woman who had her head wrapped in a big bandage and one arm in a sling. The newspaper said Rachel Shelby had been injured in the wreck. Harold was sure he was looking at the woman who had the money.

The woman and the old cop climbed into the cop's car and drove out of the parking area.

Taking his time, Harold slid out from beneath the car and dusted himself off. The cop's car was moving straight up the street. Harold climbed into Sam's car and followed, hanging far back, just keeping the cop's car in sight.

The cop drove to the interstate, turned up an access road, and pulled into a motel.

Harold hooted, wondering if the old cop was about to get some nookie. He drove on past and parked on the street. Leaving Sam's car, he climbed a low, grassy embankment and walked across the motel parking lot.

The ice bin and soft drink machines were located in a niche between the two wings of the motel. Harold fished in his pocket for change, allowing his gaze to take in the right-hand wing.

The old cop and the woman got out of the car and went into the room at the far corner. Two deputy sheriff–like guys were standing near the door. After less than a minute the old cop came back out. He talked for a moment with the two deputy-like guys, then left.

Harold walked down the row of rooms to where the deputies were standing. They looked up at him, neither friendly nor unfriendly.

"Either of you guys got change for a dollar?" he asked.

"Don't believe I have," the nearest one said. "You can get change up at the front desk."

"Thanks," Harold said. He walked away.

He had learned what he wanted to know. The patches on their arms said DEPUTY SHERIFF. Both were armed with big revolvers, but they wore their holsters shoved back toward their asses. Both pistols were strapped down. Harold was sure that with his .357 S&W he could take both of them before they could get off a single round.

He went to the front desk, received change from a prissy-looking guy, and returned to the machines. He put in the money and punched the button for root beer. He stood by the machines for a time, drinking the root beer, thinking about the setup.

The little tough bitch's mama had promised no cops.

And here they were, all over the place.

He figured the money must be in the room.

Why else would they have two deputies on the door?

He finished his drink and put coins in for another. The can banged down the chute with a sound that carried across the parking lot. He knew the deputies were watching him. He did not even glance in their direction. He wanted them accustomed to seeing him around. After popping the top of the can, he walked to the front of the building, rounded the corner out of their sight, and returned to Sam's car.

He drove onto the interstate and tooled thirty miles and more eastward, to where the little tough one's movie was showing. He bought a ticket and sat amid a few adults and a bunch of kids who shouted, laughed, and talked throughout the movie. Harold had a hard time concentrating on it.

The little bitch onscreen was much like the one chained to the cot back at the barn. Yet somehow the one onscreen was different. Of course he knew they told her what to say. She constantly cracked jokes and spouted funny stuff. But the way she conned people was much the same. And he was surprised to see her sing and dance. She had not mentioned that.

She was tough in the movie too.

Harold left the theater disturbed. He could see now why they were willing to pay a lot of money to get her back. Everybody in the theater had paid five bucks to see her, and that was happening all over the country.

He could not begin to guess how much money that might be.

He stopped for a Big Mac and fries. With the little tough bitch on his mind, he ordered some more stuff put in a sack to go.

Driving back west, he pulled off onto the access road and again went by the motel. The two deputies were still on duty.

He drove to an all-night café. Groups of teenagers were hanging around, the boys and girls flirting with one another. Harold parked Sam's car on the fringes, eased out, and walked off into the darkness, down the deserted streets.

He approached the motel from the rear and slipped into the narrow lane between the building and a high fence. The space was occupied only by a Dumpster and a boat mounted on a trailer. Clinging to the shadows, he eased forward until he could see the whole parking lot.

The motel was quiet. Most everyone seemed to be racked out for the night. Across the way the two deputies were sitting on the hood of their car, smoking and talking. Harold remained motionless and watched.

After a while two more deputies arrived and the first two left. All quieted again.

Harold figured that nothing more would happen until morning. He was about to leave when a big black car drove up and parked in the vacant space in front of the room. Four men got out. One was the old cop. The others looked like cops too. The four walked up to the door, knocked, waited a minute, then went in.

Again Harold's head was filled with a thousand thoughts, all flying in different directions.

Who were those men? Why were they coming to see the little tough one's mama at this time of night? What was going on?

She had promised no cops.

He had not really believed her. But now he had proof that she was a lying bitch. Anything he did to her, she deserved.

He could hardly contain his fury.

And in his anger a plan began to form.

He would stay a while longer and see what happened.

Tomorrow he would give her one last chance before he lowered the boom.

Rachel sought to put her argument into few words. "Mr. Simmons, I'm convinced that if we renege on our promises to this man, he will react violently. We could further endanger Suzanne needlessly. We can *meet* his demands. All we must do is ensure that he meets ours."

"I'm not suggesting we renege," Simmons said. "Our goal will be to prolong the negotiations, buy time."

"I doubt he'll tolerate delays," Rachel insisted. "I read him as a direct, simple man. Impatient. Short-fused."

They were seated around Rachel's motel room, using all available chairs. Noonan, Booker, and the other FBI agent, Todd, were allowing Simmons to do most of the talking. Rachel was annoyed by the silence of the three. She badly wanted support, especially from Booker. "Mr. Reeves, how do you feel about it?" she asked.

"I believe Tom's right," he said. "The profilers, all our experience, convinces us we're dealing with a very dangerous individual, one who lacks any compassion for human life. As I told you yesterday, I think there's only a remote possibility for a successful swap. Tom is bringing three dozen special agents into the case. So we should keep the dialogue going as long as possible, give them time to do some work."

"Inspector Noonan?"

"Mrs. Shelby, with the additional manpower and expertise, we could have a meaningful breakthrough in the investigation at any moment. I sincerely believe that prolonging the negotiations is the *only* way we'll get your daughter back safely."

"The FBI profilers issued a warning to us tonight," Booker added. "They predict this man won't be taken alive, that he'll take as many of us with him as he can. We don't want to give him a chance to do away with Suzanne. There's a strong likelihood he will if we corner him."

Most of the time Rachel could shove her emotions aside when necessary. But occasionally she failed. Booker's warning had broken through the barrier. A moment passed before she could speak. "How can they tell he's so violent just from the tape?"

Simmons answered. "Voice stress analysis. General tone. Word use. Comparison with what we've learned from similar killers."

"They have him pegged as an erratic type," Booker said. "He doesn't seem to fit neatly into any of their categories. His violence could crop up in ways we can't predict."

They sat through a brief interval of silence. Rachel knew they were awaiting her response. But she was not yet convinced that delay should be their strategy. She wanted to know more. "If we stall the talks, what technique will we use?"

"You handled him so well, I'm almost hesitant to give you pointers," Simmons said. "But as a general rule, any device that puts the burden on him."

"Like the test question?"

"Of that nature. And if you see two avenues opening up, take one and save the other for later. We don't know how much time we'll need."

"I'm not sure I'll recognize the opportunities," Rachel said. "I'm accustomed to closing deals, not prolonging them."

"We could have a trained negotiator at your side."

Rachel thought of the difficulties. "No, I wouldn't want the distraction."

"Let's try a few scenarios," Simmons suggested. "Nate, Booker, J.H., and I can take turns playing the role of the subject. We should be able to give you an idea of what to expect."

For more than an hour Rachel endured impromptu exchanges with the men, polishing her technique. At times, as they fell into their roles, the improvisations grew disturbingly realistic.

Each long session was followed by critiques, suggestions, and at times arguments.

The meeting did not end until almost midnight.

"I think we're as ready as we'll ever be," Simmons told her as the men prepared to leave. "There's no way of knowing when he will call again. But I'd guess sometime today."

Rachel asked one last question. "What should I do if I think I see a genuine chance to make a deal."

Simmons looked at her for a moment before answering.

"Mrs. Shelby, I'll be blunt so I won't be misunderstood. Just keep one thought firmly in mind: Once this subject gets his hands on the money, Suzanne is dead."

She's got an awful lot on her," Booker told Pete. "She may snap. She's close to it."

Pete was resting his head on the back of his chair at the edge of the patio, gazing up at the stars. "What makes you think so?"

Booker struggled to put the indescribable into words. "The look in her eyes. Like a caged animal. Just think about it. She must have died a thousand deaths in the last few days. Finding the kid's clothing was traumatic. Now there's the strain of talking with the killer, with Suzanne's life at stake."

Booker, worn out from his long day, had been unable to sleep. He had remembered that this was one of Pete's rare nights off. He had phoned and suggested to Pete that they get together and drink themselves numb.

"She'll be by early in the morning to have the dressings changed," Pete said. "I could insist on a tranquilizer."

Booker considered the possibility. "Might be best if you didn't. We need her sharp for the telephone."

"Couldn't someone else handle the calls? That's as wearing on her as anything."

"Too late. If anyone else answered, the subject would hang up. He seems to have a thing about cops. Rachel has played him well so far. We're hoping she can develop some rapport with him."

A coyote howled in the distance. Booker waited for an answer. The silence lingered. No potential mate around tonight for that lonesome lobo.

"Do you really think the kid's alive?" Pete asked.

Booker had been asking himself that question for days. "I was losing hope fast until today. Now I think she is."

"God knows what kind of shape she's in," Pete said.

For Booker, that thought stirred old memories. "It's unbelievable what some people will do to kids," he said. "I worked a case down by Idabel thirty years or more ago. In the deep woods down there. Wasn't a kidnapping exactly. Fellow's sister died. He wound up with her kids. For punishment, he burned them. Kept a hot poker in an old wood stove. This one little girl, he'd burned her ears off. Nothing but stubs left. Wasn't a square inch of the kid's body that didn't have scars. I was young and bushy-tailed then. I could've killed that son of a bitch as easy as looking at him. He only got twenty years on it. Probably out a long time now, working on other kids."

Booker and Pete sat for a while in silence in the peace of the rural night. But Booker's story apparently stirred memories for Pete. "Worst I ever saw was a scalded baby at Bellevue. The mother's live-in boyfriend did it. Deliberately. The baby lived three days, suffering every minute. That was before the days of burn units. I tried hard to save it. When it died, I came unglued. The chief resident took me into his office and chewed my ass. He said if I insisted on becoming emotionally involved, I'd never be worth a damn as a doctor."

"I'm sure glad you don't become emotionally involved any-more," Booker said.

Pete laughed. "Well, I don't. Not often. Just sometimes. A little compassion is good. But too much clouds your mind, makes you try what you shouldn't."

"Anger is what trips up an investigator," Booker said. "You get so mad over what some creep has done that you feel you've got to get him. So you start cutting corners and seeing evidence that isn't there. Stretching the evidence. That's an occupational hazard."

"Has your anger been a problem in this case?"

"I'm fighting it. An angry investigator is a bad investigator. There's just so damned much frustration in police work."

"I suppose there would be," Pete said. "With the courts and parole boards turning them loose as fast as you bring them in."

"It's the whole setup," Booker explained. "You spend a lifetime in police work before you begin to understand the true situation. The public thinks of crime as a war between criminals and the police. It isn't that way at all. Bottom line, crime is interaction between the criminal and the victim. Usually the cop is only a by-stander. Most of the time he just comes along afterward and tidies up. You can't go after the bad guys until they've been bad guys. You're always saying to yourself, 'If only I had been there.'"

"You can't blame yourself for not being there. That's absurd."

"You don't see what I mean. I'll give you an example." Booker hesitated. He had never shared this private agony with anyone. "My partner and I once investigated the rape and murder of a twelve-year-old girl. We worked up a suspect. But we couldn't find enough to nail him. I kept digging for months and found he'd been a suspect in three other kiddie rapes and murders, all similar, some in another state. Everywhere this guy went, kids died, and he walked on every one. I kept my eye on him. A year or so later he married a divorced woman with a daughter. A pretty little girl about eleven. I knew that situation was a time bomb. Sure enough, the girl showed up at a clinic a few months later with signs of sexual abuse. The mother lied, the suspect lied. Nothing was done. My partner and I almost had a fistfight over it, but I felt I had to step in. I went to the child protection people, told them all I knew. They said it wasn't enough to intervene, even to go out and do an inter-view. I went to the courts. There was doubt about the woman's divorce. The judge flat told me to keep my nose out of it. I wrote a report for the Bureau. All it got me was a reprimand. It seems that by keeping an eye on this guy, I was placing the Bureau in jeopardy of being accused of violating his civil rights."

Pete chuckled. "You probably were."

"A few months later the kid's body was found in a ditch. She'd been beaten some, but that wasn't what killed her. The guy's prick had ruptured a vein and she bled to death."

"Probably either the iliaca or femoral," Pete said. "Rare, but it happens."

"That was before DNA. The mother lied. The suspect lied. We couldn't get it all together. The DA declined to file. Not enough evidence. So the guy walked again. A few months later he and the wife moved to another state. I've lost track. But you know something? After Betty died and they shoved me out of the Bureau, that case was still hanging heavy on my mind. When I look back, that case along with a few others seem to outweigh all the convictions. Those failures turn my whole career into one long exercise in futility."

"Don't be ridiculous," Pete said, a trace of anger in his voice. "If it weren't for you, I'd probably be on death row, waiting for my appeals to run out."

"Your case was easy," Booker said. "The first time I talked with you, got some idea of what you were about, I knew you didn't do it. Patricia helped. She was fairly green in this game at the time, but after her very first interview with you she came straight to me and said, 'Booker, he didn't do it.' No ifs, ands, or buts."

"The rest of the world seemed to think otherwise."

"That was mostly television hype. After the first two or three days almost everyone in the Bureau was looking elsewhere."

"Still, from what I've heard, and from my own experience, I know there's no reason for you to consider your career as anything but remarkable."

Booker had never tried to explain the dark side of his life. He remained silent for a time, assembling the words he needed. "I closed some good cases," he admitted. "But after all is said and done, you tend to forget the good cases. It's the open files that stay with you, lay on your mind like a raw wound. I knew that child was going to die. I knew her stepfather was going to rape her. I knew he was going to kill her. But I screwed up. I didn't nail him."

Pete remained quiet while he made the connection. "I get the uncomfortable feeling you're hoping to use this Shelby case to shift the balance."

Booker did not answer. Pete had hit close to home.

Pete sighed. "Booker, neither of our professions is made for a perfectionist. Things happen. You don't always have control."

Booker was becoming uneasy talking about it. "I'm not a perfectionist," he said. "It's more complicated than that. We're talking justice. Justice for the defenseless, the helpless. That's what you've sworn to do as a cop. That's why your failures stay in your mind, eat you alive."

Pete seemed to consider that for a while. "I can see that the life of a contentious cop might become a living hell."

"It comes with the territory," Booker told him. "I've always known that. There's nothing to do but accept it."

Again they fell into a companionable silence. The moon was setting, reflected on the surface of the pond. An owl called from the distant fence line. Nightbirds sounded from the water's edge.

The turn of the conversation had left Booker disturbed, filled with thoughts he could never share with anyone. Again he thought of the long, dark nights with a gun in his lap and a gnawing horror in his head. Twice, with cocked pistol, he had come close to suicide. With both Betty and his career gone, there had seemed to be no reason to continue living.

He had been saved, pulled back from the brink, by childhood memories of his paternal grandfather. The old man had lived well into his nineties, overlapping Booker's own life by a full ten years.

During his grandfather's boyhood, all Cheyenne were raised as warriors. He had made several raids into Texas and into Kansas. He fought in battles with Custer near a fort in Kansas and on the Washita. He made a name for himself in the tribe by stealing a large band of horses from the Comanche. He had lived through the reservation times and the thievery of the U.S. Congress and its Dawes Commission. He had been born into one world, and Booker had known him as he approached death in quite another. His final years had been spent searching for the meaning of life. From his grandfather, Booker learned that the greatest injustice the whites did to the Indians was not the theft of their land or the death of the buffalo, but the destruction of their spiritual life.

"The medicine of our grandfathers no longer works," he told Booker. "I don't know why. I have looked at all the religions of this world and this is what I think: The Jesus road is the only one that goes all the way through. So I am walking the Jesus road. I want all of my sons and grandsons to walk it with me."

Booker had solemnly promised to walk the Jesus road. But he never did. Not seriously. He was always too fucking busy, working his way through college, taking all the shit dished out to his race in those days. He had survived, and earned a place in a world his grandfather could never have imagined. But he had broken a promise. He had never walked the Jesus road.

Now he was too fixed in his ways to make a sincere appeal. He still retained some integrity. Surely Jesus was tired of gathering in old farts who changed their minds at the last minute.

Booker hoped he was made of sterner stuff. In the olden days, Cheyenne warriors, like their samurai cousins, made it a practice to contemplate death every day. They sought a death that would define their lives.

If Suzanne were not found, what would be remembered of the life and death of Booker Reeves?

Would the long, dark nights return? Would the memory of his grandfather be enough to pull him back again? Or would he finally go over the edge?

Booker shuddered at the thought.

The moon had paled in the western sky. Dawn was near. Pete had gone to sleep in his chair. He was breathing deeply and effortlessly, his mouth partially open.

The coyote again howled in the distance. This time, after a moment, his call was answered. Booker found comfort in the thought that no matter what, life goes on in the world.

Quietly he eased off the patio. Another day was starting. Soon people would be up answering phones, answering questions. Booker had to be there, crowding as much work as possible into this new day. He started his car and eased away from the house in low gear, hoping not to awaken Pete, who needed the sleep.

17

Rachel was so thoroughly briefed that she felt totally in control when the kidnapper called again. "Let's get this out of the way," she told him. "Do you have Suzanne's secret name for the headmaster of her school?"

"Poot-Bah."

The wave of relief destroyed Rachel's concentration for a moment. Only Suzanne or David could have supplied that name. The headmaster was a martinet, widely called Pooh-Bah by the children. School legend insisted that he once had audibly passed wind during the silence of a full-measure rest at a piano recital. In talking with David one night, Suzanne had referred to the director as Poot-Bah and David had almost laughed himself sick. That had remained a secret joke between them, never shared with classmates out of concern it might get back to the headmaster.

Rachel waited until she again could speak without a trace of emotion. "All right, you have Suzanne. I have the money. How will we make the exchange?"

Again came the curiously clipped words. "Put it under the bridge. Then I'll turn her loose."

"I told you, that won't work. I must have Suzanne safe and firmly in hand before I can turn over the money."

The reply came in an instant shout. "Don't jerk me around, you bitch. You want her, you pay!"

Rachel had a momentary image of a small boy pitching a temper tantrum. She fought to remain calm. "I'm *not* jerking you around. Calling me names will get you nowhere. There's no need for that. We're in this together. Haven't I treated you with respect?"

He did not answer. After a lengthy silence Rachel sensed she should take the initiative. "I have a suggestion on how we might make the exchange. We could meet on a remote road, somewhere of your choosing. We could stop a distance from each other. I could bring the money halfway between us. You could bring Suzanne halfway. I would step back a few feet. While Suzanne comes to me, you could examine the money. We then would return to our cars and leave in opposite directions.''

Booker had suggested the plan as a ploy for delay. He and the other investigators strongly doubted the kidnapper would accept the plan.

But the silence seemed to indicate he was giving it serious thought. The line remained silent for a long interval. ''You'd bring the cops.''

''I promise, no cops. But I won't come alone. I would expect to have some protection with me.''

''Cops. You'd have cops. I know you have cops. You're jerking me around.''

''No, I'm not. I'm telling you up front what to expect. I don't know how I could be more honest than that.''

Again the line was silent. ''I don't know,'' he said. ''I got to think about it.''

Rachel recognized an opening for delay and took it, even though her inclination was to go ahead and try to talk him into the exchange.

''All right,'' she said. ''You can think about it. I'll be thinking, too, about how we can do this. But I want to emphasize, I must know that Suzanne is safe, and she has to be in my hands before I turn over the money. Do you understand?''

For an answer, the kidnapper hung up.

The abrupt end to the conversation unnerved Rachel.

It seemed to convey a finality.

Hopkins and Booker were on the other phone immediately. ''That went very well,'' Hopkins said. ''It bought us some time.''

Rachel was not so certain it had gone well. ''Was I too much the authority figure? I felt I shouldn't let him get away with calling me a bitch. But I'm not sure I should have responded so firmly.''

''I think you played it about right,'' Hopkins said. ''But we'll be getting an analysis.''

''He's still solidly hooked,'' Booker said. ''There's no mistaking that.''

''What if he calls back, accepts the offer?''

''I doubt that'll happen,'' Booker said. ''He's too afraid of a trap. But I've talked that over with Simmons. He agrees that we'll at least go through the motions. We'll arrange to keep him in the cross-hairs of the best marksman we can find, just in case he tries anything funny.''

Rachel was fast losing even the minimal faith she once felt for the delaying tactic. She kept hearing the kidnapper's voice, his peculiar mannerisms. In today's short conversation she thought she had gained new insights that left her filled with a greater sense of urgency. ''Booker, I think we should have an alternate plan ready, one he'll accept. I read a lot into his hesitations today. I strongly get the impression he knows he's in over his head. He's frightened and confused. His patience is wearing thin. I think he's on the verge of what the profilers warned us about. Violence.''

''You could be right,'' Booker said. ''But, Mrs. Shelby, we're getting close. All we need is one solid break.''

Harold hurried to put distance between himself and the phone, not by the most direct route. Instead of pulling back onto the interstate, he guided Sam's old car almost a mile westward from the truck stop, along the service road, keeping a close watch in his rearview mirror.

He was angry with himself. Once again he had failed to look ahead, see what might happen, and be ready. He should have known they would not agree to his plan to leave the money under the bridge. If he had done it right, he would have been ready with a string of demands: put the money under the bridge, and no cops, or you get her back in pieces. Which would you rather have for starters? A finger? Or an ear?

That would have got them moving.

He arrived at the hogback where the interstate sliced through a hill. There a rural road crossed over the interstate. Harold came to the stop sign, made a left turn, and drove across the interstate. As he came to a stop on the other side, he looked back to his left, toward the truck stop, and froze.

Unmarked cop cars were swarming into the truck stop like cockroaches. He counted six. Two more were pulling off the interstate. Some of the cars held two men, others four. The first cops to arrive were walking away from their cars. All were in plainclothes. But Harold knew they were cops from the way they rubbernecked everything and never looked at one another.

He was in plain sight. His intention had been to go on down the rural road, away from the interstate.

But if the cops noticed him and he drove away, one of the cars would come to check him out.

When cornered, rattlesnakes never try to get away. Sam had taught him that. They come toward you and edge around you until they are in the clear.

Harold turned back toward the truck stop and the cops. He pulled on left, onto the down ramp and the eastbound lanes of the interstate. As he passed the truck stop he allowed himself one glance at the cluster of cars and the men.

They were cops. No doubt about it.

Again the bitch had lied.

No cops, she had said.

Yet there they were.

He drove on, monitoring the traffic around him, keeping a close watch in his rearview mirror.

He reached into the glove compartment for his .357 magnum revolver and placed it in his lap. The hard cold steel felt good. If the cops came up from behind, or if he ran into a roadblock, he was ready.

He was tempted to take the next exit, hunt a phone, call the bitch, and tell her off. But he knew that would be a dumb thing to do. Even dumber than believing her in the first place.

People had called him dumb since he was a little tyke. It was time for a change. For once he should look ahead and see exactly what would happen if he did nothing to prevent it.

Sam's money was about gone. The bills were coming due. The pickup and car were wearing out.

Unless he did something damned quick, the red barn, the cars, would be gone. He would be afoot, just like before he met Sam. He would have no place to keep Sam and the snakes.

He could see that he had nothing ahead of him but fixing flats in service stations, stacking hay on farms, racking balls in pool halls, and shoveling shit out of cow lots.

He had been jerked around all of his life.

He was tired of it.

From now on he would jerk some other people around.

Starting tonight.

Awakened from sound sleep, Rachel reached for the ringing phone, assuming it would be Booker. For a moment she did not recognize the hysterical voice. "He called! Oh, my God, Rachel! He called!"

Rachel kicked off the covers, swung her feet to the floor, and switched on the lamp beside her bed. Two twenty-five in the morning. Three twenty-five New York time.

"Mother, calm down. Who called?"

"That monster! And the words he used! Horrible!"

"The kidnapper? Are you saying the kidnapper called you?"

"Just now! The phone kept ringing, woke me up. I thought it was a wrong number or something. I answered, and there was this voice. Oh, Rachel, it was awful!"

Rachel reached for a pad. "Mother, this is important. What exactly did he say?"

"Just filth! I can't use those words over the phone. They'd cut us off."

Rachel tried to keep her own voice calm. "They won't cut us off. Mother, I must know. What did he say? What was his reason for calling?"

"He said, 'You tell that lying bitch to keep the cops out of it and give me the money, or I'll turn her little bitch into a turd.' "

"Turd?"

"Four times he said it. I'm not mistaken."

Rachel knew she must get the exact wording. She persisted. "Mother, start at the beginning. Describe the entire conversation."

Judith made an effort. Her voice dropped closer to its natural register. "First, I answered. He was shouting. Just filth! I'm asleep, right? I can't make any sense of it. I'm thinking it's an obscene call. Like those you got. Remember?"

"Yes," Rachel said.

Once, years ago, she had been besieged for a month or more by an obscene caller.

"I'm about to hang up, when he said what I told you. When he said the words cops and money and what he would do, I knew. I asked him, 'What did you say?' And he said it again."

"That he would turn her into a turd?"

"Yes. Rachel, he knew my unlisted number! He must have connections!"

"I'm sure Suzanne told him. She *wanted* him to call you. She knew it would help us find him."

And Rachel also understood the call was a cry for help from Suzanne.

"What happened next?"

"He shouted and yelled some more. Some parts I couldn't understand. Either he was on a bad phone or he didn't speak clearly. But he warned me that if I went to the police—the cops—the next time I saw the little bitch she would be a turd."

"What else?"

"That was all."

"How did the conversation end?"

"He shouted again what would happen if he didn't get the money. Then he hung up. Rachel, he knows where I live! I'm here alone!"

It was the first time Rachel had ever heard her mother express fear. The revelation profoundly disturbed her. She found herself in the unusual role of comforting her mother. "I'm sure the call was long distance. You're not in any immediate danger."

"Such a monster! And to think he's got Suzanne!"

She began to cry.

Rachel debated what to do. The kidnapper had warned against going to the police. But she understood she had no option.

"Mother, listen, this is what I want you to do. Call nine-one-one. Tell them you must talk with the FBI duty officer for Manhattan. I'm not sure an FBI office will be open at this hour. But surely they'll have someone on call. Tell the nine-one-one operator that it's an emergency, that it involves the Oklahoma kidnapping of Suzanne Shelby."

"Rachel! He warned me not to call the police!"

"We must. It might help Suzanne. The FBI may be able to trace that call. They've explained to me that every small piece of information helps to form a pattern. Can you do that? Now?"

"If he learns I called the police, he'll kill her! I know he will!"

Rachel saw that she must reveal the true situation. "Mother, the police, the FBI, say that if they don't find him first, he'll kill her anyway. They don't give me any hope he will let her go even if we pay the money. They're almost certain he has killed several other little girls. So we have no choice. Please do this."

For a time Judith could not stop crying. "All right. If you think best," she managed to say between sobs.

"Listen to what I'm saying. The FBI will come and interview you. Tell them exactly what he said. Don't dodge around the filth. The wording is important. They do psychological profiles based on the exact wording. Do you understand?"

"Yes."

"As soon as we hang up, I'll notify the FBI here and they'll get together with the agents in New York. We don't have any time. I'll call you back, make sure you're all right. Okay?''

Judith was regaining her composure. "All right."

Rachel immediately dialed the motel desk and put through a call to Booker's room. He answered on the third ring. She told him what had happened.

He groaned. "They screwed up. I was afraid they had."

"Screwed up what?"

He answered reluctantly. "The FBI pinpointed the location of the phone while the subject was still on the line with you. He was at a truck stop a few miles west of town. They tried for an apprehension. They just missed him. He apparently saw them. That's what set him off."

Instantly Rachel was furious. "They did that? Right after I had promised him no cops! No wonder he's on a rampage! Booker, I told them I would hold them responsible!"

Booker spoke gently. "Mrs. Shelby, they missed him by less than three minutes. If it had worked, we'd probably have Suzanne back by now. It was a risk they felt they had to take. I really can't fault them for trying."

"But doesn't this change the whole situation?"

"I don't know. Tell me what he said to your mother."

Rachel relayed the conversation as Judith had described it. Booker interrupted only once.

"Turd?"

"She said he used the word four times, and that she wasn't mistaken."

"Curious," Booker said. "Go on."

Rachel finished Judith's account of the conversation.

"What will happen now?" she asked. "Does this mean he won't call anymore, that the negotiations are off?"

Booker was silent for a time. "We'll want to hear from the high-powered thinkers in Washington and Quantico. But two points strike me right off. He said, 'Keep the cops out of it.' And he said, 'And give me the money.' I think he's hanging tough. He's scared. But he wants the money. I believe we'll hear from him again."

"Is there any way we can keep the cops out of it? Completely hands-off?"

"No. But it's high time they pulled back and kept a low profile. I think I can make them see that."

"They must! If we don't keep in contact with him, we'll lose everything."

"I'll call Simmons," Booker said. "I'll see what I can do."

The squad room was jammed. Booker marveled briefly that a five-minute phone call from Oklahoma to a little old lady in New York could spill half the cops in western Oklahoma out of bed and create such a ruckus. He made his way through them, nodding a greeting and speaking to most as he went.

Nate, Simmons, and their administrative assistants were gathered around a desk in a back corner. Simmons was on the phone. Around him everyone seemed to be awaiting the outcome.

"Well, they ripped it," Booker said conversationally to Nate.

"Booker, they had to try. They asked me, and I concurred."

"Sure they had to try. But they didn't have to go in like Gangbusters."

Nate snorted. "Gangbusters. Just what I'd expect from an old fart like you. Booker, you're dating yourself."

Booker let it pass. But he felt the truth of it. The old radio show of his childhood, coming on the air with the sounds of sirens and gunfire, may have helped to push him into police work.

Simmons hung up the phone. He rocked back in his chair and addressed the crowd around him. "I want everyone who was in on the bust yesterday to think back. The subject saw us. Why didn't we see him?"

No one answered.

"I want a report from everyone who was there. Go back over it in your head. I'm sure at least one of us saw him. As soon as it's daylight, we'll reinterview everyone at the truck stop. We'll track them down wherever they are and see if they can't remember more. Let's get on it."

The group moved away. Booker took advantage of the jostling to move close to Simmons. "What do the profilers make of the turd angle?" he asked.

"They're stumped. Maybe they'll come up with a theory after they have time to think about it. But awakened out of sleep, they haven't the foggiest."

"Maybe it means he'll beat the shit out of her," Nate said. "Turn her into a turd."

"I don't read that context into it at all," Booker said. "It's driving me nuts. I think he slipped, told us something. We're just too dense to see it."

"Can you think of any regional use of the word that might apply?" Simmons asked.

Booker and Nate looked at each other.

"I've never made a deep study of it," Booker said.

"This subject's got a perverted mind," Nate said. "Maybe he's got a twisted slant on shit."

"He seemed to be referring to something specific," Booker said. "It's an anomaly. It has meaning."

"What do the Quantico boys think will happen next?" Nate asked. "Is the subject still playing the game?"

"The consensus is that he'll make at least one more try. The question is, do we move in, or do we back off?"

"Tom, for God's sake, back off!" Booker said. "One more mistake and we'll lose him for sure, along with Suzanne. We may have fucked up royally yesterday."

"Correction. We damned near caught him," Simmons said. "What I can't understand is how he disappeared so fast."

"No one in the restaurant saw anything at all?" Booker asked.

"Only seven people in the place, counting the waitress, fry cook, and the gas pump attendant. Only four customers, sitting at a front booth together. They all check out clean."

"The phone is around to the side," Nate explained to Booker. "No one inside the restaurant was paying much attention. But they probably would have noticed a car driving up. There wasn't any traffic in the parking lot."

Simmons pulled a drawing from beneath a stack of papers. "He could have pulled in here, at the west side of the restaurant. No one in that truck stop would have seen him if he walked around the back to the phone, returned to the car the same way, then drove west up this side road. But if he'd driven down to the entrance to the westbound entrance ramp, he would have attracted their attention."

"So he drove up this road," Nate said. "Then where?"

"We had units coming from the east and west. They were keeping an eye out for anyone moving away from the truck stop. My theory now is that he drove west to this overpass, and crossed over the interstate, then turned back east."

"Wouldn't someone have seen him?" Nate asked.

"Not necessarily. I went out and looked over the terrain. That's a moderately high hill. He would have been screened from the cars coming from the west."

"A matter of seconds," Nate said. "He's one lucky son of a bitch."

"Maybe more than lucky," Booker said. "Patricia warned us that ignorance doesn't always mean stupid. She said she would expect him to be crafty. We've seen him do several crafty things." He pointed to the sketch. "That little maneuver may be one of them."

"Anyway, we almost got him," Simmons said. "We're fairly sure he'll call back. We can call in volunteers, surveil every public phone along that whole damned highway. We can have helicopters up, airplanes. We can pinpoint him, track him, box him in."

"You think he's deaf and blind?" Booker asked. "You think he can't make a cop? He's done it every time. He seems to have good radar for cops."

"We could more or less bottle up the interstate, monitor every vehicle entering or exiting clear through this region."

"Look at your map," Booker said. "Look at all the rural dirt roads. He doesn't have to use the interstate."

"Airplanes could cover those back roads."

"And he'd see the airplanes. Tom, if we spook him this time, that's it. This is our last chance. He'll kill Suzanne and lie low for a while. We won't pick up his trail again until he snatches the next kid."

"I tend to side with Booker on this one," Nate said. "This guy now knows we're monitoring the phone. He'll be alert. I'm afraid we'd spook him before he could make the call."

"Then what the hell do you two want to do?"

"Let's return to the original plan," Booker said. "Play him along. We know he's getting antsy. We could go ahead and set up an exchange, if that's what he wants. That'll smoke him out. Then maybe we could take him. It wouldn't have to be Desert Storm. A half dozen good men could do it."

"What makes you think he might surface for an exchange?"

"The money. That's what keeps bringing him back. It won't be easy. He'll use the girl as hostage. Separating him from her will be the trick."

"I have a .375 bolt action Remington with a scope and a boattail hollow point load that would separate him real quick," Nate said.

"We could have the FBI SWAT marksmen down here by this afternoon," Simmons said.

"I think that might be a good idea," Booker said.

"And just let the phone surveillance go?"

"Yeah."

Simmons shook his head. "Booker, I don't know how I can justify backing off at this point."

"You said you were willing to take some heat."

"Believe me, I'm taking it. Believe me. Over the billboards. Over the reward-ransom thing. If all goes sour, it'll be plain I've mishandled the case."

"Tom, the plan to set up an exchange has logic," Booker argued. "We'll know the time and location. We can have the exchange site booby-trapped with personnel, hanging back out of sight. We can close all avenues of escape. We'd have him boxed. We'd only have to concentrate on keeping the girl alive."

Simmons lowered his head into his hands and kept the palms over his face a moment. "Okay, Booker, we'll play it your way," he said. "This won't be the first time a SAC was relieved in the middle of a major case. When do we brief Mrs. Shelby? Later this morning?"

"We'd better do it now," Booker said. "My gut feeling is that this fellow is about at the end of his rope. I expect him to call early today."

While Nate and Simmons touched bases with their assistants, Booker called Rachel to set up an immediate conference in her motel room. From her first moments on the phone he gathered that she had only a fragile grasp on herself.

"Are you all right?" he asked.

"I've been on the phone with my mother. The FBI questioned her for two hours. I know this seems unbelievable, but she's just now comprehending what may happen to Suzanne. She's taking it very hard."

"You want to put off this session until later? After breakfast?"

"No. I'm the worse for sleep. But I can listen."

On the drive out to the motel Simmons expressed his anger over the quality of work he was receiving from a few of his borrowed agents. "One of the special agents we brought in from Des Moines saw a car on the overpass to the west of the truck stop. He didn't bother to mention it until now. Said he thought it was one of ours."

"Description?" Nate asked.

"He saw only the top of it. Sun was behind it. So he didn't even get the color. He said he believes it came down the ramp onto the eastbound lane. But of course he didn't monitor as it went by. Real live wire."

Booker could imagine the zinger that would go into the agent's service jacket.

"Did he see how many people were in the vehicle?" Nate asked.

"He had the impression of one. He's not sure."

"That was probably the subject," Nate said. "It explains how he got out of the net."

Dawn was still an hour away. Early morning traffic was light. Nate slowed only briefly for red lights, then ran them.

At the motel, the two deputies were seated in folding chairs. Nate pulled into the empty parking space in front of Rachel's door. The space was reserved for her transportation, so she would not have far to walk in the crowded parking lot.

Rachel opened the door to Booker's knock. He followed Simmons and Nate into the room.

She had made coffee. Booker noticed that she had bought a portable coffeemaker much like Patricia's.

"Would you gentlemen care for a breakfast roll?" she asked.

They declined, accepting only the coffee. As she filled the cups, deftly working with one hand, Booker covertly watched her, monitoring the changes in her since their first meeting a week ago. The dark bruises on her left cheek and eye had faded to a yellowish green. She had lost weight. She now was far too thin. Yet there was an energy, a vitality about her that seemed almost defiant. Devoid of makeup, in head bandages and utility bathrobe, Rachel Shelby looked especially young and vulnerable.

Remembering how dispirited she had sounded on the phone, Booker wanted to go to her, hold her, and comfort her. Under the circumstances, that was impossible. He stifled the impulse and sat quietly.

She served the coffee, sat in a chair facing them, and spoke to Simmons. "Were you able to trace the call to my mother?"

Simmons gave her a abrupt nod. "A pay phone at a service station in El Reno. The station was closed. The streets would have been deserted at that time of night. He used a telephone credit card number. We're running it now. We anticipate it was stolen."

"You can buy stolen numbers most anywhere in bars and pool halls," Nate said. "It probably won't give us much."

"So what do we do now?"

Simmons explained that the profilers expected the kidnapper to call again. He outlined the change in strategy, from delay to cooperation.

As usual, Rachel was ahead of them.

"I interpret this to mean that your investigation has stalled and that you now have little hope of finding him before he kills her. Is that right?"

Simmons evaded a direct answer. "We think cooperation will move us into a new situation, keep him interested. If he surfaces for the exchange, we'll be there."

"Wouldn't that put Suzanne in even greater danger?"

Simmons could not talk his way around that one. He remained silent. Nate looked away.

Booker felt the question should be answered. "Mrs. Shelby, with all angles considered, we agree that this plan gives us the best chance of recovering Suzanne."

He did not add that without the plan, he doubted they had any chance at all.

18

Harold circled the block, approaching the public telephone from different directions, passing it three times.

He saw nothing anywhere that looked like a cop.

The phone stand was attached to a utility pole adjacent to the bus station, only one block off the main drag. Passengers were coming and going in and out of the bus station, milling on the sidewalk, waiting. The next bus, Amarillo to Oklahoma City, was not due for fifteen minutes. He would be off the phone long before then.

He parked behind the building so he could drive down the alley and be a street over in a second if he saw cops coming. He walked to the phone, put in a quarter for the tone, and dialed.

The little tough bitch's mama answered on the second ring.

"Did Me-maw tell you what I told her to tell you?" he asked.

She answered in that firm, calm, precise tone he found so infuriating. "She said you called. She gave me the message."

"You tell the cops to lay off?"

"I did. Believe me, I didn't know about the police. When I learned, I was angry too."

Harold figured that was pure bullshit. "You're lying," he said. "I know you was lying before. Are you lying about the money?"

Her voice became less prissy. "I swear to you, by almighty God, all I believe holy, I didn't know the police were going to do that. I also swear I have the money. Just as I described it to you. Two suitcases. Full. I further swear by all that's holy that you can have it if you'll deliver Suzanne safe."

Harold felt good. He had her groveling now. "You better not be lying about the money."

"It's here, waiting. Have you thought any more about how we can make the exchange?"

"Yeah. Tomorrow. Two o'clock. Go six miles north of Camargo. East two miles. You bring the money. I'll have the little bitch."

"Let me make sure I have this. I go six miles north of what? Camargo?"

"Yeah."

"Then two miles east."

"Yeah."

"How will we make the exchange? The way I described it yester-day?"

"Yeah."

"All right. I'll see you at two o'clock tomorrow."

Harold hung up the phone.

He laughed. "You're gonna see me before then."

He walked through the waiting bus passengers. Some glanced at him but no one was paying any attention. He walked on to Sam's car, drove up the alley to the next street, and circled around to where he could see the phone from a three-block distance. There he parked and waited.

The bus pulled in, discharged a few passengers, loaded, and drove off, leaving the sidewalk empty.

Still no cops.

Harold was surprised. He wondered if the little tough bitch's mama had told the truth. Certainly today was different from yester-day.

He looked at his watch. If he left now, he could be back in plenty of time.

He drove north, up through Leedey and Camargo to Woodward. There he skirted the town, taking the familiar roads toward the northeast.

Darkness came before he reached the red barn. He unlocked the door and went inside for the equipment he would need.

The little tough bitch was lying full-length on the cot. "Did you bring me anything to eat?" she asked.

He had forgotten. "I'll bring you something after a while." He laughed. "Wait'll you see what I'm bringing you. You'll bust a gut."

"I'm starving. Don't you know that? I won't live much longer."

He laughed again. "Tell ol' Sam about it. Sam ain't et in six weeks."

"I'm not a snake."

Harold thought that was funny. "You're gonna be before long. Now, shut up before I shut you up. I've got to think."

He gathered the gear from the back of the car and put it on the worktable. Speed loaders. Handcuffs. Plenty of ammunition. Sledgehammer. Prize bars. Gloves. Shotgun. A box of double-ought buckshot.

He changed into his khaki outfit, carried the gear out to the pickup, put it under an old tarp, and chained the doors of the barn.

Driving back south, he took his time. Yet he arrived at the interstate too early. So he stopped and ate a Sizzler. He ordered one to go for the little tough bitch. She was far from starving. But he had no doubt she was hungry. And the steak might be her last meal.

He drove around until a half hour after midnight. He then tooled over to the motel. Circling around behind the buildings, he entered the parking area from the rear and pulled the pickup into the semi-darkness next to the fence at the back.

Leaving the pickup, he walked along the street side of the motel to the soft-drink machines. As he expected, the two deputies who now had seen him several times were on duty. They sat on folding chairs in front of the door.

Harold felt even more certain that he was right.

Why else would they be sitting there, if they were not guarding the money?

He lingered at the machines, monitoring the parking lot. He saw no other cops. Cars were parked in front of most of the rooms, but no one was stirring. The parking space in front of the mama's room was vacant. That meant no cops were inside.

He sauntered across the parking lot toward the deputies, giving them ample opportunity to look him over. Neither one moved. Their guns were in their holsters, strapped down. Harold's own .357 magnum was tucked into his belt, nestled against the small of his back.

Five steps away from the deputies, Harold grinned as if he were about to come out with some bullshit about change for the machines. Neither deputy suspected a thing. They both looked up, waiting for him to speak. Harold reached behind him and took a firm hold on the revolver.

Rachel was in her shortie pajamas, brushing her teeth, when she heard the first explosion and felt the concussion.

She stood frozen in indecision. Close behind the first came another explosion. Two more followed in quick succession.

Only then did she recognize that the explosions were gunshots.

She ran to the phone and dialed the front desk. She heard the rings, but no one answered. A loud, pitiful groan came from just outside her door. She was tempted to peek out from behind the drapes. But she knew that would be foolish.

She was still holding the phone when she heard the car engine roaring. It was coming toward her door. She stood petrified.

Then with a thunderous crash the door to her room collapsed inward, frame and all. Debris sailed across the room and shattered the big mirror over the lavatory. A big chunk of plaster just missed her head.

She dropped the phone and ran past the broken glass into the dressing area.

The roar of the engine was deafening. A large metal pipe protruded through her door about knee high. Beyond, in dim light, she saw a radiator grille.

Again the engine accelerated. The pipe and grille pulled back. Heart pounding, Rachel waited, hoping that all the racket would bring help.

As if in response to that thought, a man stepped through the shattered door, pistol in hand. He was in uniform. Rachel immediately assumed him to be her rescuer. She started toward him. Then she saw the unmistakable look of triumph on his face.

In that instant she knew she had met the monster.

She fled into the bathroom, locked the door, and retreated to the far corner.

For a time she heard him rummaging around in her room. Then footsteps approached. The bathroom door shattered, the remnants banging against the wall.

The man's booted foot was still raised.

He screamed at her, "Where's the fucking money?"

"It's not here," Rachel shouted back. "It's in a bank vault."

"You're lying! Where is it?"

"I told you! In a bank vault. It's not here. Go ahead and look!"

"There ain't no suitcases!"

"They're in the bank!"

He seemed stymied. "Can you get it?"

"Not tonight. The bank's closed."

Rachel saw the hate in his eyes. He moved toward her. "You bitch! You lied! You said you had the money!"

Rachel raked his face with the fingernails on her good hand. Then a blow sent her reeling backward into the bathtub. Her head hit the wall. Even in a moment of semiconsciousness she remembered Dr. Peterson's warning about further injury.

The next she knew she was on the man's shoulder. He carried her through her room and out the front door.

She grabbed for what was left of the door frame but missed.

He carried her around the truck. They passed a man lying on the pavement in a dark pool. Rachel recognized him. The body of the other deputy lay farther into the parking lot.

Rachel's mind went blank with the sheer horror of the moment. The man threw her into the cab of the truck. Pain shot through her bad shoulder. Then the man was inside the truck, striking her with his open palm.

"Down!" he shouted. "On the floor!"

The blows to her head propelled her in that direction. She did not resist. She sought protection for her head beneath the dash.

Again the truck engine roared. They moved out of the parking lot with tires squealing.

They sped down the access road toward the intersection where she had wrecked her car. She could not see the street but she recognized the direction. At the intersection he slowed, then accelerated. She felt the truck climbing the entrance ramp to the interstate.

She comforted herself with the thought that after all the noise an alarm would have gone out. Surely by now they would be radioing ahead, watching all roads.

From the sound of the engine and the road vibrations, she knew they were traveling fast. Wind whistled through the open window on the driver's side. The monster was still shouting at her, laughing, excited. Above the wind she caught only an occasional word.

She wondered how she should react in order to stay alive. What would he want her to feel? Fear? Revulsion? Admiration?

Not knowing what to do, she did nothing. She crouched on the floorboards, watching him.

From what she could see in the reflection of passing headlights, he was not a bad-looking man. He could not be called handsome, but he was tall and his features were good, except for his mouth. Suitably dressed, with a smooth line of patter and less flab, he should be able to score nightly in any of New York's gathering places.

She wondered what had warped him, turned him into such a monster. She knew her survival, and that of Suzanne, might depend on finding the answer.

He braked and the truck slowed. Moments later she felt the truck descending from the interstate onto an access road.

Her hopes sank. If they made it away from the interstate, she could not expect rescue anytime soon.

They traveled for at least two hours on smooth pavement. Then for a while they bounced along on much rougher roads. Occasionally gravel hit the underside of the truck. The farther they went, the rougher the road became, until hard bumps sent pain shooting through Rachel's head. At times she felt dizzy. She did not know if this was the result of the blow at the motel, or if she was experiencing some of the dire symptoms Peterson had warned her about.

She lost track of time. The rugged road seemed to go on forever. Daylight came. Rachel occasionally saw the tops of trees going by at the roadside.

At last, after a bumpier few minutes, the truck slowed to a stop. The monster stepped from the truck and stood with the door open. "Out," he said.

Rachel struggled onto the bench seat. He seized her broken arm and pulled her out. She was so stiff and cramped, she could hardly stand. She wore nothing but the shortie pajamas—not even a bra. Somewhere in the manhandling she had lost her shower shoes. She was barefoot.

He propped her against the truck while he hunted for something in the back. Rachel examined her surroundings in the light of early morning.

They were parked in front of a large red barn. Behind her, to one side, a weathered, abandoned house slumped behind an overgrowth of vegetation. The windows were gone and the porch sagged almost to the ground. The house and barn were perched on the edge of a deep canyon.

"Walk!" the monster said, pushing her toward the barn.

He took a ring of keys from his belt, opened a padlock, and pulled a chain through the metal door with considerable racket. From inside the barn Rachel heard the clucking of chickens.

Jerking her bad arm, he pushed her through the door, spun her around, and threw her sprawling into a stall filled with hay. "You lied again!" he said. "I ought to kill you right now."

Watching him, studying him, Rachel realized that he had difficulty forming words. He seemed unaccustomed to speech. That accounted for the long pauses, the clipped words, and the hesitations on the phone.

She knew with fearful certainty that her life depended on convincing him that they were both victims in this. "The police lied to *me,*" she told him. "They *promised* me they would keep hands off."

With the sound of her voice a wail came from the far corner of the barn. "Mommy! Mommy! Is it you?"

Suzanne had not called Rachel mommy since the age of two. But it was Suzanne's voice.

Rachel felt both relief and dread. "Baby!" she called. "Are you all right?"

"Shut up!" the monster shouted, more to Suzanne than to Rachel.

Suzanne quieted. That was not like her. Rachel wondered how much Suzanne had been abused to achieve that level of discipline.

She felt she must establish some kind of rapport with the monster before the situation further deteriorated. She was still sprawled full-length in the hay. She sat up. "Look, I played fair with you," she said. "I expect you to be fair with me. I have the money. We can still make a deal. Just you and me."

He looked at her a moment, worked whatever it was in his mouth, then knelt at her feet. She looked down, not knowing what to expect. He encircled her right ankle twice with a chain and padlocked the links.

Without speaking, he walked to a table and began ridding himself of the gear he had carried in from the truck.

Rachel's eyes were still adjusting to the relative dimness of the interior of the barn. Big cages lined the far wall, all the way to the corner where she had heard Suzanne.

She was puzzled. The cages seemed far too big and too high for the few chickens in each. The air was heavy with pervasive, rank odors she could not identify. To her right came the low hum of an electric motor, a refrigerator sound. Canvas structures like upside-down tents lined the rest of the wall, on into the corner behind the workbench. Rachel could not imagine their purpose. Some kind of belts hung in rows to the right of the upside-down tents. As her eyes adjusted, she recognized them as snakeskins.

She shivered.

She had never felt comfortable even with alligator handbags and shoes. Snakeskin was beyond the pale as far as she was concerned.

The kidnapper returned, carrying a small stool. He sat in front of her, facing her. She was still seated in the hay, her right leg stretched by the chain.

"Where's the money?" he asked. "What bank?"

Rachel was determined to tell this man the truth. Even the appearance of an untruth might be fatal, both for herself and for

Suzanne. "The small bank on the corner, just down the street from the motel."

"You can get it?"

"Yes. Only one person has access to it. A man from the movie studio. I have another friend who can get it from him and deliver it. He can help."

"The old cop? The one that hauls you around?"

With a chill, Rachel understood that she had been stalked, perhaps for days, by this man.

Why had no one seen him?

"Ex-cop. He's retired. He has no official capacity."

"He works with them. He runs around with them."

"That's true. But I pay him. He'll do what I tell him. If I ask him not to tell the police, he won't."

"They listen on the phones. I know that. I'm not stupid. How you going to tell this guy to keep the cops out of it?"

Rachel thought of a way. "I can reach him through a person I trust. Believe me, I can get the money for you if you'll let us go."

He was frowning. A wet brown stream ran from the corner of his mouth down to his chin. "How do I know you ain't lying again?"

"You don't. But think about it. We both want what the other has. You want the money. I want my daughter and myself out of this, safe. We both can get what we want if we work together on it."

His frown deepened. He breathed through his mouth, running his tongue along his teeth while he considered what she had said. Rachel caught glimpses of a dark wad in his mouth.

"If I turn you loose, how'll I know you won't talk?"

Rachel took refuge in diversionary argument. "I don't know your name. I have no idea of the location of this place. That money can take you a long way from here. To another country, where the police would never find you." From his thoughtful expression, she sensed that the time had come to push. "I have only one stipulation." She was aware he probably was unfamiliar with the word. She used it calculatedly. "I demand to see my daughter, right now, to be sure she hasn't been harmed. After I see her, we can talk, work this out."

For an answer, he went to the workbench and got the key. He opened the padlock on her ankle and half dragged her the length of the barn.

Suzanne was perched on a cot beside a big cage. She was chained by the ankle. And to Rachel's horror, she was naked.

Rachel ran to her and kissed her. The left side of Suzanne's face was bruised and swollen. Ugly open sores ringed her ankle where the chain had rubbed. Suzanne began to cry.

Rachel held her. "Baby, are you all right?" she asked. "Has he hurt you?"

Suzanne shook her head. Rachel knew they both were not talking about blows and chains, but worse.

Rachel looked up at the man. "I demand clothes for her."

From his slow grin, she understood: Humiliation was a major weapon in his arsenal.

"He goes without clothes half the time," Suzanne said.

Rachel wondered briefly why he had not removed her shortie pajamas. Logic furnished the answer. Sexually inadequate, Patricia had said. Never a normal relationship with a woman in his entire life. Suzanne's still-flat chest, lack of pubic hair, and smooth crease were not threatening to him. Her own mature womanliness was.

She filed that knowledge away for possible use.

She also remembered that Patricia had said to keep his mind busy.

"Look, there's no need to mistreat her. All we need to do is find a way for you to get the money and for us to go free. We must work together on this."

His voice again took on the tone of schoolboy belligerence. "You let me worry about that." He pointed a finger at her. "And I'm telling you. If you're lying again, she'll get et by ol' Sam here."

Rachel thought she had misunderstood. "Sam?"

"The big snake," Suzanne said in a small voice. "There."

Rachel followed Suzanne's gaze and barely stifled a scream.

A huge snake lay not five feet away in the darkness at the top of the cage.

The man was amused. He struck the cage with a fist. "Hey! Sam!" he shouted.

The snake stirred and raised its huge head.

"Sam ain't et in a long, long time. He's plenty hongry. If you're lying again, you can watch while he eats her."

Rachel poised her tongue to say that a snake could not eat a person. But she stopped short.

She had no idea what a snake that size could do.

He had promised to turn Suzanne into a turd.

Was that possible?

Suzanne read her thoughts perfectly. "He says Sam has eaten six girls about my size. The smaller big snakes over there eat chickens all the time, whenever they feel like it."

Aware that knowledge might be her only weapon, Rachel sought a roundabout way to ask about this place, this man. "What are those canvas things over there?"

"Rattlesnakes," Suzanne said. "This is the snake man. He catches snakes for a living."

And kills little girls, Rachel thought.

"Now you know my name," the snake man said. He jerked Rachel to her feet. "Party's over."

He dragged her back to her stall and snapped the padlock on her ankle.

Keep his mind busy, Patricia had said. Rachel rushed into a plan only half-formed. "Listen to me. We can do it this way. You can take me to a phone. I'll call my friend. She can get word to the person who can get the money. He can leave half—two hundred and fifty thousand dollars—anywhere you say. Then, after you let Suzanne go, he'll deliver the other half. You can take me with you, to someplace where you're safe, before turning me loose. How does that sound?"

"The old cop would tell them. He'd fuck it up."

"No! He couldn't. He's obligated to me, to Suzanne. I hired him to keep us safe. He'd know that this is the way to do it."

From the snake man's frown she could see that he was thinking seriously about it. She felt she should block his thoughts from other areas. "This is the only way. If you try to rob the bank, they would be on to you before you got out of town. You've been there. You know the town is full of police. And they'll be angry now that you've killed two of them. This way, we could do it without the police knowing."

"The old cop would tell," he said again.

"He wouldn't," Rachel insisted. "Not if I tell him not to."

The snake man turned and walked away without another word. He went to the worktable. Soon Rachel saw that he was cooking heroin, preparing himself a fix. Once, years ago, she had edited a novel that dramatized the procedure in detail.

Reviewing her impromptu plan, she could find nothing she would change. The first step would free Suzanne. That was her prime consideration. And she had planted the idea that he could use her as a hostage.

Otherwise, unless she continued to be of some value to him as a hostage, he would kill her.

She had told only one possible lie.

In truth, she was not sure how Booker Reeves would react.

The fact that Booker had been a policeman all his life would affect his thinking. She could not predict the results.

The snake man sat in an old chair and gave himself a shot. He then leaned back in the chair and closed his eyes.

Suzanne began to cry. Rachel wanted to voice some words of comfort, but none came.

After a time the refrigerator clicked off and the interior of the old barn stilled. The chickens quieted. Suzanne's soft sobs and the occasional slithering of snakes were the only sounds.

19

Booker's pain went far beyond the visceral. It penetrated his soul, the core of his being.

He knew he would never forgive himself.

The abduction of Rachel Shelby revived memories of other tragic mistakes he had made through the years.

Once, back in the fifties, a convicted murderer had slipped his cuffs, grabbed Booker's pistol, shot him, and left him for dead. Before the killer's capture ten days later, he raped and murdered two high school cheerleaders.

Booker had been careless snapping on the cuffs. He had not noticed that the killer placed three fingers along one wrist.

As a result, two innocent victims died.

Booker still felt that pain after more than three decades.

He had made other tragic mistakes. But nothing came up to the level of this one. "We should have seen it coming," he said to Nate. "All the signs were there. He was too quick to agree to the exchange. Just plain stupidity on our part."

"Booker, I've got two men down," Nate said. "I'm in no mood for second-guessing."

"I'm talking about me. I should have seen it coming, been over there in that parking lot, waiting for him."

"Then we'd probably be burying three instead of two. He's slick, this one."

They were waiting for Simmons to get off the phone. Crime scene photographs and trace evidence from the motel had been sent to Quantico. An analysis was expected momentarily. The crime scene crew had picked up several latents, but they appeared old. Booker held no expectation they would yield a solid lead.

All occupants of both wings of the motel had been rousted and interviewed. The results were meager, and confirmed a trend

Booker had noticed. In the old days, suspicious noises made people look out their front windows. Now urban gang wars, movies, and television dramas had done their work. On the first hint of trouble, people ducked. Most hit the floor.

No one had seen anything. Not even the desk clerk, who admitted he had dropped to the carpet at the first shot and stayed there until he heard the pickup truck leaving the parking lot. Only then had he peeked out.

An old pickup, he said, maybe blue, maybe black. He could not see how many passengers were in it.

"I can't understand how he got the drop on both Henley and Grimes," Nate said. "Two good, experienced men. I've worked with them. They wouldn't have been caught napping. You've worked with them, haven't you?"

"Grimes, a couple of cases," Booker said. "I knew Henley only to speak to. But I can see how it might have happened. The guy looked normal. He probably walked right up to them and they didn't suspect a thing until he pulled that three fifty-seven. They probably thought he was going to ask how to get back onto the interstate, or where he could get a hamburger that time of night."

"We're long on theories, short on a collar. And two good men went down with half the law officers in this part of the country sitting around with their thumbs up their asses. Booker, now we've got to get this guy."

Booker did not comment. He had never shared the view of his colleagues that an officer down necessarily escalated a case. To his mind, law officers were obligated to put their lives on the line every day. Risk came with the job. To some extent, the same could be said for convenience store clerks, jewelry salesmen, bank cashiers, and armored car personnel. But a child was a completely innocent victim. Booker did not rank any crime higher. Not even the killing of a fellow cop.

Booker's view was in the minority. When the subject came up in cop shops, Booker kept quiet.

And while he blamed himself for Rachel's abduction, he also blamed Henley and Grimes. They should have been more alert. The latch on Henley's holster was still fastened. No doubt he was shot first. Grimes had managed to get his strap unlatched. But his pistol was still in its holster.

Dumb, dumb, dumb.

Booker also blamed everyone connected with the investigation. They all should have been thinking ahead to what the subject might do next.

Instead, they had allowed him to con them with his quick agreement to the exchange.

Now Rachel Shelby was gone, maybe dead. The son of a bitch probably would not keep her alive for fun and games. If Patricia was right, this one had no use for grown women.

Simmons got off the phone and leaned back in his chair. "Okay, I've received a verbal preliminary. The profilers think, from the way Mrs. Shelby's room was tossed, that the subject was after the money and that the abduction was secondary."

Nate and Booker looked at each other.

Brilliant, Booker wanted to say.

But he was in no position today to criticize.

"What about the latents?" Nate asked.

"We have a few names. We're checking them out. Nothing looks promising."

"So the bottom line is, we're right where we were two days ago," Nate said. "We've learned nothing new from this."

Simmons did not answer.

"Do they have any theories on what he'll do with her?" Booker asked.

"They think that ordinarily he'd get rid of her fast. But they say we may have two factors working for us. First, he may try for the money, using Mrs. Shelby. Second, they now have him pegged as a sadist. They believe he may want to torture and kill the kid in front of Mrs. Shelby."

Booker closed his eyes for a moment. He had been thinking along those lines.

"Anyone been through her papers over at her office?" he asked.

"Not yet. Even with the extra manpower coming in, we're spread thin."

"I could go over and do that," Booker offered.

"What would you expect to find?"

"She was well organized. She kept notes. I'm thinking that this subject has been stalking her. She may have written something down she thought too insignificant to mention."

"Okay. Go ahead and do that. We're expanding the search, trying to find witnesses to his route out of town, so I'll be out of pocket here for a while. If you find anything, tell Hopkins. He'll know how to reach me."

"I figure she's already dead," Nate said. "He was bound to have been plenty pissed when he didn't find the money. He doesn't seem to have much of a hold on his temper."

"That could be," Booker said. "But she's a good talker. She

handled him well on the phone. I'm just praying she can con him, stay alive long enough for us to find him.''

Booker left the police station and drove to Rachel's office. A new onslaught of television trucks and news people had descended. They were clustered around the building, filling the parking lot and spaces at the curbs. Booker wasted several minutes finding a place to park.

Several from the media recognized that he had something to do with the investigation. Cameras turned in his direction. Questions were shouted. Booker raised his voice. ''I'm not authorized to make statements. Talk to Chief Laird.''

The office door was locked. Booker tapped on the glass. Pete's cute emergency room nurse came and opened the door for him. He could not remember her name. Her eyes were red and she looked like hell. The office was full of volunteer workers. Plainly all had been crying. Some still were.

''I'm Donna Sewell,'' the nurse said. ''We all felt we should be here. But without her we don't know what to do.''

''My advice would be to close the office, at least temporarily,'' Booker said. ''It has served its purpose.''

''Is there anything new?''

The other volunteers were listening. Booker felt he should offer as much hope as he could. ''Not yet. But don't forget that half the officers in the state are working on it, not to mention the FBI.''

He walked on toward the back of the office. Donna followed.

''I thought I'd look over her notes, see if there's anything that might be of significance,'' Booker explained.

She led him into Rachel's office and turned on the light. ''Her desk is just like she left it yesterday,'' she said. ''None of us felt like being in here.''

She gave way to tears. Booker found himself in the grip of an almost overwhelming urge to put his arm around her and comfort her. But he just stood silent. She shook her head by way of apology and, with tissue to nose, went out, leaving him alone.

He stood for a moment wondering if this sudden recurring impulse to comfort young women was part of the process of becoming a useless old fart.

He sat at Rachel's desk. During his career he had gone through the private effects of hundreds of crime victims. Never before had he felt so strongly that he was prying. Rachel's slim presence seemed to be hovering over the desk.

He opened a notebook filled with her neat handwriting. The precise notations seemed intimate and personal. Booker read for several minutes before regaining his professional distance.

The first notebook concerned her interviews with various people in the news media. She analyzed each as to potential audience and effectiveness. She had made specific notes on the interviews, citing attempts to trap her into saying what she did not want to say.

The list went on and on. But for Booker's purpose the only revelation was a greater appreciation for the depth and scope of her accomplishments over the last few days.

A yellow legal pad contained material more rewarding. In her painstaking way, she had listed all the points made by Patricia and Hopkins on how to handle the kidnapper.

A few she had underscored.

Farther down were notes that at first seemed sheer gibberish. There were headings such as "Playing to his esteem," and "Playing to his need for belonging," and "Playing to his self-awareness."

She had drawn boxes. Under "His security needs" she had written "Promise him *repeatedly* that the police will stay out of it."

Delving deeper into the material, Booker came to understand that she was employing her own elaborate system of negotiation, probably the same she used in her business.

She had factored in the advice of Patricia and Hopkins and emerged with her own unified plan.

Booker shook his head in admiration. As usual, she had been far ahead of everyone. Her deft handling of the calls had been no accident, but the result of much hard work.

Farther down, she posed questions: "Patricia says he probably was abused in childhood. Would there be any way of reestablishing rapport with his childhood image? Soothing those wounds? Would it help to try to establish a *maternal* role? Or would that be too dangerous? Must ask Patricia."

She had made other, extensive notes. Booker read through all carefully.

He had finished with the notebooks and was fishing in the desk for any other items of possible importance, when one of the three phones on the desk rang. Startled, he belatedly identified the ringing phone as the straight line from the police department. He answered.

"Simmons just called in," Hopkins said. "He was wondering if you found anything."

"Nothing that means much at the moment," Booker said. "She kept extensive notes and observations. They may tell us something later."

"Could the profilers use them?"

Booker considered briefly. The profilers were trained in that area. He could have missed something. "They might," he said.

"Bring them over. We'll fax them. And you've had two phone calls I should mention. Pete says he needs to talk to you. The other was from Rachel's mother. Mrs. Mermin."

Booker thumped the desk. "Damn. I should have called her this morning. We shouldn't have let her learn about it on the news. I just wasn't thinking straight."

"None of us was. You have her number?"

"Somewhere. But you better give it to me."

He took down the number. Hopkins seemed reluctant to end the call, even though Booker heard another phone on his desk ringing. "Booker, she's a smart lady. I really think she might be able to talk the guy out of killing her. At least for a while."

Booker knew Hopkins was addressing him personally and not just discussing the case. He appreciated the gesture.

"That's my thinking," he said. "I figure we've got twenty-four hours, maybe a little more if we're lucky, to find her."

"I think we will. Everyone has already signed for a double shift tonight. Everyone! Just hang in there, Booker. We'll get him. I've got to go."

He hung up. Booker sat for a moment debating which call to return first.

He opted for Pete. As he expected, he first had to answer the inevitable question. "I'm sorry, Pete," he said. "There's nothing new at this point."

Pete's voice was low and strained. "We kept it from David for a while this morning. But he became suspicious. I had to tell him. Booker, he took it pretty hard. I had to sedate him. Now I'm concerned. I can't keep the kid sedated forever."

"I have a callback here from his grandmother. Should I suggest that she come down?"

Pete hesitated. "What I'm telling you now is doctor-patient, privileged information: Rachel doesn't get along too well with her mother. And she feels that the grandmother's relationship with the kids is not up to par."

Booker was surprised. He wondered how David felt about his grandmother. "Still, she's family," he said. "David may need family around him, especially if worse comes to worst."

"That's true. Maybe we shouldn't interfere if she wants to come. She tried earlier, and Rachel stopped her. Rachel said she didn't want her mother butting into all she had to do."

That was understandable. "That's out of the way now," Booker pointed out. "I won't suggest she come. But if she's inclined, I'll say it might be a good idea. How would that be?"

"On target, I think. What I wanted to ask, I'm thinking of moving David out to my place. There's really no reason for him to be in the hospital now, and it's depressing for him. Miata could mother him, and he'd have Miata's kids to talk with. What do you think?"

"I'm sure Rachel would like that. But if the grandmother comes, there might be complications with him out there."

"We could put her up too. That way they'd have more time together. From what I hear, she wouldn't be able to get a room in town anyway."

"Want me to extend the invitation?"

"Why not? Go ahead." Pete paused. "Booker, what do you think on the odds of finding her?"

Booker saw no reason to lie. Not to an old friend seriously involved, and who really wanted to know.

"Pete, I'm convinced this asshole is the most vicious killer I've ever run across. But our theory now is that it may be to his advantage to keep her alive for a while. If we get a break within twenty-four hours, I think she has a chance."

"Well, I've seen you work miracles before, Booker. I'll be praying you can work one more."

Years ago, back when Rachel was a teenager and thought she might become a commercial artist, she was sketching one afternoon in the primate house at the Bronx Zoo. Engrossed in her drawing, she belatedly became aware that she had won an admirer. A male monkey was prancing back and forth in front of her, showing off an erection.

She had stayed late to complete a drawing. She was alone in that portion of the primate house. She sat mesmerized through the bizarre ritual, until eventually the monkey tired of the game and rejoined his companions.

Rachel had thought the monkey's exhibition the most humanlike act she had ever seen from an animal.

Now, as the snake man paraded in the buff, Rachel thought his behavior the most animallike she had ever seen in a human.

Moments earlier, before taking off his clothes, he had given himself a narcotic fix. She sensed that the chickens had something to do with his performance, but she did not know exactly what. The chickens in a center cage were raising a tremendous clamor, squawking and running from one corner to the other, tumbling over one another in their haste.

A moment later, to her horror, she understood why the chickens were in such a panic.

One of the large snakes was gliding slowly down from his perch. His movements were almost glacial. As his head dropped lower and lower, the chickens went into full-scale hysteria.

The snake man hurried to the cage and sat in the lotus position on the bare cement floor. His giggling and chortling rose even above the noise of the chickens.

Rachel knew she was being introduced to the snake man's fantasy. Yet she could not interpret it. The scene was disorienting, and made no sense to her.

The stalking, the frantic squawking, the laughter, continued for an interminable time.

Then abruptly the terror of the chickens ended. In a motion too fast for the eye to follow, the snake struck, snaring a chicken by the neck. The snake man shouted his exhilaration. The snake's coils tightened around the victim-chicken.

The other chickens quieted and scattered.

Moments later the victim-chicken's third eye closed and its feet stuck out stiff. Slowly the snake changed position, coils working. The jaws unhinged and the swallowing began.

Rachel could not bear to watch.

After the chicken disappeared into the snake, the snake man rose and resumed his marching. He pounded on the snake cages, shouting. For a while he seemed to be paying no attention to anyone but himself. But gradually he moved toward Suzanne's cot.

Rachel's view of that corner was blocked by the side of her stall. She heard the snake man repeating, over and over, "Come on, you little bitch. Come on!"

Never in her life had Rachel felt so completely helpless. She wanted to yell and scream at the snake man. She wanted to threaten him. But she was certain that if she broke his self-immersion in his fantasy, she would awaken his violence. She sensed that she must ignore her feelings, trust to her intelligence, and keep a tight rein on herself. Suzanne had said the snake man had not hurt her. Rachel made herself follow Suzanne's lead.

She would not yell unless Suzanne did.

Suzanne remained silent. Rachel heard the snake man's heavy breathing, his occasional grunts.

In a few minutes he returned. He did not even glance in her

direction. She remembered Patricia explaining that the kidnapper no doubt viewed his victims as inanimate objects, dolls to use for whatever he did with them.

On a few dates during her early adult years, Rachel had found herself treated almost totally as a sex object and ignored as a person.

But this was the ultimate.

Thinking back, she could see that from the moment of her abduction the snake man had been vacillating across a borderline. He was forced to deal with her as a person in order to get the money. But in all other respects he had ignored her. She recognized the need to keep pulling him back across the line to thinking of her as a person, to thinking of the money. She called to him. "Have you thought about my plan? Are you ready to go get the money?"

He turned and looked at her blankly. He frowned. "Shut up!" he shouted.

Rachel persisted, aware she was risking a beating. "Remember, if we work together, I can get you half the money. You'll get the other half when Suzanne is free."

Again he shouted. "Shut up!"

His face was red, like that of a small boy in a tantrum. She remembered his outburst on the phone. She had no doubt he was capable of murderous rage.

So she shut up for the moment.

He walked away talking to himself. "I got to work. That guy in Phoenix needs them heads."

Methodically, he lined up a series of Styrofoam containers. Still naked, he walked to the canvas pits and snared a rattlesnake with his bare hands. Holding the head, he milked the venom into a beaker while the snake coiled around his arm. He picked up his knife and adeptly whacked off the snake's head and rattles. He hung the snake's body on a hook and slit the skin lengthwise along the belly. In one smooth, fluid movement he removed the skin. He raked out the entrails and cubed the meat. After scraping the skin, he applied a chemical fixative.

Rachel was impressed by his skill. His movements were efficient. Heads went here, rattles went there, meat elsewhere. From his earlier erratic behavior she would not have thought him capable of such organized effort.

She wondered if someone else possibly could be associated with the business, someone who had established the procedure.

The snake man worked without letup. His movements made the only sounds in the old barn. The snake with the lump in its middle had climbed back up to the top of its cage. The chickens remained silent.

Lulled by the monotony, exhausted from fear and tension, Rachel lay back in the hay and wept silently, fighting panic, making herself search for some way to get Suzanne and herself free.

The snake man came and kicked her shins. "Come on," he said. "Let's go."

He had dressed in his uniform. He knelt, unlocked her chain, jerked her to her feet, and pushed her ahead of him out the door.

The night was cool, the sky clear, the stars dazzling. In her pajamas and barefooted, Rachel shivered from the chill. The snake man guided her to the pickup, pushed her inside, and climbed in behind her. "Down!" he said.

Rachel dropped to the floorboard to avoid the blows she knew would come. He started the truck and they moved slowly down the rough canyon road. There was no hint of exhilaration about him tonight. He seemed preoccupied, unreachable.

He drove grimly. For a while Rachel tried to keep some sense of distance and direction. But that proved impossible. The roads twisted and turned, and his speeds varied.

Gradually the roads improved. The snake man drove faster. After an hour or more, reflected lights indicated they were passing through at least the outskirts of a sizable town. The snake man drove on.

A few minutes later they again were traveling through darkness.

Rachel estimated that they were on the road more than two hours before she recognized maneuvering that indicated they were pulling onto the interstate.

After a half hour or so on the interstate, the snake man slowed. Rachel felt the pickup drop as they traversed an exit ramp. For several minutes they seemed to be circling. At last the snake man stopped. "Out!" he said.

Rachel raised her head from beneath the dash. They were parked on a dark, lonely street a few feet from an old-fashioned phone booth—the kind with a glass box, floor, and a folding door.

"Out!" he said again.

"Where will I tell them to leave the money?" she asked.

He gave the instructions in a flat tone, as if by rote, working the cud in his mouth in rhythm with the words. "Go to Vici. South six. East two. Hollow tree. North of road. Ten o'clock tomorrow."

Rachel repeated the instructions. He pulled her out of the truck.

The gravel of the roadbed knifed into her feet. She stepped gingerly into the phone booth. He pushed in behind her and closed the door. His odors enveloped her.

"You know the number?" he asked.

"Yes," Rachel said. Every phone in town was assigned the same three-digit prefix. That made the last four easier to remember.

"You dial," he said. "I'll listen. No tricks."

He inserted a coin for the dial tone and held the receiver firmly between them. At such close range, he smelled strongest of snuff, stale sweat, and the chemical he used to tan the hides.

Rachel dialed Donna's number. The phone rang five times before Donna answered. Donna's voice sounded heavy with sleep.

"Donna, this is Rachel. I'm calling to ask a big favor."

"Rachel! Where are you! Are you all right?"

"Yes. But, Donna, I'm not free to talk. Please listen. This is important."

As Rachel expected, Donna's discipline as a nurse came to the fore. Immediately she was focused. "Tell me."

"Please go to Booker. Quietly. Get him away from the police, everyone. Tell him I've made a deal."

Rachel outlined the terms.

Donna hesitated. "That gets Suzanne released. But what about you?"

"Donna, please. This is the deal I've made."

Through the earpiece, Rachel could hear the snake man breathing into the mouthpiece.

She hoped Donna also heard it.

"All right. I'll tell Booker. You can count on it. But I've got to ask. Is Suzanne okay?"

"Yes. Patricia was right about everything."

The snake man jerked the phone away. For a moment Rachel feared he was ending the call. But he frowned, shook his head no, and again put the phone to her ear.

Rachel hurried to finish before he changed his mind. "Donna, I've got to give you the instructions on where Booker is to put the money. Do you have paper and pencil?"

"Just a second." Rachel heard rustling. "Okay."

Rachel gave the directions.

"The money must be there by ten o'clock tomorrow morning. I've lost track of days. Not the morning after the night we're in now. The next one."

"Thursday. By ten A.M. Thursday. Okay. I'll tell Booker."

"Tell him we absolutely must keep the police out of it. And, Donna, please don't tell anyone else about this call."

Again the snake man jerked the phone. Rachel held on.

"You can depend on me," Donna said.

"I know I can. That's why I called you."

She opened her mouth to say more, but the snake man put a hand on the button and broke the connection.

He hung up the phone.

"In!" he said, gesturing toward the pickup.

Rachel stepped back through the gravel, climbed into the truck, and slid onto the floorboard beneath the dash without being told to do so.

He started the truck. "What'd you tell them?"

"Just what you told me. You heard me."

"Who's this Pat whatever her name is?"

"Patricia. She's a friend. She kept telling me Suzanne was safe. I was just confirming that she is."

"They better not go to the police!"

Rachel did not respond. She arranged herself as comfortably as possible for the long ride back to the red barn and thought of the risks she was taking.

She trusted Donna.

But she was not at all sure what Booker would do.

20

The narrow dirt road climbed over a high hill and sloped gently down to a creek almost a mile away. A succession of wet years had left all vegetation lush and green. The creek bottom was especially fertile. Fields of alfalfa, corn, wheat, and cotton filled the landscape into the distance. Below the hill, at the far side of a strip of cotton, a lone hollow cottonwood rose beside the creek.

Cautiously Booker looked back to confirm that his car was well hidden. He had driven it close to the creek, behind a rank stand of brush. He was relieved to see that even from this angle, at the top of the hill, the car was out of sight.

The sun was a half-hour old and warm, burning dew off the grass at roadside. But the cuffs of Booker's trousers were still wet and flopping from his walk through the fields.

He had left the suitcase in the hollow tree, an old cottonwood split years ago by lightning. Even from this distance a corner of the suitcase showed dark against the tree trunk.

He glanced at his watch. A quarter to seven. He faced a long wait. He walked on down the hill, searching for the proper place to bed down.

Toward the bottom of the hill the roadside ditch had been carved deeper by decades of spring torrents. There, profuse grass, weeds, and wildflowers provided suitable cover. Considering the proximity of the hollow tree, fifty yards across a strip of tender green cotton, Booker estimated that the subject would stop close to this spot. He selected a place where he could lie flat and remain hidden from the road, yet could sit up for a good view of the entire landscape.

Already the day was growing hot. Booker slipped off his jacket and used it as a pillow. He placed his hat upside down in the grass, removed the transponder from his shirt pocket, and placed it beside his handheld radio.

The transponder was an expensive gadget just now coming into use. Bumper beepers had been around for years, but they were limited in range and effectiveness. This new gadget sent signals to a satellite. The manufacturer claimed that its location could be pinpointed within a hundred yards.

Booker had been tempted to plant the device in the suitcase with the money. But he had been told that if the suitcase was carried into a metal building or underground, the capabilities of the device would be compromised.

So he had decided to try for the subject's bumper. He figured that if he could manage to plant the gadget on the vehicle while the subject went for the suitcase, the subject could be tracked home to his hideout.

The FBI SWAT team then could make a quick assault in force.

Booker stretched full-length in the grass, rested his head on his makeshift pillow, and waited.

Stakeouts were never easy. But through the years he had learned patience. To pass the time, he watched the bees and insects working the wildflowers, the birds passing overhead, the cattle grazing in a pasture beyond the creek.

During the next two hours two pickups passed. They were the only vehicles on the road. Neither slowed. One was two-tone green and of ancient vintage, the other newer, red over white.

A few minutes after nine a vehicle approached from the west and slowed as it came down the hill. Booker lay flat, hardly daring to breathe. Not until it was safely past did he raise himself up for a peek. The pickup was old, a faded, once-dark-blue GMC. The front bumper was reinforced with five-inch pipe, the kind used to break through Rachel's motel room door, and the kind described to Patricia by the witness under hypnosis.

Booker saw only one occupant in the truck—a male subject wearing a gimme cap. At the bottom of the hill the truck picked up speed, went on past the small bridge over the creek, and vanished among trees to the east.

A few minutes later the truck returned, traveling even slower. Again Booker lay flat until it had passed. It went on over the hill.

With the third pass Booker thought the driver again planned to drive on, for he went past where Booker had estimated he would stop. But farther down the road the driver braked and pulled the pickup to the side of the road.

After a minute the driver's door opened. The man in the gimme cap got out. Booker cautiously watched him through the weeds.

The subject was taller, bigger than Booker had expected from the descriptions. The man walked around the truck, kicking the tires as if gauging air pressure, while rubbernecking the road and surrounding fields. His gaze kept returning to the direction of the hollow tree.

Booker did not see a gun. But he had to assume that the man was armed.

Abruptly the subject left the truck in a fast jog toward the hollow tree. Booker grabbed the transponder, gathered his feet under him, and estimated time and distance.

By parking farther down the road, the subject had wrecked Booker's plan to dash from cover, plant the transponder, and return to hiding, all in less than fifteen seconds. Now, with the truck farther down the road, he was forced to make a forty-yard sprint in the open.

He did not hesitate. While the subject's back was turned, Booker ran for the truck, transponder in hand.

But before he had taken six steps he heard a new sound. At first he thought it was a loud motorcycle approaching from the other side of the hill. He dropped to a squat in the weeds.

The subject also heard it. He stopped twenty yards short of the hollow tree.

The sound continued to build.

Instead of a motorcycle, a yellow airplane zoomed over the hill hardly two hundred feet off the ground. Its roar filled the creek bottom. Canting left, it passed close to the subject, rocking its wings in greeting.

For a moment Booker wondered wildly if the subject had an accomplice who had come to pick up the money. But he saw that the subject had panicked and stood pistol in hand, watching the plane bank over the creek for a return pass. Booker then wondered if Simmons and Nate had set up some kind of an operation, leaving him out of the loop.

But at that moment he saw the pipes along the bottom of the airplane wing and understood: The plane was a crop duster. The pilot was testing the air currents near the ground, preparatory to spraying the field of cotton.

The subject's back was still turned. Booker had only a moment to decide whether he should stay out of sight or place himself between the subject and the truck.

If he ran for the truck, he would set off a gun battle.

Of that he had no doubt.

If he went down, he would take Rachel and Suzanne with him.

That also was certain. The subject would view Booker's presence as an ambush, a betrayal. If he killed Booker, he would not allow Suzanne and Rachel to live.

And if Booker killed the subject, the location of Rachel and Suzanne might not be found until too late.

Booker could see no way he could win in a shootout.

Quickly, while the subject's back was still turned, he ran and jumped headfirst into the ditch.

He made two miscalculations. The ditch was deeper than he thought and his body was far less resilient than it had been thirty years ago. He hit the bottom—six feet down—with a force that drove the air from his lungs. Sharp rocks cut into his skin. He tasted dirt. For a moment he felt consciousness fading.

Yet he managed to climb far enough back up the side of the ditch to peer through the weeds.

The subject was running toward the truck. Booker brought his .357 Colt Trooper up and pulled back the hammer, still uncertain whether he had made the right decision.

The subject reached the truck, climbed in, started the motor, and dug out, throwing dirt.

For an instant Booker held the pistol sights fixed on the subject, his forefinger resting heavily on the trigger while all the arguments pro and con again went through his head.

The range was borderline long. He might miss. If he wounded the guy and he got away, Rachel and Suzanne would pay with their lives. If he killed the guy, where was his justification as a law officer? His own life was not in danger. Furthermore, the killing would place two additional lives at risk.

Also, there was a chance either Suzanne or Rachel were in the truck, bound and gagged on the floorboards. He might inadvertently hit them.

He held his fire. The truck raced off to the east. The yellow plane continued to circle the field as the pilot concentrated on how he would lay his swaths. The pilot probably saw nothing illogical about the man running from the field. No one in his right mind would stand and allow hundreds of pounds of chemicals to rain down upon him.

Booker lowered the hammer on his pistol. His forehead was bleeding profusely from a cut. His rib cage hurt. Sharp pain came with each breath.

He walked back up the hill to where he had left his coat, picked up the radio, extended the aerial, and pressed the transmit key.

"Subject was frightened off by a crop duster. He didn't make it to the tree. He has left the scene, headed east."

"You place the gadget?" Simmons asked.

"Negative on that. Didn't get a chance. The plane came out of nowhere."

"Why didn't you radio? We could've sprung the trap."

Booker did not want to admit that he had been away from his radio. "Better this way," he said. "If we waste him, we'd probably lose the victims. Let's give him time. He may be back."

The radio remained silent while Simmons considered his options. "Ten-four on that," he said after a moment. "All units remain in place. We'll wait."

Booker sank back into the weeds. His chest hurt. His forehead was still bleeding. He felt miserable.

Now, after what had seemed to be a marvelous opportunity, they were right back where they had started.

Harold fled eastward into the South Canadian bottoms, monitoring his rearview mirrors constantly.

He saw no sign of pursuit. But with airplanes up there, he did not know what to expect.

When he reached the river he abandoned the pickup. He waded the wide, shallow stream and climbed a knoll on the opposite bank. There he found a place in a tangle of brush where he could keep watch while he figured out what had happened, and decide what to do.

He had no doubt that the airplane had targeted on him. The pilot had leaned out of the cockpit and looked right at him. The wing waggle clearly had been a signal for someone.

He was sure that by running and getting away so fast, he had escaped a trap.

For a while he was so scared that he had no room left for anger. But as time passed, and he saw no pursuit, his confidence returned. So did his fury.

Once again he had been jerked around, lied to, betrayed.

He kept remembering the earnestness of the little tough bitch's mama. He had to admit that when it came to lying, she was world-class.

The problem was, what should he do now?

He could see that they had never intended him to get the money. They had used it only to jerk him around. The little tough bitch's mama had sweet-talked him over and over with it, and twice he had narrowly escaped capture.

It was high time he wised up and forgot about that money.

If he had stayed with what Sam taught him, he would never have gotten himself into this mess and reached the point where he was so desperate for money.

Sam was the only true friend he had ever known. Even his father, and even Buster had deserted him. But not Sam. If he returned to Sam's teachings, he might yet survive.

Tomorrow he could send the guy in Phoenix the heads and rattles. The leather place would probably pay if he sent them the hundred large, high-quality skins he had just processed.

If he shipped the meat and venom, those places also would recognize that the quality was up to Sam's standards. They probably would pay.

If everyone came through with money for the merchandise he had on hand, he would be able to pay his bills.

All he needed to do was to return to what Sam had taught him. There was another strong argument for doing exactly that: Until this reward deal came along, he had never worried much about cops. Now they were all over the place.

Thinking through all the angles, he could see that only the little tough bitch and her mama could identify him. If he got rid of them, he would be in the clear.

The hours passed. At sunset he waded back across the river to Sam's truck. He drove carefully out of the river bottom, keeping a sharp lookout for cops.

Gradually his fear eased. Apparently he had lost them.

To be certain, he wound around on back roads through the night, stopping often to watch his back trail.

When he returned to the red barn at sunup, he checked for tire prints. He found none.

Concentrating on all he had to do, he went into the red barn. The little tough bitch's mama called to him. "Did you get the money?"

With his head so full of stuff to do, he hardly heard her.

She raised her voice. "What happened?"

The tone was the one he had heard all of his life: *Where have you been? What have you been doing? Where are you going?*

On and on.

He walked over and knocked her flat. "Shut up!" he said.

She scooted backward the length of the chain. "Why are you angry? What happened?"

"You lied, is what happened. Your friend told the cops. They were there."

Her voice rose as she started her lying again. "I *didn't* lie! I have no idea what went wrong. But look, we can work this out! We can try again!''

She was good. He had to hand her that. Yesterday he might have believed her. But never again. He was through with her. But he would wait till later to kill her. He wanted her to see Sam swallow the little tough bitch. He would have both of them screaming at the top of their lungs. That thought made him feel good.

''I got to get some sleep,'' he said, more to himself than to her. ''Then this afternoon I got a hell of a lot of work to do. And when I get done, me and ol' Sam are going to have us a party.''

21

Even with the painkiller Pete had given him, Booker found sleep impossible. He kept seeing the kidnapper in his sights, feeling the pressure on the trigger. Repeatedly he went over the pros and cons, and still he was not convinced he had done the right thing. Nursing his pain, agonizing over his snap decision, he was still wide awake at six when Nate called.

"Booker, we've just received word from Quantico. They've located a university professor who thinks he may recognize the bite pattern on the kid found up in Kaw Lake."

Booker sat up. Already he felt better. "What does he think it is?"

"He says he's not certain, no plainer than the pattern is. But he suspects it may be a big snake. Python or anaconda. Obviously we need to talk to him soonest. Simmons is still plenty pissed at you over the money deal. But I've told him you're way ahead of everyone on the autopsies on the priors, that it'd take anyone else hours to catch up. I convinced him you should do the interview. You feel up to it?"

"Hell, yes."

"How soon can you get down here?"

"Ten minutes."

"The professor said he'll be into his office at a quarter to eight, his time. That's forty-five minutes. You might grab some breakfast on the way in. It looks like a long day."

But after Booker hung up the phone and began moving, he found he was in worse shape than he first thought. Pete had warned him. When the X rays turned up negative on broken ribs, Pete had said separations could be just as painful. As Booker showered and dressed, every move was torture. By the time he left the motel, he managed only coffee and a danish on the way in.

250

The professor's name was Arnold Collins. Terri put the call through. The professor came on the line friendly and gregarious. Booker assumed the professor had been backgrounded. But he went through the motions anyway, introducing himself, and establishing that the FBI had assigned him to do the interview. Only then did he launch into the questions. "You believe these autopsy photos show a python bite?"

The professor's voice was loud and breezy. "Either that or an anaconda. You don't see much else that big. Offhand, from the size and what appears to be a double row of impressions, I'd say it's from a reticulated python."

"What was that word? Ret . . . ?"

"Reticulated. That means the scales form a netlike pattern."

"How big a snake are we talking about?"

"Longest I've ever seen was thirty-four feet. You hear of them up to forty. But I take those reports with a large grain of salt. There are legends in the back country of pythons up to a hundred feet. There's archeological evidence for pythons of that size. But I think that's all folklore now. The longest you'll find today will probably be closer to thirty than forty."

"Are they the largest of the snakes?"

"The *longest*. The anaconda—a boa, a kissing cousin—is usually bigger. Some of those boogers run up to three, four hundred pounds. Two hundred's about average, full-grown. But they're shorter. Twenty, twenty-five feet, max."

"Professor, I'm fairly ignorant about this. You say boas and pythons are cousins? How close?"

"They're of the same family, scientifically called Boidae." He spelled the word. "I'm sure they share the same evolutionary ancestor. Their habits, temperament, and what you might call lifestyle are about the same. But one curious fact. There are very few places in the world where the habitats of pythons and boas overlap, and then not extensively. Main difference—the way we separate them— is that the boas are born live. The pythons lay leathery eggs. After that there's not much difference. They all kill by constriction."

"What do they eat, generally?"

"Depends on the habitat and the size of the snake. You see, there are about eighty species of pythons, and many, many subspecies. Some are no bigger than your ordinary garden snake. Three feet or so. They'll eat mice, bugs, lizards, other snakes. In the wild, the bigger snakes feed mostly on rodents, small mammals, even birds with the tree-climbing varieties. They're slow-moving. But most have good camouflage. And they can strike like lightning."

Booker felt he should back into his next series of questions. "Do the bigger ones eat anything the size of, say, a moderate-sized pig?"

"Oh, sure. Pigs, calves, young deer. All authenticated. And there are persistent reports from all over the world of boas and pythons killing and devouring full-grown oxen, horses. But I know of nothing of that size that has been authenticated."

Booker felt he had paved the way for his big question. "Humans? Do they kill and devour humans?"

Collins hesitated. "Again, there are persistent reports. But as far as I know, none has been confirmed. In the back country the natives usually attribute any disappearance to pythons or boas. Certainly, the hazard is there. In the literature I see warnings to zoo people and collectors that no one should attempt to handle a big snake alone. There have been fatalities. I don't remember the specifics. Happened years ago."

"Zoo people killed?"

"Yes. You see, big snakes are extremely temperamental. Like any wild creature, they can revert in an instant. People try to turn them into pets. They're not pets. Not in any sense of the word."

"Children? Would they attack children?"

Booker noticed that Collins did not hesitate this time. "The warnings I mentioned usually stress that children should never be allowed around big snakes unsupervised. I don't know if there have been fatal incidents with children."

"Could they swallow a child? The size of a small eight-year-old? Sixty pounds or so?"

Again Collins did not hesitate. "I don't see why not. Certainly, they could handle a meal that size. There are fairly authentic reports of child victims in the wild. And of course they can be tricked into eating most anything."

"Tricked?"

"In a sense. From what we can determine, their eyesight is not good. In fact, until fairly recent times, geologically speaking, they spent most of their lives underground. They have no eyelids. The eyeball is protected by an outer shield, much like a contact lens. So their eyes never close, even when they're asleep. That can be disconcerting, when you're around them, because they always seem to be looking at you."

Collins apparently had lost the thread of his explanation. Booker reminded him. "You were telling me how to trick them."

"Right. They're almost blind, you see, except for nearby movement. So they depend mostly on their sense of smell, which is quite good. They run their tongues out into the air, capture molecules of odors, then run their tongue into holes in the roof of their mouth called Jacobson's organ. By and large, they tend to eat a restricted diet. I've never reared one. But in the literature the authorities say that if they're raised on chickens, they tend to stay with chickens. If you want to feed them rabbit for a change, you smear chicken smell on the rabbit, or vice versa. That way you can trick a snake into changing its diet."

"So if you primed a child with a certain smell, the snake would probably kill and devour the child."

"Exactly."

"How often do these big snakes feed?"

"Generally, if they are fed small meals—rats, gerbils, small chickens—maybe every other day. Large meals, pigs and so forth, probably every other week. If you waited a month, six weeks, they'd be hungry enough to eat most anything, and they'd be in a bad mood. I'm speaking generally. Like I said, they're temperamental. Sometimes they'll just quit eating for a while. No one knows why. They can fast a month or so without appreciable loss of weight. There are recorded instances of big pythons going for a full year and more without feeding. But to answer your question, a big python should be fed a substantial meal every two weeks for good maintenance. If you wanted to make sure he was ready to kill and devour a large meal, such as a child, you would wait six to eight weeks."

Booker made a note of this and circled it.

Six to eight weeks was exactly the cycle that fit his theory of a serial killer.

"Professor, you keep using the phrase *kills and devours*. Do these big snakes eat only what they themselves kill?"

Collins gave a mock groan. "Now you've stumbled upon our dirty little secret. We don't talk about it much. But yes, as a general rule, a big snake won't eat anything unless it does the killing. I say as a general rule, because claims exist that some snakes have been trained to eat fresh-killed food. Personally, I'm dubious. I believe those claims are made to forestall the animal activists. Generally speaking, a snake such as a python will eat *only* what it kills."

"And exactly how does it kill?"

Collins implied by tone that he thought this a dumb question but was too polite to say so. "You put the rabbit, chicken, or whatever into the cage with him. He stalks it and kills it just like in the wild. We don't enjoy talking about this. And I wouldn't want to work with anyone who did enjoy it."

Booker persisted. "Kills them how, specifically?"

"Constriction. Pythons, boas, all Boidae possess strong coils. They don't actually crush the victim like most people think. They just squeeze, keeping the pressure on, preventing the intake of breath, until the victim expires."

That answered the question of little Kathy Simpson, who to all outward appearances had just stopped breathing. Booker moved on to the other medical mystery, little Brenda Wallace's body partially covered with saliva.

"While doing this, do they emit a lot of gastric juices?"

"Oh, I know what you're talking about. There's a common belief that they cover whatever they eat with saliva, make it slick, so it'll go down easier. That's a myth. I think I know where that comes from. If they're interrupted in feeding, or if whatever they're devouring is too big, they'll just throw it up. From time to time, people have seen dead pigs or calves covered with saliva. That's how the myth got started."

Booker moved on for a possible explanation of the abductions where no bodies had been found.

"Suppose a big snake killed and swallowed a child. What would be left?"

Collins did not understand. "Left?"

"Would there be bones? Any residue?"

"Oh, my, no. Nothing hardly at all." He paused. "You see, these snakes defecate much in the same way as other creatures. The anal opening is about where the body narrows into the tail, a division clearly delineated. The anal scale covers an opening there called the cloaca. All waste material is eliminated through that opening."

"Excuse me, Professor, but are we talking about plain, ordinary, garden-variety shit? Turds, so to speak?"

Collins laughed. "Well, it's really not quite that simple. Actually, there are three types of snake waste. First is the regular excrement, what you're talking about. Second, there's a grayish-white mass that's mostly uric acid. You see, big snakes have no facility to drink liquid. So they retain all moisture possible. This white mass is really urine, emitted as a solid. Third, there's a compacted mass of undigested material—fur, feathers, hair, whatever. I'm speculating, but I'd imagine that with a human, you'd get back only hair, remnants of teeth, and very little else."

For one of the few instances in his long career, Booker momentarily lost his objectively while on the job.

The kidnapper had promised to turn Suzanne into a turd. Apparently he was equipped to do exactly that.

Booker forced his mind back to the case. "If I wanted to buy a big snake, a really large one, where would I go?"

"To the classifieds in trade journals. Or you'd just ask around. Understand, with eighty species there's a lot of variety. About a dozen species are readily available to collectors. Your reticulated python—a big one, thirty feet or so—would be relatively difficult to find, but not impossible. Carnivals, sideshows, and collectors sell and trade them quite frequently."

"They're not registered?"

"Oh, no. Theoretically, there's restriction on international trade, under CITES—the Convention on International Trade in Endangered Species. But only eight species—mostly boas—are currently listed as endangered. The rest are restricted to prevent trade in skins. All CITES nations impose export curbs. But there's smuggling. And of course trade within each nation, including ours, is uninhibited. To sum it up, you can buy a python most anywhere if you pay the price."

Booker could think of nothing else at the moment. He gave Collins the usual notice that he would be calling back if he thought of anything else.

As he ended the call, Nate and Simmons came over to his desk. As they approached, Booker observed that both looked as if they had just emerged from a ten-day drunk. The case was taking its toll. Back during the oil field theft that led to Iran, Simmons had easily handled pressure from the State Department, the CIA, even the White House. Now he looked as if he had just had all his tail feathers pulled. Booker felt a moment of self-reproach. Simmons's thirty-year career was on the line. Booker knew much of the heat on him stemmed from the billboards and the hollow tree debacle— ideas Booker had proposed and championed.

"Get anything?" Nate asked.

"It's falling into place," Booker told them. "Our man has a reticulated python, plenty capable of killing and swallowing a child. It all fits. That's why his disposal pattern changed, and why we're no longer finding the bodies. A year or so ago he started turning them into snake shit. The snake threw up the one covered with saliva. That's how little Kathy up in Kaw Lake was suffocated without damage to soft tissues. The snake just squeezes, keeps you from breathing. And the timing fits. Collins says you would starve a snake six to eight weeks to make it eat a big meal. That's been the killer's interval. And his snake's about due for another feeding."

"That should finally convince Washington that we have a serial killer on our hands," Simmons said.

"How will we find him?" Nate asked.

"Through the snake. The professor says exceptionally large pythons are relatively rare in this country. So we can start calling, find out when and where they were bought and sold, maybe who bought them."

"We'll put every phone on it," Simmons said.

Within minutes, the first queries went out to the snake magazines, and from there the search expanded. Every phone in the squad room was put to use as investigators interviewed collectors and dealers, tracing the sales of large reticulated pythons.

Soon more than a dozen snakes were being traced. The owners proved difficult to locate.

"If you think about it, that shouldn't be surprising," Booker told Nate and Simmons. "Anybody that keeps a twenty- or thirty-foot python would hardly be your ordinary guy next door. These people probably live off to themselves. If they're with a carnival or sideshow, they're probably on the road most of the time."

Field investigators were dispatched to check out the leads, concentrating on Oklahoma and the surrounding states.

With the search in operation and functioning smoothly, Booker tried a different approach, one he hoped might save some time. He remembered that carnivals usually visited each town in the region during the annual rattlesnake roundups. His work with the OSBI had introduced him to mayors, police chiefs, and civic leaders in most of those towns. He began phoning those acquaintances, seeking the names of the carnival owners, especially those who had offered "snakeariums" among their attractions.

Booker was convinced that the killer was local, and that at one time or another he may have tried to buy a snake from one of the carnivals.

After a half dozen calls there came a moment of sheer serendipity—one of the rare instances in Booker's career when he asked precisely the right question of exactly the right person.

He was talking with a Ford dealer who for several years had served as committee chairman with his town's chamber of commerce, directing the local Rattlesnake Derby. The dealer gave Booker the names and addresses of several carnivals that had come to town in recent years.

Then Booker asked the right question.

"Actually, what we're hunting is a subject who may have purchased a python or similar big snake from one of those shows. Do you recall anything like that?"

"You're talking about the snake man," the dealer said. "Sure, I remember him."

Booker activated his tape recorder. He did not want to miss a single word. "The snake man?"

"A fellow who comes around every year and takes space for a booth at the derby. About three years ago a carnival from Texas had a big snake. A really big one. About twenty-five feet or better. The snake man drove them crazy, wanting to buy it. You can check, but I think he finally did."

"You remember this snake man's name?"

"I'm not sure I ever heard it. He claims he works for an old man who used to come around. Sam. Sam Chambers, I believe his name was. Sam always paid cash for the booth. Paid a good price for the best rattlesnakes. I haven't seen Sam in several years. This younger fellow, the one they call the snake man, always takes the booth in Sam's name, says he's still working for Sam. I've never had reason to question it."

"What does he look like?"

"About six feet, I'd say. Maybe a little more. Borders on pudgy. Lots of hair. Or did have. Losing some of it. Face normal-looking except for his eyes and his mouth. He has a way of staring at you that pisses some people. Looks right through you. And his mouth is odd-looking, just a sort of wide slit across his face. Chews tobacco or dips snuff, I don't know which. Dribbles on his chin a lot."

"Color of hair and eyes?"

"Both brown, I guess."

"What kind of personality?"

The auto dealer laughed. "Weird. That's the only word that comes to mind. Never talks more'n necessary. Now, the old man, Sam, was a windbag. Talked all the time. This younger fellow first showed up with him four or five years ago. Wait a minute. I remember Sam calling him Harold. I don't think I ever heard a last name."

"You know where Sam was from?"

"No. He talked a lot but never said anything. You know what I mean? Never nothing about himself. Always about how the government's doing people in, or how the banks are taking everybody to the cleaners. That usury should be a sin. Things like that. I remember some of us talking one time, after the derby, about how Sam never mentioned where he was from or where his business was located. If you asked him something specific—and I did a time or two—he'd laugh and say he just operated out of his hip pocket. I assumed he was dodging the IRS, paying cash all the time. But I figured it was none of my affair.''

"Business? What kind of business?''

"Rattlesnakes. That's the reason he bought only the best. Most of the snakes at the derby wind up barbecued. Sam bought the best-looking snakes, sold the venom to labs, skins to leather outfits, meat to specialty foods, even the heads and rattles to curio dealers. He always seemed to have money.''

"You haven't seen Sam in a while, huh?''

"No. Someone was telling me they once asked Harold about him and Harold said Sam was sick. That's been some time back. Harold's been taking good care of the buying. We did have a little trouble with him a few years ago. But we got that cleared up.''

"Trouble? What kind?''

"He was scaring some of the girls. Acting like he was about to toss them a rattlesnake. Flirting, I guess. He did it so much, some people got hot about it. We told him to quit it, and he did.''

"You say Harold didn't talk much. Any idea why not?''

"I always figured he was tongue-tied or something. Or maybe that wad in his mouth just made him tight-lipped. But he definitely seemed to have trouble with talking.''

Booker ended the interview and called the carnival owner in Texas, who confirmed that Harold had bought the python.

The carnival owner could not remember Harold's last name. "I'm not sure he ever told me,'' he said. "He paid cash for the snake. I remember that. So there wasn't a check or anything. He really had a yen for that snake. Kept boosting his offer till I felt I had to sell.''

He said he had not seen Harold since.

"We lost money that year. We made too many of those snake roundups. For some reason, county fairs, rodeos, and frontier day celebrations seem to work better for us. That's where we go now, mostly.''

Booker ended the interview and took his new information to Nate and Simmons. "I think I'm on to him,'' Booker told them. "His name's Harold. No one at this point remembers a last name. He runs a rattlesnake business for a man named Sam Chambers, who may or may not be alive. No one knows where the business is located. We need to check with the people who buy that crap— venom, skins, meat, heads. They should be able to give us an address.''

"Sounds promising,'' Nate said. "But, Booker, we're running

down three or four hot leads on big snakes. I'm not yet prepared to single in on just one."

"Nate, this is our guy," Booker insisted. "He hunts rattlesnakes for a living. So he's mobile. He has a speech impediment. He owns a big reticulated python. And one source said he likes to scare girls. All we need to do is find who he sells to. There can't be many outfits that buy crap like that."

Nate considered the information. "All right. I'll give you three or four men to put on it."

Within thirty minutes Booker's small task force obtained a Woodward postal box number from two sources who said they had dealt with Sam Chambers.

In talking with one of the specialty dealers, Booker received an indication of why the box number was used. "Sam is insistent on payment by money order," the dealer said. "That's always been a hell of a lot of trouble for us. Sometimes it takes two or three money orders to pay for one shipment. I always figured Sam operated off the books to keep from paying income tax. But he always sent good merchandise. Or did until recently. He's fallen off some. Getting old, I guess."

No one could supply a street address. Neither the Woodward phone directory nor the chamber of commerce listed such a business, or a resident by the name of Sam Chambers.

That aroused the interest of Nate and Simmons.

"We'll get a bench warrant to see if there's an address connected with that box," Simmons said.

While waiting, Booker called the Woodward County sheriff.

The sheriff remembered Sam Chambers. "I didn't know the man. But I worked the case. Someone dumped him at Woodward Hospital, back at least three or four years ago. He was into the last stages of a massive coronary. Didn't last two hours. Whoever dumped him never came back. We had the devil's own time finding out anything about him. Eventually we learned that he lived alone in a little rental house. We went through all his belongings there with a fine-toothed comb. We couldn't find any mention of relatives, bank accounts, acquaintances, anything. He wasn't on the tax rolls. He'd never voted. No phone, no credit cards, no credit record, no nothing. Just a driver's license, using that address."

"Vehicles?"

"Neighbors said he drove a car most of the time, and sometimes a pickup. We never found either. No vehicle was registered in Oklahoma under that name. We didn't spend a hell of a lot of time on it, because we found no evidence of foul play. It was a natural death.

No question about that. Autopsy showed his heart was in terrible shape. Had been for years. We buried him as a pauper.''

"Anyone mention seeing a young man who may have been his assistant?''

"No. But that could've been who brought him to the hospital.''

"Did anyone mention his business? Where it might be located?''

"We never learned what he did. He had a business?''

"He apparently was a rattlesnake dealer.''

Booker explained briefly how the business worked.

The sheriff laughed. "Well, I'll be damned. Rattlesnakes. I guess it takes all kinds, don't it?''

Booker told the sheriff about Harold, and what was involved.

"We need to locate this young man in the worst way. He's holding the woman and her daughter, if he hasn't already killed them. We'd appreciate it if you could reopen that old case, ask around and see if anyone knows anything about Sam's assistant. We believe he went right on with the business, and that it's still in operation around there somewhere.''

The sheriff promised to get right on it.

Booker next researched the methods Sam and Harold used to ship their merchandise. He called the laboratory that bought the venom, and a company that bought the meat.

They said the goods sometimes came UPS, and sometimes Federal Express.

The fact that the merchandise was packed in dry ice seemed to be the best bet. Booker went with it. He soon located the place in Woodward where Sam, and now Harold, bought dry ice.

"That fellow was in here just yesterday, or maybe the day before,'' the manager said. "We usually see him every few weeks.''

He did not have Harold's last name or an address.

"He always pays cash and turns down a receipt. I always thought that kind of odd. You'd think he'd want a receipt to prove expenses for tax purposes. But he don't. Sam always operated the same way.''

With the cooperation of a helpful telephone operator, Booker crisscrossed the address of Sam's rental house and located one of Sam's neighbors.

The man remembered Sam well. "We never saw much of him. He was gone most of the time. He just seemed to use that house for sleeping. Never had any visitors that I knew of. We'd hear him come in late, then he'd be gone early the next morning.''

The neighbor confirmed that Sam was a voluble talker who never revealed anything about himself.

He did not know Sam's occupation. He did not recall ever seeing anyone of Harold's description.

Booker told him about the rattlesnake business.

The neighbor expressed surprise. "Now, that might tie in with something I remember. I was dove-hunting one day way up to hell and gone in the Cimarron bottoms. I saw Sam's old pickup moving along one of those back roads at a good clip. Saw it two or three other times up there, on other hunting trips. I always wondered what the hell he was doing up there."

"Could you pinpoint that road for me?" Booker asked. "We think he may have a place where his business was located."

"I'd have to think about it. I've hunted all over up in there. Different trips. Dove. Quail. Deer. Even turkey. If I had time to think about it, I probably could draw you a map. That'd be well into Woods County, way up above Quinlan. That's awful rough country up there, you know."

"If you could draw me a map, I'd sure appreciate it," Booker said. "I'll be up to Woodward later this afternoon. I'll come by and pick it up."

After ending the call, Booker consulted a road atlas.

Many years earlier he had pursued a murder suspect into the Cimarron breaks northeast of Woodward. The atlas confirmed his memory. Most areas of Oklahoma were studded with the names of close-knit farming and ranching communities. But not the Cimarron bottoms. Thirty and forty miles of blank space accompanied the river's course. No towns, few paved roads.

Booker felt a kinship with the region. When Custer came down out of Kansas to murder many of Booker's ancestors on the Washita, his 7th Cavalry was supported by the 19th Kansas, a regiment of volunteers who lost their bearings to the Cimarron terrain and their horses to a stampede. They almost starved before they were rescued. That was rough country. If Harold's hideout was located somewhere up there, it would be well isolated.

Nate came by Booker's desk. "We've run into a delay on the bench warrant. We should have it before long."

"I doubt we'll get anything with it," Booker told him. "The postal box will probably check back to the rental house. I'm getting a good picture of Sam. He knew how to cover his tracks."

He told Nate of his interview with the sheriff, and with Sam's former neighbor. "I think I'll go on up there," he said. "I may be able to backtrack from the neighbor's sightings of that pickup."

"Booker, you're jumping to conclusions again. We're tracking down three other weirdos who own big snakes. They all look good.

One also owns an old blue pickup. I'd like to get more information before we single in on one.''

"By then it might be too late for Rachel and the kid. Nate, this is our guy. I feel it in my gut."

"Hell, it'll be good dark by the time you get up there."

"At least I can get oriented, and be into the area by first light."

"All right, I won't stop you. But take a radio. And use it this time. Keep in touch."

Booker gathered his gear and started for the door.

Nate was not through. "Booker, if you get onto him, don't do anything foolish. Keep remembering what a decrepit old fart you are now. Call for backup, and wait."

Booker nodded and walked on out the door.

He was not sure what he might find up in that country. But in the last hour he had learned much, much more about Harold. All past suspicions were now verified.

The next time he had Harold in his sights, he would not be inclined to hold his fire.

22

The snake man slept through the morning. Rachel lay awake, trying to imagine what had gone wrong. After considering all possibilities, she could conclude only that Booker Reeves had not kept the secret, and that the FBI had made yet another botched attempt at capture.

Whatever the reason, the bait of money no longer worked. Just the mention of it now sent the snake man into a red-faced tantrum.

Rachel slowly came to understand that if she expected to get herself and Suzanne out of this, she must turn to other devices.

But what?

She had no weapon. She was chained and helpless. Time was running out. The snake man had said in no uncertain terms that tonight he would feed Suzanne to Sam.

The episode with the chicken had thoroughly convinced Rachel he was capable of such horror.

Furtively, while the snake man slept, she hunted through the loose hay in her stall, seeking anything she might use as a tool or weapon.

She found nothing.

In late afternoon the snake man awoke. He paid no attention to her or to Suzanne. He seemed upset and muttered to himself as he worked.

Again Rachel was impressed by his efficiency and neatness as he carefully placed the Styrofoam containers in boxes and surrounded them with dry ice. After sealing the boxes, he carried them out to the pickup. He chained the door and left without saying a word to her.

As the sounds of his truck faded into the distance, she called to Suzanne. "Precious? Are you all right?"

"I guess," Suzanne said. "But I'm so hungry! He only brings food when he remembers. Usually he doesn't."

They had talked all through the night while the snake man was gone, calling to each other the length of the barn. Suzanne had described the snake man's eccentricities, his perversions. Rachel had been appalled, yet somewhat relieved.

His conduct thus far could have been far worse.

Rachel had told Suzanne of the massive manhunt, of the extensive coverage on television and in the press, and of the reward posted by the studio. She tried to encourage Suzanne, telling her she thought the snake man would take the money and turn them loose.

Now clearly that was not to be. Rachel assumed that Suzanne had heard the exchange after the snake man's return and was aware the plan had gone awry.

"Maybe today he'll remember food," Rachel called.

"I doubt it," Suzanne said. "You heard him say he and Sam are going to have a party tonight. You know what he means, don't you?" She began to cry.

Rachel felt she should offer what hope she could. "Suzanne, I can distract him. He's not the smartest man in the world. I'll get his mind on something else."

"I don't think you can. He's been planning this ever since he brought me here. He talks to Sam like a person. I don't think you can talk him out of it."

"I'll try, precious. I'll do *something.*"

After a moment Suzanne's voice came as a wail. "Mommy, I'm so scared!"

"So am I, precious," Rachel admitted. "We'll just have to be brave."

Rachel estimated that the town they had passed through was an hour away. She assumed that would be where he would go to ship the boxes. If so, she had two hours to devise a plan.

Systematically, she visually examined every square foot of the barn, searching for any tool or weapon.

Rakes and long-handled snares were leaning against the wall less than fifteen feet from her stall. She could see nothing else that might be useful.

Again she attempted to pull her foot free, even at the expense of some flesh. But the chain was snug. The links were strong. The ringbolt was set solidly in the concrete floor.

Thinking back, she remembered that the snake man had gone to the workbench to get her padlock and key. He again walked to the bench for the key when he took her to Suzanne's cot.

She moved to each side as far as her tether would allow and studied the workbench. And there, on a nail at the side, hung a key ring. It was five long steps beyond her reach.

Cautiously, she unwound the turban bandage from her head, leaving the dressing precariously in place.

But the bandage was not nearly long enough. She ripped it into strips and braided them into a rope, flimsy but of sufficient length.

She had no weight to use for tossing. After several failed attempts, she twisted a handful of straw into a solid mass and tied it to the end of her makeshift rope.

For a while she repeatedly tossed the bundle at the nail, attempting to knock the key ring loose. Her efforts were futile.

She could see that hitting the key ring would be a matter of chance and might take forever. She switched her attention to the rakes and snares.

After countless attempts, she at last snared the tines of a rake with the straw bundle. She tugged gently, fearful her fragile rope would break.

The stack of rakes and snares tumbled to the concrete floor with a resounding clatter.

"What are you doing?" Suzanne called.

"I see a key ring," Rachel explained. "I'm trying to get the rakes so I can reach it."

"If he finds his stuff moved around, he'll beat you with his fists," Suzanne warned. "He only needs an excuse."

"I know," Rachel said. "But I must try."

The straw bundle was still caught in the tines. Gingerly Rachel pulled the rake to her.

The handle was not long enough to reach the keys. But she used it to pull a long-handled snare into her grasp. She then bound the handles of the rake and snare together.

Lying on her back on the concrete floor, using her feet, she worked the combined poles far enough to bang the end of the rake against the side of the table. Her improvised device was heavy. After several attempts her injured arm rebelled. She was forced to rest.

"Did you get it?" Suzanne asked.

"Not yet," Rachel said. "But I think I'm close."

She resumed, and at last the keys fell to the floor. Rachel raked them to her.

The ring contained two identical keys. With trembling hands she put one into the padlock on her ankle. The lock snapped open and she was free.

She ran to Suzanne. The key easily went into Suzanne's padlock but refused to turn. Rachel tried the other key.

It would not work either.

"I think he keeps my key on his belt," Suzanne said.

"Maybe there's a duplicate here somewhere. I'll look."

The drawer on the workbench contained only metal spoons, a few used plastic razors, large rubber bands, hypodermic needles, and a dark brown lump Rachel assumed to be heroin. She fished in the farthest reaches of the drawer but found no keys.

She searched the hooks holding the snakeskins, the sides of the stalls.

Nothing.

Suzanne began to cry. "Mommy, run! He'll be back any minute!"

"No," Rachel said, still searching. "I'm not leaving you."

"If you get away, you could bring the police!"

Rachel stopped to consider.

That was an option. But she could see flaws. Darkness would come before long. If she stuck to the roads, the snake man would find her. If she left the roads, she would become disoriented, lost.

Either way, she probably could not bring the police soon enough to save Suzanne.

"I'll try to find tools to get you loose," she said.

Suzanne was still crying. "He keeps everything in the truck. The other day he went out for a hammer and some nails to make a divider in one of the pits. When he was through, he took the tools back."

Apparently Suzanne was right. Rachel searched the barn and could not find even a screwdriver. She remembered that the snake man carried a knife in a sheath on his belt. She could find no other.

She thought of the old car beside the barn and started outside to search. But the barn door was chained shut. She was locked in. Pushing against the door, she found that the chain was not totally snug. Using her feet from a sitting position, she managed to create enough of a gap at the bottom to slip through. She was starting through the gap when Suzanne screamed. "I hear him! He's coming!"

Pausing, Rachel also heard the far-off whine of the old truck. She hurried back to Suzanne.

"Listen, he won't know I'm free. I'll put the chain back on my ankle, loose enough that I can slip it off. I'll wait for the right time, and do something to get us out of this. But we both must be good actresses for the next few minutes. Do you understand?''

Suzanne pushed her away. "Hurry! Hurry!''

"You understand? Not a word! Not a sign!''

"Yes! Yes! Hurry!''

Rachel ran to the other end of the barn and returned the rakes and snares to their leaning stance against the wall. She picked up the scattered straw that had fallen on the floor and rehung the keys on the nail.

The truck came up the hill toward the barn.

Still searching for anything she might use as a weapon, she frantically examined the space behind the snake cages and pits.

Nothing.

She went to the big refrigerator, thinking he might keep a knife there.

The shelves contained only cartons. In the corner a cardboard box bore a warning label of skull and crossbones, and in red letters the words:

CAUTION
SNAKE VENOM

Rachel opened the carton.

It was filled with stoppered test tubes containing milky liquid.

She ran to the desk for a hypodermic needle. With shaking hands she opened one of the vials and drew some of the creamy liquid into the needle.

The truck ground to a halt outside, brakes squealing.

Rachel replaced the stopper, put the vial back into the carton, closed the refrigerator door, and ran to her stall.

Hurriedly she hid the needle behind her in the hay, circled the chain around her ankle, and closed the padlock, leaving enough slack to slip her foot free.

She was not sure how deadly the venom might be. But she was sure that if she could manage to stab him in the neck and inject the venom, the poison would be at least partially paralyzing.

She stretched out on the hay, concerned that the snake man might see that she was winded and perspiring, and that her head bandages were in tatters.

But when he entered the barn his attention was totally on Sam the snake. Carrying a small bucket, he went to Sam's cage and pounded on the metal. "Hey, Sam!'' he shouted. "You hongry enough? You ready to eat?''

He did a little dance in front of the cage. "Sam! We're gonna part-tee! 'Nuff of this shit!"

Rachel rewrapped her head, hoping the snake man would not notice that her bandage was now in much narrower strips. When she finished, she called to him. "You could still have the money, you know. We can still make a deal."

He whirled on her. "Bullshit! You think I'm stupid or something?"

Rachel felt encouraged that if only for the moment they were communicating. She had pulled him back over the line. "You never told me what happened last night. I know it was a mistake of some kind. I'm sure my friend tried to get the money to you."

"No mistake. They sent a fucking airplane."

He put the bucket down by Sam's cage, spread his arms, made airplane noises, and zoomed back and forth in front of Sam's cage.

Rachel again raised her voice. "Did you look in the hollow tree?"

"Never had no chance. Fucking airplane run me off."

Again he made airplane sounds and zoomed around the room. Rachel knew she was losing him. She frantically sought a way to preserve the thin thread connecting him with reality. "Why don't you go back and look? I'm sure it's there. I'm sure my friend left it."

He zoomed close to her, leaned near, and made a face. "Don't need it. Me and Sam's gonna be all right."

He zoomed to the workbench and threw down his cap. He kicked off his shoes. He shouted to Sam, "Now we're gonna have us some fun."

He lit a propane-fueled Bunsen burner and prepared his shot of heroin.

Rachel's mind froze.

The bizarre ritual was starting.

He placed the needle on the bench and went across the floor barefoot to Suzanne's cot, carrying the small bucket. The wall of Rachel's stall blocked her view. For a moment she could not see what was happening.

"Now we're gonna find out if this little bitch is half as tough as she thinks she is," the snake man said to Sam.

Suzanne screamed.

A moment later the snake man came into view dragging Suzanne.

Rachel's hand closed on the hypodermic needle. Suzanne was yelling, struggling. Rachel slipped off her chain, preparing to run and stab the snake man in the neck while his back was turned.

She knew her chances were slim. He probably would hear her

coming at him. With his size and strength, he could knock her unconscious with one blow.

And if that happened, she would be of no help to Suzanne.

In that instant, seeing the impossible odds, Rachel changed her plan.

She remembered the snake man's routine of the other night, when the snake killed and swallowed the chicken. At the start of the snake's long stalk, the snake man had gone to his chair and given himself a fix.

Later, Suzanne had confirmed that this was his routine.

"I brung you a present," the snake man shouted to Suzanne. "Sam likes pigs. So I brung you some pig shit. We gotta turn you into a fucking little pig."

He picked up the bucket and with a broad brush began smearing Suzanne with a dark green liquid.

Suzanne dodged, screaming, trying to avoid the pig manure. "Mommy! Mommy! Help me!"

The snake man's back was turned as he held Suzanne with one hand and smeared her with the other.

While he was diverted, wrestling with Suzanne, Rachel ran to the workbench. She switched the needles, leaving the one filled with snake venom in place of the one filled with heroin.

She was gambling that she would have time to get Suzanne out of the cage before Sam seized her.

Suzanne continued to scream. "Mommy! Mom-mee!"

Rachel steeled herself, knowing she must keep herself under control. Success depended on adhering to her plan. She must not distract the snake man from giving himself that shot of snake venom.

The snake man opened the door to Sam's cage and shoved Suzanne inside.

Suzanne ran to the far corner and looked out at Rachel. "Mom-mee! Help me!"

As Rachel watched in horror. Sam's head lifted.

He began to move.

"Go get her, Sam!" the snake man shouted. "Eat her up!"

The snake man did his little dance in place. Rachel knew he was impatient to go take his shot and peel off his clothes.

She made herself sit quietly and wait.

Suzanne ran from one corner of the cage to the next, trying to stay out of Sam's vision.

"Mom-mee! Why don't you help me?"

The snake man turned and hurried toward his chair, making a sound somewhere between a giggle and a laugh.

Rachel held her breath, certain he was on his way to take his shot.

But at the workbench he stopped. He picked up the key to her lock and came straight to her. "Sam and me's gonna give you a ringside seat."

He knelt to unlock her chain.

Rachel knew in that instant she had made a terrible mistake. She hit him across the back of the head with her arm cast.

Her arm went numb. He rose and hit her with his fist.

She saw stars as she tumbled backward into the hay.

He unlocked her chain, apparently not noticing the slack. He grabbed her by her good arm and dragged her toward Suzanne's cot. Rachel resisted, but he was too strong. He threw her across Suzanne's cot, next to Sam's cage, and locked the chain around her ankle.

She rained blows on his neck and face. He hit her again, knocking her back onto the cot.

"Damn you!" he shouted. "You'll never whip me again! I'm gonna kill all your little bitches!"

Even in her terror, in the midst of Suzanne's screaming, Rachel recognized that the snake man was fully into his fantasy, whatever it was.

She tried to shatter it. She shouted back at him. "What are you talking about? I've never whipped you! I don't have any little bitches!"

For answer, he hit her again. From the crazed fury in his face Rachel fully expected to be beaten to death in the next minute.

But at that moment Suzanne's screams acquired new pitch and volume.

The drama beginning inside the cage interrupted the battle outside. Sam was sliding down from his perch, his long tongue shooting in and out.

Suzanne scuttled to the other side of the cage.

The snake man laughed. "Hoo-ee! Go get 'em, Sam!"

He hurried to his chair to take his shot.

And in that moment Rachel fully understood what a tragic mistake she had made.

Again she was chained and helpless. If the snake man mainlined the venom and collapsed, she would be unable to rescue Suzanne.

Even in death the snake man would win.

From only a few feet away she would have a ringside seat as Sam killed and swallowed Suzanne.

And she would not be able to stop it.

"Mommmm-eee!" Suzanne yelled.

Sam was moving toward Suzanne, his big head swinging.

Again Suzanne ran to the opposite corner of the cage.

The snake man laughed. "Takes hours, sometimes. All night, sometimes. But ol' Sam always gets 'em, don't you, Sam?"

The snake man was in his chair, working with a rubber band.

Rachel thought wildly of calling out, warning him.

But she could not win either way.

If he died in the chair, Suzanne would die.

Yet, if she warned him, he would still kill them both.

She remained silent. He inserted the needle. Slowly he pushed the plunger with his thumb.

For a moment there was no reaction.

Then abruptly he stood and staggered toward the work bench. "What . . . ?"

He was unable to finish the sentence. His eyes widened. The wad of snuff fell from his mouth.

His gaze was locked on Rachel. "You! You!" he shouted.

He started toward her, walking spraddle-legged like a drunk. "My daddy had your number! I'm gonna get you now!"

He drew the knife from its sheath at his belt.

In the near corner of the cage, Suzanne turned to look at the snake man. "Mommm-eee! Run!" she shouted.

And in that moment, with Suzanne's attention diverted, Sam struck.

His jaws closed on Suzanne's shoulder.

Suzanne's screams became unintelligible as she fought to pull loose.

Sam's coils quickly encircled her.

The snake man staggered on toward Rachel. Ten feet away he stopped. For a moment she thought he would collapse there. But again he came on, holding the knife in front of him at waist level. "You bitch! I shoulda done this a long time ago."

As soon as he came within reach, he slashed at her.

Rachel dodged and retreated back against the cot, as far as the chain would allow.

Again he jabbed.

Unable to retreat farther, Rachel grabbed the blade with both hands. He tried to raise the knife to stab her in the chest. She held on. He pushed the knife, trying to reach her chest, her heart. But he was growing weaker. She forced the blade down.

She saw rather than felt the blade go into her abdomen.

For an eternity Rachel and the snake man were locked in a demented dance. He kept stabbing. She kept pushing the blade away.

At last the snake man gasped. He fell backward against Sam's cage, hung there for a moment, then dropped facefirst to the concrete floor.

Rachel collapsed onto Suzanne's cot, certain she was dying. She had seen the blade go deep into her abdomen. She felt weak, on the verge of passing out.

But her eyes focused on Suzanne.

Sam was still holding Suzanne by the shoulder. His coils were working, tightening. Suzanne's eyes were glazed. Her face was dead white. She did not seem to be breathing.

Rachel struggled to her feet.

In his superhuman effort to kill her, the snake man had done her two favors.

He had brought her the key.

And he had brought her the knife.

After several attempts with her blood-slippery hands, Rachel managed to roll the snake man's bulk over far enough to reach the keys at his belt. Her hands refused to function properly. Frantically she hunted through the keys, seeking one of the right shape. She tried three in the padlock on her ankle without success. But the fourth worked. Free at last, she picked up the knife and staggered around the corner of Sam's cage to the door. There she had to drop the knife again in order to use both hands to search for the key to the cage door. At last she found one that worked. She threw open the door.

Only Suzanne's head and feet were visible. Sam's coils encircled the entire length of her body. Her face was dead white. She did not appear to be breathing. Rachel was terribly aware of the absolute silence. She picked up the knife and entered Sam's cage.

She knew nothing of snake anatomy. But she assumed that Sam would be most vulnerable at the base of his skull.

There she stabbed, using both hands and all of the strength in her arms and shoulders. It was like stabbing into a big roll of heavy carpet. The knife refused to penetrate. Sam did not appear even to notice.

She shifted her attack to his eyes, driving the knife point time after time. At last she drew blood. Sam released Suzanne's shoulder. Abruptly his massive head swung in Rachel's direction. Before she could maneuver out of his way, he struck, his jaws closing on her arm cast. He jerked her toward him, pulling her off balance. She felt his scales raking skin from her arms.

Then with lightning speed his coils released Suzanne and encircled Rachel. She slashed at the snake's body, making long, deep cuts. Twice Sam's writhing made her slippery hands lose their grip on the knife, but each time it remained in Sam's flesh and she was able to grab the handle again.

She was growing weaker. For a desperate moment she thought she was losing the battle. Sam's coils completely encircled her from waist to knees, and he was trying for her chest. She kept slashing at the places where he applied the most pressure. Blood gushed from her deeper slashes. She knew she was winning the battle.

At last Sam released her arm. His coils dropped away. Writhing, he retreated, climbing into the dead branches at the top of his cage.

Rachel could no longer stand. She sank to the floor and crawled to Suzanne.

Suzanne was not breathing. Whimpering in fear, expecting Sam to return at any moment, Rachel repeatedly blew air into Suzanne's lungs.

For agonizing seconds Suzanne did not respond.

Then she choked, struggled for air, and began breathing on her own. She cried with deep, terror-ridden sobs. Her body was racked by a shuddering that bordered on convulsion.

Rachel's strength was fading fast. But she knew she must get Suzanne out of the cage. She dragged Suzanne across the rough concrete floor, toward the cage door. An eternity seemed to pass before she could get Suzanne through the door. But at last she managed to return Suzanne to the filthy cot.

There Rachel held her, whispering repeatedly into her ear. "We're safe, precious. It's all over. We're safe."

How long they lay embraced, Rachel did not know.

Gradually Suzanne's trembling eased. She wiped her eyes. "Where's Sam?" she whispered.

"He went back to the top of his cage," Rachel told her. "He's badly hurt. I may have killed him."

"And the snake man?"

"There," Rachel said. "On the floor. He's dead."

Suzanne looked. "Did you kill him?"

Rachel avoided the thought. "I switched his needles. He gave himself a shot of rattlesnake venom."

Rachel felt she was close to passing out. She knew she should assess matters, get organized, seek help. "We're not out of the woods yet, precious," she said. "The snake man stabbed me."

Suzanne became aware of the blood on her. "Where?"

Rachel pointed. "I don't think he hit anything vital. If he had, I wouldn't be talking. But, precious, you'll have to go for help. My hands are cut. I can't possibly drive the truck.''

Suzanne moved to get up. ''I'll go now.''

Rachel held her. ''No. It's still dark. You'd only get lost. It'll be daylight soon. Then you can go. Listen to me. If I become unconscious, wait until daylight. Go out to the road and turn right. You may have to walk miles. Seek help from the first person you see.''

Suzanne was regaining her color. ''I doubt anyone will have anything to do with me. I'm covered with pig do. I could eat a bar of soap.''

Rachel laughed. She felt encouraged. Suzanne was sounding like herself again.

''I wish David were here,'' Suzanne said. ''He'd say funny things and make us feel better.''

''He'll be sorry he missed the excitement,'' Rachel predicted.

They lay cuddled for a time without speaking. Rachel worried over how much blood she was losing internally. She feared she might be bleeding to death. But she did not want to send Suzanne out into the dark. She knew it must be close to morning.

Suzanne turned to look down at the body of the snake man. ''What made him the way he was? Do you know?''

Rachel no longer wanted to think about it. ''I have absolutely no idea.''

Suzanne continued to look at the body. ''Someday I'm going to make a movie about him.''

Rachel winced. ''I'd think you could find a more palatable subject.''

''He was awful,'' Suzanne agreed. ''But there was something really sad about him. I'll bet if you could learn what made him the way he was, he'd be a sort of country Hamlet.''

Rachel laughed. She felt a rush of love for this precocious child-woman who had so enriched her life by being her daughter. ''I'll have to wrestle with that thought for a while,'' she said.

''I think it's getting daylight,'' Suzanne said.

Rachel followed her gaze. Faint light was showing through the cracks in the metal sides of the old barn.

Rachel felt relief. There was a chance Suzanne might find help in time. ''Then you can go now,'' she said. ''I don't know how far you'll have to walk. If we're lucky, you may meet someone on the road before you go far.''

''I wish I had some clothes.''

Rachel considered the problem. Her shortie pajamas were filthy and covered with blood. She lacked the strength to peel the snake man's shirt off him. She had no idea where he kept his spare clothing, and she was incapable of making a search. "I'm sorry, but I can't help you there," she said.

"Maybe I can find something in the truck," Suzanne said.

At that moment Rachel saw movement in her peripheral vision. Suzanne's eyes widened. She screamed. "He's out! Oh, God, Mommy! Sam's out!"

Rachel turned to look. Sam was on top of his cage. His bloodied head was gliding downward, suspended in air by several feet of his body.

With instant horror Rachel recognized the extent of this new danger. Concerned with Suzanne, she had left the knife in the cage, and the cage door unlatched. Whether by design or accident, Sam was blocking the passageway between the cage and the wall. Suzanne would not be able to reach the barn door. Nor could they get past him into the cage.

"Mommy, what'll we do?" Suzanne yelled.

"Help me turn the cot over," Rachel said. "We'll get between it and the wall and use it for a shield."

Rachel was too weak to be of much help. Following her directions, Suzanne did most of the work. They angled the overturned cot against the wall and wedged themselves behind it. Sam kept swaying his head in the passageway, inching toward them. Rachel and Suzanne placed the thin mattress over them for whatever protection it would give.

They snuggled down in the narrow space. The cot springs were skimpy, leaving large holes in their makeshift barrier.

"Won't he be able to get in here with us?" Suzanne asked.

"I don't know," Rachel said. "But if he does, I'll fight him. I want you to promise. When he concentrates on me, I want you to go for help. Promise?"

But Suzanne seemed not to have heard. She was watching Sam. "Oh, God, Mommy! He's coming! He's coming."

Rachel looked. Sam was now fully onto the floor, moving rapidly toward their corner.

Suzanne began to scream.

23

With dawn breaking over the canyons of the Cimarron, Booker saw the enormity of the effort that would be required to search the entire region thoroughly. He thought of different methods. None seemed satisfactory. With sufficient manpower they might check out subscribers to the power lines, one by one. But that would take time. No doubt many meters served only deep well pumps and other nonresidential usage. And there was a chance Harold might not be on the power line.

Booker considered making a radio appeal to Simmons and Nate for an air search. He had about decided to go that route, when he caught a glimpse of some kind of red structure well away from the road.

It was the first possible habitation he had seen in several miles. From the map Sam's neighbor had drawn, Booker estimated he was close to the spot where Sam's car had been sighted.

A low hill blocked his view. Booker stopped his car and walked to the top of the ridge for a better perspective.

The red structure was an old metal barn. Nearby stood an abandoned house, weathered gray and missing many shingles on the roof. A pickup and a car were parked in front of the barn. With the pale morning light, Booker was not certain whether the pickup was faded dark blue. But he was certain he had found Harold. Remembering Nate's admonition, he was raising his handheld radio to call for backup when he heard the screams. With the distance the sound was faint. But there was no mistaking the terror.

Booker ran back to his car. He did not waste time searching for the road leading to the barn. Jumping his car across the shallow ditch, he knifed through a barbed-wire fence and drove across the rocky, mesquite-filled pasture, bouncing over fallen deadwood and pincushion cactus, winding his way around the thicker shinnery.

Several times his car hit high center and stalled. Each time Booker backed up, pushed the accelerator to the floorboard, and barreled his way over the hump.

By the time he reached the barn, two tires were flat. He pulled to a stop behind the pickup, leaped out, and ran for the barn door, pistol in hand. He did not stop to use his radio. The screams, now at close quarters, left no doubt as to the urgency. He yanked the door open and plunged into the barn.

The transition from bright morning sun to the dim interior left him momentarily blinded. He did not wait for his eyes to adjust. He turned in the direction of the screams.

There was violent movement in that corner of the barn. Not until he came close could he make out the details.

Rachel Shelby was enveloped in the coils of a giant snake. Only her head and part of a shoulder were showing. A naked child Booker assumed to be Suzanne was pummeling the snake with her bare fists. The coils of the snake were working, tightening.

Booker seized Suzanne by the arm and pulled her away. But at such close quarters he could not shoot without the danger of hitting Rachel. His eyes had now adjusted. The snake's jaws were closed on Rachel's shoulder. He pounded the snake on the head with his pistol. As the snake released Rachel's shoulder, and the massive head swung in his direction, Booker fired. The sound of the .357 magnum in the enclosed space was deafening. The 158 grain, hollow point bullet tore through the snake's head, taking considerable brains and flesh with it. But Booker left nothing to chance. He emptied his revolver, pulverizing the snake's head.

The coils fell away from Rachel. Booker pulled her free. She was unconscious. Large dark bruises and swellings covered both sides of her face. But to Booker's relief, she was still breathing. The snake's body continued to writhe aimlessly on the concrete floor. A man lay beyond the snake, in the corner. Quickly Booker rolled him over and found that at last he had met the snake man. Booker felt for a pulse. The snake man was dead.

Behind Booker, Suzanne was into full hysterics. He knelt beside her and put his arms around her, only faintly aware of the nauseating stench of pig shit. "Honey, everything's all right," he told her. "Come on. Let's get your mother out of here. Help me get her through the doors."

It was an old trick: The quickest way to help anyone regain control of themselves was to give them something to do.

As Booker carried Rachel out to his car, Suzanne went ahead, opening the doors. At the car Booker got enough out of Suzanne to understand the situation. He wrapped her in his jacket and put her into the backseat of the car with Rachel.

He pulled out the aerial on his handheld radio. The Woodward police dispatcher was busy with morning traffic. Booker did not wait. He broke in with an emergency request for a Careflight helicopter.

Rachel awoke surrounded by flowers. She felt groggy but comfortable, relaxed, and safe. Patricia, Booker, and Peterson were gathered at her bedside.

Peterson leaned over her. "How do you feel?" he asked.

Rachel remembered the other time he had asked that question as she regained consciousness. She experienced a moment of déjà vu. She felt weak but found herself inclined to talk. "Fine," she said. "Did you do the surgery?"

He smiled and shook his head. "I didn't make it up here in time to scrub. But I got in on the closing. They did good work. You're going to be all right."

Again Rachel felt overwhelmed with the urge to reassemble her family. "How's David?"

"He's up, moving around. He's out at my place with your mother."

Rachel's surprise must have shown on her face. Peterson raised a hand. "They're getting along fine. I really think they're learning a lot from each other."

Rachel considered that briefly.

Had she been wrong about her mother and the children? Was she carrying her own animosities into the next generation?

She would have to think about that.

She turned to Patricia. "How's Suzanne?"

One of Rachel's last acts before going into surgery had been to request Patricia's professional services with Suzanne.

"In the short range, I believe she'll be okay," Patricia said. "She's been on the phone to all her friends on the West Coast. She insists she'll be able to make the movie on schedule."

"Patricia, should I allow her to go back to work?"

Patricia hesitated. "You may want to talk to your pediatric psychiatrist. But my sense is that work would help, at least in the short term, which, of course, is our immediate worry. Long-term, it's more difficult to say."

Rachel waited, knowing there was more. Patricia seemed to be choosing her words carefully.

"She could have trouble on down the road. Nightmares. Flashbacks. Insomnia. Anxiety attacks. But for the moment she's handling it. I talked with her more than two hours while you were in surgery. She made it plain she didn't want me to mess with her mind. She said she needs those memories, that they'll make her a better actress."

Rachel was warmly reassured. That sounded like Suzanne.

"She's in seventh heaven," Patricia went on. "Her room is so full of flowers, there's hardly room for the patient. The hallway outside is full. I'm sure you've heard this before, but you have a most remarkable daughter."

"I don't mind hearing it again," Rachel said.

"You see? David's fine, Suzanne's fine," Peterson said. "You are our main concern."

"So give me the bad news."

"Nothing we can't live with. Really, the abdominal stabbings aren't as serious as they seem. I doubt they'll give you any permanent trouble. The thrusts were just in and out. If he had moved the knife sideways, it would have been a different story."

"Shifting gears, the convicts call it," Booker said.

"We made a CAT scan of your head while you were out," Peterson went on. "The beatings you took apparently caused no further damage to your skull and brain. But of course we'll want to keep a close watch to make sure. Your hands are more serious. The knife sliced tendons, punctured synovial sacs, severed nerves. I won't minimize it. You face repeated surgeries and a long, painful recovery with them."

"Small price," Rachel said.

"Small price indeed," Pete said.

Rachel looked at Booker. He seemed older, worn. "Booker, I owe you my life. I'll never be able to repay you."

"Finding you two was payment enough," he said. "We were so afraid we'd lost you both."

"Thank God for the three of you," Rachel said. "I could never have made it without you. If there's anything good to come out of this, it's that I've met three wonderful people."

"Look who's talking," Peterson said.

A nurse came in the door, stopped, and hesitated. She was carrying a hypodermic needle.

Patricia rose. "I think we should get out of here and let the hospital do its work.'' She leaned over and placed a hand on Rachel's shoulder. ''We'll see you in the morning.''

As Booker, Patricia, and Peterson walked out the door together, Rachel truly understood their closeness for the first time. They had shared unspeakable horrors together and learned one another's worth. The warm thought came to her that now she was a part of this close-knit group. She was certain that the four of them would remain close friends throughout the remainder of their lives.

Pete led Booker and Patricia out through the hospital basement to his car at the rear, avoiding the press jammed around the front entrance. The town of Woodward was overrun by television crews and news writers.

''We'd better see about rooms,'' Patricia said. ''I plan to stay over a day or two and work with Suzanne.''

''I'll stay through tomorrow,'' Pete said. ''The beating Rachel received from that pervert may be more serious than we know. I want to do another CAT scan tomorrow and consult with the hospital staff, make sure they keep her under close observation.''

Booker felt exhausted yet curiously pumped up. Much work remained to be done, and he wanted to stay on the case until the final whistle. Nate and Simmons were hounding him for a complete written report of his part in the investigation and rescue.

''Just drop me at the cop shop,'' he said. ''Maybe they can scrounge up a typewriter for me.''

He gave Pete directions. The streets were crowded. Booker doubted Woodward had seen so much activity since the 1947 tornado.

''Booker, what about your transportation?'' Pete asked. ''You need to borrow my car?''

''I'll rent one,'' Booker said. ''Or get a loaner.'' He did not expect to see his own car anytime soon. The wrecker driver sent to haul it in had reported the transmission knocked out of alignment, the tailpipe and muffler gone, springs broken, shocks shattered, two tire rims beyond salvage, and the rear axle broken. He also added that the oil pan, differential, and radiator might have to be replaced.

But as Rachel had said, small price.

Pete stopped in front of the police station. The three of them made plans to get together later for dinner.

Booker was offered use of the police department's computer system. He politely declined, insisting on a typewriter. An old upright Underwood was found for him in a back closet. It worked fine.

For three hours Booker's forefingers banged away in the efficient hunt-and-peck style he had developed through the years. He began his report with his arrival at the intersection where Suzanne was kidnapped and continued to relate in detail his every theory and action down to his emergency call for a Careflight helicopter. The words came easily; he was satisfied with them.

He knew that the written report would not be the end of it. Specialists were being brought in to work the old red barn and the snake man's vehicles for trace evidence to be matched with that taken from prior victims' homes. The snake man had not been much of a housekeeper. No doubt the filthy old cot alone would yield hair, blood, and urine from several of his victims. Booker was expected to be there through the entire search. He was now generally recognized as the leading authority on all the priors.

When his report was finished he made three copies—one for Nate, one for Simmons, and one for himself, confident that in the coming years when long, lonely nights brought dark thoughts, it would make good reading.